# The Master of the Switch

### The Girl with the Gray Eyes
#### Book 3

## L.V. Lane

Copyright © 2023 L.V. Lane
All rights reserved.
ISBN: 979-8-37476-6-127

This is a work of fiction. Names, characters, businesses, places, events, and incidents are either the products of the author's imagination or used in a fictitious manner. Any resemblance to actual persons, living or dead, or actual events is purely coincidental.

All rights reserved. This book or parts thereof may not be reproduced in any form, stored in any retrieval system, or transmitted in any form by any means—electronic, mechanical, photocopy, recording, or otherwise—without prior written permission of the author.

Editing by Steph Tashkoff
Cover by Saintjupit3r

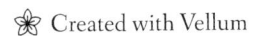

❦ Created with Vellum

# Contents

Introduction . . . . . . . . . . . . . . . . . . . . . vii
Content Advisory . . . . . . . . . . . . . . . . . . ix

Chapter 1 . . . . . . . . . . . . . . . . . . . . . . . . 1
Chapter 2 . . . . . . . . . . . . . . . . . . . . . . . . 9
Chapter 3 . . . . . . . . . . . . . . . . . . . . . . . 13
Chapter 4 . . . . . . . . . . . . . . . . . . . . . . . 19
Chapter 5 . . . . . . . . . . . . . . . . . . . . . . . 28
Chapter 6 . . . . . . . . . . . . . . . . . . . . . . . 33
Chapter 7 . . . . . . . . . . . . . . . . . . . . . . . 41
Chapter 8 . . . . . . . . . . . . . . . . . . . . . . . 46
Chapter 9 . . . . . . . . . . . . . . . . . . . . . . . 54
Chapter 10 . . . . . . . . . . . . . . . . . . . . . . 62
Chapter 11 . . . . . . . . . . . . . . . . . . . . . . 68
Chapter 12 . . . . . . . . . . . . . . . . . . . . . . 74
Chapter 13 . . . . . . . . . . . . . . . . . . . . . . 91
Chapter 14 . . . . . . . . . . . . . . . . . . . . . . 95
Chapter 15 . . . . . . . . . . . . . . . . . . . . . 104
Chapter 16 . . . . . . . . . . . . . . . . . . . . . 111
Chapter 17 . . . . . . . . . . . . . . . . . . . . . 120
Chapter 18 . . . . . . . . . . . . . . . . . . . . . 124
Chapter 19 . . . . . . . . . . . . . . . . . . . . . 127
Chapter 20 . . . . . . . . . . . . . . . . . . . . . 133
Chapter 21 . . . . . . . . . . . . . . . . . . . . . 137
Chapter 22 . . . . . . . . . . . . . . . . . . . . . 144
Chapter 23 . . . . . . . . . . . . . . . . . . . . . 149
Chapter 24 . . . . . . . . . . . . . . . . . . . . . 153
Chapter 25 . . . . . . . . . . . . . . . . . . . . . 157
Chapter 26 . . . . . . . . . . . . . . . . . . . . . 167
Chapter 27 . . . . . . . . . . . . . . . . . . . . . 172
Chapter 28 . . . . . . . . . . . . . . . . . . . . . 176
Chapter 29 . . . . . . . . . . . . . . . . . . . . . 179
Chapter 30 . . . . . . . . . . . . . . . . . . . . . 184

| | |
|---|---|
| Chapter 31 | 188 |
| Chapter 32 | 195 |
| Chapter 33 | 201 |
| Chapter 34 | 205 |
| Chapter 35 | 209 |
| Chapter 36 | 214 |
| Chapter 37 | 223 |
| Chapter 38 | 229 |
| Chapter 39 | 233 |
| Chapter 40 | 240 |
| Chapter 41 | 244 |
| Chapter 42 | 250 |
| Chapter 43 | 256 |
| Chapter 44 | 260 |
| Chapter 45 | 273 |
| Chapter 46 | 280 |
| Chapter 47 | 286 |
| Chapter 48 | 293 |
| Chapter 49 | 299 |
| Chapter 50 | 304 |
| Chapter 51 | 313 |
| Chapter 52 | 319 |
| Chapter 53 | 325 |
| Chapter 54 | 328 |
| Chapter 55 | 333 |
| Chapter 56 | 337 |
| Chapter 57 | 341 |
| Chapter 58 | 346 |
| Chapter 59 | 351 |
| Chapter 60 | 357 |
| Chapter 61 | 367 |
| Chapter 62 | 373 |
| Chapter 63 | 375 |
| Chapter 64 | 378 |
| Chapter 65 | 384 |
| Chapter 66 | 387 |
| Chapter 67 | 395 |
| Chapter 68 | 398 |

| | |
|---|---|
| Chapter 69 | 406 |
| Chapter 70 | 417 |
| Chapter 71 | 421 |
| Chapter 72 | 429 |
| Chapter 73 | 438 |
| Chapter 74 | 446 |
| Epilogue | 451 |
| | |
| About the Author | 453 |
| Also by L.V. Lane | 455 |

# Introduction

This is not a romance, although it does have a HEA, but before that, I'm going to introduce you to a man you should run far away from and never want to see again.

Don't believe me?

I knew you wouldn't, but later, when this is all over, I'm going to say I told you so.

# Content Advisory

Extremely dark, graphic content, mind-games and manipulation, SA, violence, and gore.

References to past stillborn baby by side character.

Heroes in this series range from sweet to pitch black.

# Chapter 1

## Shadowland

### Hannah

I hated the sea, the consequence of a childhood boat trip, the memory of which I'd buried under layers of avoidance. I remembered boarding with a sense of excitement, an ice cream clutched in one hand, the reassuring grasp of my mother's hand in the other.

I was seven. It was the day my parents died.

The memory had faded over the years, but I remembered the way the swaying motion of the boat had made me nauseous as the weather turned and the craft rolled against the choppy sea. The rolling gait of the horse beneath me produced the same swaying motion, worsened by my exhausted state from fleeing the tent where Karry had died. Exhaustion overwhelmed me, further exacerbated by many hours of hard riding.

My body demanded all of my limited energy, consumed with the roiling sickness in my stomach that the sips of water and the occasional bite of food hadn't eased.

I needed to see Ella. My desire was childish, I knew this, yet I desperately needed my sister all the same.

A determination settled inside, a vow to make Bill pay for what he'd done to me and for what he allowed Karry to do in his name.

This inner desire for retribution battled against my foggy mental state of where I was and where I'd been. Tanis had handed me a ri leaf earlier to help with the pain, and another a few hours ago. The pain was manageable, but it only added to my groggy state.

I clung to the mental lifeline of the alpha pressed against me, the solidness of Tanis' body and his rich pheromones that filled my nose and senses. But as I drifted in and out of sleep, I often imagined myself still with Karry, expecting to see his leering face as he delivered another blow before my mind would scramble to accept that it was over, and Karry was finally gone. The relief of remembering I was safe and free was profound, washing through my body in a heady adrenaline rush.

Questions filled my mind in bursts between the mental chaos of processing what had happened and drifting snatches of sleep. The questions felt important but couldn't be grasped coherently for more than a moment. Tomorrow—I would worry about questions tomorrow.

Tanis remained quiet behind me for much of the journey other than the odd brusque order to eat and drink; likewise, his few commands to his men were clipped and to the point. His limp when collecting me, the bruises on his face, and scuffed, swollen knuckles all told a story.

We rode into a small clearing as the light faded. Here we would camp, and I dismounted in an apathetic stupor, relieved the day was drawing to a close. Tanis motioned someone over before turning to speak to Garren.

"Oh, Red," I said, going into his arms and instantly calming. I hadn't noticed him earlier, but then I hadn't noticed many things. I

## The Master of the Switch

was glad Red was here... that all three men I cared about were here. And it was also nice to see a friendly face when Tanis was so abrupt with me, and Garren seemed distant.

"You must be exhausted. Let's get a bedroll set up for you." He took a bedroll from the back of his horse and spread it out on the ground. "Do you want anything for the pain?"

"No thanks," I said. "The leaves are making me a little woozy and I'm not in any pain." Only a slight white lie about the pain, but it was manageable, and I liked a foggy mind less.

Red offered me a food pack.

"I'm not hungry." I thought I might throw up if I tried. "I'll have some water, thanks." I sat, and my weary muscles twitched and shook in relief.

Red sat down beside me and passed me a water bottle.

Sipping enough to wet my lips, my eyes turned to where Tanis was engaged in a heated discussion with Garren. Their features and build held many similarities and, in the fading light, there wasn't much to distinguish them other than Garren wore his sandy hair shoulder length while Tanis wore his dark hair shorter.

Beyond them, a soldier lit a small fire, although the presence of rations suggested it was to discourage animals rather than for food.

"They're doing alright," Red said around a mouthful of his cracker. "Which is surprising after what happened at Thale."

My sluggish mind snapped to alert. "You mean...What do you mean, exactly?"

Red looked away. "The morning we left Thale."

"Because I went to Tanis' room?" My face heated, and I questioned my desire to seek details.

"It's not my business." Red stared down at his half-eaten cracker before pushing the remnants back into the pack.

I didn't like his tone, the words, or the way they placed a distance between us: like he wasn't mine anymore. Was that what he thought? That I'd left him and Garren and was with Tanis now?

Was that what had happened?

3

My head hurt as I tried to work out the sequence of events. "Red, I still care about you. I just—" I what? Whether I liked to admit it or not, I'd gone to Tanis' room, refused to leave, then asked him to fuck me. And I still didn't know a damn thing about Tanis' feelings toward me; whether I was a one-time thing, whether his determination that he wouldn't share meant I was now exclusively his.

Then there was Garren and his fury when I'd gone to Red behind his back. He was my alpha. He'd made it super-clear an omega should speak to her alpha before taking other males to her bed. The very next day, I'd gone and done exactly that with his brother!

My stomach turned queasy, and it had nothing to do with the injuries, exhaustion, or lack of food in my stomach.

"What happened the morning you left Thale?" I asked quietly.

Red sighed. "I suggest you ask Tanis. At least I'm assuming Tanis is the one you want to discuss it with and not Garren."

His words stung. I searched his profile, feeling sicker than before.

"Sorry, that didn't come out quite how I meant it to." Red glanced toward Garren and Tanis, who continued their discussion. "Garren was angry the next day. Someone must've told him you were with Tanis, and after the armory—everyone knows that was about you."

I had known, sort of. My conversation with Tanis that evening had been convoluted, and then I'd forgotten... or purposely erased it.

"I'm not sure how it happened, but they both drew swords on one another the morning we left Thale. Apparently, it's a pretty big deal, like nearly killing each other level of seriousness."

I swallow hard. What had I done? "And they've been fine since?"

"Fine is a strong word. More tolerant of each other, but getting better. I know Garren was upset when Tanis surrendered to the Rymorians."

"He did what?!"

My squeaked question hung in the air as the shadows around me deepened. Lifting wary eyes, I found Tanis standing there. His dominating presence seemed particularly potent in the waning light. I'd been sitting in front of him on a horse all day. Yet, my mind decided

### The Master of the Switch

now was the perfect time to drag forth all our encounters, the most memorable of which was me pointing a gun at him back at Station fifty-four. This unwelcome ramble down memory lane concluded with the final night in Thale when I'd slept with him. My face flooded with heat.

Tanis remained broodingly silent. Red jumped to his feet and grabbed another bedroll from his horse without another word.

"Finished eating?"

I studied my unopened food pack before glancing back up at Tanis, my mind now grappling with what Red had just told me. I nodded.

"Good. Time to sleep." He walked over to his horse.

Two men stood to my left, ready to take the first watch. Everyone else had moved to their bedrolls, including Garren and Red who sat talking opposite me. My chest squeezed painfully when Garren didn't so much as glance at me.

Too tired and drained to worry about this now, I shuffled to the center of my bed and lay down, resolute. Suffering taught a person a lot about perspectives. However emotionally uncomfortable this was, it was a million times better than being with Karry.

I glanced over my shoulder to find Tanis placing his bedroll behind mine. "What are you doing?"

"Sleeping. And, upon Garren's overly firm insistence, I'm sleeping next to you."

There was no mistaking his dry undertone, and I wondered how it was possible to experience such a familiar, Tanis-induced sense of chagrin after the horrors of the last few weeks.

My eyes shot toward Garren, the only person still sitting up, who was now staring back at me, his locked jaw clearly visible even in the gloom. "It's none of Garren's business," I said, which was an outright lie, and made me feel like a prize bitch. "I don't enjoy sitting next to you on the horse; I certainly—"

Putting his arm around my waist, Tanis yanked me back flush against his body.

My mind shut down to everything but the comforting feel of his powerful body and his scent flowing over me and setting every molecule of my body into a riot.

He purred.

An unmistakable dampness gathered between my legs, and my emotions fluctuated between embarrassment and heady delight.

"Red said you threatened to kill Garren after—after we—" I stopped, unsure why I'd broached the charged subject even as a distraction from my wayward body.

Tanis grunted and muttered under his breath before responding, "That was kind of Red. I must talk to him about that tomorrow."

"Did you?"

"I never threaten to kill someone. I *was* going to kill him."

"That's..." was he joking? "not normal."

"Nobody ever confused me with normal," he said, tone amused.

"Why?"

"Why am I not normal? I was born that way, I guess."

"No, why were you going to kill him?"

The silence stretched before he replied. "Because I'm the leader, and because Garren is not."

That didn't explain anything. "I know you care about him." The camp had become quiet, and my words were a whisper. I watched Garren lay down and put his back to me. "People don't kill someone they care about, even if they're angry, even out here."

"Perhaps knowing I killed his three older brothers without any remorse will clarify my personality failings for you."

I frowned. "That's not very nice."

His sudden laughter surprised me and sounded loud in the quiet camp and the darkness enveloping us.

"I'm not normal, and I'm not nice. Those insults are coming thick and fast tonight, but I'll take them over a tyrant, although the latter is more accurate."

"I don't believe that," I said softly, lulled by his purr in a way that

## The Master of the Switch

disconnected me from the words. "If you killed them, then you had a good reason."

His arm tightened, pulling me back against him more snuggly, and I reveled in being safe and protected, in the simple intimacy, even as I ached and longed to have Garren and Red close, too.

"Ah, Hannah, how do you retain an idealized impression after all you've seen me do? I spend my time killing people in an endless self-perpetuating cycle that seeks only to stop them killing me first. I've killed many people, too many to count or remember, and I'm certain not all of them would meet Hannah's 'killing them is justified' criteria."

I acknowledged the truth of his words, yet I no longer had a steady grip on what was right now that I'd killed someone myself. At least, I thought I had. "I don't care about other people. I care about Garren."

"Are you trying to piss me off?" His tone held an equal measure of anger and curiosity.

I fidgeted and tried to make a gap between us. My efforts only succeeded in sapping the last of my energy. By the time the silent battle ended, I was hot, irritated, utterly exhausted, and closer than before.

"I just feel bad that I caused conflict between you."

"Don't," he said brusquely. "It would have happened sooner or later."

"You threatening to kill Garren?"

"It wasn't a threat, and that wasn't what I was talking about." He sounded testy again.

What was he talking about, then? The desire to gain distance rose, but I was too tired to do more than fidget.

"Stop fighting with me! I realize you're not happy with me beside you, but you've just..." drawing a deep breath in, he resumed the sentence, with a softer tone, "been through a traumatic experience. Me sleeping beside you isn't negotiable, so you may as well get over it so we can actually get some sleep."

"What if Garren had killed you?" I couldn't say what prompted that question, but the thought of Tanis dying left me as cold and panicky as it did when I thought about Garren's potential death. I should have told Garren I wanted Tanis. He'd made allusions as to suspecting my interest. It wouldn't have been so hard a conversation. I was a foolish, defective omega, broken by Rymorian culture and failing epically, to the detriment of everyone.

"Is that concern or wishful thinking?" Tanis asked, sounding baffled now. "Garren didn't feel like dying, and that's why he put his sword away."

"That's very arrogant."

"Confident," he countered, but I could hear the smile in his voice, and it settled me some.

"So, you really are a tyrant?"

"I am. Now, go to sleep."

Yesterday, I'd been at Karry's mercy, and my life was filled with terror.

Today was a different day, so I closed my eyes against the fading light, letting exhaustion take me.

The old Hannah would have been far more concerned. But I wasn't that person anymore, and the new Hannah was simply grateful to be alive.

As the silence settled, a wave of fear came rushing in, yet the arm around me was heavy and reassuring; his steady, rumbly purr, comforting. Despite my earlier desire for distance, I was glad to lie beside him. It reminded me that my life had changed irrevocably. I focused on the places we were connected, making them an anchor that could stop the current from pulling me into another nightmare. Finally, I fell asleep.

# Chapter 2

## Rymor

### Sirius

Exiting the capsule, I stepped into the derelict underground labyrinth deep beneath Rymor, and followed a dingy stone passage that was as frigid as a tomb.

It sickened me whenever I came back here. Despite the passing years, the wound was just as deep, and my heart filled with the same disappointment that we were still fighting in the shadows. I didn't buy into the master's theory that the harbinger uniting the Jaru would make a difference, nor did I buy into the Armageddon switch as a solution. The great cities were our cities, and I had no desire to see them reduced to rubble.

Yet the master had lifted his head from his books and left his home.

Change was coming, albeit too slowly for my liking. In the interim, I was determined to wreak whatever retribution I could against the people of Rymor; a quest that brought me great joy.

Eighty-two souls had been extinguished in the last bombing. Not nearly enough for what had been done to my people.

The Outliers had been disrupting Rymorian life for a long while now. Only a great pity that we were few in number, meaning our impact was small. It was even less than it should have been, given those traitorous few who came here to infiltrate, only to lose sight of the mission. These weak individuals succumbed to the lure of Rymorian society. I'd personally killed many betrayers over the years. Better to make an example to others who might find their resolve waning.

This bitterness would never be resolved while Rymorians lived. These lands and everything in them belonged to the Jaru, and I refused to share them under Rymorian terms.

Arriving at the exit door, I pressed my palm to the scanner plate. The light flashed from red to blue, and the door slid open.

"You're late," the man on the other side said. He wore full-body, black Rymorian combat fatigues with a pulse beam rifle slung over his shoulder and a handgun at his waist.

I stepped through the door, leaving the cool dusty air behind for a cleaner version. "This is not a simple journey." I pressed my palm against the inner plate, and the door slid shut behind me. "The Outliers have begun moving. I bring final orders from the master."

"What orders?" The guard's gray eyes narrowed.

"Has the meeting been called?" I asked. I was about to update our team, but not with the master's orders. The master had chosen an unwise path, one I no longer desired to follow. I was unconvinced it would yield the results the master hoped for and thought it more likely to herald our doom.

"Yes," the guard said. "They're assembling, and eager to hear the news."

"Good, I will update you all together." We took the elevator and ascended the sixty-plus floors to the innocuous cleaning bot factory that acted as a cover for Moiety operations.

The factory was a significant employer in the ironically named

## The Master of the Switch

Hope Town district, which made an excellent choice of location since it provided a bounty of recruits for my less congenial pursuits.

Hope Town was among the poorest suburbs in Serenity, with a transient population of drug dealers, drug addicts, and criminals of every kind, mashed up with the down-on-their-lucks and down-and-outs, who wanted nothing more than to get out. Few people stayed here long, and most worked hard to find a better situation. Those who didn't were soon beaten down by the hard life, killed or assimilated into one of the gangs. Regeneration projects kicked off every decade, but none were ever successful, and all it did was shuffle the problems around.

Yes, an excellent base, I thought, as the elevator doors opened, and we arrived at the floor reserved for the secret side of our operation. Seven people were in the conference room in person, and a further thirty-four via a virtual connection.

The room was hushed as I entered, and expectant faces turned my way.

"The Outliers have left for the plains," I said. "The master is leading them to the harbinger, and the catalyst for our salvation. The master has instructed us to stay firm in our resolve in these testing days to come." The master had made no such comment, but I was certain the master's quest would fail, and he would likely never be seen again. "He asked that we heighten our efforts, since should he fail, the responsibility for redemption will fall to us. We must make all possible roads to recover both the missing codes and genetic markers."

Nods and murmurs of agreement greeted my words. Those who chose to fight and destroy the Rymorian people from within were not afraid to die for the cause. Many already had. Still, I thought the master was taking a greater risk in seeking to control the harbinger.

"Our priority is a list of government officials with the necessary clearance levels. But we will also be focusing efforts on general disruption. Rymorian security forces are in Shadowland, leaving their internal security weak. We find ourselves in a time of great change, perhaps the greatest time of change in the planet's history. Rymor no longer has an operational wall, and our intelligence suggests this is a permanent failure. We cannot hope to be whole unless we can save our regressed brothers and sisters. To do that, we must retrieve the genetic markers; a mission of great urgency given the escalating war. Now is not the time for caution or half measures. Now is the time for action, for bravery, and even for risks."

The faces staring back at me were lit with the same fervor afflicting me. While the Outlier's philosophy was peace, we suffered an inner conflict. We fought a constant battle against the darkness within us. I thought I liked the darkness well enough. It was time to embrace our true selves; to embrace any action needed to claim our lands and life once more.

# Chapter 3

**Richard**

My young assistant's cheerful face greeted me when I entered my office's reception area. "Your first appointment is waiting for you, Senator Dance."

Halting just inside the door, I suffered a familiar sinking sensation that had accompanied far too much of my life lately, as a stream of terrifying scenarios crashed through my brain. "First appointment?" I adjusted my collar to mask my hesitancy. I had been sure my calendar was empty today.

"Yes, Senator, he's waiting in your office," my assistant said, oblivious to any potential alarm the unexpected visitor's arrival had caused.

I forced a smile past tight lips. "Must have slipped my mind." I remained frozen in place while I considered my options. Would I find one of the chancellor's black-suited hitmen waiting on the other side, poised to deliver a quick death through a silent weapon, or would I be taken away, like Dan Gilmore, the renowned technical Grand Master, and never seen again?

Although I had once been Bill's most trusted advisor, and my greatest source of stress my latest wife filing for a divorce, I no longer filled that lofty role and, nowadays, whether my current wife decided to stay or go was the least of my concerns. I spent long moments weighing my limited choices, aware that my assistant must think my behavior odd. Then I realized that the location was inconsequential to my fate, given the reach of Bill's control throughout Rymor. If whoever waited within had indeed been sent by Rymor's chancellor, fleeing would only exacerbate the situation.

Resolute, but without great comfort, I steeled myself to continue into my office... and found Nate lounging with relaxed aplomb in one of my easy chairs.

My brows lifted in surprise, and I drew in a shaky breath. "A little notice would be nice."

"Come on, Richard," Nate said, a huge grin lighting his young face. His rich auburn hair had begun to grow out, and flopped over one eye. "Where's the fun in that? Besides, you enjoy surprises."

"I hate surprises," I said, wondering if my heart could handle Nate's poor sense of humor after my many ill-spent years of fast living and four marriages.

Nate's grin grew. "Yes, I know."

I collapsed into the chair opposite. "I hope you're here to tell me what the hell is going on. Last time we spoke I'd just been bundled out of the secure facility where they were holding Dan, after a sudden and suspicious interruption." My eyes narrowed on Nate. "That was two weeks ago, and I've not heard a word from you since. Bill has disappeared, and the government hasn't had a single official update on the progress of the war. It's a shambles."

"A fair summary," Nate agreed. "Right, let's get you up to date. Dan escaped the facility five days ago. He's staying with Coco Tanis and me."

I closed my eyes and offered a silent, heartfelt prayer. "I'm relieved to hear that... Wait. Coco Tanis, as in John Tanis's mother?"

"That's the one."

"What on Serenity is she doing with Dan and you?!"

# The Master of the Switch

"She's been a friend of Dan's for many years. They share common concerns. Bill was about to arrest her and, after what happened to Dan, I couldn't take that risk. Not the kind of leverage we want to give Bill while he's at war with her son."

"Goodness!" I said inadequately. The famous geneticist had lived a quiet life after her son's exile for his part in a terrorist attack. As far as I knew, she had always distanced herself from those dramatic events ten years ago.

"Yes, and especially given the way events have heated up since we last spoke," Nate said. "John Tanis was taken into the custody of Kelard Wilder, which is why they cut your meeting with Dan short. They put all government agencies on immediate alert and terminated meetings with non-personnel as a result."

"Well, I'm relieved my sudden ejection from the building was nothing to do with us, but now you say they have John Tanis? Is the war over?"

"No, far from it," Nate said. "Four days later, we lost power from Station fifty-four again."

"What?" I frowned. "That's terrifying. How did that happen?"

"An explosive device of some kind."

"Was it deliberate?" I asked blankly, grappling to accept this catastrophic news.

"Dan's still investigating, but a Rymorian access code was used to gain entry. The damage is comprehensive, possibly irreparable."

"God help us."

"Yes," Nate replied seriously. "It may need something that drastic. With the station down the satellites are down, too. The reason you're not getting any updates on the war is because there are no updates on the war, except the ones I have, which have improved since Dan's arrival. He knows how to access a lot more information than I do, but I'm learning fast."

"And what do you know?"

"John Tanis wasn't captured. He surrendered to Kelard Wilder in return for Rymor's withdrawal from Shadowland."

"But that's astonishing," I said.

"Yes, it doesn't fit his profile; unless it was a decoy to distract the Rymorians while Tanis's men took the station down. We don't know who is behind the station yet. It's possible whoever did it was working with John Tanis. Yet despite Wilder's suspect interrogation techniques, Tanis refused to leave. Theo believes Tanis surrendered under the genuine hope it would halt Rymor's attack."

"Theo? Theo who? You're not referring to Bill's missing first assistant, are you?" I asked slowly, ignoring the interrogation part, which had conjured up images of torture. Rymorians didn't torture criminals, even one responsible for a brutal terrorist attack, which had left twenty-seven dead.

"Yes, the very same."

"What the hell is he doing in Shadowland?" I began to feel a little light-headed. This was the worst Nate visit yet, and the others hadn't exactly been calm.

"Theo is kind of like me. We're related."

"You're related to Theo? That's the most preposterous statement I've ever heard!"

Nate produced a crooked grin. "Come on, Richard. I think I've made far more preposterous statements during our short acquaintance."

I snatched a deep, fortifying breath and scrutinized Nate. Now I felt like an idiot! While their personalities were very different, there were many physical similarities. Theo was professional and neat, while Nate's style was casual, but now, with hindsight, it was still obvious. "So, he's Dan's son? The same as you?"

"Sort of," Nate elaborated vaguely, and his eyes did the shifty thing that always made me nervous. "It's complicated."

"Hmm, as you've mentioned before. Most things are with you. So, how did Theo get into Shadowland and find John Tanis? And more importantly, why?"

"Because we infiltrated Bill's records. I'm now confident Tanis was never behind any terrorist attack," Nate said, warming to the

# The Master of the Switch

topic, "While Tanis is no paragon of virtue, he hates Bill and may be the only person who can bring that madman down. And Theo traveled through the tunnels. There are miles of them linking Rymor to Shadowland—a mystery for another time. Most are abandoned and in a poor state of repair, but plenty remain intact enough for Theo to have been able to make his way to the Rymorian camp in Shadowland. An interesting aside, Bill has been using the tunnels to visit the abandoned fortress at Talin, which is why he's absent much of the time. Thankfully, Bill's activity is far to the north and away from the sections of tunnel Theo needed to use. Theo discovered Kelard Wilder interrogating Tanis in ways that would break every human rights law we have. The station's destruction allowed Theo an opening, and he persuaded John Tanis to leave the camp."

"Tanis is free again? How did they escape?" I asked. "Surely such a nefarious man was securely guarded?"

"Dan gave Theo a stop code for the Rymorian weapons," Nate said, matter-of-factly. "So, I expect there wasn't a lot they could do."

"You've disabled the weapons!" The scale of this operation was well beyond all my prior suspicions. "Where is Theo now?"

"He's still with Tanis. We received a brief communication from him via a waypoint, a couple of days after they fled the Rymorian camp. He didn't go into a lot of detail—I think because of Dan." Nate's steady gaze held mine. "Hannah is in the reluctant company of a criminal Bill enlisted to do his work in Shadowland... As you can imagine, Dan is frantic."

"But is someone going to help her? Theo?"

Nate nodded. "Yes, I believe so. The waypoints aren't a great source of communication. Dan is working to regain satellite communication so he can talk directly with Theo. Otherwise, we'll need to wait until Theo initiates contact via a waypoint again."

Dan's affection for Hannah was well known, and I could imagine how distressed the renowned Grand Master must be. "Is Dan well? After what we did? After what *I* did to him?"

"He's perfect." Nate's smile held genuine warmth. "Not too steady on his feet, but that will come with time."

"That's a relief, and a positive note among so many troubles." I tried to park my worries in order to allow the information to settle. It was a lot to take in. My brows drew together. "Why do I get the feeling you're not here simply to give me an update?"

"Richard, you realize this is just the beginning, right?" Nate said. "We have many more steps to take."

"Yes, I had a feeling you were going to say that," I muttered. Such dangerous times, and yet I was still hopeful for a future free from corruption and deceit. "I want to help, Nate, in any way I can. I'm committed. I was the moment Dan entered my office and asked me to help. I've needed time to accept it, and a few nudges from yourself to embrace it. As I'm sure you're aware, you're my only appointment of the day. I suggest you make the most of it and tell me what I need to know."

Nate smiled, the one I'd come to think of as his winning smile. "I'm so glad you said that. Now, where do I begin…"

# Chapter 4

**Shadowland**

**Tanis**

The clamor of people moving should have woken her, but Hannah remained fast asleep. I was the leader of Shadowland. I should be gifting her the finest nesting materials and feeding her treats. She should be exhausted because I'd spent all night fucking and knotting her, not because a sick bastard had used her as a punching bag.

I sighed. We would leave soon, and the gray of dawn was just starting to bring light enough for travel, so I crouched and gave her a gentle nudge. She stretched languidly, blinked open her eyes, and then scrambled backward in a frantic rush.

I suppressed a smile. "How are you feeling?"

The bustle of the camp snagged her attention. "Okay, I'm okay." She attempted to finger-comb her wild hair, but her fingers snagged, and she gave up.

"You certainly slept well enough."

Her indignant glare made me chuckle and instilled a sense of normality, along with relief that they hadn't broken her with their cruelty, that she wasn't a cowering wreck. Even as it gutted me that she had suffered, I also felt fierce pride. No alpha wanted a weak omega. We wanted an equal: one who had power and strength in ways that we did not.

"We found a scanner, among other things we retrieved from Karry's camp, but it's been configured for his thumb print, and I don't know any work-around. Unless you do?" The bruising on her neck had worsened since yesterday, turning a spectacular shade of purple.

She pressed her fingers to her throat. "Not without hooking it up to a computer. My throat aches, but I don't think it's worse than a bruise. What does it look like?"

"Like somebody tried to choke you out," I said seriously. "If it doesn't improve, we have a healer at the main camp."

"It's okay, Karry didn't always heal me."

She said this so matter-of-factly that I wanted to kill the bastard again. Only it hadn't been me who had done that deed. "He's gone now."

"Did I kill him?" Her pretty gray eyes held mine for longer than I was comfortable with.

"Do you really want to be the one who killed him?"

Her gaze lowered to her hands. "I'm not sorry if I did."

"That wasn't what I asked."

"I think I killed him," she said uncertainly

"Sorry to disappoint you, but *I* killed Karry." I stood and raked my fingers through my hair. "I'm certain I killed them all." I hadn't been thinking straight yesterday, and that scared the shit out of me. If Garren hadn't halted my killing spree and refocused my attention on locating Hannah, I might not have found her in time, and she would have been dead.

Time to change the subject. "We're heading to meet with the rest of Garren's section... At Julant."

## The Master of the Switch

Her chin shot up at the mention of the village, and her eyes searched mine.

"I'm sure she'll still be there." Assuming the good people of Julant hadn't driven Molly out for terrorizing the other children.

I'd found Molly hidden in a farmstead decimated by a Jaru attack. The slaughtered remains of her family had been among the wreckage, but somehow, and against the odds, Molly had survived.

Much to Tay and Han's amusement, she had formed an instant attachment to me, cemented by my killing of the 'bad Jaru' as Molly called them. With nowhere else to take her, I'd left her at Julant's orphanage. But only two days later, the kindly proprietor had begged me to take Molly with me since the little girl had a propensity for trouble Hannah remained oblivious to.

I wasn't one for premonitions, but I felt that an impending sense of doom surrounded the upcoming visit to Julant.

Before we reached Julant, the matter of claiming Hannah had to be resolved. I beckoned Red over. I still wanted to strangle the fucker for throwing his hat in an already crowded ring. But it was done, and I could handle Red with her easier than Garren, which made no fucking sense when she'd been with Garren from the start. "We'll be leaving soon. Get yourself ready."

As I left Hannah with Red, I noticed Kein chatting with Garren. Despite the fact that he had been absent for many weeks, the scout's horse waited beside him, ready for a swift exit.

"Kein, good to see you," I said as I approached.

"Likewise." Kein grinned. "I heard about your adventure." He passed a critical assessment of my battered appearance. "You'll be pleased to hear the station is broken. Permanently, according to Joshua. Rymor is once more without a protective wall. Our mission went well enough, until a Jaru skirmish while Joshua was inside the station. They were armed with tower-dweller weapons, and we lost sixteen men. Danel took the losses badly. He's at Han's camp with the rest of the Rymorians. Garren mentioned you have a way to stop their weapons."

"Yes, we do." I was more relieved than ever about Theo's arrival. The decimation a single Rymorian weapon could do to my soldiers was terrifying—Wilder's men had been armed with thousands. "My information flow has suffered in your absence. Any other news?"

"Javid is tracking their movements from the north. The Rymorians turned west as predicted."

"Han's keeping track of the access point," Garren added. "But if they try to leave, there won't be much he can do while we have the disabler here with us."

"What about the main Rymorian group?"

"Slow moving." Kein shrugged.

"Good, I'll reassess the situation when we get to Julant," I said. "Our supporters inside Rymor have taken control of the waypoint communications, and we'd better hope that continues if we don't want more Rymorians in Shadowland. This is personal to me, and I want to be there when we take the Rymorians down."

"They had fun with you, so I can see why this is personal," Garren said. "Glad they did though, you'd be dead now if they had any brains, and, for the record, I still think you handing yourself over was a stupid idea."

"I think that was supposed to be an insult, but I'm not completely sure." Kein grinned before turning to me. "Where do you need me next?"

"Update Han on our discussion and meet me at Julant."

Kein nodded, his expression softening as his gaze settled on Hannah. "Did you kill the one who did that to her?"

"No, Hannah had already killed him." I'd lied to her about it. At the time, she'd narrowly escaped being raped by the man in question and was covered in enough cuts and bruises to make my guts churn. Not the best time to inform her that she was a killer and, despite her recent bravado, I didn't intend to change my mind. "She doesn't realize she killed him. I would rather it remained that way."

Kein's brows rose. "She came through it all alright?"

## The Master of the Switch

"Yes." Her strength of character was a thing of wonder. "I think she's going to be okay."

Kein smiled. "I look forward to talking with her when we're less pressed for time." He vaulted into the saddle without waiting for me to confirm the conversation was over, then called out as he rode away, "I'll return via Javid."

"I didn't tell him to visit our father." I stared after Kein.

"No, I think he decided that all by himself," Garren said, smirking. "You know how Kein loves to gossip." His attention shifted over my shoulder. "Maybe leaving Hannah with Red wasn't such a good idea."

I turned to find Hannah in the throes of an animated rant. Red stood opposite, vigorously shaking his head with one hand gripping the hilt of his knife.

"I'm going to kill someone," I muttered as I began walking. Garren's laughter followed me.

"What's going on?" I demanded.

Red threw his arms up and stalked off without saying a word.

"Hannah?" I asked.

"It was nothing." She refused to meet my gaze.

"It didn't look like nothing."

"I told him I wasn't hungry, but he insisted I should have something to eat."

"You should eat, but that wasn't what you were discussing."

She scoffed. "And you're a walking lie detector?"

"No, you're just a terrible liar."

"I was a good enough liar to fool Karry."

"No, you didn't; that's why he kept asking you questions."

"And then *I* killed him."

"No, you didn't."

"You know, you're a terrible liar, too." Her lips began to tremble, and her eyes glistened.

"Well, that's irrelevant since I'm telling you the truth. Now, sit down, eat some food, and stop asking Red for a weapon. You're not getting one." The entire camp was watching us, but I stood my ground and met her glare with my best stony expression.

Hopefully, being a dick would distract her from the burning who-killed-Karry question.

"You're such an asshole," she muttered before stalking off to retrieve her ration pack.

I blinked after her. Did I come out on top of that?

When I turned back, I found Garren smirking, again. "Nicely handled," he said.

My eyes narrowed on him. "Fine then, since you're an expert, she can ride with you today."

That wiped the smirk right off his face.

## Garren

"Ride with me?" I repeated, to be absolutely clear. Was this some kind of test? A trap? He'd let Red touch her, although I'd seen how he bristled at them sharing a hug. I knew exactly how he felt. "You think this is any easier for me? I returned to Thale to find her in bed with Red."

"You shared her?" he asked. Only it wasn't a question.

"Yeah, after I'd gotten over my rage." I'd used her roughly, rutted her like a beast against the wall and then the floor, and she'd taken it as her due. "Red's a pushy bastard for all he's a beta. He won't walk away. And besides, she's bonded to him now." I shrugged. "He follows instructions well, if you know what I mean. And smaller cocks are useful for breaking in her—"

Tanis lifted a hand and heaved a breath. "Don't finish that or I swear I'm going over to rip his small cock off."

I chuckled. Tanis wasn't used to playing well with others nor sharing when it wasn't under his terms. Tay didn't count. He had no deeper feelings toward her than friendship and her place as a wolf

### The Master of the Switch

guard. She slept with other men, including me. An alpha female, she never hinted at wanting or needing more until she did.

He'd dealt with her harshly, but there'd been no point in leaving confusion about her place. It helped me in some ways, too. Whether I liked it or not, he was part of this. I wasn't going to win any intelligence awards. I was simple in my needs and not always fast when reading subtleties. Tanis and Hannah were inevitable. I'd thought he might try to take her from me at first. He might still, but I thought it wouldn't go over well with Hannah if he did, so he was fucked either way.

"This wasn't what any of us planned," I said. "But it's happened. I'm still pissed at you for fucking her behind my back. I'm pissed at her for fucking Red behind my back, too, only she didn't know better that time. When she went to you, she did."

"If it makes you feel better, she only came for information on the war," he said. "I'd been drinking Red Alrin and told her to leave—ordered her. She refused. But I'd always wanted her, and it went sideways from there." His eyes shifted to Hannah. "As you say. It's done now. I'm still an alpha who can't have children, and we're still at war. The future is far from rosy or certain. I should walk away. It would be better for her if I did, before the bond grows deeper. But I can't. Maybe time and circumstances will change that... She can ride with you today. Tomorrow she'll ride with me again. But Garren, you don't fuck her. Not until I say, and not unless I'm there. I was ready to kill you over her before, and nothing has changed. I don't have control over myself where she's concerned yet. So don't push me on this. Advise Red of the same."

∽

## Hannah

I sat fuming after Tanis's dressing-down and ate the nut cracker in an angry rush that left a heavy lump in my belly.

"You're riding with me."

My head swung around just as Garren plucked me from the ground... and deposited me in a saddle.

His saddle.

I frowned, trying to work out what this meant.

But I was tired, and I couldn't.

"Don't think rubbing your sweet ass will get you fucked," Garren said seriously. "Tanis is a surly bastard at the moment, and he'll be pissed if you can't keep your hands to yourself." He winked at me as he drew the reins over the horse's head and mounted swiftly behind me.

"I wasn't going to," I said weakly, but then Garren's scent and familiarity washed over me, and it was like we were right back at the start again. Only so much had happened since then. The world had changed, and so had I.

Around us, the rest of the party, some fourteen people in all, were also mounting.

Was this Tanis giving me back to Garren again? I'd wanted to slap his arrogant face a few minutes ago, but now I was desolate at the thought of being passed off. Yet the feel of Garren around me, his solid presence, and his strong warrior body, had immediate and predictable results. My mind played catch-up, showering me with the images of that wild night back in Thale when Garren had fucked me in front of Red and then shared me with him.

The horse danced as he turned it on the spot and nudged it into a walk.

I couldn't help myself. I pushed my ass back, feeling an instant thrill when I met an unmissable and very hard bulge.

His growl was ticked-off alpha, and that also made me wet.

"Are you angry with me?" I glanced back.

His arm tightened around my waist before he lowered his hand slowly until he could cup my pussy through my pants. "Yes," he said. The horse's gait made his fingers rub against my clit, already growing sensitive from the light stimulation.

### The Master of the Switch

"How angry?" I breathed, surreptitiously rubbing against his hand, reveling in the sensations rushing through me. After so much darkness, it was a wonder to feel this again.

"How pissed I was about Red, times a hundred."

"Oh," I said, my ardor cooling some, although he didn't take his fingers away and, to my shock, rubbed them back and forth, making me hot and urgent again.

"Tanis has ordered me not to fuck you, so a punishment fuck is out of the question. You definitely don't deserve to get off, so that's off the table too. So I think I'll settle for taunting you all day long. Then tonight when Tanis takes you back, your scent will break his iron control and he'll stop treating you like you'll break, and then we can move on to the punishment fuck."

"Oh, god," I said weakly, not liking the thought of denied gratification, but totally on board with everything else, including the punishment fuck; because that couldn't be all bad, right?

Garren worked the heel of his hand against my crotch—I bit my lips to stifle my moan.

"I'm sorry," I said. "I don't know what I was thinking. I should have come to you."

"Should have," he said. "Didn't. I promise you're going to be a whole lot sorrier by the end of the day."

# Chapter 5

**Rymor**

**Nate, illegally created being**

The labyrinth linking Rymor to Shadowland was vast and complex, with an estimated total length of nearly three thousand miles. The dozen or so main tunnels close to the Shadowland boundary were in good repair, but the rest had decayed, their entries long ago sealed and tagged and, for the people of Rymor, they were no-go zones.

I wasn't letting any of this stop me. The tunnel I was navigating today was derelict, but I knew where at least one of its pathways ended because my bio-engineered brother, Theo, had traveled this way several weeks ago.

The ancient crumbling walls were cast into stark relief by my flashlight. While I thought it was unlikely to collapse suddenly, the cracks suggested it was a possibility.

"Sending twenty field scientists into Shadowland with weapons is crazy," I said, not for the first time. When Scott Harding had said

## The Master of the Switch

he wanted to send people into Shadowland, I'd foolishly assumed he meant one or two.

"It was the best I could do to keep it to twenty," Scott grumbled. "The whole team wanted to go."

"But twenty?! Like, this isn't a sight-seeing trip. Do you not think questions might be asked if twenty members of a small, but incredibly notable, government agency all suddenly go off grid?"

"Keep your voice down!" Scott hissed, pointing his flashlight in my face. "My team's ready to go and, besides, you can manage the systems to make sure Bill doesn't know they've gone."

I directed my own flashlight into Scott's face and hissed back, "I can't manage twenty households! I'm a man, not a machine!" Actually, the last part was debatable, since Dan's enhancements sort of crossed the human-cyborg boundary. In theory, anyone with cybernetic devices was, by definition, a cyborg, but I supposed there was some room for interpretation of the law.

Also, I wasn't technically human to start with, so who knew what that meant, philosophically or legally.

Scott suddenly grinned and slapped me on the shoulder hard enough that I fumbled my flashlight. "We've all got our part to play, pretty-boy. You've got to watch the surveillance, I've got to put up with that dickhead Wilder and that asshole Jordan, and the team here need to save their fellow field scientists."

I lowered my flashlight, defeated, and turned to my right where twenty field scientists stood, several feet away, awaiting the outcome of our intense discussion. I flicked the flashlight over them, and twenty expectant faces blinked back. "Well, I suppose they're here now."

I'd been reconnoitering the tunnel ahead while Scott had followed my markers from behind. Only now, with hindsight, did I recognize my mistake. Had I been with Scott back in Serenity, I might have thwarted his insane plan.

"Right, let's go!" Scott hollered down the tunnel, and twenty pairs of boots stomped enthusiastically forward to join us.

I turned and took the direction leading toward Shadowland as Scott fell into step alongside me.

"Any more news on the station?" Scott asked.

"The station? Ah, no, it's a complex and intricate assembly of ancient technology, which would be hard enough to fix had it not been destroyed by a bomb."

"Well, we can't leave the wall down," Scott said, scowling. "Once Tanis finishes with the Rymorians out there, he's going to come looking for Bill, and one psycho is enough for any country."

"Yes, I agree, but there's only so much we can do when we're working surreptitiously."

We reached a section where a collapse on the left had caused soft gravel to spill from the ruined wall to the opposite side, forcing us to slow to navigate the slippery ground. Ahead, the tunnel opened into a vast cavern with the same featureless walls. I mentally searched for the controls, and light flooded the area as my cybernetics made contact.

Scott scowled at me, his broken nose and lean build against the semi-derelict setting combining to make him look more street-thug than the head of a prominent government department. "Did you do that?"

I gestured toward myself. "All part of the package."

Scott grumbled under his breath.

A capsule track sliced the room in two. An easterly exit led in the direction of Rymor and had collapsed, burying the track and part of a transport capsule. A westerly track led deeper into Shadowland and housed another capsule.

"How did you get the capsule working?" Scott asked as the team spread throughout the cavern.

"It was still operational."

"It'll hold fifty, easy." Scott frowned. "Why would we ever need to transport so many people in and out of Shadowland?"

"An interesting question," I agreed. "And one I have no answer

# The Master of the Switch

for. It's clear there was once an awful lot more interaction between Shadowland and Rymor."

"But you have a theory?" Scott's eyes narrowed on me.

"Not a conversation for now." I nodded at the field scientists, who had begun converging on the capsule.

"Okay, team, gather round and listen up," Scott hollered. They shuffled over and fixed their attention on their boss.

The lockdown had left them itching to return to the job they loved. Scott had confided in me that his team was angry they were being accused of leaking technology into Shadowland.

Ironically, they were about to do the very thing they'd been accused of, breaking the law and their code, both of which held them to observe but never interfere. All were fitted with trackers and transmitters, allowing them to communicate with Scott via the waypoint towers found throughout Shadowland. I just hoped this didn't come back to bite us. With luck, ordinary Rymorians need never know about the risk Scott's team was taking.

"Nate is uploading your systems with the tunnel plan. We've not been able to contact our people out there to let them know you're coming, but we'll keep trying."

Grave faces stared back, but I could also sense their excitement at being part of such an important operation.

I finalized the data load and then pressed my palm against the plate on the capsule door. The door hissed and popped open. "It's an hour ride, followed by a one week walk underground," I said. "A collapse has compromised the capsule track toward the end. Although the damage isn't bad, the capsule can't get through. Unfortunately, you have a challenge at the end. The exit elevator isn't working and there are a lot of stairs."

The team offered good-humored grumbles. "How many floors?" one man asked.

"Two hundred and eighty-three."

Further grumbling ensued.

"Okay, you know what to do." Scott raised a hand to quieten them down. "I know you're putting your lives on the line for this. Most of you have families, and that makes it difficult; not that it's easy either way. It's killing me not being able to come with you, but some bastard has to stay behind and manage that ass-wipe Jordan." That received a few guffaws from the group. "We all want to return our colleagues home safe and clear their names, and that's why we're here breaking rules." They nodded in silent agreement, their faces solemn. "Let's get this done. Keep in contact where possible, and most importantly, keep safe."

A small but enthusiastic cheer went up, and the team filed into the capsule, with handshakes and back-slaps for Scott and me. By the time they had finished, I was battered and bruised, and relieved when the last man stepped inside.

The doors closed, and the capsule accelerated down the Shadowland track.

I turned to find Scott watching me.

"So," Scott said, conversationally, slapping his hand on my shoulder and making me jump. "You were going to tell me your theory as to why Rymor once transported so many people in and out of Shadowland..."

# Chapter 6

**Shadowland**

**Hannah**

Garren made good on his promise; or was it a threat? Tanis slept beside me again, and no amount of subtle fidgeting could crack his stoic façade. I woke up irritable, wondering about this new hell I found myself within.

We rode at a brisk pace toward Julant for the next few days and, while hard riding was nothing new, my lingering injuries made it worse. Our small procession consisted of fourteen people, with two riders ahead of me, and the rest snaked behind.

Yesterday, I'd ridden with Garren again, which had been an exercise in torture. If he felt any ire at Tanis' don't-fuck-her order, his manner didn't reflect it.

Today I was riding with Tanis again.

I'd asked to ride my own horse. I hated riding double and riding in front was even worse since it made me feel like a hapless child. My request met with no reaction other than Tanis pointing at his horse.

The prospect of a day in the saddle with Tanis was almost too much to bear. Almost. But I would still rather be here, wherever here was and however hard the ride, so long as Garren, Red and, particularly, Tanis, who had saved me from Karry's men, were near. Possessed by this new self-preservation instinct, I found myself linked to them by an invisible thread. I remained conscious of where they were and how many seconds it would take them to reach me should some form of terror manage to get past the dozen other armed men.

This unhealthy fixation worried me and was further exacerbated by Tanis' proximity while we rode. The rational part of my mind realized it was the after-effects of facing my mortality and that, in a sane, normal world, I would have had time to come to terms with what had happened. Then again, in that other world, it wouldn't have happened at all.

After an hour or so of brisk cantering, it was a relief when we slowed the horses to a walk, which presented an opportunity for me to eat or doze. The air was hot and muggy, but the forest birds were in fine form and screeching up a storm—sleep was out of the question. I pulled out my ration pack and picked at the nutty cracker for a time. Dissatisfied after a few bites, I put the pack away.

My body was recovering, and although my clothing offered a welcome barrier to the view, the bruises still ached. My wrists were another matter. The gold and purple welts and angry cuts drew my eyes. I pulled my cuffs down to hide them.

"Stop thinking about it," Tanis said.

I thought about telling him to go fuck himself (or me, or give me to Garren for the punishment fuck that was coming) but somehow I restrained myself, knowing it would not end well. What I spent my time thinking about was none of his business, but our conversations hadn't gone well of late—they hadn't gone well ever—and instead, I said, "How do you know I was thinking about it?"

"You stiffen when you stare at your wrists. You also fidget with your cuffs, and you sigh a lot when you do so," was his detached assessment.

## The Master of the Switch

I wondered then about the man I wanted to tie myself to. How much did I really know? Not a lot, I decided. Did he still possess any emotions or had his violent life scoured them out? Although he'd once lived in Rymor, he seemed to have forgotten what ordinary people were like.

"I can't help myself." My eyes were drawn to the evidence of those most recent harrowing events. "I could have died."

"Welcome to Shadowland. People die here all the time."

That was cutting. I'd spent too much time angry during the last few days, between obsessing about Tanis, being aroused by Garren, missing the simple comfort I'd shared with Red and only Red, and wallowing in the heady, anxious delight of being alive only to then worry how long that might last. "Nearly dying may have become normal to you, but for ordinary people, it's a life-changing event."

"Was that you asking to ride with Garren again?"

I was going to do something regrettable... like stab him with his own knife.... if this forced proximity continued another second. "I want to ride on my own!"

"And I don't have time to stop and pick you up when you fall off."

"I've fallen off a horse exactly once: on the day the Jaru attacked, three weeks after I entered this godforsaken country. My aversion to the bruises on my wrists is my own business—I can't stand that they kept me tied."

"You're not exactly dangerous with your hands free."

I suffered a moment of startling clarity. "Is this a misguided attempt to distract me?"

"Maybe," he replied, and there was no mistaking the smile in his voice. "I'm pretty sure you're thinking violent thoughts toward me right now. Better you hate me than sigh as you stare at your wrists."

That took the wind out of my rant. "Your methods could use some finessing," I finally said.

"I'll work on it," he said.

Only, I didn't want to do him violence anymore, and even his abhorrent attempts at distraction made me teary. My eyes shifted back to my wrists. "Why did you go to the Rymorians?"

"Are you staring at your wrists again?"

"Just answer the question."

His sigh was heavy. "I went because I hoped Bill would stop at me, that I would be enough to satisfy his sense of revenge, and that my surrender would halt the war. It didn't work out that way. It never does with Bill."

"You didn't expect to return, did you?"

He didn't answer. The silence stretched, and I knew the answer already. He wasn't expecting a trial. He expected to die. "Why did you come back? How did you? What did Bill do?"

"What he has always done." His voice sounded brittle. "Which is: going too far, making it personal, and hurting innocent people who should never have been involved to start with."

The words carried undertones but, like dice caught in a perpetual tumble, they never landed to reveal the score.

"What did they do to you?"

"What people usually do to prisoners," he said. "I did worse to the man responsible afterward."

"They tortured you?"

"They did, enthusiastically."

My stomach turned over, but then my brows pinched together. "Then you tortured a Rymorian?"

"Do you know who I am?" he asked, sounding confused.

"Yes, of course, I do." The horse ahead shook its mane and jangled the bit between its teeth.

"How do you think I went from knowing no one to ruling the five fortresses and everything else in Shadowland in the space of ten years? I've done many terrible things when I needed to; and when not doing them would mean the lives of people I care for. The world beyond Rymor's wall is complex, and the line between right and wrong is often blurred. Have you forgotten the first day we met? How I beat the Jaru leader while Adam lay bleeding out on the ground?"

# The Master of the Switch

I had forgotten, which was impressive considering how horrified I'd been at the time. Yet that horror was absent now, and that side of Tanis no longer frightened me.

*Had it ever?*

No, I'd never really feared him, even when he was furious, even when he had slit the Jaru leader's throat. This realization settled uncomfortably. What kind of person did that make me?

It made me grateful and alive.

"How did you do it? How did you come to rule Shadowland?" I felt calm again in the wake of my inner resolve.

"I'm an accomplished killer." He sounded amused again.

"That's all?" Could anyone but John Tanis sound amused while making that statement? I was suddenly curious as to what had driven him.

"It was enough to get me noticed by Thale's commander. Once recruited, I rose through the ranks and, after two years, I became the commander. Life was good until I had a disagreement with the fortress leader. I disagreed with him a little too forcefully. He put me in prison, which the majority of the garrison took exception to. They killed him, and that's how I became the ruler of Thale."

"And the rest?"

"The second was Techin. Its lord had heard about Thale and came to their rescue. In truth, he came expecting to find the fortress in disarray; that it would be easy pickings. I killed him, and that's how I came to rule my second fortress. The third became mine in roughly the same way a few years later. The last two were together and so were a little messier, especially given one of those fortresses was ruled by my father."

Quiet settled between us, and I lifted my water bottle to take a drink. Tanis made it sound like he'd stumbled upon his place, yet I knew it was neither accident nor luck. Shadowland was a daunting place; one I was still coming to terms with.

Yet recent events had sullied my views of Rymor, too.

*"Rymor no longer exists for you, Hannah,"* he had said a long time

ago, and while I had been pointing an operational weapon at him. *"At least not the Rymor you know. Better to forget it sooner rather than later."* I hadn't wanted to accept that at the time.

I tucked my water bottle in the saddle pack. "I don't think I can cope with almost dying again," I said softly.

"It won't happen again."

"You don't know that, and you can't guarantee that." I was tired of never feeling safe. "You said so yourself: this is Shadowland and people die here."

"You're sitting in front of me and, as I've just pointed out, I'm not exactly easy to kill."

"You won't always be near me." That irrational fear of him leaving bore down on me once more. Despite our physical proximity, I sensed his detachment from me over the last few days. It was as if our night of intimacy together had never happened. I felt stupid and confused about how this might play out. He was the leader of Shadowland and was sinfully handsome, lethal, and commanding. He probably had thousands of omegas begging him for a scrap of time. "Even Thale wasn't safe against technology."

"The dynamics of this world are about to change, Hannah. It's already begun, and I still intend to bang heads when I get back to Thale for allowing you to be taken. Now you can eat, try to sleep, or just sit quietly."

I guessed the conversation was over. I remained quiet, but I wasn't hungry, and sleep was out with such a jumble of thoughts clamoring in my mind.

I felt sad, like I was grieving for something that had never been mine. "Have you ever been in love?"

"For fuck's sake, Hannah."

"Have you?" I persisted, needing some sort of evidence from him that he was capable of such emotion.

"Yes, I've been in love," he replied, in an unexpectedly desolate tone.

## The Master of the Switch

"What happened?" The pain in his voice manifested within me; the feeling tangible, as if it were my own.

"Bill happened," he bit out bleakly.

"Did he—did they have an affair?" I couldn't let it go, reluctant to uncover the details, yet still pulled into its sordid embrace.

He remained silent but, given the history of our discussions, I was amazed he'd shared as much as he had. Tension rippled through his body where it pressed against me, and I shifted, feeling uneasy.

"No, he brought her out here." His words trickled like water over smooth stones, the emotions too intense to find purchase. "She nearly died..." he paused as a mournful weight wrapped around us both, "and then you nearly died."

I tried to connect what he'd told me, but like an overly complex jigsaw, my tired mind could not make them fit.

Did he feel obligated toward me because I had a loose connection to a Rymorian woman he'd once loved?

"Did she go back to Rymor? Do you miss her?"

"Ava returned to Rymor, and no, I don't miss her. At first, yes, but not in many years. The part of her I once cared for died out here. It changed her. It changed both of us, I guess. I couldn't go back with her. She couldn't stay out here. Not that it mattered since I terrified her afterward."

Putting a name to the woman Tanis had once loved made the pain worse. Ava's rejection made me angry. He was what he was, and he did what he did. If he didn't, then I would've been dead long ago. Besides, how could I judge him for being a killer when I'd killed someone myself?

He said the rules of my world had no place in this. At first, I didn't understand, but now, reflecting on my time with Karry, I thought I did. Only now, Rymorian life seemed far from idyllic, when the people who had hurt me were Rymorian.

"I should have killed him when I had the chance. That I left him to wreak this havoc on the world is a living grief I cannot reconcile. The thought of him ever having had happiness in his life is sickening to me... I thought I could live with the first part. She was still alive, so was Bill, and I'd reconciled myself to making a life in Shadowland, but a week later, after I let him return to Rymor, I was taken prisoner by a group of men he'd paid to kill me. I know Bill paid them because they went to great lengths to remind me of that during the long, mindless hours of torture. I spent four months as their prisoner, lost a quarter of my body weight, and acquired an impressive collection of scars. I thought I would die there—I expected to, but Kein came for me. He saved me... A few people know about the first part; only Kein and now you know what happened after."

There was no way back from the raw emotion of those last words, and my silent tears made soft splats against my clothes. He didn't tell me to stop or seek to distract me. His revelation explained much. I'd once believed Tanis hated me because of my association with Bill. Perhaps he had at first, but I no longer thought so. That night in Thale had been a mistake that wouldn't be repeated, and too much had happened for him to be impartial in dealing with someone who had claimed to have once loved Bill. I'd been betrayed. I didn't know how to make peace with it, nor did I trust my judgment when I'd thought myself in love with Bill and had missed such wanton darkness.

"Don't blame yourself," he said quietly, as if he had read my inner thoughts and saw through to the heart of my anguish. "After all, he was once my best friend."

# Chapter 7

**Talin**

**Bill**

Upon arriving at Talin a week ago, one of my first actions had been to establish an office and personal space from where to conduct my business. I'd selected a suite of rooms near the top of the fortress, in the east wing. The aged wooden floor and the glistening black stone walls felt oppressive, but the room had windows, unlike much of the rest of the building, and the outlook provided a view across the endless forests of Shadowland. It was odd to see the same trees I'd gazed upon from my Rymorian office from the context of a fortress, to see a view so familiar, so close, and to be amid that view.

The fortress of Talin wasn't visible from my more civilized office, but it still felt like I'd submerged myself into that living picture. I'd dreamt of being out here. Reality was sweeter, but there was more to do before I could fully savor my victory.

I could still communicate with Rymor and had engaged in several conference discussions during the morning. Later, I would return to Rymor. Twenty-four hours was all I could afford to be absent at such a critical stage.

The delay in hearing back from Kelard and Karry gnawed at me. Kelard had Tanis, and I wanted Tanis. I wondered how I would feel when I saw him again.

Guilt, love, regret, and anger all had a place.

Seeing Tanis again, winning against him, might even soften the other disasters unfolding in my life. The wall remained inoperative, and the severed connection to Station fifty-four appeared to be terminal. The engineering grunts were scratching their heads, at a complete loss. So far, none had offered any enlightenment other than the original station fix being temporary or a subsequent related failure taking place.

Of course, I knew Rymorians had entered the station just before the second failure, and the likelihood of sabotage was high. The engineers didn't know that, nor did anyone in Rymor other than the few involved with global monitoring. The one person who might have been able to shed some light on the matter was Dan Gilmore, who was now missing, along with Coco Tanis.

Coco's disappearance had been inexplicable enough, given I had real people watching her, but Dan's escape from a maximum-security facility when he couldn't even walk was unfathomable.

The teams were scrambling to uncover how a man who couldn't walk had escaped the building without a single sighting or alarm.

The absence of first Theo, then Coco, and finally Dan painted a picture I was at odds to acknowledge. My entire operation was at risk, and the possibility that they were collaborating in some way was high. They hadn't acted yet, but they would. Theo, in particular, concerned me, given how much information he'd had access to during his five years as my employee. I needed a fresh approach, and while I didn't have answers yet, I was confident they would come.

I leaned back in my chair and turned my attention to Ella, who

## The Master of the Switch

sat today, as she always did whenever I was at Talin, on a small stool in the corner of the room. She followed me as I went about my business, a strangely comforting shadow.

As far as the people of Rymor were concerned, Ella was dead. Uncovering details of her parents' death had gifted me the perfect, plausible cover. No one would suspect she was here, and this gave me the freedom to do with her as I willed.

Her treatment before my arrival had left mental scars. Her intelligent eyes had lost a spark, and while she was clean, well, and outwardly articulate when we conversed, her former hatred of me for daring to have a relationship with her younger sister was gone. Her eyes, while not empty as expected, held gratitude.

Now I had her under my control in this state, I was unsure what to do with her. I felt no desire to toy with her in other ways nor to taunt her, as I'd initially intended. Her odd presence was simply comforting. I had won this, and there was nothing else I needed to do.

My lips pursed in thought as I studied the woman who might, at a glance, have been mistaken for Hannah. A little less wild in the hair, a little older, and beautiful, but not *as* beautiful as Hannah, Ella had once harbored open contempt for me. The abuse and torment she had suffered at the hands of the original fortress personnel had changed that. They had broken her. "Have you eaten today?"

She shot a brief, furtive look my way. "No. I forgot."

My brows drew together. Owning Ella was much like owning a pet. One had to care for their charge. Rather than feeling a burden, I liked the idea of her dependence.

Rising, I threw open the door, finding a grunt waiting outside. "Send for lunch and ask Damien to join us."

The grunt nodded and disappeared down the corridor. I closed the door again, since open doors distressed Ella. According to the grunts on duty watching her room when I was away, she never ventured out of the room although the door had no lock.

Shortly later, Damien entered, followed by a servant carrying a tray with food and drinks.

Damien Moore was an investigative archeologist who had first come to my attention several years ago when he published a journal on his lifework exploring the origins of Rymor. Subsequently, he had discovered the interstellar ship believed to have brought the first settlers here.

Together with a small team, he was about to begin a detailed study of the vessel buried in the heart of the Jaru Plains. It would have been a perilous trip had I not formed an alliance with the Jaru's despot leader, Ailey. Damien's team had all been asked to sign a non-disclosure agreement. Given how momentous the discovery was, none of them had balked.

"How are your plans for the trip progressing?" I asked, and motioned Ella to come and collect some food. She placed a few items on a plate before hurrying back to the corner.

"Exceptionally well!" Enthused by the ship's discovery, Damien's bumbling conversations had risen to borderline articulation. "We're due to head out again at the end of the week. Just waiting for the last supplies to arrive."

At least something was progressing well.

Our conversation continued in detail and was wrapping up when a knock sounded on the door. At my behest, one of the grunts entered. "Sir, two reconnaissance men have arrived. They say they need to talk to you urgently."

"Damien, please excuse me."

Damien left to complete his preparations, and the grunt nudged his head at Ella. "Do you want me to take her back to her room?"

"No." My attention shifted to the woman who was nibbling food from her plate, oblivious to the world. I didn't need to worry about hiding things from Ella. "She can stay. I'll take her back later."

The grunt left, and I pondered the news for only a moment before there was another knock on the door, and my reconnaissance team entered. They were dressed in the nondescript Shadowlander clothing worn by all Rymorians while performing such duties, dusty and stained from travel.

### The Master of the Switch

"It's about Karry." The first man said. He reached into his pocket, extracted a blackened tracking device, and held it out toward me. "This is Karry's. He's dead."

As I stared at the device, a cold, sinking sensation settled in. "What happened to my prisoner?"

The man withdrew his hand, closing his fingers around the tracker. "Gone."

"Gone? You mean...dead?" I frowned, my eyes shifting subconsciously to Ella, who continued to eat her food.

"No, taken." He nudged his companion.

A silent, glaring battle took place between the two men before the second man said, "The villagers said John Tanis came. He killed Karry and took the woman with him."

I swallowed down the sickness in my gut and looked at Ella again. She was no longer eating, but her face was perfectly blank.

I turned back to the two men. "Then you had better get back out there and find out where the fuck she is."

# Chapter 8

**Shadowland**

**Tanis**

We were closing in on Julant, and fifty additional men had joined us from Han's camp. Among other things, they'd had the foresight to bring tents.

The prospect of sleeping in a bed delighted me. Much as I could cope with the hard ground when necessity dictated, I preferred comfort. I was making a steady recovery from my time in Kelard Wilder's hands. Just a few niggling aches remained, which were negligible and should settle with the aid of a few more days—and a bed.

Hannah was also looking better... and throwing off enough pheromones to choke me. I'd been trying to give her space to heal, but between Garren's taunting her whenever they rode together, and my own rising needs, I thought that her time was up.

## The Master of the Switch

"There's no beer. I double checked," Garren grumbled at my side.

We stood amid the rapidly forming camp as tents were pitched and fires lit for cooking, which would make a welcome break from the travel rations. Two of my wolf guard stood nearby while the rest were preparing my tent. They were still disgruntled that I'd left them with Han while searching for Hannah, and were now making their displeasure known by dogging my every step.

The lack of beer *was* a disappointment. I suspected Han didn't trust me alone with Garren and beer, without someone on hand to pull us apart. I admitted demonstrating poor reasoning on that fateful morning back at Thale. I felt better about the situation now.

Garren had done as I'd asked, other than toying with Hannah while they rode together. Red was polite, but eager for any scraps of time with Hannah. The situation rankled me, but there was no point in fighting it. I needed her. They needed her, too, and if the way she rubbed her ass against my crotch was any indication, she was a cat in heat and in desperate need of dick.

"Hope that scout arrives tonight," Garren added, distracting me from my plans for Hannah for tonight. "We're a week from Julant, and this lot knows less than Kein's already told us."

"Yes, I'm eager to know if there's news from our Rymorian contacts." I remained impatient to end Rymor's foray into Shadowland, and just as impatient to turn my attention toward Bill.

"Are you going back to Rymor when we're done here?" Garren asked.

My brother was curious about Rymor, as most Shadowlanders were. I had mixed feelings about returning, especially under the guise of war. Although it wasn't a guise. I really was returning there to overthrow their appointed ruler. Still, much needed to happen between here and the end of the war.

"I think I'll have to," I replied. "If I don't, they'll regroup and return in greater force and with greater weapons. I've been lucky this time. The insider support has been invaluable. I need to press this advantage and shut Bremmer down for good. If I don't, I may never have a chance again."

Garren nodded acceptance, then grinned and waggled his eyebrows. "So, tonight's the night?"

I was about to tell him there was a pecking order, and he wasn't at the fucking top, when Agregor interrupted us.

"I've done your tent," Agregor announced. He'd integrated himself with my guards and was now their willing helper. "Do you want me to do anything else?"

"Speak to Tay and see if she needs help with the horses."

Garren studied Agregor through narrowed, suspicious eyes. "What are you doing here?" He cuffed our younger brother around the back of the head. "Did you piss Han off again?"

I braced myself as Agregor stepped up nose to nose with Garren. I thought Agregor might have gained an inch on his older brother. "Why don't you ask him when we get back?" Agregor flashed Garren his signature cocky grin before stalking off.

Garren's frown followed him. "He's been acting weird lately."

I grinned. "Really? I hadn't noticed."

"Scout's here!" a wolf guard called.

The scout nosed his horse through the tents, stopping before me, where he leaped down. The scouts were undertaking many miles of hard riding due to the scale of the operation, and I found his energy impressive. He was one of Kein's apprentices and a sign of how much communication was going on that even the younger lads had been enlisted to aid the information flow. The man pulled open his saddlebag and extracted dozens of grubby, dog-eared scrolls.

"Why not give me the whole bag?" I suggested, worrying they would end up on the ground. "You can stay here tonight. It'll take me a while to read and respond." A night? Who was I kidding? A week would be more accurate. Where the hell had so many scrolls come from?

The scout froze. Several scrolls dropped and rolled away. He

## The Master of the Switch

battled to stuff the remainder back into the bag. Then he scrambled to retrieve the fallen ones, stamping on one in his haste.

Garren grunted a curse and snatched the scrolls and saddlebag from the scout. "See to your horse and get something to eat."

The man hurried off, leaving me with Garren, the two ever-watchful guards, and a year's worth of scrolls. "Alright, let's get through them. Damn Han and his trust issues; I could do with a drink."

Garren chuckled and followed me into my tent. Inside, a lamp had been lit, and food laid out on the table.

The guards tried to follow me in.

"Outside," I barked, and with indignant glares, they returned outside.

I sank into my chair, delighted there *was* a chair, as Garren dumped the saddlebag and scrolls on the table and took the seat opposite.

He reached for the food without further invitation and regarded the scrolls hopefully.

Maybe I would be more excited about scrolls if I'd never used a retinal viewer? I emptied the saddlebag, divided the pile in half, pushed one lot toward Garren, and dragged the rest toward me.

Garren's face lit up. He loved opening scrolls, and this was a scroll bounty.

"Where the hell have they all come from?" I muttered as I picked up the first one, checked the mark, and opened it without further ado. It was from Javid, and he was pissed.

Garren started chuckling, putting the first scroll down, and reaching for another.

"Javid?" I asked.

Garren ignored me, and further guffaws followed.

I frowned and grabbed some of the food without any feeling of appetite. "If any are not from Javid, can we read those first?"

Garren wiped tears from his eyes with the back of his hand. "He found out about your escapade in the Rymorian camp." He gave his best idiot grin.

Having skimmed through Javid's colorfully emotive scrolls, the four from Han were pleasantly dry and factual. The final scroll was from Greve, who, together with twenty thousand Techin men, watched the northern border.

Greve noted that the Jaru were still massing at the border but were not yet crossing, which was good. The rest were from Javid in varying degrees of rant. Firstly, at me for handing myself over. The theme of these early communications centered on his plans to knock sense into me after he razed the Rymorian camp to the ground. The later ones, after he discovered I'd escaped, were still flavored with violent promise, along with speculation about my decision, in Javid's words, "To drop everything and race halfway around Shadowland over a woman".

"The favored son has fallen from his lofty height," Garren said, smirking.

I snatched the one Garren was grinning over. I muttered a curse as I read it. "He's at Julant?" I said, hoping I'd made a mistake.

"Right, I had better get some sleep. Looking forward to reaching Julant and the ultimate father-son showdown." Garren stood and stretched. "Unless you need some help..." He winked and nodded toward my bed like I might be confused.

I shook my head slowly.

"Fine then," he said.

As I watched Garren leave, I decided I was no longer hungry nor in a hurry to reach Julant. Then I realized something was missing: Hannah, who must still be outside with Red. She had barely touched her travel rations during the day, not that I could blame her. There wasn't much of her to start with. Her time with Karry had left nothing but skin and bones... And now I was worried about whether she ate. This was rapidly veering toward doting alpha mate territory.

Thoroughly irritated by Javid's scroll frenzy and my instinctive need to coddle my omega, I stalked out my tent and collided with a

## The Master of the Switch

guard who stood directly outside. "I don't need five guards." They shuffled about. None of them made eye contact, and none of them left. Resigned to their overzealous attention, I stared out into the camp.

My gaze landed on Hannah, sitting opposite my tent. An empty bowl rested in front of her—at least she had eaten—and an empty bedroll behind her. Red sat beside her, chatting about something or other. She looked up at him and smiled. My fists clenched as he tucked her hair behind her ear in a tender gesture that spoke of familiarity.

If there were any doubts about my commitment, it was sealed by the riot coursing through my veins. I wanted her, wanted to assert my place as first alpha, to demonstrate that I could give her what she needed, that I was better than the oaf who'd nearly landed on his ass while undressing back at Thale.

I walked over. The moment I drew close, her ripe fuck-me scent hit me, fogging my mind to every good intention. "Go and get in my tent." What the fuck had just come out of my mouth?

She looked from me to the tent and back again. "No, thank you."

I raised an eyebrow because I was in full surly alpha bastard mode and just wanted to keep her to myself.

"What?" She feigned ignorance.

"The tent, now," I said, attempting to keep my tone even.

"No!"

"It wasn't a question." I was ready to toss her over my shoulder if needed.

She stood abruptly, snatched up her bedroll, and stomped over to my tent.

I followed and nearly walked into her when she stopped dead upon entering.

"I'd forgotten about your grandiose side." Her steady gaze took in the table, still covered in a mountain of opened scrolls, then drifted down to where several had spilled out onto the floor before continuing on to the other side where the bed was; not a proper bed by any means, but better than the hard ground.

She turned away from the bed, found the furthest possible location from it, laid out her bedroll, and settled down to sleep.

It was going to be a long night.

I dragged the bedroll from under her—there was a satisfying squeal as she tumbled onto the rug-covered ground—and stalked over to the tent flap and threw it out. A muffled grunt came from beyond, but given a dozen guards were milling about around my tent, not hitting one of them would have been more of a surprise.

When I turned back, I found her scrambling to her feet.

I positioned myself in front of the exit.

Her lips formed a tight line. "You can't be ordering people about all the time!"

I rubbed the back of my neck, grimaced, and wondered if she was suffering from amnesia. "Actually, I can, and I do, and it's been working for me so far."

"The power really has gone to your head."

I laughed and reached for the buckle on my light leather armor.

"I want to sleep outside."

"No, you don't." I continued working the buckles undone before shrugging out of it. "Hannah, when have you ever done anything just because I told you to?" I threw my jacket to the right, where it landed with a soft clank beside the bed.

She stared at me blankly.

"You never do anything I ask. Don't wander off on your own; ring any bells? How about: get out of my room?" I pulled my shirt over my head and tossed it in the general direction of the body armor.

Her wide eyes blinked back at me. "You think I want to be here?" She sounded adorably confused.

"Yes, Hannah, it would seem you do." I yanked my boots off and tossed them after the other clothes.

"But what does that mean?" Her brows drew together, and I knew she was asking a deeper question, but I was certain that she was

### The Master of the Switch

still suffering from her ordeal with Karry and had neither the energy nor the acumen for such a conversation. "It means you're tired, and sleeping in a tent on a bed with a marginal level of padding, is more interesting than sleeping on the ground outside."

"Are you sleeping in it, too?"

"It is my bed and I generally sleep in it." Her frown was so serious it was hard not to smile. "Are you being coquettish, Hannah?"

Her eyes lit with a chagrined fire that was as much part of her as that wild, frizzy hair. "No, I was just—" As her words died off, she looked lost.

"Do I need to threaten to throw you out again?" I said, in all seriousness.

"I don't want to die," she said, as if this were the root of all her problems. Perhaps it was. She had nearly died more than once, but the impact had driven deeper this time.

"Don't overthink it, Hannah."

She wouldn't make eye contact with me. "I think that advice comes about six months too late."

I sighed, wondering what she would do. I was exhausted, and the nearby bed held far greater allure than a hard bedroll. "If you don't want to be here, then by all means, go back outside, but I will follow you, and I will sleep beside you."

I was expecting further arguments.

"I do want to stay with you." She sounded surprised by her words.

She wasn't the only one.

Then she dropped to her knees.

I swallowed as her small hands reached for my belt.

Fuck!

# Chapter 9

## Hannah

I was on my knees. I had no idea how I'd come to be here, but it felt right on every level.

He hissed through his teeth as the buckle came free with a faint clatter. Beyond the tent, came the odd call, footsteps, and the industry of a camp setting up but, inside, we were cocooned in another world that belonged only to Tanis and me.

He wanted me, I saw the evidence straining the leather of his pants. As I ran my fingertips over the bulge, I felt it too. Our last time seemed forever ago and held all the tangibility of a dream, a hazy jumble of scenes that had visited my dreams and brought bittersweet wistfulness when I was with Karry.

He was right. I wanted to be here and couldn't deny the pull between us, an invisible thread that always told me where he was... where all of them were. Only this wasn't about Garren or Red. Not this time, anyway.

"You don't have to do this," he said, but the tic thumping in his jaw said he wanted me to.

"I know," I replied. "I want to."

## The Master of the Switch

Obsession might have been considered an ugly word, were we not alpha and omega. It didn't feel ugly from my perspective, but natural and right. Tanis was my alpha, and I needed to be close. Only it was more than a simple connection, and therein lay the darker side. He was arguably the person in Shadowland best able to keep me safe.

Was that the crux of my obsession? Some misguided—or even guided—sense of survival?

Did it matter if it was?

My heart was hammering in my chest so wildly I could feel the pulse jumping at the base of my throat. Tanis hadn't moved, but watched me with such focus that I knew my emotional state was laid bare to him.

If I must accept the many complex nuances as to why I chose to be here, I must also ask why he similarly wanted this. After our conversation two days ago, I'd believed what we'd shared at Thale to be an anomaly: a one-off.

Was this coming from a genuine desire on Tanis' part or was it just convenience?

He'd given me a choice, said I could leave, and his only stipulation was that he would follow me.

Caught in a trance, my fingers pulled at the ties holding his leather pants, loosening them one by one, letting his rich scent wash over me. My reasons were my own. Just as his were. None of them mattered, for I couldn't deny myself what I needed, and that was to taste. The primitive, animalistic side of me that was an omega reveled in the moment, in praying to the alpha god who had saved her life.

Rymor was dead to me, gone. Tanis had told me he would protect me, and this was my opportunity to make sure he didn't change his mind. To pay homage to the male I desired as my mate. How many women and omegas must have wanted such an opportunity, and how few had got the chance?

*Submission.* As I freed the last lace, and his pants came free, I understood there was power in submission. His patience as he waited, allowing me to guide the act as he stepped out of his pants and gifted me unfettered access to his beautiful cock, was a wonder. Beneath my fingertips, I felt him tremble as I skimmed my hands over his hair-roughened thigh to close around my prize.

His chest heaved, and his fingers formed fists as I slowly pumped. Free of clothing, his scent was so much richer and spicy, my mouth watering for the taste as pre-cum pooled and then leaked from the tip.

He remained silent.

"I want to please you." That was an unexpected truth, but I no longer questioned my judgment.

"I ought to be suffering a conflict in regard to your motives," he said, voice roughened with need, "but rational thought appears to be eluding me. You know how much trouble you're in, hmm? Toying with an alpha, teasing him, making him think you'll suck his dick, and then making him wait?"

My lips tugged up. Oh, I very much liked to taunt the beast, wanted everything that might happen if I pushed him, and he broke. But my needs were great, and I also wanted a taste.

Directing the weeping tip of his cock toward my mouth, I licked up his pre-cum.

∼

## Tanis

My hips jerked forward at the first lap of her tongue, the tip flushed and sensitive as blood flooded it, making me hard to the point of pain.

I looked up at the tent's roof and steeled myself to endure, because this was a special kind of hellish heaven, having her lap my cock like it was her favorite treat, her small hand wrapped around the shaft, and her contented hum halfway to a purr.

When I'd gotten control enough to look back down, she was staring up at me, eyes hooded, her expression one of bliss.

"Suck me, Hannah. Suck me right fucking now. I want to see

## The Master of the Switch

your lips stretched around me, want to feel you swallowing around me as you take me deep."

She was definitely purring this time as she opened her mouth, and I watched the head of my cock disappear between her lips. Moaning, she sucked me deeper, her eyes closing as she bobbed her head and gently sucked, her tongue lashing the sensitive underside of my cock.

She still had her clothes on, and I'd strip her naked and eat her out so good just as soon as I could think straight.

I wasn't going to last, knew I couldn't, and closed my fingers over her silken hair, feeling the strands catch against calluses left from sword use.

Her fingers worked up and down the shaft where she couldn't reach with her mouth, tracing over the sensitive knot and driving me to an animalistic compulsion to choke her. Others had claimed her, but now and here, there was just us within this tent. I could hear the bustle of the camp beyond the walls, and I couldn't give a shit. She was going to be screaming before the night was done. I wanted everybody, especially Garren and Red, to know I was making her come, to leave no doubt in anybody's mind that she was mine.

"I'm going to come," I said, giving her warning and an opportunity to stop if she wished. Only she didn't stop, and her fingers tightened as she worked the knot.

I came, barely remembering to lock my legs, because the sensation of emptying into her throat snatched all my focus.

My fingers clenched over her hair, holding her to me as I kept coming, balls tightening again as I shot more cum down her throat. My hands were shaking, but my legs were shaking more. I pulled her off when she looked intent on going again, and heaved a deep, post-climax breath.

She hadn't spilled a fucking drop. My cock jerked and my nostrils flared as that realization settled in. I swiped my thumb over her plump lower lip. "Did you like that, Hannah?"

She nodded slowly, gazing up at me.

I heaved another breath. "Good, because now I'm going to make you pay." I tightened my fist over her hair, and her little gasp and her aroused scent saturating the air was all the answer I needed.

"Up." I hauled her from the floor and stripped her. She helped, or tried to, but mostly got in the way until I spanked her ass.

She groaned.

Fuck, I couldn't think about that. Omegas liked to be mastered, enjoyed it, and got off on it. She had certainly enjoyed it when I'd bound her hands at Thale. Yet much had happened between then and now, and a bastard had made her suffer in ways no omega should. I wanted to erase the memory, remind her that she was here, alive, and could still feel. No one had the right to take her pleasure from her; I wanted to give it back.

I took her down onto my bed and angled my mouth over hers. She opened, groaning, her tongue tangling with mine. I poured all my savage emotions into the kiss, plundering her softness. Her small hands were in my hair, gripping and tugging, not to push me away but to pull me closer. Her legs circled my waist, heels digging into my ass, and wet pussy smearing all over my stomach. There were things I wanted to do, to kiss, to touch, but this was good too, our lips moving over one another's, letting the urgency build.

Fate and destiny were meaningless to me; and if you'd asked me before today, I'd have sworn I didn't believe in love anymore. But this was a passion of an otherworldly nature tied with all I might have lost. So I kissed her, trapping her tiny body under me where she was safe, hearing her sweet moans as she kissed me with the same fever.

Breathing heavily, I dragged my lips from hers to gaze down into solemn eyes near black in the lamplight. Her lips were swollen and puffy, her cheeks flushed. Wild, silver-blonde hair made a stark contrast against the dark furs covering my bed.

For only the second time in my life, there was an angel in my bed.

I took her lips again before peppering kisses over her cheeks and jaw and circling my tongue around her ear. She shivered. I nipped at her throat... then sucked.

# The Master of the Switch

Her groan was deep and earthy, letting me know she liked me marking her. I tried to rein myself in, but it was a lost fucking cause when she responded so sweetly. Her pleasure was an aphrodisiac, from her captivating scent to her copious slick and low moans. How miraculous that she could be the same, giving omega after all she had endured.

I moved on to her tits, squeezing them together and sucking the upper swell to leave another mark in evidence of my claim.

Her nipples were already hard when I flicked one with my tongue. My reward was an arch to her back, and her mumbled begging as she fisted my hair. I sucked harder, and her cries lit a fire inside me. I moved from one breast to the other, sucking sharply, kissing and sucking again until, frenzied, her nails scored my skin.

I wanted all of her, wanted this wildness to take us both so we didn't need to fucking think.

"God, please."

I pushed her legs up and out, lowered my head and breathed in the scent before taking a long lick. With her legs spread wide and neck arched, she offered me a bounty, and I gorged on her sweet slick, getting my fingers inside her tight pussy, finding her gland, and petting until she twitched and clamped down.

"Good girl. Come for me, Hannah. I need you to fucking come."

And she did, squealing loud enough that nobody in the camp would doubt my claim.

Her pleasure tipped me over. Something snapped deep inside; the last of my sanity, perhaps.

I put her on her hands and knees, lined my cock up, and thrust deep into hot, clenching heaven. Here I fucked her, hammering into her as primal forces awakened in me, slamming her on and off my dick, grunting and growling with pleasure, as she begged me for more.

She never stopped coming, and our flesh soon made wet *smacks* with every deep thrust. When I felt her coming down, I only had to pet her clit or angle to find her slick gland, and her pussy fisted my cock again.

I held off as long as possible, until the sweat bathed my body, and my cock became so hard I thought I'd broken the damn thing. My knot grew ever more inflamed, and I gritted my teeth as each thrust became a battle to penetrate her slick, gripping channel.

My spine tingled, and my balls rose as I slipped past her entrance one last time. Her hot, silken sheath fell into climatic waves. Head tipped back, she squealed as she milked me of my seed.

This wasn't pleasure. It was a fucking revelation.

We breathed heavy through the sparking aftershocks, and I purred and held her close.

As soon as my knot softened, I wanted her again.

I didn't need to ask. Her searching fingers wrapped around my length and directed the tip to her puffy pussy. I took her slowly until I could stand it no more, and then I slam fucked her with all the aggression I felt, trying to imprint myself upon her.

She came, her scream shattering the still air.

A distant wolf howled, and we both chuckled, kissed, then laughed some more.

Only the peaceful, sated state never lasted for long, and the night was lost under urgent touches that were more important than sleep.

In the frenzy of the moment, I convinced myself that she was mine. Yet, at the same time, there was too much between here and the end of the war: too much doubt, too much risk. My alpha instincts were clamoring. The need to keep her safe and to protect her battled against the need to fuck, claim, and breed her.

Only I couldn't claim her and keep her safe, and all of that aside, I couldn't breed her, because I was sterile, as all Rymorian men were until they chose otherwise.

Garren could, though.

At a deep, primitive level, I hated that he offered her something I could not. Then there was Red, a gentle beta, a man from her world, who offered her something different again beyond Garren and me.

I was jealous; in this, I felt that I, the leader of Shadowland, offered her the least of all. Yet could any of us claim her in such a

### The Master of the Switch

tumultuous time? Was it fair to? I didn't have the answers or know the right questions to ask. I didn't have a fucking clue what tomorrow might bring; only what I hoped for.

Hopes and dreams were no basis for an enduring relationship, and life had taught me not to trust in them.

Beyond the tent, dawn was lightning in the sky.

Worries were for later. In this brief interlude, there was an omega nestled in my arms, one I desired with all my heart, one I wished to claim as mine, yet dared not do lest I put her life at risk.

I swallowed. Hannah grew restless. She was sensitive, as all omegas were, to emotional cues, and perhaps sensed my inner conflict.

I purred, and she settled down, and I felt like a fucking god because there was nothing more beautiful than calming an omega with your purr. An act that was made more special by the depth of my feelings for Hannah. I was drawn by her tenacity for life, strength of will, endurance, and authenticity, this prickly yet giving omega who was encased in a tiny, fragile, precious package.

I thought of the children we might have had were circumstances different. What better omega could an alpha wish for?

None, was the simple answer.

Outside the tent, the camp was stirring with low voices, footsteps, grunts, and shuffling, rousing me from a pleasant daydream where all this might be over, and some miracle presented me with the ability to father children and live out my life to watch them flourish and grow with Hannah at my side.

The noises reminded me that the camp and the war were my reality.

I kissed her forehead, breathed in her sweet, well-fucked scent, and took my last lingering look before rising, dressing, and leaving the tent.

# Chapter 10

**Hannah**

I woke to find myself in the embarrassing situation of being in Tanis' bed alone. The moment had a certain déjà vu.

I blinked at the roof of the tent, now made lighter by the onset of dawn and buffeted by a gentle breeze. Past the false privacy the barrier provided, I could hear the sounds of industry and conversation. Nothing was really private in Shadowland and, just like in Thale, everyone here would know where I was and what it meant. I groaned. God; I hadn't exactly been quiet. That damn alpha was ruthless, and he'd found inventive ways to send me soaring again whenever I started waning.

Underlying this embarrassment was the fact of my dramatic declaration that I wanted to please him as I'd sunk to my knees. Maybe he'd intended to do no more than sleep beside me, as he'd done every other night.

I pushed the covers back and searched for my clothes, which I retrieved from various locations with no recollection of how they might have gotten there. Dressing with shaky fingers, I decided that while sleeping on a bed in a tent should have left me rested, it had

## The Master of the Switch

done nothing of the sort. I was tired, irritable, and ached as bad as the time I'd run myself to exhaustion fleeing Karry's tent.

Being clothed improved my mood, but an attempt to finger-comb my hair revealed a sorry, knotty mess. *Great!*

Shoving my feet into my boots, I was angry with Tanis and the world by the time I slammed out of the tent.

Two of his guards waited outside the entrance. They regarded me with speculative eyes before they pushed past. Thuds, thunks, and rustling came from within as packing ensued.

They must have been waiting for me to rise, which added a whole extra level of embarrassment.

I'd forgotten how many people had joined us, and it took me a few seconds to process who they were. Tanis was nowhere in sight, nor was Garren, but I spotted Red eating and made my way over.

He sat chatting to a Shadowlander, but sprang to his feet as I neared. "Are you alright?" He inspected me in a way that said I looked every bit as bedraggled as I felt.

I shifted under his gaze and started to regret leaving the tent. "Yeah, I'm fine."

"You don't look fine." There was a touch of color to his cheeks.

"Red, please don't." I raised a hand in a silent plea for him to drop it, then sighed when he continued to stare. "I'm pretty tired."

A tic began thumping in his jaw, and I internally cursed my choice of words. "I just came to see if you had anything to eat."

"It's not right. He can't do this."

I thought about pointing out that Tanis could do whatever he liked and that no one, certainly neither Red nor I, was likely to make a damn bit of difference, but this was irrelevant given I'd thrown myself at Tanis.

"Red, please leave it alone." I just wanted some food. If I didn't eat now, I would be stuck with travel crackers.

"Hannah, you know what this is about. You know he hates Bill. You're the ultimate trophy fuck."

If he'd struck me, it would have been a softer blow. My vision blurred, and my ears rang, but I shook my head to clear it. "Is that what you think? What you really think?"

He shifted where he stood but made no attempt to retract his harsh words.

"I think I love him." I felt stupid the moment I blurted it out. I couldn't believe Tanis would use me as a sick means of revenge, but the idea still brought a sharp stab of pain. How well did I really know him?

Red ran his fingers over his face with an air of defeat. "You really know how to pick men. Garren has got his faults, but he's okay. There is a world of them queuing up who would worship you in every way and you gravitate toward the only two assholes who treat you like shit."

I hit him, my palm connecting with his face so hard and fast the resounding crack shocked us both. I'd never hit anyone in my life, but he had lit a fire inside me, and I slapped him again.

He caught my wrists and tried to stop me. "Fuck, Hannah, I'm sorry! I don't even know what the fuck just came out of my mouth. I'm sorry. I'm fucking sorry!"

His words fell on deaf ears as I fought furiously, still trying to land my fist even as I tried to yank free.

I found myself jerked away by the scruff of my neck.

"Enough," Tanis said from behind. He shook me until the fury seeped out of me, and I went limp under his hold.

"I'm interested to find out what you said to make Hannah so unnaturally violent. You're lucky she doesn't have access to a knife." He pulled me about and gently pushed me in the other direction. "Go and get ready, Hannah. Red and I need to talk."

Determined not to turn back, I stalked away... Then I stopped, finding Garren in my path. Low, angry murmurs came from behind me, but I was furious enough not to care.

Garren's expression was pensive as he stared over my shoulder before looking down at me. "What did Red say to upset you?"

"Nothing." The sounds stopped, and a sense of sadness

## The Master of the Switch

enveloped me. Red's words were out of character, and I didn't think he'd meant to be cruel. "He won't hurt Red, will he?"

The corner of Garren's mouth tugged up on one side. "No, they're just having a bit of a discussion." He nudged his head to the side. "Come on. You're riding with me today."

I stifled a churlish response about them having no credible reason to question my horsemanship. "Can't I ride on my own today?"

He rolled his eyes and started walking. "You look like you haven't slept all night, and you're not stable on a horse at the best of times."

Falling into step alongside him, I felt a rather glum expression overtake my face, as I acknowledged that I *hadn't* slept all night.

"And you're still recovering from what those Rymorian bastards did to you. I'm impressed you're doing as well as you are." As he reached his horse, he added, "I'm not impressed with Tanis for making you look half dead again." He lifted the saddle from the ground and placed it on the horse, then pulled the straps underneath and tightened the girth, while I fidgeted and hoped he would shut up. "But Tanis and I don't have serious discussions about what he does with you anymore and, unlike Red, I know how to do pissed quietly."

"I don't know why he wants me." I wished the words unsaid when Garren stopped and turned toward me. "Red said Tanis was using me. That I was a trophy fuck."

Garren grunted and lines of amusement crinkled around his eyes. "I'm going to thump the fucker myself later for that." His face softened. "Hey. You know he doesn't mean that, right? He's just... tense because he's not gotten some in a while."

"Well, I'm sorry Red's dick can't abstain while I recover!"

"It's not about that," Garren said, continuing with his straps. "And if the screams coming from the tent last night are any indication, you don't need any more recovery time. Red is worried he's been displaced, and that he's out of favor." He pinned me with a look. "That he's been relegated to a friend now you've hit the Shadowland jackpot by snagging Tanis' interest... and, believe me, you're the first woman who has."

My mouth gaped. "Jackpot? Does that word have any context in Shadowland?" This wasn't the most important part of the conversation, but the only one that moved from my brain to my mouth.

"Never really thought about it." Garren shrugged. "Red thinks he knows how things work with alphas and omegas, but he really doesn't and he's insecure." He winked. "He's a beta with a small dick, so he would be right to feel insecure, but, again, that doesn't really matter to an omega, does it? Because you've imprinted on him, too, and no matter what bullshit comes out of his mouth, you want him. Don't worry, he won't do that again. Tanis is busy setting him straight. Whatever my gripes about Tanis, he knows how to get a point across."

I went to speak, but nothing would form into words. It hadn't crossed my mind that Red might feel displaced and think I didn't want him. Not that it excused him from throwing out such hurtful words. "I still don't understand why Tanis wants me," I said quietly.

Garren drew a harness over the horse's head. "Tanis was in a bad way when he escaped the Rymorian camp, could barely stand, and had a concussion so bad he struggled to keep food down." He buckled the saddlebags into place. "He could've sent others to find you since the tower-dweller kid had a box telling us where you were. I could have gone. You were mine, after all. Tanis didn't need to deal personally with a few Rymorian men, especially when he has so many others on his land." He stopped and held my eyes. "Trust me, a man doesn't do that over a trophy fuck, nor to score a point."

His words soothed me, and new questions rushed in, but Garren's hands clamped around my waist, and he dumped me into the saddle before I could speak.

He climbed behind me with the enviable ease of a man who had been doing it all his life. Opening the saddlebag, he dragged out a dreaded ration pack. "Here, eat this." He turned my hand over and placed the ration pack in my palm before closing my numb fingers around it.

"You're going to need to keep up your strength." There was a

## The Master of the Switch

definite smile in his voice. "I have it on good authority: tonight is punishment night. Time for you to pay your dues for getting with *another* man behind my back, and right after I'd just explained to you how that was a big no. And Red just fucked up, so I'm going to make him pay worse than Tanis can do with his fist. I'm going to tie the bastard up and make him watch."

# Chapter 11

### Garren

I wanted to thump Red for upsetting her, even knowing Tanis had taken care of it.

I also wanted to thump Tanis for fucking her all night, even as I spent the day taunting her to prime her for him.

She was mine first, and she needed to remember that, no matter how Tanis crashed into our midst like a pumped-up bull scenting fertile breeding stock. So, tonight was punishment night all round, and for everyone but me.

∽

### Hannah

By the time we pulled into a clearing at the end of the day, I was restless, anxious, and needy beyond recognition. I'd napped a little while riding the horse, but it was nowhere near enough. Nothing else mattered, when all I cared about was one of my mates fucking me.

Garren dismounted first. Around us was the bustle of people,

## The Master of the Switch

carts lumbering in, calls as tents were promptly erected, and fires lit for food. He lifted me down, making a wall before me with his big body, before glancing over his shoulder at something or someone I couldn't see. "Fuck up again," he said, voice low and gravelly, "and I'll thump you twice as hard as Tanis did."

My chest compressed because I knew who would be standing there. Garren had done a good job of distracting me from Red's harsh words. As he stepped aside, I saw the evidence of Tanis's displeasure on Red's handsome face.

"I'm sorry," Red said. "So fucking sorry. If you want to slap me again, go ahead. I deserve it. But, please, don't send me away."

My lips quivered, and a weight settled behind my eyes, tears stinging and then spilling down my cheek because they had only been words, and I hated to see the bruise shining on his cheek. "I won't send you away, Red." I stepped forward and held up my hand. He took it within his larger ones and brought it to his lips. "I want you. You're part of this now. But, please, don't say things like that again."

I swallowed, aware that Garren was only a pace away, listening in as he removed the saddle from the horse. "I love you, all of you, including Tanis. Garren was first, and he will always be first, but that doesn't diminish what I feel for you."

"I fucked up," he said.

"You did."

He brushed the tears away from my cheek with his thumb, and there he hesitated.

"You can kiss me," I said.

Cupping my face within his hands, he leaned down and pressed his lips to mine, gentle and brief, before lifting his head. His eyes searched mine. "I don't deserve you."

"Of course you do," I replied. "If you didn't, I would never have chosen you."

I went into his arms and let him wrap me up. There was no rich scent like with an alpha, but I already had two of those and didn't need more pheromones fogging up my brain. Red was tall, powerful for a beta, and handsome. But my attraction to him was about so much more than looks. He was also brave and giving, an accomplished lover who, under Garren's direction, had become so much more. I tried to put myself in his shoes as we stood in the forest amid a rapidly forming camp, holding one another. I wondered how it would be to share him with two other women I might perceive to be superior.

I would hate it. I couldn't share Red, Garren, or Tanis, yet I was expecting them to share me. And how hard it must be. For all that Garren seemed accepting, I could remember his rage that night when he returned and found me in bed with Red.

Although such relationships did happen in Shadowland, Red and I came from a different part of the world. While he must be familiar with Shadowland and their ways, he was a Rymorian like me, an exile making his way in this foreign land. I thought I might have succumbed to bouts of insecurity and harsh words I didn't mean, were I in his place.

I pressed my palm to his cheek, feeling his beard rough and springy under my fingers. "I want you, Red. That night in Thale, when we were together with Garren, was the wildest of my life."

His lips tugged up. "Yeah," he said softly. "Same."

"Don't get any ideas," Garren said brusquely.

I'd been distracted and hadn't realized he'd finished with the horse, but now his scent washed over me, and I felt his presence behind me, sucking in my awareness. I shuddered as his fingers skimmed the back of my neck before collaring me. He squeezed lightly. My eyes locked with Red's, watching his widen slightly when I gasped.

"She's...um...aroused," Red said thickly, before swallowing.

"I know." I heard the smirk in Garren's voice. "I made her so. Tonight, we're going to be working through arrangements." He stepped closer, trapping me against Red.

I felt Red's cock hardening where it pressed against my stomach.

## The Master of the Switch

"She *really* likes that." Red's Adam's apple bobbed. "Being between us."

"She's an omega," Garren said, by way of explanation. "A particularly needy one. No one man was ever going to be enough."

My stomach dipped, and my pussy spasmed.

"Don't think you're getting anything tonight, Red," Garren said. "I anticipate a lot of suffering on your part. You can watch what we do with her.

Red groaned. "I don't care. I'll take anything, even watching when I can't touch. I want to watch. Would rather be there and be part of it in a small way, than somewhere else thinking about what you might be doing."

His eyes lifted from mine to meet Garren's over my shoulder. His nostrils flared at whatever he saw there.

"Take her to Tanis' tent," Garren said. "Undress her, but don't touch more than you must. Tanis and I will be along shortly. Keep your fucking clothes on, understood?"

Red nodded quickly.

Now," Garren said. "I need to talk with Tanis and set that bastard straight."

~

Garren left, and Red took me to Tanis's tent; the first one to be completed. Here he undressed me, taking Garren's instructions to the limit and beyond, finding reasons to pinch and pet me, making me gasp and whine because I wanted him to kiss me, but he refused.

By the time I was naked, I was needier than I'd been all day.

Which is when the tent flap opened and Tanis and Garren entered.

"She's naked," Tanis said unnecessarily.

"Were you in some ways confused about what was about to happen?" Garren asked.

"No." Tanis narrowed his eyes at his brother in a way that said he was thinking about thumping him. "I just like to do the unwrapping."

"Yeah," Garren said. "I bet Red did too. Given that's the closest he's getting to her all night, I have high expectations that he's done a thorough job of priming her."

Red swallowed.

Tanis chuckled.

"It's time for her punishment," Garren announced.

My pussy clenched. He'd been teasing me all day, keeping me on edge with touches, whispering what he was going to do to me while Tanis and Red watched. How I was going to come so hard. How I was going to beg Garren for his cum in front of my other mates.

*My other mates*, he'd called them, and how my body and mind had reveled in the term and his acceptance.

"Over my dead body are you going to punish her," Tanis said, voice dangerously soft.

Garren rolled his eyes. "Give me some credit here."

"I *want* to be bound," I blurted out. Garren had explained how I would be punished, that the first step was being bound, and I wanted it, all of it, even knowing I would also hate the wait.

I'd waited all day, had missed Garren so much; and if he wanted this, I wanted it too.

"No fucking way," Tanis said.

"Please. I want you to," I said. "I hate that Karry bound me, but it's different when I think of you. I trust you; I trust all of you. I liked it when you did it last time." My cheeks filled with heat.

"The fuck?" Garren muttered. "When did you tie her up? Not last night?"

"It was at Thale." Tanis shrugged, his grin definitely smug. "She was interfering, and I wanted to eat in peace."

Red groaned. "Please can we bind her if she wants that?"

Garren stabbed a finger in Red's direction. "You don't get a say in any of this after you fucked up this morning. Strip, and then shut the fuck up."

### The Master of the Switch

I bit my lip as Red began stripping.

"Fine," Tanis said. "But we keep a knife close. If she looks like she's anything but aroused, I'm hacking the damn things off and we're not doing this again."

There was too much talking in this tent. I walked over to Garren, my first mate, knelt and held up my hands.

"Ah, fuck," Red said. "I'm going to embarrass myself."

# Chapter 12

**Tanis**

I thought Red might not be the only one embarrassing himself, as I watched Hannah kneel before Garren. I'd had many moments with my younger brother during our tempestuous relationship, but the jealousy that burned in my gut tonight was something new.

I hated him, wanted to beat him to a bloody pulp, and then fuck her like a savage.

Only I wasn't a savage, and a sliver of conscience held me in check.

How close the line was in that moment between the human and animal parts of me. Alphas were not entirely human. We were genetically modified to be killers, tempered only by time and a mate. Garren was my competition. Worse, he could breed her while I could not. She was kneeling for *him*, not me, offering her wrists up to *him*, asking *him* to bind her.

Only, underneath all this seething rage was a dark, hot, and compelling tendril of desire that drove a steely hardness to my cock such that I felt like it was being strangled by my leather pants.

## The Master of the Switch

Last night she had been kneeling for me, sucking my dick like a little cum-junkie, getting off on my knot stretching out her tight cunt, and whining for more.

I swallowed hard as the lamplight showcased the scene in all its glory, and scents rose thicker: hers, Garren's, and mine. Little wonder Red was swaying where he stood, cock erect and leaking pre-cum in a way abnormal for a beta. She would change him over time and when, and if, we mated through her heat, forming a life bond, he would share that too. There were elements to sweat, saliva, and slick of alphas and omegas that worked on a beta, whether female or male, increasing stamina and sexual appetite over time.

I felt the pull to Hannah like a thread hooked in the center of my chest. My eyes roamed over her body: the curve of her hip, her pert tits begging to be sucked and pinched, and the marks I'd left on her pale skin all aroused and satisfied me in equal parts.

"You understand how this punishment works?" Garren asked.

"Yes." Her voice was the barest whisper.

"We're going to come—you're not. I won't lie about this. It's going to be rough on you. Omegas come easily, and don't like being denied."

"I know. I understand."

"Do you?" He closed his fingers gently over her offered wrists, and she instantly arched, trying to get closer, to get more of his touch.

I'd spent a lot of time not thinking about how they might be together. Tonight, it was front and center; I was part of it, and there was no avoiding the tenderness and trust between them. Jealousy surged, but so did pride in my brother, who had previously rolled through life like it was a game, now taking enthusiastic responsibility for a mate.

*Mate?*

Was that what was happening?

Was I deluding myself into believing it was anything else?

"There are three men in this tent, but, Hannah, there are not going to be any more. As it is, you're going to find yourself rutted anytime one of us looks at you. You're going to be dripping cum. By doing this, you're giving me more than just your wrists for binding. You're giving us permission to fuck you whenever and wherever we choose. You know how it works now. You tried denying me once, and how did that go?"

She shook her head quickly. "I won't deny you again. I promise."

"How did that particular lesson play out," I asked thickly.

"It was before the station," Garren said, never taking his eyes off Hannah, thumb rubbing lightly over her wrists. "She said she wanted to stop fucking. I turned my back on her, took my cock out, and started to jack off. She lasted all of a second before she was begging and clawing at me. Got herself knotted for the first time, didn't you?" He brushed the hair back from her flushed cheeks.

She nodded.

"So now you understand. Three is a lot for any omega to take and you're not going to offer your pussy to anyone else, are you?"

"No," she said. "I don't want anyone else. Only you." She glanced over her shoulder at me, then Red, before turning back to Garren. "I'm ready."

I was confident she wasn't ready.

I was also confident Garren would end up forcing her heat if he took this path to its natural conclusion.

There was a war happening and danger on every side. I should be pulling back, reminding Garren of this.

Only I didn't. Like a sleepwalker, I fetched the soft leather binding rope.

∼

# Red

I remember entering Tanis's tent once, long ago when I'd been redirected from my mission to look at the crash. It felt like a lifetime ago now, and so much had happened since. It still struck me as odd that,

## The Master of the Switch

while traveling through this country on horseback, you could find a tent with a bed, desk, chairs, lamps, and even soft furnishings that might befit a king. He *was* a king of sorts, the leader who ruled them all.

Only, here, the bed was missing, and instead, a thick mattress centered the room.

The ground was covered by a sturdy tarp to keep dampness and cold at bay and, over that, a rug and mattress piled high with thick blankets and furs.

Space, I realized, for what we were about to do. And in consideration of the fact that there were three to fit into a bed intended for two.

Or perhaps four... I was still hoping Garren would relent.

I understood why Garren was furious. He'd had Hannah to himself once, then she brought me all too willingly into the mix. A short time later, Tanis had similarly claimed a place. There was no room for others. She couldn't handle others. My blood pounded at the thoughts of others, and not in a good way.

No, she was ours and ours alone.

That I'd nearly cost myself a place might have cooled my ardor some, except there was a naked omega kneeling in front of Garren.

Tanis took her hands from Garren and slowly moved them to her lower back.

"You okay?" he asked.

"Yes." The word came out breathy. "I like your hands on me. I like what you're doing."

He began to bind them with slow, easy movements. Her chest rose, setting her tits quivering as she stared up at Garren.

Tanis enclosed her bound wrists in one large hand, and brushing her hair back over her shoulder, he settled his other palm against her throat. She waited, attuned perfectly to whatever her alphas might do. "How does it feel?"

"I-I like it." Hannah glanced back, her lips parted. "Can I come now?"

Garren chuckled. "Not a fucking chance. Take her to the bed."

Tanis scooped her into his arms, carried her to the bed, and carefully placed her back on her knees in the center. "Open your thighs," he commanded, his hand cupping the back of her head.

She hesitated only a moment before pushing her knees wide, giving me a perfect view of her pink pussy, all swollen and glistening with slick.

"Good girl," he praised.

I didn't realize Garren had moved, until I felt his hand at the back of my neck. I jumped at the touch, and my eyes clashed with his in askance. "Come," he said, his tone suggesting he was amused. "You get a front-row seat. He directed me forward, keeping his hand at the back of my neck, setting off a tingly awareness of his power and the roughness of his hand.

I considered myself a measured man. I wasn't submissive, but I sensed his dominance over me, and it sent everything inside me off-kilter.

He stopped at the foot of the bed and applied downward pressure. "Knees."

I sank to my knees, confused but definitely aroused. A look passed between Tanis and Garren. Tanis nodded and handed something over.

More binding rope?

Fuck!

Garren dropped to his knees behind me and yanked my hands roughly behind my back in a mirror pose of Hannah's. I jerked, trying to break free, but he held me tight, and I wasn't going anywhere. My cock flexed, and pre-cum gushed from the tip. Fuck, fuck, fuck! I was *not* going to embarrass myself by coming.

"It's okay to like it," Garren said, lips close to my ear.

*Did* I like it? Or was it all mixed up with the vision of Hannah: kneeling, cheeks flushed, with her eyes glued to my dick, tits jiggling with every breath, nipples berry-red and hard.

My dick was ramrod straight, bobbing wildly, and pre-cum was trickling down my balls. Was I getting off on being dominated?

## The Master of the Switch

"There we go," Garren said, patting my shoulder, and then he was binding me, winding the strip of leather around my wrists, just like Tanis had done with Hannah. My chest heaved, and sweat broke out across my skin as I stared at Hannah, noting the pulse leaping at the base of her throat and the aroused flush to her cheeks.

"Don't move," Garren said, like it was an option.

I couldn't think straight, never mind move, and I was sinking fast. Their scent was all over me, saturating the air. It wouldn't impact betas the way it did an alpha and omega, yet it still sent me high as I knelt, bound and naked, staring at Hannah, who was bound and naked and staring back at me, all spread open and vulnerable; so close, yet out of reach.

The two alphas stripped, and the air became so thick with pheromones and tension I could barely breathe.

As they kneeled either side of her, I was struck by the way their hands trembled and how gentle they were, when the word 'punishment' had made me anticipate roughness. Garren fisted her hair lightly, tilting her neck back, before claiming her lips. Tanis came down on the other side and lowered his mouth to her breast.

Hannah moaned, her stomach clenched, and slick tickled down her inner thigh and dripped onto the furs. My cock flexed, leaking pre-cum, my balls drawn so tight they ached. I'd never climaxed without physical stimulation, but I was so fucking close watching them with her. Big, powerful males, their touch possessive as they cupped her tits and ran fingers over her belly, a sharp slap against her ass. The moans and occasional growls as they trailed kisses over her shoulders, throat, breasts... and lips. Another sharp spank to the ass.

How incredible they looked together: the image of two alphas arousing an omega, the seamless pack instinct of the two males as they worshiped her. How helpless she was, and yet never doubting she was the center of their world, of all our worlds; our omega, so needy and desperate, arching into touches and kisses, letting them swallow up her cries.

Garren coaxed her to open her thighs wider, his fingertips tracing patterns against the soft skin, drawing ever closer to where the slick gathered near the top. They continued to kiss her shoulders and throat, taking turns to capture her lips. And all the while, their fingers were converging on the apex of her thighs until finally, they bumped against one another as they petted her pussy.

Her reaction was a sharp intake of breath followed by begging. "Please, please, please."

Tanis's lips were at her breast, sucking, while Garren claimed her lips, their fingers petting and building her arousal.

My heart thudded loud and fast, my balls were painfully tight, and my cock was hard enough that I felt like someone was choking me as they toyed with her.

"She's close," Garren said gruffly. Their kisses gentled, and they withdrew their touches.

She begged so sweetly, but it didn't matter, and they would do no more than kiss her until she had calmed.

Once she did, they resumed their play, sliding their fingers over her pussy. Garren paused to bring his fingers to his lips, growling noisily as he licked them clean. "Do you have any oil?"

Tanis grunted and nodded his head to the side. "In the small trunk."

Tanis tapped Hannah's cheek, drawing her attention to him. "Look at me, Hannah."

Her eyes fluttered open, but they were without focus.

"Look at me, right now."

She blinked and gazed at Tanis with such love and devotion my chest squeezed.

"Are you still with us? You still want more?"

"Please," she said." Don't stop, I couldn't bear it."

Garren returned with the oil bottle in his hand, and I swear more blood tried to pound its way into my cock because I knew what he was going to do. He poured oil onto his fingers and rubbed them together.

### The Master of the Switch

His hand went behind her, her sudden gasp telling me exactly what he was doing to her.

Tanis kissed up her cries, his hand on her breast, pinching her nipple, before slapping each breast lightly in turn, making them bounce. She whimpered and moaned, arching for more, and all the while, Garren was pumping fingers into her from behind.

"You took Red here before, didn't you, Hannah?" Garren said, one hand on her throat, turning her mouth to meet his so he could kiss up her mewling sounds. "You're going to take me here tonight while Tanis takes your pussy. You'll take both of us like a good girl. I'm not going to lie to you. It's going to be a lot, but you'll take it because we want you to, and because you chose to have three mates with great needs."

Her breathing turned choppy. Tanis's hands were in her pussy again, filling her front as Garren filled her from behind.

"She's absolutely drenched," Tanis said. "Think she's going to come if we go much further."

"Fine," Garren said. "I don't think I can last much longer anyway." He rose and presented his weeping cock to her mouth.

She opened, and I swear, as she sucked him off, it felt like she was sucking me.

I came, hot, hard and heavy, shooting cum all over the bedding and myself; with gulping breaths, grunting, and hips jerking.

Tanis emitted a low chuckle as my cock continued to jerk through the aftershocks. He rose to stand on Hannah's other side, wiping his cock over her cheek. As Garren's cock slipped from between her wet lips, Tanis surged inside, pumping slow and shallow. And all the while, my cock jerked, and my balls reached for cum that wasn't there. I'd never felt so wretched nor so fiercely aroused seeing them use Hannah's mouth, taking turns to fill her, and her chasing them with her tongue, desperate for the next taste.

My climax didn't take the edge off for long. I had barely begun to soften when I was hardening again.

I was lost as the two huge alphas filled the tiny omega's mouth with their cocks.

∼

# Hannah

I was on my knees, so close, full of scent and cock, only the cock wasn't where I wanted it, so I sucked and licked, chasing the hot male flesh, doing anything I might to make them assuage this terrible ache.

Tanis fisted my hair, holding me captive, perfectly still as he shared my mouth with Garren. They were going to come. I knew it. I could feel the tension rising, the quickening of their thrusts, and the building urgency that triggered an echo in me.

They came together, with masculine grunts and growls, too much for my mouth, the excess spilling down my chin. The rich scent made me quiver with need, my heart racing, breasts heaving, clit pulsing, and pussy aching to be filled. Even my ass throbbed in a reminder of when Garren thrust his fingers inside.

My eyes fluttered open to clash with Red's. He was kneeling opposite me in a mirror, jaw slack, eyes glazed, and nostrils flared as he heaved a deep breath. His beautiful body glistened with the sheen of sweat. My eyes lowered over his firm abdominals to where his cock bobbed, glistening where he'd come, a little still dripping from his balls.

Garren swiped his thumb over my chin and offered it to me—I sucked it down greedy, panting lightly, ready for more. Inside, I felt wild, on the cusp of something. What was beyond? Madness, maybe?

I jerked against the binding holding firm against my wrists.

Tanis closed his hand over the binding and my wrists, instantly calming me. He took my chin, turning me to face him. "Do you need the binding off?"

I blinked. Did I? "No." I shook my head. "I like it, the way it feels. Please, I can't wait."

## The Master of the Switch

"Ah, Hannah," he said. "You know this is just the beginning, right? We have a long way to go before you're reminded that two alpha and a beta is all you'll ever get."

"I don't want more. I never wanted more."

"We're going to make sure about that," Garren said. "Omegas sometimes need to be reminded of their place."

His words unraveled me.

"Are you ready to start again?" Tanis asked.

"Start?" I shook my head. "I need cock."

Red groaned.

"And you'll get it," Tanis said, lips tugging up in a sinful smirk. "When we decide."

Hands were on my breasts, pinching, petting, rolling nipples, slapping, and pinching again. Then they were in my pussy, widening my legs and making sure Red witnessed every lewd detail as they fingered me, one then the other, and then both, stretching me open so good; and all the while, I stared at Red, who was riveted by what they did.

I throbbed with need as they touched everywhere but my clit, barely brushing my slick gland and crushing all hopes of climax. When they did catch my clit, it was like an electric shock passing through me, and the light brush of fingertips over my sensitive slick gland made me turn feral and snarl for more.

They knew my needs, attentive to when I was about to come, and their caresses softened every time.

I grew ever more frenzied, losing any sense of time as they took me under, deeper, moving against them with wanton intent, begging openly until they took my mouth again, and even that was not enough.

I didn't remember the bindings coming off, only that the restraint was gone. Garren directed me to sit down on Tanis's cock.

And it was so, so good as thick heavenly flesh pierced me, opening me up, setting nerves sparking as the sweetest, most decadent pleasure surged everywhere at once.

"She's close," Tanis said. "Very fucking close. Stay with us, Hannah. You can do this for me. Take just a little more before you come because, when you do, it's going to feel so fucking good and you won't stop coming. But you have to hold it for me, just a little longer."

Out of my mind, I basked on a different plane of existence, disconnected from rational thought and wholly aware of every nuanced sensation.

Tanis rolled his hips in a slow, deep penetration that ripped a keening wail from my lips.

Garren's cock was against my ass, pushing, building pressure until, aided by copious slick and oil, he surged deep, punching air from my lungs. I squealed at the savage pleasure, planted my palms against Tanis's chest, and pushed back for more.

"We've got you," Tanis said. "We've got you. Now, come for us. Come all over my cock, right now. We want you to. We need you to."

They began to move, Tanis, then Garren, sliding in and out, a dark, wicked pleasure rising. Hands cupped my breasts, tugging on my nipples in time with the thrusts.

My climax tore through me, setting me convulsing, blinding me, and rendering me deaf. Rapture, sharp and sweet, took me to the top and tossed me over in a heady rush.

I expected Tanis to knot me.

He did not.

They both kept thrusting into me.

And I never stopped coming, gasping, twitching, crying, in pleasure so perfect, needing an outlet and finding one, as my nails raked flesh, savage in my intent to mark and claim.

The endless waves ripped me up and sent me tumbling over again. I didn't know what was up or down, could only feel the bliss of hot naked bodies, slick with sweat, and nostrils and lungs full of pheromones. My teeth nipped and then bit.

But there were too many hands and cocks, and I realized Red was free, that I now lay on my side, Red to my front. I kissed him as another cock slammed in and out of my pussy from behind, making

### The Master of the Switch

wet slapping sounds, my thigh held up high. "Hannah, Hannah, Hannah," Red mumbled, lips against my cheek before capturing my mouth.

I dug my nails into his ass, squeezing my thighs around him, needing more, harder, feeling his wet cock thrusting against my belly. I grasped it, rewarded by his ragged groan as pre-cum smeared all over my fingers.

"She needs more," Garren said gruffly.

"Open," Tanis said, his voice a low, growled command next to my ear. He thrust deep and held his knot just outside, maddening me with need. "And let Red in."

In? I shook my head.

"I can't," Red said.

"She can take it," Garren said. He was laid out behind Red. "She takes a knot. She can take your cute little cock and his."

"Ah! Fuck!" Red muttered as Garren closed his big hand over Red's cock and redirected it to my stuffed pussy. "Do you have any idea how insulting… fuuuuck!"

Garren thrust his hips forward. I groaned as the tip of Red's cock breached me.

I wriggled. Hands tightened over me, holding me still as two slippery cocks began to move in and out. It was too much. It wasn't enough. The dark stretching and the overfull sensation was like a slow-moving sexual revelation coming for me out of the dark. Pleasure rose out of the darkness, curling around me as thousands of nerves sparked and my pussy began to flutter.

I wanted Red, to feel him, to have him inside me in any way I could.

Yet it wasn't enough, the pressure was building again, and I became feral with hunger.

"Too hot." I pushed at the males around me as scents, suddenly twice as potent, washed over me. "Hot."

"She's tipped over," someone said.

*Heat?*

I didn't expect it to feel hot.

I was a burning abyss, and the only thing that would cool me was cock or cum.

∽

# Red

I'd been with alphas and omegas before I met Hannah—had been with Hannah and Garren—and had fooled myself into thinking I was prepared when Hannah's heat finally struck.

I wasn't prepared, not even close.

A feral beast had crawled under my skin and hijacked my brain. Garren's big hand was on my cock, sliding through slickness every time I thrust. His teeth pierced the flesh where my shoulder met my throat, a warning to obey, sending a shiver all the way to my aching balls.

I couldn't come. Something was fucking broken, my cock ached to the point of pain, and my balls were drawn up tight, and still, I didn't come.

My hips thrust erratically, chasing the bliss that never came.

Garren's hand lowered to my balls, cupping and then rolling them, and fuck, it felt insanely good.

"You like that?" he rumbled beside my ear. "Stretching our omega out? You like what I'm doing to your junk?"

"Yes," I grunted.

"Want me to stop?"

"No, don't stop." I thought I might lose my mind if he took his hand away. I was fucking close.

He chuckled and moved his hand away, only to palm my hip.

I knew what was coming. Anticipated it, even as tension and lust ripped through me.

Then the fat head of his cock was pressing, and I grunted as he breached my ass. "I'm going to come."

### The Master of the Switch

"You can fucking hold it until I'm all the way in."

His fingers tightened on my hip; he thrust deep.

I came, cum ejecting from my cock so hard I saw stars, my heart thundering wildly as every muscle in my body stretched taut. The dark, burning pleasure-pain in my ass as Garren began to power in and out, the sensation of my cock being crushed in Hannah's pussy as she came, the smells of lust, and the debauched symphony of grunts, growls, and groans, all conspired to take me under again.

Hannah's teeth found my throat, bloodying me, claiming me, both of us crushed between two powerful alphas.

My cock slipped out of her hot cunt, and Tanis slammed deep, his low, feral growl and her visceral wail telling me he was knotting her. I swear I'd never hated anyone as much as I hated Tanis at that moment. I wished I was an alpha, had a knot, and could feel her come over me like that.

I could only cup the back of her head as she bit deeper. Neither of us was in control of this. Neither of us cared.

As Garren stilled and flooded cum deep in my ass, my last rational thought was that I'd never walk straight tomorrow. My dick gushed a weak but intense jet of cum over Hannah's belly, but my cock grew harder instead of softening.

Garren began to thrust into me again, slow, dark and twisty pleasure.

I didn't care how anyone used me so long as they did.

∼

## Hannah

My teeth found hot flesh. Voices taunted me, telling me to bite harder. I tasted blood even as cocks continued to pump in and out, surging, sending me over again.

What followed was a frenzy as they sought to cool my fever. Rutting and claiming me for long hours until my heat finally broke.

## Tanis

"You could have given me some fucking warning," Han grouched as I emerged from the tent. My body felt like I'd been run over by a herd of wild beasts, and my mental state wasn't much better. Her scent was still smothering me. I'd gotten up and out of the bed before I began fucking her again, because, although my raw dick was all up for it, my omega was not.

I held up a hand and, ignoring him, stalked naked to the river, where I waded straight in.

He followed me. "Is it over?" He called from the bank.

I shot him a glare. Clearly, I wouldn't be wading into a river that was bracing, even at this time of year, if rutting were an option.

He chuckled. It had been years since I'd heard Han chuckle. "You look like shit."

"Thanks, I feel like it."

"Are we moving out today?"

"What time is it?" The sky was dull and overcast but hot enough that I thought it was approaching midday. Still, the cold water wasn't shocking me to alertness fast enough for my liking. "Any news?"

"It's midday and there have been no major developments."

"Fine, tomorrow then." The only thing waiting for me at Julant was war and my pissed-off father. Neither of which filled me with joy.

I rubbed absently at my chest as Han stomped off. I could feel Hannah inside, a weak connection, but still there. I'd fucked up. At least she wasn't bred. I couldn't. Red was unlikely to, as a beta, and Garren had put his dick anywhere but her cunt. My fried brain couldn't work out whether it was respect for my situation or a personal preference.

No, we'd shared enough women, Tay included, through the years for me to know he liked pussy plenty.

# The Master of the Switch

I dunked my head under the water and scrubbed my hair. When I came up for air, there was a great splash beside me, and I caught a flash as Garren dropped Hannah beside me. She came up coughing and spluttering. The river wasn't deep, but she was small, and it came up to her chest.

"That was a dick move," I scowled at Garren as I copped a handful of wet, wriggling woman. She threw her arms around my neck, and blood surged into my raw cock, which thought it was showtime.

Another splash and Red joined us. "Fuck, it's cold," he hissed, wading deeper before diving under the water.

I smirked. Hannah nipped at my throat. She was going to get fucked if she kept that up. "How are you feeling?"

"Hungry," she said, nipping harder against my throat, making my balls draw tight from more than the cold water and my cock bob in hopeful anticipation.

My hand moved of its own accord to cup her intimately from behind. She'd taken my cock and Red's together in there enough times that she had to be sore. Why did the thought of her pussy being sore and open make me want to pound into her all over again? I eased my fingers inside, feeling how open she was, pumping slowly until she clamped down weakly over me. "Yeah? Are you hungry for food or cock?"

She never got to answer. I waded for the riverbank, where I lowered her onto a soft cloak Garren must have left there. I pried her legs open and used my fingers and thumb to open her up.

"Tanis! What are you doing?"

I leveled her with a scowl before my eyes returned to her pink, slick, puffy pussy. "Inspecting what's mine," I said. Yes, I sounded like a caveman. No, I didn't care much. I'd never felt possessive about any woman in my life and didn't fully understand what was driving this behavior, only that she was mine.

"Do you think she might need a rest?" Red asked, tentatively.

Garren chuckled. "You going to tell a newly mated alpha to wind it back a notch? Good luck with that."

"How sore are you?" I watched her pussy swallow my thick fingers with ease as I swiped my thumb back and forth over her fat little clit.

"Only a little."

"You want my dick in here?"

"Yes."

Red groaned. "They can't be serious."

Garren chuckled again.

They didn't interfere, and I heard them moving off as I lined up and let my weight slowly drive me home. And there I just held, feeling her clench and flutter around me, knot swelling without any further need for stimulation. I rocked my hips against hers, rubbing against her slippery clit, taking us both forward, letting the sweet, rising climax sweep over us, her pussy tipping into heavy contraction that sucked the cum from me.

She hissed—I was guessing her sore inner muscles didn't like being woken up, but she clung, wrapping her arms and legs around me like she was worried I might pull out... like I had any fucking choice, like my body was under my command.

My knot took the option away, and I nuzzled against the nearest claiming mark as she continued to pulse around me. I kissed her, pouring into it all I felt amid these uncertain times. She kissed me back with the same fervor.

I purred for her, and she softened in my arms as the warm air tickled my sweat-dampened skin. It was quiet and peaceful in the shade of the thick forest canopy.

Troubles waited on my periphery.

Tomorrow, I promised myself: I would worry about them then.

# Chapter 13

## Rymor

### Coco Tanis

I picked up the cup of chamomile tea from the low table, closed my eyes, and savored a sip. The floral scent was soothing, which was funny, given I'd thought it foul when I first tried it.

I smiled.

"Now, that's a knowing smile if ever I saw one," Dan said, from the opposite side of the room. Beyond him, the harbor city of Tranquility provided a stunning backdrop of sparkling water and soaring towers. The monorail system here wasn't as intricate as in Serenity, but the interconnecting span bridges pulsed with the light of capsule flow, and the sky twinkled with near and distant shuttles. From his faraway expression, I could tell he was using his retinal viewer as he relaxed on the high-end retro leather couch of our temporary apartment that Nate had commandeered several weeks ago.

The new Dan still astonished me, reminding me of a young colt, awkward in its body; but he gained strength and confidence every day.

I sighed. "I've no idea how I can smile about anything when I'm worried about Nate... and Scott." My lips tugged up a little. "Not so much about Scott, now I think about it. He's been teasing me relentlessly ever since Nate and I…"

Dan chuckled. It hadn't been that long ago that he'd been bound to a personal mover. After Bill had imprisoned him, Nate and Richard had taken drastic measures to get Dan out. Steps that had turned his biology around. Where once he had been aged beyond his years, now he was young; his body steadily gaining in strength.

I still wasn't comfortable discussing Nate with Dan. I was a lot older than Nate and, well, Nate wasn't exactly normal, even if you ignored the age difference. I wasn't one for second-guessing relationship decisions, which was definitely a personal failing. It would seem one was never too old to be foolish. Nate was just so… Nate, and really, I couldn't describe my attraction to him any better than that. I artfully changed the subject. "Do you know where I first discovered chamomile tea?"

"No idea," Dan replied. "Can't stand the stuff myself. Someone told me once that it's a Shadowland tea."

"It was during my time as a guest of John's father in Shadowland." I rolled my eyes at the memory as I sipped at the floral tea. "A Shadowlander woman I met out there told me it was beneficial during pregnancy, and I was having a hard time of it, among other things."

Dan's eyebrows raised. "Is it?"

"No, not at all, but I didn't know that at the time." I laughed. Yes, I'd been gullible in my younger years, and reckless. "I hated it at first. I would gulp it down to get it over with. Then, after I escaped and returned to Rymor, I bought some. I have been drinking it ever since."

"You still miss him? John's father?"

"Yes, I do, which makes no more sense than my desire to drink chamomile tea. Javid's answer to someone having a dispute with him

## The Master of the Switch

was to kill the man. His answer to me leaving was to lock me up. We had nothing in common and a world of differences too vast to be breached by notions as mystical as love." My shrug conveyed a sense of helplessness. "He was amusingly direct, though, and when he wasn't killing people or trying to provoke someone into killing him, he could be rather charming."

I sounded a little wistful. Damn, even after all this time, I was still thinking about the abominable man who was an out-and-out chauvinist, as well as playfully formidable. After thirty years, perhaps time had mellowed my memories? My on-off relationship with Jon Sanders hadn't helped me to distance myself from the past, when the man in question was a field scientist and knew every nuance of my sad story and all about my lingering affection for my son's father. I loved Jon, and while I'd tried to convince myself that he could fill Javid's void, as the years had passed, I'd realized he never would.

I questioned whether I had used Jon. Yet the pain I'd felt when I'd thought I had lost him told me that my feelings were genuine. Only how could I love Jon when I still had feelings for Javid? I was an omega, a geneticist who had used manipulated my genes to effectively turn myself into a beta. Only at heart, I was still an omega, still remembers how it was, the wildness and the rush of being with an alpha. And now I'd allowed Nate into my catastrophic relationship mix. I knew Nate fancied himself in love with me, too. For a person who prided themselves on a level head, I went all-in regarding matters of the heart.

"Makes me glad I've never been embroiled in such things." Dan gestured at himself. "I'm still getting used to a functioning body—just standing up is a delight!"

"Yes, I imagine it is." I smiled and drank more tea. "Have you heard from them today?"

"They're still in the labyrinth. Said they would complete a bit more reconnaissance before they return," Dan said. "Scott has a meeting tomorrow, so he has to be back for that. Keeping the twenty men Scott took out there off the radar is a challenge I could do without. The monitoring on them is basic and, while it's relatively easy to make a system overlook a person for a few hours or even days, real people start to ask questions about extended absences."

"Internal security has been increased since the bomb, too. I thought we were past this, that Moiety would put their grievances aside given we're at war. A dozen people are dead, and for what reason?"

"They are getting bolder," Dan said, his tone sad.

"The current escalation of attacks feels opportunistic or desperate. I can't decide which," I said. "They yearn for something, Dan, something they're willing to die for, something they've never forgotten or let go. We're the invaders, the people who forced them from their lands. They won't rest until we're gone."

"It's been too many years, Coco, and we can't give them back what we took anymore. This world is as much ours as theirs. Did you uncover anything in your research?"

"No," I admitted, "and the lack of records is bothering me, even with your illegal access. I've spent many days searching for references to the introduction of the Shadowlanders to see if it's linked to our displacement of the Jaru. There's nothing, not a single record, and I cannot help but wonder why."

"I think most experts agree the ancients used less than congenial means to acquire this land."

"Dan, I don't know why, but I'm convinced there's more to it. Who are Moiety and why do they even care, when, as you say, so much time has gone by? Why are they still fighting, and what are they really fighting for?"

"I don't know, Coco," he said earnestly. "Too many problems, too little time."

I nodded, but the suspicion remained that I was missing a vital clue.

# Chapter 14

## Shadowland

### Tanis

We arrived at the town of Julant mid-afternoon, having traveled at a conservative pace.

I was aware that change was coming. I told myself Rymor might have withdrawn, that the war might soon be over, leaving me free to dedicate time to nothing more complex than being a mate.

However, unless someone else had taken the privilege of killing Bill from me, I knew this outcome was unlikely.

Located in the middle of Shadowland, Julant had established itself as a trading post as far back as anyone could remember. It wasn't a prominent place, but it had a dozen taverns, nearly as many churches, and a population nearing a thousand. While accustomed to the ebbs and flows of caravans and traders, Julant was straining under the volumes I'd pushed through it of late.

When I saw my father waiting for me, a thunderous expression on his face, I muttered a brief prayer of hope they had restocked the beer. I was glad I'd had the foresight to put Hannah with Garren again, since the first thing Javid did when I dismounted was slug me hard in the face.

I let him. It seemed the best option to calm him down. My eye hurt like a bastard and felt like it had just exploded in the socket, but it still functioned, giving me a watery view of the world.

Javid's fist remained clenched.

"That's all you're getting." I gave a pointed look at his tight, red-knuckled fist.

Javid suddenly grinned, and, without warning, dragged me into a hug, thumping my back hard enough that I suspected he was half-disguising another blow. "It's good to see you, son."

Thank fuck he was happy to see me!

"So that's what all the fuss was about?"

I followed my father's line of sight to where Garren was helping Hannah to dismount. Garren then stomped off to begin organizing our tents, leaving Hannah chatting to Red. The beta was attentive, and doted on her, which I couldn't even fault him for.

"Fuss?" I knew, even as I spoke, that I shouldn't be engaging my father in a discussion about this, especially not now, and that doing so would not end well. I blinked, my eye swelling and watering—my father didn't believe in pulling his punches. In the warped Shadowland universe, it was a sign of great affection.

My eyes went to Hannah, the wonder in a tiny package. My respect for her as a person was only surpassed by the complex emotions I felt when claiming her as a mate. But, love and lust aside, she was ill-suited to a Shadowland life. The bond was weak, as yet, and I still questioned that decision. I had known Garren was going to tip her into heat, and selfishly, I'd let it play out. I wasn't planning on dying anytime soon, but it was a possibility; and then what would happen to Hannah?

## The Master of the Switch

"You, racing halfway across Shadowland to rescue a woman, sounds like a lot of fuss to me."

I should have pointed out that a three-day ride hardly constituted halfway across Shadowland. Instead, I muttered, "And you have never done anything like that."

Javid grinned. "You know, she does remind me of your mother, now you mention it."

I rubbed tense fingers through my hair. What had possessed me to make that particular reference? Javid had only ever traveled the breath of Shadowland in pursuit of one woman, my mother. I could see the calculating glint in his eyes and knew it was too late to deflect his attention; that the connection had been made. "Great, I'm sure a psychologist could offer some fascinating insights into my choice of woman."

"A what?"

"Never mind, Javid." Now was the perfect time to explain I'd already mated her, along with Garren and Red, but then questions would come about how irresponsible it was to take a mate at this time. Like common sense had anything to do with it.

Besides, I'd already surmised I was a selfish prick and didn't need anyone to tell me.

"So, you're admitting she *is* your woman. Although, I'm a bit surprised you let her ride with Garren, weren't they—"

"Drop it," I growled. Too late: I'd thrown myself in the hole with both feet. Bad enough I had to contend with other men in her bed. I wasn't discussing it with Javid. I tried to distract myself by surveying the vast camp that had once more descended upon Julant. Tents jutted among the trees, Thale's blue-on-blue flags mixed up with Luka's red-on-white. "You know what happened before and the reason I was exiled to Shadowland. I couldn't leave her with the sick bastards working for Bill."

"Hmm." Javid, ever vigilant for any weak point in a conversation, was homing in for the kill. " 'My choice of woman.' They were your exact words." Javid continued to scrutinize Hannah through hooded, openly admiring eyes.

I suffered a sudden and acute urge to punch my father. This wasn't the time or place for a family skirmish, and I was certain hitting my father now would turn into a brawl. "Not that she looks like your mother, mind you, but tower-dwellers do hold a fascination. They're a puny race, for sure, yet despite their poor breeding potential, you still find it difficult to think of anything else."

I caught hold of Javid's collar, dragged my father close, and tightened it to near choking before I could check myself. "There have been many times I considered reversing the decision to spare your life, but if you're thinking about rutting her, I won't be able to stop myself."

I allowed Javid to pull out of my hold.

"Better run me through now, son. A man would have to be dead not to be thinking about it," Javid said, unconcerned. "Garren is still a part of it, I'm guessing, and the beta at her side, who seems very familiar with her. Never been much for sharing, myself, but I could be persuaded in the right circumstance. And an omega has needs. You clearly aren't satisfying her on your own."

*The fuck!*

"I've started preparing our tents. I assume we're staying here tonight?" Garren approached from my right, glancing between us. "Something happening here?"

"We were discussing Tanis' woman." Javid nudged his head in Hannah's direction.

"Our woman. We mated Hannah a few days ago," Garren said, chest puffing a little with pride.

I heaved a sigh.

"Mated." Javid feigned ignorance as he turned toward me. "Did it slip your mind, son? Still, the timing is not great. What if one of you dies in the upcoming war?"

"We're camping here," I said in a blatant change of subject. "I need to sort out what is happening and where everyone is, given Javid

## The Master of the Switch

has screwed up my plans by moving half *my* army in the completely wrong direction."

"I wasn't going to let them kill you," Javid replied mulishly. "Then I would be left with Garren, who is passing average as a leader."

"I'm right here!" Garren glared at my father.

Javid continued. "And Agregor has got his mother's brains, so no hope there. Then there's Logan, and he was dropped on his head as a baby. I was relieved when he left to join that obscure religious sect. The rest are too young to assess, but I'm not hopeful."

I laughed, partly at Garren's outraged face and partly at my father's brutal but accurate assessment of the remaining family members.

"Still, with all this fuss going on I'm wondering if those tower-dwelling bastards haven't left some permanent damage. Do you think your mother's still of breeding age?" Javid asked earnestly. "I may need a back-up plan."

It was Garren's turn to laugh, and I remembered why I avoided spending prolonged periods in my father's company.

"Scout's here!" someone shouted.

"In my tent, now," I said. "I want a new plan in place before either of you screw up anything else."

"It's not ready." Garren squinted at my half-pitched tent, "and I haven't screwed anything up for a while."

"Exactly! The next one is overdue!" But I wasn't thinking about Garren. It was the Hannah variety of trouble-brewing that I had in mind as I watched her engage in an animated conversation with Red. Her attention shifted back and forth between Julant and Red, who'd already been smitten with her before the constant rutting we fitted into every spare moment. No way he would offer credible resistance. "Finish my tent and then get everyone in there ready."

The conversation between Hannah and Red died as I approached. Red gave me a defensive glare. "She wants to go to Julant."

"Nothing short of tying her up is likely to stop her." I realized I'd failed to hide how appealing that option sounded when Red coughed to cover his laugh.

"She can go to see Molly. Then straight back here. Go with her."

I pointed my finger at Hannah. "Do not wander off alone."

I pointed my finger at Red. "Do not let her wander off alone."

Neither offered a comment, and I turned back to find my tent ready, with men stomping in and out with supplies and furnishings. Two of my guards waited a couple of paces away, two more waited at the tent entrance, and a further four clustered a little distance to the left.

Taking a deep, calming breath, I headed to my tent. Inside, it was cool, and the furniture was in place, as were Garren, my father, Kein, and a crate of beer. I raised an eyebrow at Garren, who was in the act of slugging one back.

I thought that perhaps drinking was a poor idea, given my mood. I took one anyway, because everything looked better after a beer.

I downed half the contents.

Tilting the bottle, I inspected it with a frown. "Don't they have anything but stout?"

"I thought you liked stout?" Garren said, his puzzled gaze settling on the bottle in my hand.

"I hate stout."

Garren snorted. "You drank enough of it last time we were here."

"Yes, because they didn't have anything else."

Garren grinned and grabbed his second bottle. "Well, you're out of luck, because stout is *still* all they have."

"So, where is everyone?" I turned to Kein, who also held a stout and looked even less enthusiastic about it than me.

"Fifteen thousand here, fourteen thousand with Han a day to our north—he's got both the waypoint and the gateway to Rymor locked down. Adro has another twenty ready to cut off the main Rymorian group from the east. There's another five thousand camped to the south in case the Rymorians head that way. We've got the area boxed

## The Master of the Switch

in." Kein sipped his stout and grimaced. "We've reports of Falton heading north-east. I think it's fair to assume he doesn't intend to join us."

"Heading to Talin?" How had Bill gotten word out to a fortress leader? What was he offering them for their allegiance?

"It's possible," Kein agreed.

"Greve's not far from Talin, either," Javid muttered.

Falton wasn't a huge surprise, but if Greve had joined forces with Bill, I'd just lost my two largest fortresses and nearly half my army.

"Just over twenty thousand are with Greve near the border, but he's started pulling back since the Jaru began moving south."

"It was going to happen sooner or later." Garren finished his second beer and reached directly for the third.

"Later would have been better," Javid quipped.

"Let's send a rider to call Greve back and see how he responds," I said. The Jaru movement concerned me, but Bill forming an alliance with Falton and Greve worried me more. "Make sure you use one of his scouts. Let's not lose a good man testing a theory. Have Greve followed at a discreet distance. If he's not joining me, I still want to know what he's doing and where he goes."

Kein nodded. "We've had some news from those helping us inside Rymor." He pulled a scroll from his jacket pocket and handed it to me.

It was from Theo, and I smiled as I read it. "Field scientists are coming to support us, armed and able to communicate directly with Rymor." This was about to get interesting.

"I hope your trust is well placed," Javid said seriously.

Reading down, I barked out a laugh.

"What?" Garren said, impatient—he hated waiting for scroll news.

"My mother has gone into hiding and is working with the Rymorian resistance group. She's with Scott Harding, and Dan Gilmore, who Hannah has mentioned to me before."

"I think that just made my day." Smiling contentedly, Javid sipped his stout.

Wilder had been dealt with, but there were still many Rymorians and an increasing Jaru threat.

I stilled as a possible pathway opened before me. I didn't want Hannah to be caught up in the fallout, should we fail. But could I really do what I was considering?

Did I have any fucking choice?

The pull was already there, a thread in the center of my chest connecting me to her. Every time we fucked, it drove the bond deeper. I wanted to keep her safe. I needed to keep her near.

And wasn't it the most bitter realization to know that I couldn't do both?

I'd been making hard decisions all my adult life. She had already suffered too much, and I couldn't be the man who allowed her to be hurt again.

*Separating will hurt her,* my inner voice taunted. But there were different kinds of hurt, and it was better if she lived to hate me than fall into Bill's hands.

"Kein, I want you to head back to Han tomorrow and fetch Theo here. With the Jaru on the move, I need to take out the Rymorians swiftly. I'm sending Hannah back to Han with you. She'll be safer in Rymor now."

Kein's sharp gaze turned to me. There were questions in the scout's eyes, but he remained silent and began stroking his mustache.

"The fuck!" Garren slammed his fourth empty beer bottle against the table. "Don't I get a say in this?"

"You want to keep her here? When we're about to fight a war?"

His scowl deepened, but there was uncertainty, too. "I don't fucking know. Last time we left her, it didn't end well. We should ask her what she wants to do."

"She was fucking tortured and beaten last time she fell into the wrong hands," I said heatedly. "She trusts Dan. I trust my mother. Now I'm asking you to trust me."

## The Master of the Switch

A tic thumped in his jaw. With hindsight, the tent with its attendant audience was not the best place to have had this discussion.

"You going to send Red with her?"

My gut clenched. I nodded.

Garren reached for another beer. "She won't like it... *I* don't fucking like it."

"Yeah, I know." I reached for another beer, too. Tomorrow, I was going to have a different kind of fight on my hands.

# Chapter 15

**Hannah**

The town of Julant was an odd, quirky place that I'd found endearing on my first visit. It had lost none of its appeal the second time around. Narrow, rutted, gritty streets predominated, with little wooden shops and houses on each side. Occasionally, a more grandiose house, church, or tavern broke the flow, but mostly it was squat, rickety structures spilling their wares out onto the street. In the center, a vast open expanse allowed for a huge market that, as far as I could tell, opened every day of the week.

A minor lord presided over the village. His house was a sprawling double-story mansion, compared to the other dwellings, located not far from the center and near the church to which Molly's orphanage belonged.

A dozen children of various ages lived there. Molly liked none of them.

"Can I come with you?" Molly demanded, having climbed onto my lap and offering me a bite of the half-eaten carrot she was snacking on. It was an improvement on travel crackers, but I resisted

## The Master of the Switch

and declined. She must have been the only five-year-old prepared to eat a raw carrot.

Over the top of her sweet, messy hair, Red was vigorously shaking his head.

"I...ah...I'm not sure you would enjoy being with us. There's a lot of traveling."

"I hate it here," she said. "The kids are all stupid, and Mr. Watters won't let me pet the pigs! Besides, I like traveling, especially when a cart gets stuck, and everyone starts cursing."

Red chuckled.

I shot him a glare.

We spent the afternoon and early evening with Molly, where she showed us her stick doll and her favorite places to play. Her beguiling and forthright ways worked on my resistance, but it was the proprietor's insistence that she wasn't happy, that she had talked of nothing but John Tanis and me, that clinched it.

"This isn't going to end well," Red said, as we headed back to the camp. The tense set of his jaw and shoulders said he felt he was a man walking to his death.

With the turn toward dusk, lanterns had been lit and lent the village a magical air that emphasized Shadowland's differences. Within Rymor, the brilliant artificial lighting almost negated a sense of night.

"It'll be fine," I said, although nerves fluttered in the pit of my stomach. I ignored them—I had no intention of leaving Molly behind this time. "He's not completely unreasonable."

Red gave me a sideways glance and muttered, "I think you have a selective memory."

"I'm sorry Tanis hit you." I bit my lip to hide my smile. "I had that covered."

He chuckled. "Not as much as I am, but it's okay, I deserved it."

We exited the town. Before us, the Shadowlander camp extended out into the tree line and beyond. Someone had told me a mind-blowing fifteen thousand soldiers were here.

Right before us, directly opposite the town entrance, was Tanis' tent. At my best guess, twenty soldiers were on duty outside.

"Is he seriously worried someone might kill him?" I thought out loud.

Red laughed. "No, Hannah, I don't think it's at Tanis' request. They didn't appreciate him surrendering to the Rymorians, and they're worried he'll do it again. Hence, they don't let him go anywhere alone. They appreciate even less that he took off, straight after returning, to search for you without any of his personal guards."

"Great, no wonder they keep giving me funny looks." I noticed two of his guards ahead of us had just left the village and were hurrying to the tent. Two more disappeared inside when they spotted me. "Why do I feel like they were waiting for me?"

"They've been following us all afternoon," Red said. "I guess Tanis didn't trust either of us."

As we approached, the tent flap opened, and people began piling out. First, two guards, followed by Garren, Kein, and Javid, then two more guards carrying several crates of beer. From the way they held the crates, hanging from one hand, the bottles had to be empty. Kein gave me a nod as he passed. Garren waited just outside the entrance, and then, finally, Tanis stepped out.

An overwhelming urge to run gripped me. I spun around... and collided with a guard so hard the breath escaped me in a *whoosh*. Why was he right behind me?

"It wasn't my fault," Red said. His words held a note of resignation. "I told her it was a bad idea."

"I'm not blaming you, Red." Tanis's voice was so calm, I immediately knew he knew about Molly and was furious. But he was my alpha now, my mate. How bad could it get? "I should have just tied her up. I won't make the same mistake again."

I felt more than justified in agreeing to take Molly, and turned to face Tanis. His eye, puffy and red earlier, had turned a mottled black. He nodded over my shoulder at the guard, and I sensed him move away.

# The Master of the Switch

Tanis continued to stare at me. "You can leave too, Red."

I sent a frantic glance Red's way, but he gave a brief apologetic shrug and left.

"She's not coming with us." Tanis's tone was clipped, his expression unreadable. He scratched his forehead, and my eyes tracked the clumsy movement.

"She *is* coming with us," I said with greater confidence than I felt. Weren't alphas supposed to dote on their omegas? Shouldn't he have already capitulated to my wishes? "It's all arranged."

"She's not coming," he repeated a little louder this time.

"We can't leave her here. She isn't happy. The proprietor said she still hasn't settled in." It had been so hard leaving Molly last time. No way was I going anywhere without her this time.

He scoffed. "You are joking. She's a terror, that's why they want to get rid of her. Not that it matters when we're heading toward a war!"

I glared at him. "I'm not leaving Molly!"

He scratched his head again. This time, there was a definite lack of coordination. "You're a nightmare, too," he muttered, but he didn't sound so angry anymore.

"We are taking her, though?" I asked tentatively, confident that if I could only get him alone, I could find ways to stop him from being so grumpy.

He let out a puff of breath. "Yes, you can take Molly with you, but there will be consequences."

"Consequences?" No, I didn't like the sound of that.

Fisting my arm, he started walking, pulling me with him. "Garren, get a rope," he called over his shoulder.

"Tanis, you can't be serious," Garren muttered from a few feet away.

"A rope, Garren, or I promise what I do instead will be worse."

"Where are we going?" I craned my neck to stare after Garren, wondering if he was going to fetch a rope, as Tanis had asked, or had simply walked away. Neither option sounded good. Tanis's fingers were cutting off the circulation in my arm as his pace increased.

Then I noticed the post.

I dug my heels in, clawed at his fingers, and attempted a kick, which wasn't easy while walking at this furious pace, and I nearly landed on my ass. He ignored my attempts to escape his vice-like grip. We drew ever closer to that dreadful destination, and, finally, out of desperation, I let my body go limp.

"Uff!" He hauled me over his shoulder, where I hung, confused about how I'd gotten there as the blood rushed to my head. Given his freakish size, the ground was an alarming distance away.

"What are you doing?"

His footsteps made a steady thud against the ground that bounced me around.

"You can't—"

He stopped abruptly and dumped me on the ground, where I collapsed in a heap of flailing limbs and indignation.

I looked between Tanis, the looming post, and Garren, holding a length of rope in his hand. Beyond Garren, Red stood watching, slack-jawed. Tanis couldn't really mean to tie me there now, could he?

Closing his fingers over my ankle, he unseated me, pulled my boot off, and tossed it over his shoulder.

"Tanis?!"

The next boot followed.

"Are you insane?!"

He stripped me.

I alternated between cursing him and squeals of protest, none of which made any difference to the outcome. My entire body had flushed crimson by the time he removed my panties, sending them sailing through the air. The only saving grace to my humiliation was the onset of night.

Standing back, Tanis adjusted his cock without the slightest indication of shame. My eyes locked on it, and I licked my lips. To my

## The Master of the Switch

further embarrassment, all this tussling had made me wet. With seemingly little effort, and despite my vigorous struggles, I was back on my feet with my wrists bound.

Drawing my hands high above my head, he secured the rope to the post.

"Still want to take Molly?"

"Will you untie me if I say no?" I asked myself if I would fold if he said yes. I wasn't sure.

"No, you're overdue a night to reflect on what you've done." He ran his fingers over his face, swaying a little before he jerked himself straight. "Let's see how your resolve is in the morning." He turned and stalked away.

"You have control issues!" At least no one was throwing rotting fish at me.

"Don't mind it," Garren said. "He's a bit tense and handling it badly."

I rolled my eyes. Pity it was too dark, and he probably couldn't see.

He turned and walked away. "Come on, Red, let's go and talk some sense into him. If that doesn't work, I'm just going to thump him."

I seethed. So what if I'd said Molly could come with us? His response was neither fair nor proportional to my transgression. Further, it outraged me that *he* was sleeping in a comfortable bed surrounded by dozens of guards he didn't need while *I* was here, cold and alone.

Okay, so it wasn't that cold; and I was in the middle of a camp, so not exactly alone. I tugged on the rope.

It didn't give and I roused myself into a fit of temper trying to rip it out.

My arms started to ache. So did my legs. It was late, and I was tired and irritable. I was also feeling needy. Since my heat, one of them would usually be fucking me by now.

I couldn't say if I stood there for minutes or hours, then I saw that someone was coming toward me. A guard I hadn't noticed shifted to block the man's path. They spoke in voices too low for me to hear before the guard stepped aside.

Garren stopped a few feet away.

He had a black eye.

I sighed.

"I know you only thought to help her, but the Jaru are coming, Hannah. She'd be safer here than if she were to be dragged into the middle of a war. He's going to be really pissed tomorrow, and he's going to want to make a point."

*Tomorrow?* "What the hell could be worse than leaving me here all night?"

He puffed out a breath, and although I couldn't see well, I thought he wasn't looking at my face.

"Garren!"

He chuckled. "I guess you really do like being bound." I could hear the smile in his voice. "Wishing I could see a lot better in the dark."

"Are you going to untie me?"

He leaned forward and caught hold of the rope where it was hooked to the post.

It gave suddenly.

I stumbled forward but came to an abrupt and painful halt. All he had done was allow some slack. "What? Let me go!"

"I'm not suicidal. I'll be back in a bit when all the guards have fallen asleep." He dropped a blanket over my shoulders, turned, and left.

# Chapter 16

**Hannah**

A sudden piercing squeal roused me from sleep. Before my sluggish mind could begin to assess the situation, a tiny body hit me.

"Molly?!"

It was dark, and the only light came from a lantern in the hand of a nearby guard.

"Who the hell gave you a blanket?" Tanis pulled Molly off and indicated the dusty patch of ground to his right. "Wait there." Molly fidgeted, but otherwise did as instructed.

I gave serious consideration to telling on Garren. He'd said he was coming back, and then I'd fallen asleep. How long had I been here? "Nobody, I found it here."

He made a noncommittal grunt as he caught hold of my wrists and cut the rope. Then he ripped the blanket away.

I squealed.

He dropped a pile of clothing at my feet. "Get dressed."

Glaring at Tanis the whole time, I dragged my clothing on, conscious of his silent fuming study of me; but he had Molly with him, which had to be a positive sign. "You brought Molly." Why was Molly up so late? Was it nearly morning?

"The dear orphanage proprietor feared we might forget her and was kind enough to bring her over early," he bit out.

"I'm coming with you!" Unable to contain her enthusiasm, Molly jumped up and down.

"Yes, you are," I agreed. The horrible episode was behind me, Molly was here, and everything would work out.

"Alright, Molly, Hannah needs the rest of her punishment."

Pushing my messy hair out of my face, I glanced up, flushed. "Punishment?" My flush deepened, because the last time I'd been punished I'd gone into heat. My body decided it was interested, even if my mind said, 'not yet'. "I've got nothing to say to you after you left me out here, terrified, all night while you were sleeping in your comfortable bed!"

"You've been here all of fifteen minutes. And clearly you were not that stressed if you fell asleep!" He indicated the blanket in his hand. "A blanket and enough slack to sit down wasn't what I had in mind. Follow me."

He stalked off toward the camp, Molly skipping at his side. I followed, feeling confused. Had I really only been there for fifteen minutes?

"Will Hannah be spanked?" Molly tugged on Tanis's hand. "When I'm really naughty I get my bottom spanked."

"That's a wonderful suggestion, Molly," he said, all serious consideration. "But first I'm going to burn this blanket."

"You can't burn it. It's Ga—" I clamped my mouth shut, too late. Tanis stopped walking. We had all stopped walking.

He grinned. "That was comically easy."

"I didn't say anything," I said, worried as he abruptly veered off in a new direction, one, I belatedly realized, led directly to where Garren stood talking to Red.

"I've got something for you, Garren," Tanis said as he approached.

## The Master of the Switch

Hearing his name, Garren looked up... and met Tanis's fist in his face. He staggered back, his eyes darkening with the promise of retribution as he scowled at me. "Which part of don't tell him did you not understand?"

"I didn't tell him," I said. "Also, you said you were coming back... and left me there for... fifteen minutes!"

"What the fuck is fifteen minutes?" Garren muttered.

"About how long Hannah's been at the post," Red offered.

Okay, so it really had only been fifteen minutes.

"Never mind," Tanis said, tiredly.

"Tanis threatened to burn the blanket and she blabbed," Molly said helpfully as Tanis shoved the offending blanket into Garren's hands. "Hannah's a telltale."

Garren grunted as he grabbed it.

Tanis's grin had a sadistic edge. "You two can watch the nightmare while I deal with Hannah. Molly, go with Garren and Red."

"You can't call a little girl a nightmare," I said, distracted from talk of spanking and worried about what 'dealing' with me might entail. "It's damaging."

"I am a nightmare," Molly chirped. "Mr. Watters said so after I pulled a chunk of Gretta's hair out. There was blood everywhere! I wasn't allowed any supper!"

"Was Gretta mean to you?" Despite the reference to lots of blood, I was ready to come to Molly's defense.

"No, I don't like her. She kept pestering me and asking me to play with her."

Oh my God, the child really was a monster, I thought deliriously.

Tanis gave me a knowing look. "See, she's a fucking nightmare. She knows she's a nightmare. Even Watters, the sweet, elderly patron of the orphanage, knows she's a nightmare. His parting words were: she's a nightmare. I can't cope. Please take her, I beg you."

"He did say that," Molly said, clutching Garren's hand. He frowned down at her—she smiled sweetly up. "I think he begged more than once."

"You should be more concerned about yourself," Tanis said. "We're going to talk in my tent now. Alone." He fixed Garren then Red with a look.

"She's going to get a spanking," Molly said excitedly for Red and Garren's benefit. "What's fucking? Is that a curse word? Mr. Watters says cursing leads to eternal damnation."

Garren laughed, but it faded swiftly, and an undecipherable expression settled over his face. My eyes shot toward Red, but his face was painfully solemn.

I didn't get a chance to ask more because Tanis pivoted and frogmarched me in the direction of his tent. "You're not really going to spank me, are you?"

"Why, do you want me too?" He sent me a speculative look.

"No!" *Yes*.

He smirked. "You're such a needy omega. Spanking it is."

"You can't be serious?"

The tent loomed. My breathing turned choppy as I failed to hide how much I was secretly enjoying this... enjoying being mastered, no matter the reason.

Once inside, he sat on the bed, hauled me over his lap, and spanked me.

It stung.

I wailed.

The tussling also made me wet.

"Ow! It really stings, you barbarian."

He chuckled and carried on.

"Your insults are improving, Hannah," he grunted, catching a flailing hand and pinning it to my lower back before spanking me some more. "We both know you're dripping wet and desperate for me to rip these pants down and fuck you hard."

He stopped. The sting continued to dance like flames over my skin. He turned me over slowly, and I hissed when my ass connected with his thighs.

Then I stilled because his face held a strange emptiness. He

### The Master of the Switch

brushed my hair back from my hot cheeks and lowered his mouth over mine. The kiss was slow and sweet, but it didn't stay like that for long. Warning bells were ringing, but nothing mattered when we kissed. The urgency rocketed between us, as we both fumbled to liberate the clothes.

He rose abruptly, tossed me onto the bed, and freed enough clothing to bury himself inside me. A brutal edge to what came next lit an echo in me. My pussy tipped into organismic spasms out of nowhere. He didn't stop, just hammered me into the bed, his hands bruising where he gripped my hips, and I loved all of it. I didn't stop coming until he'd knotted me. Even then, I continued to flutter around him, basking in the blissful high.

We lay in a tangle, sharing gusty breaths. Only then did the sense of wrongness return.

He rolled onto his back, taking me over him, the knot locking us together.

"You're returning to Rymor."

Blindsided, I leaned up to study his face as a chill swept the length of my spine.

He wasn't purring.

I wanted to laugh, to scoff, and tell him not to be ridiculous, but his face was so empty I knew this was real, that somehow, and some way, I was returning to Rymor.

"When?" I asked softly—did I really want to know? He was still inside me, locked intimately. How could he be inside me and speak of sending me away?

"Tomorrow, Kein is taking you."

"Red and Garren?"

"Red will go with you. Garren has no place in Rymor, and even so, I need him here. He'll escort you to Han's camp, where twenty field scientists, trustworthy ones, are waiting to take you to Rymor where it's safe."

That wasn't a good enough reason not to send me to Bill.

Nothing was.

"Garren wouldn't want this." He couldn't, could he? Garren would never let me go.

"No, he's not. But he's not the leader here, I am."

I struggled to wrench away, but Tanis clamped his hand over my ass and held me tight. "Why, Tanis? Tell me why?"

"Because it's not safe for you here."

"After Karry, I'm pretty sure I can cope with anything." I fretted. He rolled, taking me under him and pinning me to the bed.

"After Karry, and in all seriousness, I'd sooner cut off my own arm than put you at risk again. The decision is made." That cool, clipped tone was back in play.

"The decision isn't made."

"Sorry, Hannah, but this time it's not open to interpretation."

The world tilted around me, and I, sliding with it, disconnected from reality. "Just like that, I'm leaving. No discussion. No choice."

His dark eyes had a mesmerizing quality. If I'd had any doubts about loving him, they were laid to rest tonight. I loved him, wanted, and needed him.

I blinked back the tears, but they tumbled over my cheeks anyway.

He leaned down to kiss them up. The knot had softened, and he began to move.

I cried harder, but I no longer wanted to push him away. I clung to him, knowing tonight would be our last. He rocked his hips, setting everything sparking again, and then he began to thrust.

We fucked like the world was ending tomorrow. In all the ways that mattered, I felt like it was.

The onset of dawn brought an end to the interlude and to Tanis and me.

My cheeks were damp from weeping, and my body was sticky and suffused by aches. We lay on our sides, facing one another, our bodies pressed close and entwined. He purred for me, and I never wanted him to stop, wanted to stay here, forever lost in this moment.

"What about Molly?"

## The Master of the Switch

A tired smile tugged at his lips. "Still worrying about Molly? Right now?" His smile faded. "That's for you to decide."

His lack of direction felt worse than if he had simply told me Molly couldn't go.

I hated him for deciding this and for not giving me a choice... but obviously not enough. "I'm safer with you. We both are."

"Not now the Jaru are coming, and there are still the rest of the Rymorians that Bill sent out here."

"I won't be safe in Rymor." My breath stuttered as the stifling panic came rushing in. "I can't be. What about Bill?"

I pushed at his arms, wanting free of him yet feeling a thousand times worse when he allowed me some distance. I sat up, and he followed, collecting my small hand within his. God, how could a touch break my heart so?

"They aren't taking you back to Bill. There's a resistance group. A man you mentioned before as a friend, Dan Gilmore, is working with them. We have only one device that can disable the Rymorian weapons and there are several groups here. In total, nearly ten thousand Rymorians, all of them armed. It could all go wrong very easily and then you would be back with another equivalent of Karry. Why put yourself at risk when there are people within Rymor who can keep you hidden?"

Dan? Those words erased the last of my resistance. Could I see Ella?

"A man named Theo helped me to escape the Rymorian camp. He's working with Dan Gilmore and has been spying on Bill for the last five years—I believe you know him? It was Theo who told me Karry had snatched you from Thale. Bill fitted you with a tracker before you left. Theo can remove it once you're at Han's camp."

So that's how Tanis found me, and how Karry found me, too. I wanted to argue, but at the same time I recalled those odd, sensitive glances Theo had sent my way, that suddenly made sense. Why had Dan kept this from me?

"I need to get things ready," Tanis said. He kissed my forehead before slipping out of bed.

I listened to him getting dressed, lost in my thoughts. As the tent flap closed on him, leaving me alone, I put my head in my hands and wondered what the hell was happening to my life. Whenever I thought I was moving forward, it kicked me back to the ground. If I went, I could see Ella and Dan—only Dan had kept terrible secrets from me.

I couldn't dwell on that right now.

Heat wafted in from the tent opening, flapping in the gentle breeze. It would be another hot day. Resolute in the face of no alternatives, I pulled my hands away from my face and raked my fingers through my knotty hair. At least I could get it cut.

I dressed.

Garren would ride with me to Han. Two days, that was all, and then he would also be leaving my life.

When I pushed out of the tent, I found thirty men and women gathered in the clearing, preparing to leave. A sense of purpose surrounded them, with horses being saddled, supplies packed, and the clamor of bellowed orders. I'd witnessed such scenes often enough to recognize the underlying order of what at first appeared chaotic. Tanis stood to my right, talking to Kein, but on seeing me, he stopped.

My attention shifted back to the group, and I spotted Red with Molly, packed and mounted. Garren was waiting with his horse. My lips trembled when I saw only resigned sadness on his face.

When I turned back, Tanis was striding toward me, and everything inside me squeezed. He was handsome, a warrior, an alpha, and an extraordinary version of both.

He stopped before me. "Are you ready?"

I shook my head. No, I wasn't ready, and I never would be. "You said Rymor no longer existed for me. You said I should forget it." My eyes clouded over, and my brows drew together, "And, finally, as I accept a life here, you tell me I have to leave."

## The Master of the Switch

"Shadowland was never your home, and you never belonged here."

My chest compressed. Somehow, I remained upright when all I wanted to do was beg him to let me stay. It was gone—my life, my heart—utterly gone. No more tears fell. I had no more energy for sorrow or anger, nothing but an all-consuming numbness that had sucked in my whole world.

His face was as closed as it had ever been. He was already removed from my story. I could see that now, and I wondered if we'd ever even shared the same page.

He was sending me away and, worse, ripping Garren from me too. At that realization, the emptiness became absolute.

"Take care of yourself, Tanis. It's what you do best." The slightest crack showed in his stony façade, evidenced in the tightening around his mouth. I took some comfort in that, determined to give him nothing more, no demands or wild declarations. Dignity was all I had left, and I wrapped its cloak tightly around myself.

A person didn't get over such events, and I turned to where Garren waited, solemn. There were reins in his hand, not to his horse, but to a smaller one. I took them from him without a word and mounted. Today, I got my own horse.

I refused to look back, feeling the weight of Tanis' gaze on me. The command to ride was given, and the party began to filter through the camp and then out into the winding pathways of the Shadowland forests. Those pathways led to Han's camp, and the field scientists. And all too soon, I would be back in Rymor.

I had wished for this so often. *"Be careful what you wish for,"* I whispered.

That warning, like so many others, had come far too late.

# Chapter 17

**Rymor**

**Nate**

It was early morning when Scott arrived at my commandeered apartment and immediately launched into complaints about the day ahead. He wore a suit today, and combined with his whipcord build and crooked nose, it gave off a criminal overlord vibe.

"I can't believe they put that moron Andrew Jordan in charge of homeland security," Scott said heatedly.

I stifled a yawn, pushed my floppy fringe out of my eyes, and downed my coffee from the vantage of the kitchen counter, which was currently propping me up. We had been working late into the previous night, and although I needed little sleep, I did need some mental downtime. I felt depleted and wasn't in the mood for a Scott rant.

"Don't you think it's a little early to be drinking?" I gave a meaningful glance at Scott's coffee. "You just said you were meeting Andrew Jordan later and you don't get along at the best of times."

## The Master of the Switch

Scott's eyes narrowed. "Good point, Nate. Where's the scanner?"

"You can't keep using the scanner to remove alcohol from your bloodstream. It's illegal," I said. Scott enjoyed strong coffee. What I hadn't initially realized was that he often added a little something extra.

Scott jumped up from where he had been lounging on the couch and went to retrieve the scanner from the home hub. "Illegal is my middle name since I met you, Nate." Joining me, he slapped a hand affectionately against my shoulder.

I scowled at my sloshing coffee, dumped it on the counter, and snatched the scanner from Scott. I configured it to prevent the incident from being recorded on the medical database. "I will eat this scanner if you don't have another before you leave."

"A challenge, eh?" Scott took the scanner back, pressed it against his arm and shuddered as it did its magic. "Dan still in bed?"

"Yeah, we were up late last night trying to decipher the communications between Bill and his Shadowland forces. Blocking them is easy, breaking encryption is another matter."

The far bedroom door opened, and a sleepy Dan shuffled out, grinning. "Finally got the satellite connection up so we can communicate again." He raised his hand to his mouth as he yawned and headed for the printer. "I'll work on hooking everyone's retinal and personal viewers up—as soon as I get a coffee."

"At least you've got some good news," Scott said. "Jordan proposed deploying field scientists to patrol the wall. If that happens, our cover is blown."

"When did he decide that?" I demanded. "Why are you only telling me this now?"

"I just found out," Scott said defensively. "I received an emergency meeting invite an hour ago. The redeployment of field scientists is the first item on the agenda."

"I'll have a word with Richard," I said. "He's still on the action committee."

"Interesting that he called the meeting when Bill isn't here. Our illustrious chancellor left for Talin about two hours ago," Dan said. "I've got an alert on the exit he's using."

"He's going out there more often," I said. "That's twice this week already; it can't be easy for a chancellor to leave in a time of crisis. It's like he doesn't care anymore."

"Well, it's going to be a lot harder to shut Jordan down without Bill there," Scott said. "About the only good thing I can say about Bill is that he hates that dickhead Jordan as much as I do. Bill hates the field scientists too, and he won't want them involved with the war. Without Bill, I'll have a fight on my hands."

"Does Richard have any insight into what's happening with Bill?" Dan took his coffee out of the printer and came to join us.

"No, but he's found evidence of dissension, with surprising offers of support among members of the upper council," I said. "It seems councilman Carl Stevens isn't as well liked as Bill believes."

"Heard a rumor he's into paid companionship." Scott grinned.

"Yes," I agreed. "He's also free with his bribes, and if that doesn't work, he's happy to progress to the threats."

Dan paused with the coffee halfway to his lips. "I hope you're not getting Richard into danger."

"No more than any of us, Dan," I replied. "Unfortunately, we all need to take risks. Richard's careful, and I've been monitoring the people he's had dealings with as a precaution."

"What are you going to do if one of them isn't quite the supporter Richard believes them to be?" Dan asked.

"I'm hoping it doesn't come to that." I sighed. "I guess if it does, then we're going to need to act, but don't ask me what acting means or what I am prepared to do."

Scott grinned. "Don't worry, Nate. No one is expecting you to get your hands dirty. I suffer no such problem where Jordan is concerned." He cracked his knuckles. "Right, I'm off to battle Jordan. Wish me luck, because if negotiations don't work, bribery won't work either with that self-righteous asshole, and I'm skipping straight past the threat stage and onto action."

### The Master of the Switch

Now Scott even sounded like a criminal overlord!

Scott slapped me on the shoulder again, making me jump. "Don't overeat today, you need to save some room for a scanner." He winked as he headed out.

"It won't come to that, Nate," Dan said once we were alone.

"Yes, Coco once accused me of having the IQ of a door scanner. Eating a medical scanner feels a lot like cannibalism."

Dan laughed. "That wasn't what I meant."

"I know," I said tiredly. "And I wish I felt as flippant as I sound. Do you have any idea how much danger we're in? We've twenty men out of the country, and the wrong outcome of this meeting could put our plans and lives at risk."

"Which is why I intend to listen in," Dan said. "If I suspect it's not going Scott's way, I'll shut the meeting down. If nothing else, it will buy us some time." Then he grinned and added. "Now come on, you have an encryption you need to break."

# Chapter 18

**Sirius**

Maurice Fuller had once been the oldest member of the Senate. Several months ago, he left that position to become the security council director. While he was influential, it was his access privileges that interested me.

Harmony was among the less populous Rymorian cities. The apartment's windowed wall revealed the brilliant blue waters of the eastern shores of Rymor. In the distance, a chain of green islands dotted the water.

Maurice had come here for a holiday.

A holiday, now very much over.

Maurice's wife sat before the window, gagged and bound to a dining chair. Her presence added an additional motivation for Maurice, and her tear-stained face and wild eyes further aided that aim.

I was questioning Maurice, and the conversation wasn't progressing well for anyone involved.

Five of my best agents accompanied me: two by the door, one behind Maurice and his life partner, and one beside me who oper-

## The Master of the Switch

ated the controller. They all waited, their faces impassive, for my next order.

I nodded, and the collar was activated again.

On the other side of the room, Maurice's wife emitted guttural sounds of horror from behind the gag as Maurice danced about in his chair, thrashing against the bindings like a tormented puppet. His wrists were red and bruised from fighting the restraints, but they had bound him tight, and no amount of struggle would deliver freedom.

I nodded again, and my agent deactivated the device. A pain collar was an ingenious creation that left no physical damage to the wearer. The pain came in waves of the perfect duration to prevent the wearer from losing consciousness. It had been a common sight during the pre-enlightenment slavery era and was an excellent form of management. Slavery had been banished long since, but the skills to craft such devices were easily restored. I thought it was meeting my current needs well. It was possible, with training, to block the pain, but such tolerance could take years to master. Maurice didn't have that much time. The pain levels were excruciating; sooner or later, everyone sought to comply with the controller's wishes.

Maurice's head lolled to one side, his mouth open, and his breathing faint and shallow. A thin sheen of sweat covered his face; he appeared incognizant of his surroundings. We had given him a cocktail of drugs to aid the loosening of his tongue, but so far, he was proving stubborn.

"I need the list," I said.

Maurice roused himself, his pale, hooded eyes meeting his partner's. "I don't have it," he rasped out.

I was yet to be convinced of this. I nodded to the man standing behind Maurice's wife.

The agent collected another collar from his bag.

"What-what are you doing?" Maurice hissed. "I've told you I don't have any such list. I don't have the clearance." He began sobbing, his face crumbling as he turned toward his thrashing wife. "No, please no."

She began grunting wildly behind her gag as the collar enclosed her throat.

I studied Maurice's reaction with cold eyes while my agent clicked the collar into place.

"Please, you must believe me! I don't have it!"

"Proceed." I nodded to the agent. The gag muffled the ensuing screams, but it was still an intensely disturbing sound. Her cries became lost behind Maurice's desperate begging. He rocked and bounced his chair, seeking to force his way over, banging it furiously until the man behind him intervened to hold it still.

Maurice was insensible when the collar ceased its torment, and the man behind him cuffed him hard to bring him back.

"The list," I said patiently.

Maurice began sobbing again.

"The list," I repeated.

Nothing. Perhaps Maurice didn't have the information I needed? My lips compressed. This displeased me. "Again."

This time I let the device follow its entire course, and several minutes passed before its safety mechanism kicked in and it deactivated to prevent death.

Silence descended on the room, broken only by his wife's shallow, ragged breaths and Maurice's pitiful sobs.

"This is your final chance," I said. "You can tell me now or be certain I will gag you and deliver many hours of pain before I allow you another opportunity to speak. You may trust you will speak eventually. Everyone does."

"I-I don't have the list." Maurice's eyes lingered on his wife before turning, haunted, in my direction. "But I can tell you who does."

# Chapter 19

## Shadowland

### Hannah

Molly rode with me on the second day. The little girl had talked the entire way, which provided a nice distraction from the turmoil in my mind. It took us two days to reach Han. As a scout approached to inform us that we were no more than a few miles away, Garren ordered our small party to stop.

Lifting me down from the horse, he took me a little away from the party.

"I'm not coming to the camp with you," he said. "I can't do it. If I do, I know I'll do something stupid. I want to fucking strangle Tanis sometimes, but he's right, you need to be safe, and I need to be here for him."

I'd been determined not to cry again, but now panic clamored inside me. The thought of separating from Garren was a living form of grief. He was my first, and he would always be my first. If I loved Tanis, I loved Garren just as hard.

He purred and pulled me into his arms, and then the tears did spill.

"We'll find a way when this is over," he said.

Only I didn't believe him, and I didn't see how he could have faith in what he said. We were from different worlds. We were different people, and I feared that once I set foot inside Rymor, I'd never be able to leave again. How would I be able to? I'd conjured up a million and one fanciful scenarios where I'd have a reason to come here again. Not one of them would fly.

When I'd gone into heat, I'd been glad I hadn't gotten pregnant. There had been too much uncertainty, and it definitely wasn't the right time. Now I wished that I had, wished for something to tie us together greater even than the mating bond.

He gathered my hand and pressed it over his heart. "You are in here, Hannah, until the day I die."

"Don't die," I whispered. My lips trembled, and tears pooled in my eyes. "Promise me you'll find a way for us to be together when this war is over, Garren. I can't live without you."

"I promise," he said.

He kissed me, and I clung to him.

But then, too soon, he was setting me away.

A storm was coming for this planet named Serenity. I'd been through storms before, and they were universally cruel.

"Take care of her, Red."

Then he was vaulting into his saddle and riding away, and I had to pick myself up once more.

∾

We rode on.

Molly offered me her cracker. "Don't be sad," she said. "Tanis will get the bad Jaru, and come get us again, just like he did last time."

My smile was weak at best. This time it wasn't as simple as the Jaru, and Tanis wasn't infallible.

### The Master of the Switch

With every step of the horse, I was aware of Garren pulling away from me, of the distance between us, and the growing ache in my chest.

I wanted to turn and ride after him.

I didn't.

And then it was too late as a sprawling camp came into view. As we reached the center, Han pushed out of his tent, along with his younger brother Danel.

From their left came another group with Adam, Jon Sanders, Joshua, and the remaining Rymorians. There were others I immediately placed as field scientists, and standing in their midst was another familiar face—Theo.

"You okay?" Red asked, helping lift Molly down then holding the horse as I dismounted. His compassionate eyes searched mine, one hand resting on my shoulder, the other taking Molly's hand.

"Yeah," I said and leaned in to accept a hug. It hurt whichever way I looked. We were all trying to navigate this relationship—this failed relationship.

At least I had Red.

Only I recognized that Red wasn't enough, that the two alphas who had cast me away were the balance I needed in my life.

When I could force myself to leave the comfort of Red's arms, I turned my gaze to Theo.

It was a shock seeing him here, but not as shocking as the discovery that he'd been working with Dan and spying on Bill. A silent understanding passed between us as he met my gaze. We had things to discuss.

I crouched down to Molly. "There is a man I need to talk to. Will you wait with Red for me?"

She nodded. "Can I have travel crackers?" she asked Red.

Red chuckled and ruffled her hair. "Kid, you're the only person who likes them. You can have as many as you like." He turned to me. "Take your time, Hannah. I know you are eager to talk about Dan and to find out how he's doing. I'll get Molly some food and see if I can settle her down. Come get me if you need me."

"Thanks," I said.

He took Molly to join Han and the field scientists, leaving me alone with Theo.

His smile was tentative. "We need to talk, Hannah."

I nodded. My throat was tight and my chest aching, now Garren was gone, but I wanted to hear what Theo had to say. It was so strange but, in seeing Theo, I felt a connection to all I had left behind, parts of me that had been lost during my long exile in Shadowland.

He indicated for me to join him, and I fell into step. "We'll go to my tent. We won't be disturbed there." His smile was warm, but his eyes were troubled. "It's good to see you again, Hannah. Dan's been so worried about you. He still is."

Those words put me at ease, like a little bit of Dan was here with me. He was still Theo, the same Theo I knew, but there was more to him now.

To my surprise, he stopped at a tent with two guards stationed outside. On entering, I found a single bedroll to the right and technology stacked in messy piles to the left. "Is that Rymorian?" I frowned, feeling instantly stupid since it was clearly Rymorian. *That explains the guards.*

"Um, yes." His lips compressed, and his eyes cut to the stacked technology before returning to me. "There's something important I need to tell you, Hannah. Please sit down."

My mind went on instant alert. "What is it? Is it Dan? Is he well?"

He gave his head a swift shake and gestured toward the bedroll. "Please, Hannah."

I did as he asked, terrible fear rising.

"It's Ella," he said.

"Ella?" My mind grappled in confusion. What could be wrong with Ella?

Theo ran his fingers through his hair and then crouched before

## The Master of the Switch

me to take both my hands in his. His familiar, sensitive eyes locked with mine. "I'm sorry, Hannah, but Ella is dead."

"No!" I shrank back from him, outraged. How could he say such a thing? Ella wasn't dead!

"I'm so sorry, Hannah. So sorry."

I wished he would shut up or go away, but he was still there, still apologizing. My throat choked up, a tight lump forming. I swallowed, eyes filling and lips quivering. "How?"

"She searched for you. Bill had people watching her. They took her to a detention center and a week later she was dead," he continued gently. "They claimed it was a suicide bomb and that she was part of Moiety, but she never left the facility where they held her, and she certainly had nothing to do with any bomb."

No! *Oh, God. Not Ella.* This couldn't be happening. Why would anyone kill Ella? Why? My mind became a wild jumble that refused to process the terrible news. My sister was gone, and it was my fault. I did this to her. I'd made her look for me!

My head felt too heavy to support. I ripped at my hair, threw my head back and cried.

I wanted to rip apart.

I wanted to hurt physically, to tear the skin from my bones. I felt Theo's hand on my shoulder as his soft apologetic words spilled out.

Nothing should hurt this much, nothing.

My breathing became labored as my thoughts turned to Nicholas and my two beautiful little nephews. My throat constricted further, denying me access to air. Gasping, I fought for breath.

The hoarse sounds of me suffocating filled the tent and my mind closed to everything but the desperate need for air.

∼

A sensation of floating roused me from the blackness. I felt calm, although I knew I should not. A terrible sorrow lay just beyond my mental grasp. My throat was sore, and the middle of my chest felt raw.

My eyes struggled to open and focus, but after a few blinks, Theo's worried face shifted into view.

"Damn, Hannah, that was the scariest moment of my life." He drew a deep breath that I envied. "And that's saying something, given the last few weeks."

"What happened?" My voice came out slurred.

"You stopped breathing," he said, his face flushed in the artificial light. My eyes lowered to the medical scanner in his hand.

My eyes were so heavy, it was all I could do to hold them open.

"Panic attack," I mumbled. "They happened a lot when I was a child." My eyes grew heavier. "After my parents died. They said they were working for Moiety." Slurred words poured forth, a cathartic unburdening. "That they were responsible for the bomb. That I was meant to die there with them." I squeezed my eyes shut, pushing past whatever he'd administered to calm me. "Ella said it was true that they were members of Moiety, but not about the bomb." My voice softened to a whisper. "Ella said they loved us dearly and would never hurt me or anyone else. She made me promise to remember that, even when we stayed with our aunt who was more concerned about what," I drew a painful breath, "everyone would think."

On a distant level, I understood the magnitude of my confession. I'd never told anyone about my parents or mentioned what had happened, not since we'd left my aunt and uncle's house. We had taken new identities and built a new future.

That was gone now, just like my sister.

Fear danced at the edge of my consciousness, but the drugs pulled me down, and I sank into their welcoming embrace.

# Chapter 20

## Talin

### Ella

I sat in the corner of the room and watched Bill discuss his plans with the slimy leech that was the self-proclaimed Lord of Tain.

"Aligning yourself with me will provide many mutual benefits, not least that we both want Tanis dead."

A tall, broad-shouldered, handsome man who wore his cloak of power well, Lord Falton sat opposite Bill. He desired revenge against Tanis for murdering his father six years earlier. Who could blame him? Revenge and justice were normal human responses to such a tragic event, after all. In this respect, he shared a common enemy with Bill, and an immediate rapport had developed between them.

I kept my eyes lowered, and my attention fixed on my hands as I sat out of the way and observed.

Bill enjoyed having me close at hand. He enjoyed ordering me to pour him some wine or to do any of a million other menial tasks he could ask of me as and when it pleased him. My subservience was part of his fantasy, a fantasy I was confident he would much prefer Hannah to enact. In my sister's absence, I was second best.

*Oh, Hannah, how did I find myself here?* It wasn't the first time I'd thought about my much-loved sister nor questioned my stupidity in pitting myself against the Chancellor of Rymor. I could have wept for the tragedy, yet that would have made me weak, and I'd spent far too much of my incarceration in a state of weakness.

I had convinced myself I was stronger since the physical abuse had stopped, but the truth was, I hadn't been tested again. Bill hadn't touched me, which surprised me. For now, he wasn't acting on the interest I could see in his eyes. Perhaps it would change. If it did, well, I would worry about it then.

Once, I had hated Bill. Yet, he had saved me from my tormentors and, oddly, I was grateful to him.

"It's been a pleasure to meet someone who hates that bastard as much as I do." Falton had a coarse accent and a confident manner. This was only his second visit, but I'd already identified several fascinating psychological disorders.

While he did want to avenge his father on the surface, I suspected he had little genuine affection for the deceased man. As for Tanis, Falton harbored poorly disguised jealousy for what Shadowland's leader had achieved. Falton had convinced himself Tanis was a dog who needed putting down, that Tanis's subjugation of the five great fortresses was the result of luck, and that he was, in fact, Tanis's superior in every way. Underlying this belligerent self-belief were his buried doubts and fears. In the dark pit of his hidden psyche, he despised Tanis because he knew the man was his better.

I knew nothing of John Tanis other than his notoriety as a terrorist and member of Moiety who was sentenced to exile for his crimes and, subsequently, what little I'd learned of his adventures here. Still, Bill's hatred of Tanis was visceral, and I felt inclined to like anyone who inspired Bill's ire. As for the fate of Falton's father, I had decided his son was an egocentric maniac, and therefore it was

## The Master of the Switch

quite likely his father was the same and so had thoroughly deserved to die.

Falton fascinated me, and I was delighted that he had returned so I could study him again—it was something to do.

"You mentioned others might join us?" Bill asked. He motioned to me, and I hurried to refill their cups.

I was conscious of Falton's study as I performed the task, but his interest was fleeting, and his attention shifted back to his drink. "Tower-dweller wine?"

"Indeed." Bill's practiced smile didn't reach his eyes.

Falton was enamored with all things Rymorian, which Bill had quickly seized on as a bargaining chip. Bill's skill in manipulating people was impressive. He clearly had no intention of getting his hands dirty and so was blatantly pandering to Falton's ego to set him up as a future battle leader. Falton had no idea he was being drawn into a situation likely to lead to his demise; if not by John Tanis' hands, then Bill was ruthless enough to throw Falton to the wolves when he was done using him.

"Yeah, I think there are others that'll come over. Maybe not the lords themselves, but some of their men for sure."

"That's excellent news," Bill said. "I'll need skilled workers and soldiers if I'm to consolidate my base here. I would welcome any of Tanis' deserters, and would, of course, reimburse you for acting as a mediator."

Falton's gaze settled on his wine again. Not only was he egocentric, but he was pretentious too and obviously delighted by the idea of bringing exotic Rymorian fares to his people.

I had yet to learn where Bill was taking this alliance with the fortress leader, beyond his desire to see Tanis dead. He had brought troops into Shadowland with weapons sufficient to take out John Tanis, a fact I'd discovered due to my inclusion in every meeting he had. When Bill left, I was confined to my room.

Yet this all felt so much bigger than the destruction of Tanis. He had a plan, I was certain; but I was at a loss as to how it might unfold.

He was a psychopath, or at least harbored numerous psychopathic traits, I reminded myself. He didn't need a reason to draw people into his circle. He did it because he enjoyed the opportunities it might give him. Later, he might use, kill, or discard Falton; whatever offered some level of pleasure or could assist his plan. Until then, it appeared he would continue to woo the unwary man.

Somewhere far from here, I had a husband and two sons. I didn't let myself dwell on them often because it hurt too much. But in the quiet times, when Bill wasn't here, my mind would stray. The pain was physical, an ever-present ache in the center of my chest, and an inconsolable grief that followed me around. So many times, I nearly asked Bill, almost begged him to let me go back, to see them, or even just speak to them.

To see a fucking picture so I could at least know they were well.

I didn't.

I'd gone toe to toe with him once, and my life had been destroyed.

He thought I'd been broken, which was true, but I wasn't the mindless creature he'd first met in that terrible room, and my instincts told me not to reveal it yet.

# Chapter 21

## Shadowland

### Hannah

The journey below ground was kicked off by descending what felt like a million steps. There were two hundred and eighty-three floors, but I'd lost count after twenty, when my legs had started to tremble so badly I'd wished someone would offer to either carry me or kill me. Either option would've been fine.

After the stifling heat and vivid blue skies of summer in Shadowland, the labyrinthine tunnel system was dark and cold, and the sensation of being closed in made even the oppressive experience at the fortress of Thale seem relatively sublime. Molly hated it, but then so did everyone.

Encased within its depths, I soon lost all track of time. Days had no meaning.

I also realized how ill-prepared I was to care for a child, especially one as willful as Molly. We took turns carrying her for most of the trip but allowed her down at slower points. The two men at the front, charged with calling out warnings about any debris or blocks in the tunnel, were often called on to intercept Molly's flight. My nephews, who were mischievous rather than naughty, had amused me with their antics. Molly's open rebellion took childish misbehavior to another level.

Finally, after enduring days of her tantrums, squealing, and running off if anyone left her unattended for more than a second, at my wits' end, I'd taken Molly aside and sat her down.

A somewhat adult conversation had ensued, during which Molly revealed she was missing her pet pig named Grunt, whom she had fed and petted back on her family farm. She hated her siblings, especially the baby, who had always cried. From what I could decipher, there had been many siblings, and her parents had limited time for any one child. This left her chores, which included feeding the animals, as her time of greatest joy. Further to this bizarre tale was Molly's insistence that she hated pigs in general, along with a neighboring family farm known as the Turners, who kept and smelled like pigs. However, Grunt had possessed a black spot on one ear, which made her special.

"Other kids annoy me," Molly confessed, impassioned. "I'd rather play on my own."

I knew that all children were different, and that, while my nephews thrived in social situations, some preferred their own company. Molly had been through much, and concessions were in order. A pig was out of the question, but I promised to find something living Molly could care for once we arrived.

I had yet to figure out what.

Despite my trials with Molly, I genuinely desired better than an unhappy orphanage for the little girl, and her antics provided a distraction from grieving over Ella. My sorrow pressed a suffocating blanket over every waking minute, and those fleeting moments when Molly could make me laugh, or wring my hands in frustration, were escapes from the black pain.

I'd experienced two more panic attacks since Theo had given me

## The Master of the Switch

the news, but nothing for the last few days. They had weaned me off the medication, and Molly's indomitable presence had helped me to find a new purpose.

There would be time for proper grieving once we reached Rymor. Time to reflect, even if I might never understand or forgive myself. Until then, I had someone who needed me as much as I'd needed Ella all those years ago, and I wouldn't let my sister's memory down.

According to Adam's locator, tonight would be our last night in the tunnels. Tomorrow we would reach Rymor, and my heart lifted at the prospect of seeing Dan. We made camp in the usual close cluster of bedrolls, with a couple of flashlights on because we all agreed no light was terrifying. Molly brought her bedroll, which Red had been carrying, over to me in her matter-of-fact way and tucked herself down without a word.

Red placed his roll down on Molly's other side and passed me a ration pack. "Has she eaten?" he asked.

"Yeah." I looked without enthusiasm at the ration pack. "I've no idea why Molly likes these hideous things so much. I can't wait for proper food."

We shared a brief smile, and a world of meaning shadowed that simple look. I missed Tanis and Garren. I also hated them.

Worse, I was terrified I might never see them again.

My heart was broken on so many levels it was a wonder it continued to beat.

Grief came in many guises, I had come to realize. I was grieving for two men I considered my mates and grieving for a sister I'd lost.

I heaved a breath, and Red was instantly at my side, folding his strong body around me, filling some of the terrible emptiness I felt.

"You'll get through this, Hannah, I promise," he said. "You'll get to see your nephews and brother-in-law. As for Tanis and Garren, well, Tanis is a possessive bastard; there's no way he's going to stay away. Garren will come to his senses whether Tanis does or not, and then Tanis will follow."

"But how?" I said, "when we're on different sides of a wall and a war."

"I don't know how," he admitted. "Only that if either of them has a mind toward doing something, it's going to be done. I always thought I understood Shadowland and about alphas and omegas, only I really didn't. I guess with hindsight, I can now see it will take me a lifetime of learning. Being with you, and being with them with you, has been the most amazing experience of my life."

"You said I was a trophy fuck." The accusation popped out.

His hands tightened, and I felt his lips against my hair. "I was angry and jealous. Trying to figure out where I fit in when you had two alphas. Tanis is an intense guy, and he doesn't give much away, at least not to me. Maybe I was hoping that was the case, that he didn't really want you, and that without him, my place would be more secure. I was a mess; confused. I fucked up. I'm so fucking sorry. Nothing justifies what came out of my mouth or the hurt it caused you."

"That's in the past now, Red. We've all done and said stupid things. I always wanted Tanis, even when I was with Garren, and then with you. The thought that he had simply been using me tore me apart."

"I know." He rocked me gently. "He set me straight in no uncertain terms, and thumped me for good measure."

"Then he sent me away," I whispered. "Why did he send me away if he cares?"

"God, don't, Hannah. Don't beat yourself up over this again. I can't explain his actions other than I believe he is seeking to protect you. We're all trying to navigate what is a complex relationship; we are all going to fuck up along the way."

The shuffling and quiet conversation of the team penetrated the furor in my mind, and I scrubbed my damp cheeks before nodding to Red that I was okay. He released me. After having been with an alpha, I'd thought no beta could compare. I'd used him recklessly when Garren had left me alone. He'd just said we would all fuck up

## The Master of the Switch

along the way, and yeah, I knew I was guilty of that too. Red was a gentle balance against the dominance of Tanis and Garren. When the four of us were together, it was heaven on earth.

I grabbed my forgotten cracker and shoved a chunk into my mouth, aware that following this train of thought would lead my body to respond. My omega needs would have to wait. Either way, I wasn't ready to be intimate with Red without Garren and Tanis here.

With a gentle squeeze of my shoulder, Red moved off to chat with another team member, giving me space, instinctively understanding what I needed. How had I gotten so lucky with him?

Seeing Adam sitting close, I turned to him. "You must be glad to return home tomorrow."

"I am, although it's going to be strange entering Rymor without seeing my family." Adam rarely talked about his personal life, but I knew he had a wife and children waiting for him.

The secrecy surrounding our return gave me concerns, even with Bill supposedly in Shadowland now. I also struggled to come to terms with Dan's part in this, that Theo had been spying on Bill. "Hopefully, it's just for a little while."

It had made me sad to leave Theo. I had questions about his undercover activities watching Bill, and Dan's involvement in that espionage. He'd insisted Tanis would need his support in countering the Rymorian forces if they were to avoid bloodshed. Whatever Theo's hopes, I doubted Rymor would surrender without a fight. Then there was the huge Jaru army on the move.

"Yes, let's hope so," Adam said. "I'm looking forward to hearing what Scott Harding has to say. He's a good man and I trust him, and if he's working with Dan Gilmore, who you've vouched for so many times, then that's enough for me. We knew the situation was bad. Having someone inside who we can trust is a blessing."

Yes, it was a blessing and, although Dan had been forced into hiding, Scott remained working and had access to information. There were others too, Theo had said, and although the steps were being taken in secret, it gave me hope this might one day be over.

"We're going to need an alliance now," Adam continued. "The Rymorian relationship with Shadowland has to change."

When my head snapped up, Adam looked at me and shrugged.

"We're terrorists now," I said. "You know that, right?"

Adam sighed and put his uneaten rations aside. "We did what we thought was right. Everyone knew what Joshua was doing—well, everyone except you—and I'm sorry about that last day in Thale. I can't tell you how sorry I am. I should have come to you and told you. I've no idea why Joshua implied you'd been updated—" His gaze shifted to where Joshua sat on the opposite side of our small group. "Maybe it was stress. We were all pretty stressed."

"You knew he was going to blow it up?" I asked, ignoring the bitterness that surrounded conversations about Joshua.

Adam shook his head, and his haunted eyes returned to me. "No, not until after it was done. But we were out of options, Hannah. It's hard to say whether the destruction of Station fifty-four and the wall have had any impact or will yet play a part in halting Rymor's attack, but I believe it will. Rymor has no reason for war, and bringing weapons out here is wrong. Destroying the station is equally immoral. But, in desperate times, people take desperate steps."

"It's done now." I felt betrayed by Joshua. First, there had been his snide comments about me sleeping with Garren, then he'd blatantly lied to Adam about me. Yet Joshua's betrayal paled beside Tanis'. "I guess Tanis is a hard man to refuse."

In all the time I'd been traveling with Tanis, not once had he mentioned ordering Joshua to destroy the station. Whenever I thought I had figured him out, I found out something to make me realize I didn't. How could he leave Rymor so vulnerable? I'd let Red convince me that Tanis cared, that this wasn't merely an opportunity for revenge. Yet I was emotionally invested and aware that I had made mistakes before when I'd let my heart rule my head.

Despite all that had happened to me, I didn't wish the people of Rymor ill. I had left to fix the station—fixing it had been the most

## The Master of the Switch

elating moment of my life. It had cost us so much to fix it and so much more to destroy it again.

"I think you forget who he is, Hannah," Adam said, his voice soft yet carrying easily to my ears. "If you're not helping him then you're in his way. I know you were with him. That you're an omega and that grants privileges over others. But you're not that naïve, Hannah: his reputation for killing people who oppose him isn't exaggerated. If Joshua had refused, Tanis would have persuaded him, by whatever means it took. He protected us, then he helped us. He didn't have to. It's hard to refuse someone who has saved your life, even without the added pressure of that person being someone like Tanis. I don't believe he intends to destroy Rymor, but I do believe he has plans for Bill. I hope, for Rymor's sake, nobody stands in his way."

Red's return and the lights being turned down ended the uneasy conversation.

Only, the dimming of the light brought attention to a faint glow from far ahead.

"What's that?" Adam said.

My heart took an unsteady beat.

Perhaps it was an illusion, or a reflection? Several field scientists stood and drew their weapons. Red stepped in front of Molly and me.

The faint light was getting brighter. Someone was coming.

# Chapter 22

### Ailey, Jaru Warlord, Harbinger

It was another blisteringly hot day, and the thick hide tent did little to take the edge off, even under the semi-shade of the soaring, parched trees.

A woman was riding my cock, and my broad hands clamped tightly on her hips, slamming her up and down with enough force that her cries were only partially pleasure. She was the wife of one of the tribe leaders. I could no longer remember for certain, but I thought I might have killed him. She was pretty enough, with wide brown eyes, though they were screwed tight as she focused on her task. Her name was Nemi, and her braids and tits bounced as I thrust into her.

Her nails dug into my abdomen, half to steady herself, and half with the onset of imminent release. I'd been enjoying her for the last few months and had come to recognize the signs.

She came around me, her scream loud enough that anyone nearby would hear. I pounded into her harder until I grunted out my own release.

## The Master of the Switch

She collapsed over me, and we panted, our bodies made slick with sweat.

I hated this region. Always fucking hot, always sweating, and so many flies that if you didn't keep your mouth shut, the bastards were bold enough to try and crawl in.

Nemi grimaced as she heaved herself off and wobbled over to the side to find the water skin. She offered it to me, and when I waved her away, she gulped down several mouthfuls.

It was five years since I'd seen my daughter. I couldn't remember her face anymore. She was better off without me. Unfortunately, she needed me if she didn't want to find her throat slit in that tower-dwelling bastard's country. I knew Bremmer would follow through with the threat if I had the guts to tell him to go fuck himself.

I scratched at my sweaty chest and watched Nemi slip out before I dragged myself up and pulled on my lightest clothing. It stuck to my skin and made my temper flare. I pushed out of the tent and squinted against the glare. The recent forays in Shadowland had been a relief after the arid Jaru plains.

A couple of Rymorian men stood near a cooking fire to my left, and seeing me, they hurried over. "There's been trouble while you were busy," the taller of the two said. His eyes met mine as he spoke then shifted away.

"Trouble? What kind of trouble?" I searched the nearby camp, wondering at the source. Hide tents, smoking cooking fires, women bent over tasks, and grubby children playing in the dirt. Bare-chested warriors, tattooed with clan markings and kill emblems, gathered in clusters to grunt among themselves. Only two fights—one man lay, bleeding out, but the other encounter was no more than a mild scuffle.

I was impressed with the level of calm for such a stinking day.

"The Lyuni elder was—"

Grunting, I pivoted and stalked back into my tent.

The Rymorian continued, his voice muffled by the tent wall, "not happy about the progress toward—"

I exited the tent with my sword in my hand.

The two Rymorians shrank back.

"It's considered bad luck to harm an elder," the shorter man said.

Fuck luck, bad or otherwise.

I knew they were following on my heels, hoping to avert my course of action, but the elder would soon serve me better as an example. The camp was vast and sprawling, and I headed toward my horse, barking orders to a nearby Jaru man to prepare it. It was a beast of an animal, and it took two men to get the saddle into position as another man hurried to put the harness into place.

"What are you going to do?" the shorter Rymorian man asked, as they scrambled to prepare their horses and mount.

Tribespeople scattered before me as I thundered through the camp. My blood pumped, and fury hammered at the base of my skull, driving me deeper into the red haze with every thud of the horse's hooves. By the time I reached the Lyuni section of the camp, I barely registered where I was or what I was doing.

Lost in the fog, I arrived at the elder's tent. Those gathered around cowered. I only realized I'd drawn my sword when I saw the slaughtered bodies of his guards. The elder's woman was next, and I hacked her down with the same vicious intent, before catching the elder's neck in my thick fingers and shaking him like a rag. "You dare to question me?" I roared at the man, spittle flying.

I sneered, as his feeble fingers clawed at my wrist, and tossed him to the ground. Prowling after him, I poked him with my sword, delighted by his cries, poking him again and driving him to run. I followed with measured steps that dogged the elder's clumsy flight, tripping him, then stabbing him again to urge him on.

People scattered in the wake of the elder's screams and my grim intent. I continued with my sport, poking and slicing at him, drawing blood and further screams. When the man slowed down and fell to begging, I stabbed deeper until that no longer worked, and then I dragged him to his feet and pushed him on that way.

## The Master of the Switch

By the time the elder had reached his limit, we were far from his tent and in the area of another tribe.

The game was over. The man could barely crawl. Snarling my frustration, I pinned the elder under my boot and brought the sword down to hack at the base of his skull.

The head came free after the second hack, and I kicked the offending lump away.

My fury abating slowly, I returned to the present, once more aware of my surroundings, the camp, and the wary faces watching.

"Hear me!" I turned a circle, taking in those who gathered. "I am your leader and the harbinger who will take you home." I raised my sword above my head and stared down at the crowd. "No one is above my law, no one. Not even an elder." I lowered my sword and spat on the headless body for good measure.

The two Rymorians who had followed me waited at the edge. I towered over them; but I towered over everyone. I was a half-breed Jaru-Shadowlander. I was a misfit who had conquered those people who had shunned me as a child.

We would cross the Shadowland border soon, and the advanced scouting parties would begin wreaking destruction along our intended path. Bill thought we were heading to confront the Shadowland army, but I would only fight the Shadowlanders if they got in my way. The wall was gone. The last man Bill sent had said as much... right before I killed him. Ever since, I'd been making new plans.

To keep Bill happy, I needed to crush the Shadowlanders. To keep the Jaru happy, I had to lead them to their lost homelands. I wasn't a thinking man, but I could see plenty of ways this could fail. Keeping the conflicting needs aligned required a combination of grit and balls, and I had plenty of both.

Karry was dead. I'd received word a few days ago, and although I'd often wanted to strangle the skinny, mouthy little bastard, we had shared a mutual hatred of Bill.

Karry had told me not to trust Bremmer, but I already knew that.

Bremmer was never going to let me or my daughter go. I was too important for the tower-dweller's plans. The original deal had started with a simple task, then another. My daughter wasn't safe. She could already be dead or sold to some skin trader, which made my gut fucking churn. If she wasn't, I had one option to keep her safe, which wasn't happening while I was on this side of the wall.

It was time to meet my destiny.

It was time to make Rymor mine.

# Chapter 23

**Rymor**

**Nate**

Weapons and frightened faces pointed my way. "Hi," I said, offering what I hoped was a non-threatening smile.

"Nate!" One of the field scientists holstered his weapon, and the rest followed his lead. "Good to see you, man. Why the hell didn't you call it in?"

I recognized four of the men Scott Harding had sent, but the rest remained unknowns and were doubtless the ragtag survivors of both the shuttle crash and the land-based venture into Shadowland.

"Sorry, my transmitter broke and the satellite won't work down here." I patted my backpack where the now smashed viewer resided. "There was another collapse an hour back and it caught me by surprise. Smashed the viewer, which is impressive given it should be indestructible."

They welcomed my arrival with the obligatory slaps to my

shoulder and back. My traveling gaze stopped on the woman I recognized as Hannah, even if her short hair had grown into an unflattering style. An omega like Dan, she appeared tiny beside the field scientists, and was painfully lean. A child stood at her side, holding her hand.

I cocked my head to the side as I looked at them. No, she hadn't been away *that* long.

"It's a long story," the man standing to Hannah's right said, with a smile. "Adam Harris." He offered me his hand. "You look remarkably familiar."

"Ah, yes… My name is Nate." I eyed the man I would've marked as a field scientist from his stance, even without recognizing the name. "I'm related to Theo."

"Theo?" Hannah shuffled closer, the little girl still holding her hand. "It's okay, Molly." She glanced down as she spoke, and smiled at the child.

Despite the abominable hair, she had a strange, broken, beguiling beauty.

"Yes. Theo," I replied, unsure of what she was asking.

"Are you also a spy?"

"A spy? No." I blinked. "Well, yes, I suppose I am, now that I think about it."

She smiled.

"Nate's the best." One of Harding's men slapped my shoulder again, and I gave the man a flat scowl.

"Sorry," the man mumbled, then added. "What's the news from H.Q.?"

"No one has noticed your absence yet. The war has also slipped from the media interest, with more terrorist attacks taking the focus. Jordan proposed deploying field scientists to patrol the wall. Thankfully, Scott was able to reject the motion, but we were worried for a while."

"Why the hell would they deploy us to the wall?" Adam asked.

### The Master of the Switch

"Because a hundred thousand Jaru are heading into Shadowland, and with no operational wall, it's too close for comfort."

"A hundred thousand?" Adam was second in command to Scott Harding, and a natural sense of leadership surrounded him.

"At least," I replied. "We have a lot of news to share, but Scott will be waiting at the exit to give you an update in person. Which is —" I checked the time on the retinal viewer. "About six hours away."

"We're due a rest break," Adam said, "And as much as I want to push through, we do need a few hours' rest."

"Understood," I said. "A few more hours won't make any difference either way."

"Did Harding mention any plans?" Adam asked.

"There will be a debrief with yourselves. And afterward, I believe some of you will be returning to Shadowland."

"What about me?" Hannah asked.

I smiled. "Hannah, you and Joshua have no reason to return to Shadowland; nor would I advise it." I had an odd feeling this statement disappointed her. "Besides, I think Dan will be devastated if you disappeared again."

She turned to the girl whose hand she still held. "It's just that I brought Molly with me."

"I don't see a problem. Hiding missing people and interlopers has become my primary skill."

"A useful skill in our current predicament," Adam said dryly. "Right, let's get some rest, and then we can finally set foot on Rymorian soil."

Some of the team moved off, but Hannah and the silent little girl drew a little closer. "How's Dan?" she asked, and in those simple words, I sensed the depth of her feelings. Dan had first met Hannah when she wasn't much older than the child clinging to her hand. Over the years, that relationship had grown into one of deep affection.

"Different... but he is well." I knew my words were cryptic. Dan told me to break the news of his transformation and other things to her gently. "He tried to stop the war. They took him in for questioning, and held him at a secure government facility with limited visitor rights." There was so much I could say about my guilt at not reaching Ella, about how hard it had been watching Dan go, but lost for the right words, I said none of it. "There was no way to get him out, not bound to the mover as he was, so I asked a friend of Dan's to help me, and we cured him."

"Cured?"

"His disease," I said. "He no longer needs a mover. He's able to walk."

Her mouth fell open.

I grinned.

Hannah laughed and threw her arms around me in an enthusiastic hug.

I patted her back awkwardly, not sure what else to do. She pulled away and hugged the little girl at her side. "Molly, this is so exciting!"

Molly giggled and hugged Hannah back.

I reached for my backpack, figuring that was enough news for now. The bit about Dan appearing half his age would hopefully be a minor shock. "He sent you a present."

"He did?" She watched me expectantly.

"Dan insisted I bring some..." I continued to rummage through my pack until I found what I was looking for. I pulled out the popular confectionery snack with a flourish.

"Oh, God! I think I'm going to cry." She stared at the proffered item with reverence. "Thank you." She took it with the utmost care. "Come on, Molly, let's share the treat, then you need to get some rest. Tomorrow is going to be a big day. I'm certain you're going to find eating chocolate even better than petting a pig."

Petting a pig? I was left to wonder at her curious statement, even as some field scientists settled to rest and others joined me to talk about the news. Weren't pigs indigenous animals used as a food source? Was it a Shadowland colloquialism I was ignorant of?

It must be, I decided. Who would ever want to pet a pig?

# Chapter 24

## Talin

### Ella

I followed Bill along the corridor as he talked with a Rymorian man called Pope whom he had placed in charge here. I was indifferent to Pope, since he left me alone. In comparison to Wyatt, the ringleader of my abusers, I viewed this man's lack of interest as a blessing.

Falton's visit had gone well. Bill had left in a buoyant mood, but after only two quiet, Bill-free days, he was back. Things were not going so well for him today.

"I can't stay here long," Bill said to Pope. "A matter requires my attention in Rymor and I need to return as soon as I'm done here."

"Understood," Pope replied. He was a tall, lean man with closely cropped gray hair and rough stubble on his chin. "We've pushed on with the exploration into the Jaru plains, but without satellite communication, it's going to be tricky now they've left radio range. Ailey is up to something. There were no tribespeople to meet the team, and no Rymorians either. The plains are spooky quiet, according to reports."

We arrived at Bill's office, and I followed them in, seating myself in the corner near the window.

Whenever the guards heard that Bill had arrived, they would collect me and take me to meet the underground transport capsule. There, Bill would greet me with a smile and a polite inquiry about how I felt. Afterward, I would shadow his movements until he left again. Today, he barely glanced at me before he began questioning Pope. Most of the conversation escaped me, but I caught snippets here and there. Someone was arriving from Shadowland, one of his reconnaissance teams, I thought, and I got the impression the news was expected to be bad.

"We're bringing them through now," Pope said. "They wouldn't give me the message. Said they needed to talk to you in person."

"And Ailey's whereabouts?"

"Still on Jaru lands awaiting your order. More tribes are joining him. The last estimate was around a hundred and fifty thousand, but with the exodus we're seeing, it could be closer to two hundred thousand. Like a fucking horde of locusts they are, stripping the land bare." Pope scratched at his chin. "I don't know what's going on with Ailey. Perhaps that's why he sent no one to meet Damien. Perhaps the message never got through. The Jaru aren't exactly peaceful... I wouldn't want to second-guess what's happening."

"A refreshing change from your predecessors." Bill smiled for the first time since arriving. "Don't worry. I don't trust Ailey either. I have leverage over him, but he was always unreliable, and controlling the Jaru is not an easy undertaking. If he keeps moving them in Tanis' direction, I can live with the rest."

There was a sharp knock on the door. Pope stomped over and flung it open. He spoke to someone outside, shut the door again, and turned back toward Bill. "Five minutes."

Bill nodded. "I don't know when I'll be able to get back, but I'll keep in communication with you while I'm gone." He gazed out the

## The Master of the Switch

window. "Arrange to shuttle back anyone who doesn't want to make this a permanent transition."

The meaning behind the words was lost on me, but Pope's eyebrows shot up into his hairline. "You're gonna blow it?"

Blow what? I fought to smother my interest by studying my fingers. Maintaining an indifferent air had become increasingly difficult.

Bill shrugged. "Maybe. It depends what the team has to say when they get here. But I'm aware of the dangers. I made the backup plan for a reason."

"Do you want me to take her with me when I go?" Pope nodded at me.

A stretched silence followed.

I didn't want to leave. Whatever the much-anticipated reconnaissance team was about to say, I wanted to know. My survival might well depend upon it.

I lifted my eyes to find Bill watching me. Did he see my duality?

"You like to be near me, don't you, Ella?" he coaxed softly.

I nodded hoping that would suffice and get his attention away from me. Then I noticed Pope watching me with narrowed, calculating eyes. Was Pope suspicious? Would he mention his suspicions to Bill now, or disclose them later when I was out the way?

The sharp rap on the door made me jump.

"Yes, take her to her room," Bill said.

Three men stepped inside. They were tall, dressed like Shadowlanders, and dusty from travel. That was as much as I saw because Pope collected me and ushered me out of the room.

The silent walk to my quarters was broken only by the ring of Pope's heavy footsteps against the stone floor. Every step increased my sense of foreboding. He was suspicious, but was it a mild, quickly forgotten kind of suspicion, or something worse?

It was a relief to reach my room and break the tension.

Pope stopped at my door, his hand settling on the handle without turning it. My heart began to thud, and I stared at his hand, aware of his silent study.

"I've not been here so long, but I know what they did to you."

My breath caught in my throat. Was Pope making a threat?

"I don't know how you were before, but I know how you were just after… and you're not the same anymore. Bremmer is blind to it. Got you up on some weird-as-shit pedestal." He let his breath out in a little hiss, then leaned in close and whispered in my ear, "I'll keep your secret, Ella."

Then he turned the handle, pushed the door open, and stepped aside.

It creaked as it swung wide, and I fled inside. It shut with a thud, and for the first time since I'd arrived here, I thought I heard the sound of a key turning in the lock.

# Chapter 25

## Rymor

## Hannah

After a brief discussion with Adam, we parted ways with him in the underground complex, agreeing that Red and Molly would come with me.

Adam was shocked to learn that I'd mated with Red and Garren, moreso when I admitted I'd also mated with Tanis.

"My heat came unexpectedly," I said. It hadn't. Garren had forced it. I asked myself how I felt about that, and the truth was that I'd loved every moment and had no wish to take it back. "I don't know if I'll see Tanis or Garren again, and I can't bear to be parted from Red. The separation from my alphas is already taking a toll. Please, I know there will be questions, but I'd appreciate it if you could keep this private."

"Of course, Hannah." His brow creased with worry. "Can you see a doctor?" He turned to Nate. "Is there someone who can help her?"

"I'll talk to Dan about it," Nate said. "Life is pretty messy at the moment, but if it's possible, we'll find a way."

Only I didn't want a doctor to give me something to ease the empty feeling. I wanted my mates.

Red, Molly and I took an underground shuttle deep beneath Tranquility. I knew Nate was wiping us from the systems as we travelled, but I was still terrified someone would intercept us. It was late at night, and it was a blessing that Molly slept through much of the journey, barely lifting her head from Red's shoulder when we arrived at Nate's commandeered apartment.

"Hannah!"

In a state of shock, I gaped at the young man before me. "...Dan?"

Nate wore a shifty look. "The, ah, cybernetic devices worked even better than we thought."

He wasn't kidding.

"When you said he was cured, Nate, this wasn't quite what I expected. Dan, this is incredible!" I hugged him tightly. "I can't believe you didn't do this before."

"It was experimental, Hannah." He hugged me back in a way the old Dan never could. "Worked a lot better than I anticipated. Not sure Rymor is ready for the cure to aging. Opens a can of worms."

I laughed, too happy to care about future dilemmas.

I introduced Red, who, carefully, so as not to disturb Molly, shook Dan's hand with a smile and nod. A woman emerged from the kitchen. Greeting Nate with a gentle hug, she introduced herself as Coco.

"Why don't we get your little charge settled?" Coco said, smiling at Molly, who remained fast asleep.

But I hardly acknowledged her, because being here, back in Rymor, made me realize how much had changed. Most of all, it brought home to me again that Ella was gone, and I sank under the sudden and acute weight of my loss.

Red, ever attentive, was instantly at my side. One-handed, still

### The Master of the Switch

juggling the sleeping little girl, he wrapped his arm around my shoulder. "Are you okay?"

I nodded.

"I don't believe you," he said, giving me a wry smile that reminded me how lucky I was to have such an amazing man in my life. "Want me to settle Molly down? Give you and Dan a chance to talk?"

I nodded. "Yes, please."

"I'll show you to the guest rooms," Coco said.

"I can't stop thinking about Ella," I said, as Coco guided Red as to where to take Molly.

"I know, Hannah." Dan put his arm around my shoulders and guided me to the couch. "Do you want a drink? Something to eat?"

"I should eat, but I can't remember the last time I enjoyed a glass of wine."

"I'll get it." Nate headed over to the printer. "Any preference?"

"I don't care about the specifics as long as it doesn't remind me of Bill's family estate."

"Ah, the Soan region," Nate said knowingly. "The finest wine region in Rymor, but we can print something even better."

The retro-leather couch was plush, and the most comfortable thing I'd sat on for many months. "I'm not sure drinking is such a good idea. But I don't think it can make me feel any worse."

"It's going to take time, Hannah." Dan's face softened with sensitivity. "An awful lot of time, and the best it will give you is acceptance."

I took the glass from Nate, swallowed past the lump in my throat, and lifted it. "To Ella," I said and raised the glass to my lips.

"To Ella," Dan and Nate both replied.

It was an excellent wine, but I cared only that it warmed me. I hadn't eaten properly for days and had consumed Nate's snack stash before we were halfway through the day. Not the most balanced diet.

Nate excused himself to check if Red or Molly needed anything, and as I watched him leave, Dan sat opposite. Similarities between them were apparent, now that Dan was younger. "I never knew you had a son. I can't believe you kept that a secret."

Dan rubbed his chin in an oddly nervous gesture. "It's a complicated story, Hannah. Perhaps we should leave that for another night. Maybe you could tell me about your adventure?"

I sipped my wine, enjoying the pleasant fuzziness it spread. My grief needed to be broached in stages; too much at once would tear me apart. So I did as Dan asked, skimming over my six month journey through a land so wildly different from Rymor. As I gave my side of the story, Dan updated me on what had been happening in Rymor and, little by little, we filled in the broad strokes of the whole picture.

There was editing on my part regarding personal or violent details which, truthfully, didn't leave much to tell. And what it *did* leave must have confused Dan. He let me talk without interruption, seeming to know I needed this. As I spoke, I realized I'd come to love Shadowland and its people.

"I never thought I would return home," I said, once we had exhausted the main events. "I accepted that I wouldn't, and now it feels strange being here, like I'm experiencing a vivid dream."

"That's going to take time, too." Dan's tone was gentle.

"I miss her so much." The tears threatened to spill again, but I blinked them back and forced myself to carry on. "I kept thinking about the argument we had just before I left. Most of all, I wish I could tell her how sorry I am for leaving without letting her know." I sipped from the glass that Dan had refilled several times. "It hurts so bad to know I can never hug her or talk to her again. She's left a gaping hole in my life. I can't imagine how bad it must be for her husband and my nephews." I drew in a ragged breath, dashed the tears from my cheeks. My sister had so much more life to live—someone had taken that away. "Why did I ask her to find me? Why did I do that?" I felt I was begging the universe for answers it couldn't give.

Dan came and sat beside me and took my hand in his. "Dear

## The Master of the Switch

Hannah, this is not your fault. You couldn't have known. None of us could."

"I'm doing okay, Dan. Honestly, I am. I know this is normal, and as you say, it will take time to accept. But I'm not the same person who left six months ago. Not the same, in so many ways, and that both scares me and makes me proud. I know Ella would have been proud, too."

"She would have been insanely proud," Dan said. "We all are." In a blatant shift to a lighter topic, he asked, "So, will you tell me who the mysterious Molly is?"

I smiled, a reflex which often accompanied thoughts of Molly.

"Molly is an orphan. The Jaru killed her family. And... I know she doesn't belong here, but I don't think I do anymore, either. She didn't have anyone, she was unhappy, and I couldn't leave her there."

"You do belong here, Hannah, and it sounds like Molly belongs with you, even if that's here. You're exhausted, so why don't you get some rest?" he said gently.

I nodded.

"There are two spare bedrooms down the hall. I expect your man is hiding down there, giving us a bit of time."

I smiled. "Probably."

"You're mated to him?" Dan guessed correctly. "I didn't think it was possible with a beta."

"There is a bit more to it," I said. "But I think that will have to wait for tomorrow."

"I'm here when you're ready. I should go see what that maniac Nate is doing." He rolled his eyes. "It's been pretty hectic keeping the systems diverted with so many in Shadowland."

I chuckled at his candid comment. There was still half a glass of wine, and I was enjoying the fuzzy warmth. "I think I'll stay here for a little while longer. Watch the city lights and finish my wine before I join Red."

He nodded, seeming to understand I needed time alone. I was so grateful to have him in my life. "It's so good to have you home,

Hannah. Come and get me if you need me. Don't worry, whatever the time."

The highs and lows of the day faded into the background as I settled further into the soft retro-leather comfort of Nate's couch. The window offered a stunning view of the harbor city of Tranquility. I let my mind be filled with the view, watching the twinkling lights, so familiar yet I had not seen them in such a long time. Alone, now that both Nate and Dan had left to whatever mysterious espionage things they were up to, I drank more of the excellent wine.

The buzz was pleasant. I didn't drink often and felt decidedly tipsy.

I wondered if I should go and wake Red up.

Whether Molly had her own room.

God, I'd missed alone time.

I'd also missed intimacy.

Only, the comfort of just being still couldn't hold my focus for long, because Ella was still gone, and the guilt in having any joy when she did not was crushing. Perhaps being alone wasn't such a good idea after all.

A door clicked behind me, and Coco entered. "May I join you? If I'm interrupting, please say."

"Please do." The interruption was more of a relief. "Is Molly okay?"

Coco smiled and nodded. "Out for the count. Her door is open a crack so Dan and Nate can hear if she wakes."

"Thank you." I felt relieved to know she was being watched.

"I was going to introduce myself properly earlier." Coco took the couch opposite me. "But I thought I should let you and Dan talk first. I've been a friend of Dan's for many years, and he talks about you often."

Her smile was welcoming, her age indeterminate in the way of many wealthy Rymorians. Her voice was crisp, cultured, and familiar, although I was sure we'd never met.

## The Master of the Switch

"From my brief conversation with Red, I believe you might know my son."

"I do?"

"My surname is Tanis."

I lurched upright in the chair, nearly spilling my drink, realizing I was a bit more than tipsy. "No."

She smiled and shrugged. "I'm afraid so."

"You look nothing like him," I said, with unintended accusation.

Coco's lips twitched. "Yes, he looks more like his father. Perhaps you met Javid out there?"

"I tried to avoid him." Damn, that came out a little harsh. "Garren looks far more like Javid than Tanis does. Sorry, everyone just calls him Tanis; which is a little odd now I think about it." I frowned and gulped some wine.

"Garren?" Coco asked.

"Yes, Tanis' brother."

She raised a brow. "I never considered that he might have a brother. Seems a rather foolish assumption now. Are there more siblings?"

How did we get onto Tanis' brothers? "A few less after Tanis killed three of them." What the hell was I saying?

"Oh dear." Coco's face paled. "Do they not get along, then? John and Garren?"

"They're fine most of the time." I recognized that I was no longer in a condition for complex conversations, but could not pull myself back. "They just fight... occasionally... they're both very much alive, which is amazing given how much they both seem to enjoy baiting one another." I gulped more wine. "It got a bit complicated because I was sleeping with Garren, and then I slept with Tanis, and I still don't understand how it happened because I only went to his room to ask him a question." Why can't I stop talking? "Afterward, they nearly killed each other." I took a moment to get the timeline straight in my head. "Or was it before?" I rubbed at my brow. "No, it was before *and* after." I felt immensely pleased with myself for remembering this. "Then they both left for the war, and a man working for Bill kidnapped me, and I didn't see either of them for weeks. When I did see them, Tanis had decided he was my mate, and not Garren, mostly because he's the leader, and the power has gone to his head."

Did I really say that out loud?

Coco's face was a picture of horror.

Yes, I definitely said that out loud.

"Sorry, I'm just venting. The last time I saw Tanis he tied me to a post and left me there all night." Okay, so it was only fifteen minutes but it felt like all night. "Before sending me back to Rymor. Garren didn't stop him, so he's in my bad books too. Despite the post incident, I didn't want to leave—we didn't part on the best of terms."

Much to my confusion and surprise, I realized Coco's face had softened, and I could tell she was fighting a smile. I studied my empty wine glass and tried to fathom it out.

"You love my son," Coco said.

It wasn't phrased as a question because I was sure Coco already knew.

"It's more of an unhealthy obsession based on him saving my life—twice." My mouth appeared determined to throw out all the parts I'd carefully edited from my conversation with Dan. "Once from a Jaru who was about to plunge an ax into my head, and once from a Rymorian trying to strangle me. After the second time, I was never quite the same."

"My goodness!" Coco's concerned eyes widened.

I fell quiet at last. There were many more times that Tanis and Garren had saved my life, both directly and indirectly. The two mentioned were simply the most memorable.

"You've been through so much, Hannah," Coco said, her voice gentle. "As much as the subject is uncomfortable, you should talk about it. You'll never be able to come to terms with it if you don't. I know we're in hiding, but a professional therapist would be far better than myself or Dan. When you feel you're ready, I'm sure Nate would be able to work out a way."

# The Master of the Switch

I stared at my empty glass again. I knew Coco's intentions were kind, and my account had been a little unbalanced as well as putting her son in a less than favorable light. The weight settled at the back of my eyes again. "Tanis surrendered to the Rymorian forces in an attempt to stop the war. They tortured him for days, and by the time Theo helped him to escape, he was in a bad way. He rode for three days to save me after Theo told him I'd been taken. I didn't know that at the time, but now that I do, I've no desire for a therapist to straighten me out."

When I lifted my eyes, I found Coco's face filled with such love and warmth that it was all I could do not to cry.

She came to sit beside me, took the empty glass from my hands, placed it on the low table, drew me in, and held me.

"I suppose that means I *do* love him, which is really hard because he can be a self-righteous asshole, and I'm obstinate, and the two personalities don't mix very well."

"I'm sure they mix fine," Coco offered, and there was a definite smile in her voice.

"Then Garren forced my heat, and I ended up mating Tanis, Garren *and* Red."

She snorted an inelegant laugh. "Yes, Red did mention the mating. Alphas are a strange breed of being, as I found out the hard way with John's father. They mate for life, and it takes a lot to break that bond for a beta. I'd say it's impossible for them to separate from an omega, save for taking actions that I wouldn't recommend."

I shuddered, thinking about the doctor I'd seen when I first showed the signs of being an omega. No, I had no desire for that.

"You're hurt he sent you away because you're an omega and the bond goes both ways. The only explanation I can find is that his need to keep you safe outweighed the need to keep you near. That both alphas agreed means the threat to your life out there must have been very great."

I wanted her to be right, although the hope didn't make the pain any less potent.

If they'd asked me, I still would have stayed.

A heartfelt sigh escaped me. No one had held me like this in many years. Gentle fingers stroked through my hair, and I felt like a child again, being comforted by Ella.

*Ella, I cannot think of Ella now.*

Silent tears rolled down my cheeks.

"You have endured so much, and have been so very brave and amazing, I can see why my son would love you too, just like Red and Garren do," Coco said. "How could they possibly not?"

# Chapter 26

**Hannah**

After that rather candid conversation, and at Coco's urging, I went to bed. "Don't worry about Molly. We will look out for her. If she wakes up and needs you, I'll come and get you, okay?"

"Thank you," I said. Tanis' mother was nothing like Tanis himself. I wanted to remain angry with him. I still hated that he had sent me away so coldly and so finally. Yet, her determination that he loved me went some way to softening my resolve.

I thought Red might have fallen asleep, but he was waiting for me, lying on the bed, naked save for a towel.

"You okay, baby?" He rose immediately, coming to cup my cheek and kiss my forehead.

"Yeah." I stepped back, wrinkling my nose because he smelled wonderfully clean, and of *him*, whereas I did not. "God, I could kill for a shower. Was it good?"

He grinned. "Amazing. My skin started to wrinkle, I was in there for so long."

"Yes, please!" I stripped off my clothing.

Red's laughter followed me… and then so did Red.

I giggled as the stall door shut him in with me. "You're already clean. Don't be hogging my water."

He wrapped his arms around me. "Now I'm all dirty."

I squeaked.

"Are you drunk?"

"No." I giggled, making a mockery of my denial. It felt good, and I laughed again.

Then I gasped because his cock was hard and poking into my lower back. We both stilled, the water pelting over us, cocooning us in a private world.

"Let's get you all cleaned up," he said, lips against my ear.

I went from warm to burning hot in an instant. It had been so long since I'd felt Red inside me, and I needed not to think. "Please just fuck me."

"Uh, uh. Not happening, baby. Maybe by the time I've finished cleaning you, you'll have sobered up."

Damn the beta male and his ability for restraint.

He washed me like I was the most precious thing in the world, soaping up my hair and rinsing it before starting on my body. Slow, deliberate caresses ignited a fire inside me. Kisses, and light strokes, designed to drive me ever higher, all carefully avoiding the places I most wanted him to touch. I was a hot, needy mess when he finally cupped my breast from behind.

"Someone is eager," he murmured against my ear.

"Please don't make me wait any longer." I tried to grab his cock. He pinned it tightly against my back and took his time cupping my breasts and pinching over my slippery nipples until they were hard and throbbing with arousal.

"God, yes!" My legs went weak as he snaked one hand down and played in my slick folds.

"What a filthy omega you are," he said. "All slick and needy. Do you want me to make you come?"

"Please, yes."

### The Master of the Switch

He sank to his knees, pinned me against the wall, and lifted one leg over his shoulder.

Mumbled nonsense poured from my lips as he lapped at my swollen clit. My fingers fisted his wet hair, and I forgot how to breathe. I came in seconds, and a great gush of slick poured out.

Smirking, Red rose, his beautiful cock sticking straight up.

This time I snagged my prize, my mouth already watering for the taste.

He snapped the shower off with a groan, carefully peeled my fingers from his cock, and ushered me out of the stall. I whined the whole time he dried me with the decadently soft towel.

Taking my hand in his, he switched off the bathroom light, leaving the bedroom bathed in the city lights beyond the window, and walked me to the foot of the bed.

"I love you so much," he said and lowered his lips to mine.

Everything inside me softened hearing those words, and I opened to the kiss, entwining my arms around his neck, letting him set the pace. As our tongues tangled, I remembered why I loved Red, how considerate a lover he was, and how that was merely a reflection of the man himself.

He drew me tighter into his arms, deepening the kiss and taking all my worries away. Tomorrow, I would need to face my life and troubles, but for now, I was exactly where I wanted to be.

∼

## Red

She was soft and compliant in my arms, and I never wanted the kiss to end. I'd been so worried about her. Ever since we'd left Tanis and Garren, it was like the blows never stopped.

She was broken to have left her other mates.

She was broken by her sister's death.

I couldn't do a damn thing about either of those things, and the sense of helplessness was stifling.

But this, here, tonight, with her in my arms, kissing me, eager for intimacy, gave me hope that we would get through this.

"Please, Red," she murmured against my lips. "I need to taste you, too."

Fuck! Like I was going to deny her request? Like I had that much strength?

I let her guide me where she wanted me, back on the bed, where she crawled between my thighs. Fingers closing around my dick, she guided it to her mouth... and sucked me straight to the back of her throat, humming around me with joy.

"Ah, fuck!" I groaned softly, conscious of where we were, of keeping quiet because it was late and people were sleeping. "I'm not going to last, baby."

She swirled her tongue around the head as she bobbed up and down. I didn't have a fucking chance to stave it off. I came straight down her throat, white-hot pleasure delivered one heady gush at a time.

Her lips popped off as I was still panting, and she crawled over me, directed my dick toward her weeping pussy, and sat down.

I hissed. My cock was sensitive and hard. How the fuck hadn't it gone down?

Maybe because there was a beautiful woman, one I loved deeply, riding me, hips moving with sensual grace as she took what she wanted. My cock, like the rest of me, lived to serve her and only her. Fingers in her hair, I brought her lips to mine for a hot kiss, pinching and tugging her nipple with the rise and fall of her hips.

Her pussy was slick and tight over me, and my dick was stone hard. Our breathy sighs accompanied roaming hands, touching, squeezing over hips, breasts, and thighs.

"Are you going to come for me, baby?" I whispered against her lips. My thumb found her clit and swiped side to side over the fat, slippery little bud.

## The Master of the Switch

She nipped at my ear, then throat, stifling her groan.

"Come for me, Hannah. Come all over my cock."

With her teeth against my throat, her velvet sheath squeezed lovingly over my length in sweet contractions that made my balls tighten, and my dick shot a weak but intense jet of cum deep in her pussy.

She collapsed on top of me, and our lips met to share a lingering kiss.

I pulled the covers up, tossed them over us, and tucked her head against my chest.

She heaved a deep breath and let it out on a purr, comforting herself. There was no sweeter sound, and I wished I could reciprocate, could purr for her like her alphas might.

The tears came. I'd known they would, and I rolled over, drawing her smaller body against mine, holding her through the storm.

"Hush, baby. It will get better, I promise."

"How? How can it possibly get better? Why does it hurt so much?"

I didn't have the answers she needed, so I held her, stroked her hair, and let her sorrow run its course.

Wrapped in my arms, she drifted into sleep.

She was so brave, so precious, and I'd bonded to her, courtesy of her alphas and her heat. But I couldn't do this on my own. Hannah needed more than me. I just hoped her alphas had a plan, because I was terrified that no amount of bravery or tenacity could carry a grieving omega through her loss in the absence of her mates.

# Chapter 27

**Bill**

The grand auditorium in the government district of Serenity gave off a melancholy vibe. I had frequented the venue on numerous occasions, from business functions to charity balls. Today it had a somber mood that the crystal lighting and smartly dressed guests couldn't disguise.

"Such a bright young star," Grace Claridge said. "There will need to be an inquest into such a tragedy."

I offered the appropriate response, but my mind was elsewhere. The political elite and the politically aspiring filled the auditorium, and the light marble floors reflected back the black that predominated their attire. While I was sure some did care about Margaret, many just wanted to be seen doing the politically correct thing. Whatever their motivations, they were here to pay tribute to the late Margaret Pascal.

The pressure of her involvement in the Station fifty-four action committee and the war, and the impacts which such testing times had on a young woman's blossoming career had monopolized conversations since she had been found dead in her apartment. Now every-

## The Master of the Switch

thing was being seen as a potential trigger, and everyone was being counseled within an inch of their life.

"Suicide is so tragic, and avoidable with help. A great pity no one realized the pressure she was under," Grace continued. "An educational program to raise awareness of mental health needs to be at the top of the next senate agenda."

I murmured my agreement, conscious that Grace was studying every nuance of my demeanor. Grace was a wily old senate member, and I thought it likely she knew about my relationship with Margaret and was engaging me tonight to test a theory.

"Ah well, perhaps onto better news: how is your assistant doing? Has Theo returned from his extended leave yet? Such a polite and articulate young man. I'm sure I cannot be the first senate member to express envy you found him first. If he ever seeks a less spirited employment situation, do send him my way." She smiled. "Although I'm sure he would find working for me incredibly dull after more than five years with you."

I forced a smile. "Perhaps not. He is still enjoying extended leave."

Grace had been one of my early supporters and among the most influential members approached by Richard when canvassing for me many months ago.

Her support had waned, and her lines of questioning had gained barbs of late. I also thought she knew something was off with Theo's leave of absence. Perhaps Richard had told her? They were long-time acquaintances, which was what had led Richard to approach her. Now I thought about it, it seemed odd that there were no tags in my system regarding Richard visiting or communicating with Grace. Had I missed them?

"Not such a bad time to be taking leave," Grace continued. "What with the bombing last week. I wonder if any of us are truly safe? Then there was that unfortunate incident with Maurice and his wife. It's just frightful! Maurice being a former high-profile senate member, the media relished exposing his gambling debts. With so much going on, the lack of news on the war has likely slipped the minds of ordinary Rymorians. We still don't have an operational station or a protective wall. I thought it would be fixed by now." She shook her head sadly. "I should be disappointed in myself to be so naïve at my age."

My return smile held no warmth. "Gaia was a little overzealous in their restrictions. Our forces are hamstrung. I believe you're a named contributor?"

She gave a regal incline of her head. "It pays to support Gaia, and I canvassed heavily for concessions. Bill, I don't believe you would have sent a single Rymorian weapon beyond the wall without my rigorous work and full backing. I placed my faith in you. I hope it wasn't an error on my part." She took her leave under the pretense of noticing an acquaintance.

Her barbs lacked any subtlety. But was she angry the war wasn't over, bitter that she had supported my use of weapons, or was it something else? It was hardly worth worrying about, though, now that Karry was dead, on top of which there had been no communication from Kelard for three weeks.

Two weeks ago, I'd been at Talin in the northern reaches of Shadowland, where I'd received news of Karry's demise. The reconnaissance team had found the village where he'd died along with most of his team.

Karry had been confirmed dead.

And I no longer had Hannah.

The villagers offered the information without any need for persuasion. Shadowlanders had arrived and slaughtered all the tower-dwellers except for a woman and two men they took prisoner.

The Shadowland group who had killed them had been led by John Tanis.

Then, yesterday's reconnaissance team had returned and informed me that they had found the burnt-out remnants of Kelard's camp.

The worst part, the part that made me seethe until I could almost

## The Master of the Switch

not think straight, was that Tanis had taken Hannah from Karry. Tanis had rescued her.

Tanis, who was no longer my prisoner and very much at large.

The how or why he came to be there didn't matter. Nothing did now. I doubted Karry had been gentle with Hannah, although I'd given clear instructions on what he could and couldn't do.

Would Hannah hate Tanis, and Shadowland, the way Ava had? Or would she see him as her savior?

I'd been wondering how my stratagem would play out, and the outcome was bitter, especially after being so close. Whatever Kelard Wilder's situation, it was clear it couldn't be good. I thought it was probable Kelard was dead or Tanis' prisoner.

My quest for war on Shadowland was over.

The wall was inoperative, and the station was destroyed.

Everyone I'd sent out there had failed.

All I had left was Talin, a Jaru army, and one, maybe two, tenuous alliances with fortress leaders who had once bowed their heads to John Tanis.

My career would not survive failures of this magnitude, nor could I keep them out of the public eye for long. I would be held accountable and possibly put on trial.

The irony wasn't lost on me. I was the man who had issued the exile decree to Tanis, and I was about to voluntarily exile myself.

# Chapter 28

**Peter**

Global Monitoring, a white, light, circular room with four desks facing a huge viewer wall, was located deep in the base complex of Majestic Tower. Once upon a time, the night shift was a quiet time. Now the day shift was quiet, and the night shift was non-existent. Of the four desks, only two were used. So it had been for many months, and so it would be for many more.

Global Monitoring was broken. There was no other word to describe the disarray of my once mundane job, and no credible alternative peeked with hopeful intent over the horizon.

I sat at my desk, staring at the desk viewer. Officially, I was surveying recorded footage taken before the satellites were lost... for the second time. Unofficially, I was watching the fishing channel on my retinal viewer, where they were discussing fly fishing techniques. A little fly fishing would have been nice.

While I was otherwise occupied, my young colleague Tom was up to something, but I decided to turn a blind eye. A decision I hoped didn't come back to bite me. A person could only take so much stress, and both of us had passed beyond the point of breaking and had

## The Master of the Switch

emerged into a listless stupor. I knew there was a deep, underlying wrong with the troubles engulfing the world. The war was a farce, and the public had no idea the station had been restored and then lost again. Only a select few realized the power restrictions, which had been faked for a while, were symptoms of a far broader problem; specifically, that there was no wall.

The situation was unsustainable. Yet for some reason, the media failed to debate the real issues, which was odd given the frenzy when Station fifty-four first shut down. Now, they had succumbed to complacency. The war was happening somewhere else to someone else. Rymorians were more interested in the latest installment of *Celebrity Bathrooms*. Really, who cared what people with too much money did to otherwise functional parts of their pretentious homes?

Apparently, the people of Rymor did.

But the reason I knew Tom was up to something was because he had stopped complaining. At first, I'd believed his unusual quietness to be symptomatic of depression.

It took a while before I realized Tom's quietness wasn't an unhappy quiet but more industry with purpose. Tom was busy doing something he told me nothing about. When asked how his analysis was progressing, the answer was enthusiastic—"Great!"

I could've pushed the matter, but ignorance was bliss.

I also secretly hoped Tom had the balls to do something.

"Got any plans for your off days?" I asked.

Tom's fingers were a blur over the interactive surface of his desk. "Yeah, I'm meeting some friends over in Tranquility."

"Tranquility? Didn't know you had friends there. What do they do?"

Tom froze, which snagged my attention.

"Yes, a group of us are heading over." He grinned in my general direction. "My friend's birthday and his parents have a holiday apartment overlooking the harbor. Think it'll be a blast."

"Sounds great," I agreed, while not for one moment believing him. "Never visited Tranquility. More of a fisherman. Not much fishing around Tranquility. Prefer the lakes, but I expect it's a bit boring for a youngster like you."

"Well, I enjoy the lakes too," Tom agreed, then muttered a little quieter, "Prefer anywhere to here at the moment."

I chuckled. "I've missed your grouching, Tom."

Tom rolled his eyes. "No, you haven't. Besides, grouching achieves jack shit, as you would say, and I've already learned all I can about that."

I chuckled again, enjoying the banter after the prolonged abstinence from regular conversations. I would leave Tom to his secrets.

Yet my underlying concerns remained.

We had been working together for a few years, but in recent months I'd come to regard Tom as an unlikely friend amid the troubles. I hoped Tom understood the risks. I hoped, too, that the young man wasn't putting himself in danger.

# Chapter 29

**Nate**

The headquarters of Rymor's Global Operations was located in Tranquility's central business district. There were many arms to the operation located throughout Rymor, including Global Monitoring, Field Reconnaissance, Communications, Analytics, and Records Management, all controlled under the watchful gaze of Gaia.

Field Reconnaissance was based here in Tranquility, the closest city to the wall, as were the research and manufacturing facilities for the clothing and equipment used by the field crews, commonly referred to as field scientists.

In Rymor's distant past, these people had actually been scientists who happened to work in the field. They traveled through the indigenous lands, researching everything from plant and animal life to geology. The modern field scientist's role had become skewed from their original purpose. While a reasonable percentage of them were capable of scientific research, most were purely reconnaissance operatives sent to observe indigenous activities in the hidden lands beyond the wall.

Global Operations' offices were as unpretentious as their appointed leader, Scott Harding. I eyed the tall building, with its simple but elegant design, and decided I liked it. The reception floor was open and bright, housing a variety of lunch and coffee venues, along with a visitor registration area and public meeting rooms.

I, of course, skipped registration, being a unique kind of visitor who didn't announce my arrival.

Scott was in his office, an opening in his calendar having appeared, courtesy of me. I told myself I ought to stop doing this, but I had to admit, stealth was fun.

After introducing myself to Scott's rather austere assistant, I entered Scott's office, where he greeted me with a scowl.

"What the fuck are you doing here, you crazy son of a—"

I raised my hands, halting Scott's tirade. I gestured toward myself. "Scott, it's me, Nate, stealth guy."

Scott's jaw locked so tight it was a wonder he didn't crack a tooth, but after a short period of silent fuming and glaring, he snapped, "Answer the damn question."

"I'd be happy to, Scott." I sat down in the comfortable-looking visitor's chair. I wasn't disappointed.

"Why don't you make yourself at home?" Scott said, sarcasm dripping from every word. "Being as the homeland hit squad is about to haul us away."

"There's no hit squad. It's just me, plus some interesting information I've come into contact with."

The door opened, and Scott's assistant entered carrying a coffee and a plate of mini muffins. "Here you go, Nate. I hope the muffins are okay?"

"The coffee, wonderful! And muffins, too. Thank you." I took the drink and helped myself to a muffin. "Damn, these muffins are the best," I added around a bite.

Her severe face broke into a smile. "You're very welcome, dear. No bother at all."

## The Master of the Switch

Scott raised an eyebrow as he stared after his retreating assistant. "What did you do to her?"

"I, ah, just spoke to her." I stuffed another delicious muffin into my mouth.

I offered the plate to Scott, who shook his head as though appalled.

"Well, don't talk to her. I like her the way she is, stark, efficient, and a little bit scary. I rely on her to keep visitors to a minimum. I make Jordan wait out there with her an extra five minutes before our regular meeting. I've seen him quaking a time or two when she shows him in. One contemptuous curl of that woman's lip can reduce a grown man to a gibbering wreck. If word gets around that she's dishing out coffee and muffins, I'm screwed."

"Sorry." I finished the last of the mini muffins with a groan of contentment. "She makes these for her grandkids. Said she had a few left over."

"Someone had sex with that woman?" Scott said, raising a disbelieving eyebrow.

"More than once, three children, eight grandchildren, and a long and illustrious secondary career in amateur dramatics. She created the fake persona you see based on the job advertisement and subsequent interview with yourself." I smiled warmly. "She finds playing the part fun."

Scott shook his head as if coming out of a trance. "How long were you out there?"

"About three minutes."

"The news?" Scott said through gritted teeth.

"Yes, the news." I pulled myself back to the matter at hand. "Someone is about to leak footage, lots of footage, along with lots of damaging data about the war, the station, and pretty much everything that's been going on in Shadowland."

"Who the hell has access to all that?" Scott demanded. "Not you?"

"No, not me, unless I was to take a trip to Global Monitoring and, as I recall, you expressly forbid me from doing so."

"Fair enough; so, someone in Global Monitoring? Or... higher up? I can't think who is higher up. I thought they reported to Bill, now. There are only two people on active duty in monitoring since Bremmer stepped in and virtually closed them down. Like Field Operations, they're pretty much dead. Peter is a wreck, and I don't even have my 'friendly' assistant to blame for that, Bill did that all on his own. And Tom is just a kid, enthusiastic but harmless."

"I fear six months of sitting on a burning platform of information has finally taken its toll. Tom met with a web hacker group, the ones who expose corruption from time to time. They were only too happy to deliver the ultimate exposé."

"I've not had access to Global Monitoring for months. Bill cut me out of the loop for supposed security reasons. Exactly how much do they have?"

"A lot. And when I say a lot, I mean everything you could imagine they have, with a few extra delights thrown into the mix. The station's operational periods will be of particular interest to the public, given the government lied about it and further made it pivotal for their war. Then there's the shuttle crash footage, including evidence of interference from a waypoint near Valoret in southern Shadowland. Most notably though, and the one that will send this country into a tailspin, given we no longer have the wall, a 99.998% probability reading on Jaru with Rymorian weapons dated a few weeks ago."

Scott didn't say anything, not even to curse. He reached to rub his brow and released a shaky breath. "I've no idea what to say. Is this good or bad? Can we shut it down? Should we?"

"Is this good for us? I don't know," I said. "But for our chancellor, William Bremmer, I would suggest it's unrecoverable from. As you know, troop communication was also coming to Global Monitoring via the waypoints, but since we shut that down, they've received nothing. They may not yet know that John Tanis is in the process of

## The Master of the Switch

mopping up the Rymorian troops out there, but they will fear the worst. Once the people of Rymor put that lack of communication, together with the lack of a protective wall, and the hostile indigenous armies on the move in the form of an eighty thousand Shadowland army and a hundred and fifty thousand strong Jaru war conglomeration, I'd say we are about to have widespread panic on our hands. Whatever happens afterward, I guarantee Bill won't be around to watch it."

Scott ran his fingers through his short hair. "Tanis never had his sights on Rymor, and I was happy enough to hand him the Rymorians out there in good faith, while the station was operating and the wall in place. He wants Bill, and without the station, he's going to come straight here looking for him."

"So." I leaned back in my chair. "I think it's better if Bill is out there, too. He's not going to hang around waiting for a trial he may or may not be able to wriggle out of. The guy may be wealthy and have more strings than a puppeteer, but he's losing traction with several key supporters, thanks to Richard's work, and he's already halfway to living out there."

"You want to let this play out? Let the leak go public?"

"Yes, I do," I replied. "I need to talk to Richard, then tonight at the apartment we can discuss any insights he has. The leak is scheduled for noon in two days, which gives us some time. If Bill does decide to flee the fallout, there's only one place he'll go, and Tanis is going to go straight there after him."

"Talin," Scott said, in more of a statement than a question.

"Talin," I agreed.

# Chapter 30

**Bill**

It had been a month since I'd visited my mother. The last occasion had been a surprisingly pleasant affair. Rachael Stevens had accompanied me, and we'd sat on the veranda and watched my mother feed her fat pugs treats from the table while Rachael had tried not to laugh.

The grapes were plump on the vines now, and summer was slipping into fall. I hadn't seen Rachael in weeks, and Senator Carl Stevens was under investigation for blackmail and corruption, which was an unfortunate end to our profitable relationship. I didn't know what had happened to my usually faultless monitoring system, but I could make a guess, and it was related to a missing personal assistant and his twin.

There were no warm flagstones beneath my feet today, and the fat pugs lounged at the foot of my mother's bed as a nurse plumped her pillow before easing her gently back.

My mother was pale and frail, and I waited, helpless and angry, before the huge bay window, one hand in my trouser pocket while I surveyed the medical report on my viewer. I placed the viewer on the

## The Master of the Switch

table as the nurse, having finished assisting my mother to sit up, collected her things.

"I'll be outside if you need me, sir. The doctor visited this morning, and he'll return this afternoon if you wish to stay and speak to him."

I inclined my head but offered no confirmation as to whether or not I would be here. Alone with my mother, I retrieved a chair from the seating area near the window and placed it beside her bed.

I unbuttoned my jacket and sat down. "How are you feeling?"

My mother's serene expression suggested the antidepressants were working.

"Oh, you know, I'm a little tired. I had to cancel some of my charity commitments, and that was sad." She smiled.

I took her hand in mine, studying the smooth bony surface. When did she get so old?

"What happened?" I asked.

"I don't know." She stared without focus at our joined hands. "It's been a while since I needed help." Her eyes lifted to meet mine. "Sasha has not been well, you know."

The damn pugs! "So I heard," I said absently.

"I never expected her to kill herself, but when I saw her picture in the paper... Found dead in her apartment... Taken her own life... I didn't know what to think."

"Sasha is still here, Mother." I indicated the dog curled at her feet, sensing as I did so that the situation was beyond repair and that my mother was no longer talking about Sasha.

"Sasha?" My mother's confused gaze settled on the dog. "Your father dropped by earlier. He's so busy at the moment, and I know his work is important to him, but I miss him." Her voice softened. "I do miss him."

I sighed, and a dull thud kicked off in the base of my skull.

"It was his fault that the poor woman killed herself. He can be cruel. I always knew it; a wife always knows. He brought her here

185

once. Poor Margaret, he drove her to her death. You could see she adored him."

I closed his eyes. "Father never met Margaret."

She shook her head, losing herself to spiraling confusion. "I know that. It was you who brought Margaret here, and now Sasha is dead." She laughed gently and so out of context with the conversation that it made my gut clench. "Do you think dogs go to heaven?"

"I'm quite certain they do," I replied. "But see, Sasha is here." The fat pug remained at her feet. The dog was listless, but then it had never been anything else.

"Oh, so she is!" my mother cried in sudden delight.

She lapsed into silence for a while, her glazed attention on the pug.

"You're so much like your father. I hoped you wouldn't be." She patted my hand. "I loved you anyway, even though you killed him...I was sad when it happened, so sad, but I understood."

I bowed my head as her words settled. I'd never intended to become a monster; it had just happened along the way. As for my father's death, well, I'd definitely intended that.

I'd felt no love for my father, admiration sometimes, and respect, for certain, but not a hint of love.

Instead, I'd directed all my love at John Tanis, idolizing the way he thrived without a father. It even influenced my decision to commit that heinous act. I wanted to be like Tanis in every way.

Wanted Tanis to return my adoration.

I regretted how our relationship had played out. I also regretted all those botched attempts to end his life, and that I'd failed. I still hungered for Tanis' death, although I knew I would regret it infinitely more.

My mother started sobbing, which alarmed me when I considered the cocktail of drugs she had been given, which were supposed to keep her calm.

I squeezed her hand and rose to seek the nurse. As promised, she

## The Master of the Switch

was waiting in a chair outside the door and returned to check on my mother at my request.

"I can give her medication, but it will leave her drowsy."

I nodded and watched the nurse check my mother's vitals before administering a further dose. My mother calmed, and the nurse helped her to settle back down into bed. Within moments, my mother's eyes drifted closed, and an expression of peace crept across her face.

The nurse stepped back. "She will rest now. I'll talk to the doctor about it when he arrives."

At my nod, she left, and I took my mother's hand again, running my fingers over the smooth surface before leaning down to kiss her forehead.

Then I turned away and left the room, knowing I would never see my mother or our family home again. It was an ending but also a beginning; and I would have my revenge, whatever the cost.

# Chapter 31

### Richard

An armed escort brought me to Grace Claridge's State Tower office soon after the data leak, which was no surprise. I'd been drip-feeding her information for a few weeks, and the leak confirmed everything I'd said and more.

She sat opposite, her face grave and her demeanor tired. The room was the typical elegant affair that most of the upper ruling elite acquired, tempered by a fine collection of artworks that lent an additional level of sophistication. Grace wasn't born to money, like me; she had risen up from a poor beginning and a troubled childhood in one of the roughest districts of Serenity. She still dedicated much of her time to child protection charities and worked tirelessly for that cause.

"Richard, I think it's time we discussed your source," Grace said. Our location might have been the informal sitting area of her room, but both her words and the manner of my arrival made it clear that a formal discussion was taking place.

I'd known Grace would call me in, and I had discussed how to handle it in detail with Nate, Dan, and the other members of the

## The Master of the Switch

Rymorian resistance group—a group I was now part of and had aided in numerous ways.

I swallowed and decided I wasn't cut out for this espionage lifestyle.

Into the stretched silence, Grace said, "Richard, Bill Bremmer is missing, and we've had an information leak of stunning magnitude. I need to know everything, and would prefer we do this here." Her sweeping arm indicated the relaxed setting of her office. "You're not so naïve as to think there will be no consequences if you don't. You know too much, Richard, and our country is in a precarious position."

I nodded and swallowed again. My throat was itchy and dry, and I reached for the glass of water on the table and gulped a little of it down.

The city was under curfew, the streets were empty, and the good people of Rymor had been sent home from their workplaces and told not to return. There was a storm brewing. The police had managed the few isolated incidents so far but, with the majority of the troops in Shadowland, they didn't have the numbers to cope with widespread unrest.

It would only be a matter of time before the masses realized this.

They should have realized it by now.

"How much of the leaked information did you know about?" Grace Claridge asked, tone encouraging. Despite her earlier threat, I believed she only desired the truth.

I sighed. I'd been carrying this exhausting burden for months, and it was time to come clean. My once frivolous life, touched only by the occasional bout of Bill drama, was now relegated to a distant past. The funny thing was, I didn't regret the changes and had no desire to return to my former ways.

"It's complicated," I said, stifling an inappropriate laugh when I realized I sounded like Nate. That man would be the death of me in one way or another. "I had better start at the beginning."

"Please do." Grace gave a benevolent incline of her head. Her unassuming exterior might have seen her mistaken for someone's sweet grandmother, but Grace was anything but sweet, and her agile mind could scythe down anyone foolish enough to underestimate her.

I didn't underestimate Grace. It was the reason I had approached her to support Bill... and one of the reasons I'd contacted her again when I grew concerned about the validity of the rationale for the war.

"I was approached several months ago by Dan Gilmore, a long-time acquaintance of mine. The renowned technical grand master was party to information he shared in confidence with me."

"Given the situation with Station fifty-four, I dare say everyone in Serenity knows his name," Grace said. "It was brought to our attention in the first briefing on the war that Dan Gilmore was one of only four people capable of fixing the station, or he was until he went missing."

"Two months ago, he informed me that Station fifty-four was once more operational," I said. "He explained to me that he'd spoken to Hannah Duvaul while she was at the site."

Grace arched one delicate brow.

"He had no evidence, but I believed him, and subsequently took the news to Bill. The war was in motion, the approval all but complete. Bill knew about the station but chose not to make it public. He didn't know about Hannah."

A slight tightening of Grace's lips gave an indication of her displeasure.

"As you may know, Dan was brought in. Officially, it was to help with the investigation. Unofficially, they treated him like a criminal and held him in a secure facility with limited visitor access and no right to leave. I visited Dan there and was shocked to discover the extent of his isolation. I was unsettled by Bill's knowledge of the functioning station, sickened to discover he still intended to proceed with war, and felt terrible that although Dan had asked for my help, it had resulted in his incarceration.

"I became increasingly worried for Dan, for Rymor and the people of Shadowland, gravely so, but I'd no idea what to do. A young

## The Master of the Switch

man, who claimed to be related to Dan, approached me. He was an odd fellow, and he had access to a substantial body of confidential information and could do things most people could not."

"What sort of things?" Grace asked, leaning a little closer in her seat and giving me her undivided attention.

"Covert infiltrations. Espionage."

"A hacker? He's part of the group who leaked the monitoring reports?"

"No, not exactly, and he's certainly not working with them. I would say Nate is unique, but that's another story. No, my involvement with Nate was to aid him in smuggling a device to Dan that would allow him to escape. I was worried about Dan, and about what Bill might do, so I decided it was the best course of action."

"A risky endeavor whether your suspicions about Bill were correct or not."

"I know, and believe me, I've never been so terrified. I took the device to Dan, but I didn't get the chance to explain to him what it was. My visit was interrupted, and I was forced to leave." I took another sip of water, returned the glass to the table, and tried to compose myself again. "I found out later, from Nate, that we were interrupted because John Tanis had been taken into Kelard Wilder's custody. Four days later, a bomb was detonated in Station fifty-four."

Grace nodded, indicating for me to carry on.

"I've been aware of much that was happening, but not everything. Nate chose to share with me at his discretion."

"He was using you?" It was only half a question.

"Yes." I shrugged. "Undoubtedly so. Two days ago, I met with Nate and Dan." I didn't mention then that Dan appeared half his former age and was walking. One thing at a time. "They told me about the leak, its content, and scheduled release. The data came from Global Monitoring. As you might imagine, the magnitude of the cover-up had been weighing on the conscience of one of the monitoring team, and he supplied the information to the hacking group, Liberty."

Her expression remained shuttered, and I tried to steady my nerves before progressing to the most damning part.

"I've been working with this group for two months. We discussed what to do about the leak, and we decided to let it run its course."

Her stony façade cracked, and the fine lines around her lips deepened. "Richard, do you realize what you've done? What you've allowed to happen? You should have come to me. You should have trusted me."

Sadness filled me to overflowing. "No offense, Grace, but it's been hard to trust people. And if you think Bill wouldn't have had you killed, then you are not the woman I believe you to be. No, it had to come out."

Her expression was grave, but her eyes glistened. "Better to risk my life than to risk the whole country."

"This country has been at risk for a long time, Grace. The leak is just the tip of the troubles, and you need to be part of the solution if we are going to save Rymor. The group I've been working with includes other notable people, not just myself and Dan. I need to tell you before we go any further that they've been in contact with John Tanis for much of the last two months. I only discovered this a few days ago."

Her eyes widened, and she expelled a disbelieving snort that turned into a laugh.

"Richard... do you know, this is so outrageous that I cannot believe it is anything but the truth... John Tanis, the terrorist our chancellor persuaded us to go to war with?"

"The very same," I replied, uncertain if her laughter was a good indication of her mood. "He saved the Rymorians sent by land from a Jaru attack and helped them to reach the station. He also sent men to search for those missing from the shuttle crash. He found the survivors. Most are back in Rymor in a secret location, but I believe some of the field scientists involved have returned to Shadowland."

Grace's focus had become absolute. "Hannah Duvaul is in

## The Master of the Switch

Rymor? Bill's former partner rescued by a terrorist?" Her tone was disbelieving, but she had a delighted smile.

"Yes, I met her two nights ago."

She nodded, thoughtful, her eyebrows mobile as the many revelations sank in. "I need to speak to her, to all of them. Do you think I can? Will they risk leaving their hiding place?"

I let out a shaky breath and nodded. "Yes, I believe they will."

"I need to know all of what has already happened as well as what is happening now, Richard. If we are to have a chance of saving this country that we love, I will need their testimony, so that the temporary ruling council can make a judgment. A fast judgment, given the absence of our appointed leader; and one I would like you to be part of." She glanced to her right and out the window where the city of Serenity stretched out to the horizon.

Unspoken words danced tragically between us—billions of people, an entire civilization, on the brink of collapse.

"They need a focus," she said. "If we're to survive this, if we're to stem panic and fear, they need a fresh motivation, and it has to be a momentous one."

"What we need is a Shadowland army between the two hundred thousand strong Jaru army on a path toward the wall and us." It came out more dramatically than I intended. In my defense, she *had* asked for something momentous. "I did mention the leak was only the tip of what we are facing. The turmoil that grips us now is nothing compared to the decimation an army of Jaru could do."

I noted the mistiness in her eyes and the faint tremble of her lips.

"Dan has established a connection to the satellites. The Jaru are coming. There is no wall, and the only thing between them and us is John Tanis and his army, assuming we can persuade him to help."

To my admiration, Grace dragged her iron control out of whatever hidden reserves she had, and her expression once more became composed.

"I need to speak to Dan Gilmore, and Hannah, and any others that have returned, and then I need to call a meeting and pray that the people with influence will listen to my counsel despite how wrong I was last time."

"We expected as much," I said. "Grace, I need to let you know that the resistance group will have been listening to everything we have just said."

I wasn't surprised when, on cue, the door to her office opened and Nate walked in.

# Chapter 32

## Shadowland

### Tanis

The Shadowland forces weaved a haphazard path through the lands, collecting the defenseless Rymorians with gratifying ease. It had taken two weeks, but I was now confident every Rymorian, and every Rymorian weapon, that had been sent for me and the people of Shadowland was safely in my possession.

"There has been no trouble since we made the example," Tay said. She had been overseeing the prison camp, which now held an impressive ten thousand Rymorians under the watch of several hundred Shadowlanders. "They have proven much easier to manage here."

I'd left the main base earlier and ridden to the camp with my section leader, Danel, spending most of the day inspecting the site, talking to those stationed here, and performing the morale-boosting duties that leaders did for the troops who got the less glamorous end of the war stick.

It had been hard to control so many prisoners in the dense forest. Then there was the problem of feeding them, which prompted me to relocate them closer to the farmlands north of Valoret. The tall grasses and undulating hills made containing and watching them easy. I stood studying the impromptu prison camp established in a fallow field. It was cramped but, while living conditions weren't pleasant, it was better than being dead.

Keeping my army and prisoners fed was a logistical undertaking of some magnitude and one of the less exciting aspects of war. A steady stream of caravans brought supplies to the prison camp and army. For once, Mayal, the wily old king of Valoret, wasn't slow in delivering the goods. The memory of my last visit during the heavy rains of spring was doubtless fresh. The city had nearly fallen to a Jaru attack. Only the timely arrival of my army had saved them. The new Jaru threat worried even the hardiest Shadowlanders. All were eager to aid those seeking to halt the attack.

Paid protection came in many guises, I mused.

I raised a brow when I noticed Tay's smirk. "You're not supposed to enjoy it," I said.

"Oh, was I not?" she replied innocently. "I need some compensation for babysitting Agregor."

"How is he doing?" I asked.

"Enthusiastic in seeking your approval," she said wryly.

"Not like Garren then," I muttered.

"Not like Garren," she agreed.

Behind me came the sound of a horse approaching, and I turned, pleased to see it was Kein, the scout who managed to know everything worth knowing in Shadowland.

"You were right to suspect Greve," he said as he slipped from the saddle.

I let the information settle, dismissed Tay, and motioned Kein to accompany me as I returned to the center of the camp where I'd left my horse. "A shame. I liked Greve. He had a way of getting to the

## The Master of the Switch

point. Now he's just one more problem." Did I need to deal with Greve now, or should I continue my plans for Rymor and Bill?

The four units of my army had collectively traveled further north and east during the pursuit, taking Shadowland's position closer to the wall: the wall that no longer protected Rymor. Not only were they without a wall, but I'd also captured many of their forces.

The once prosperous country had many traitors in its midst. If not for the assistance of Theo, Scott, and those few others, I would be dead, and the people of Rymor cowed. Committing so many of their limited forces to the attack had been an oversight, and more so given that they had lost their technological advantage. It was time I turned my attention toward Bill, and more than time this was over. Only, Bill was reportedly in Talin, protected by two formidable allies, Falton and Greve.

"He definitely joined Bill?"

"He's at Talin," Kein said. "He crossed the gorge at the Yandue River. There's nothing else there except Talin and the Jaru Plains. I heard his scout offered a different story when he returned a week ago."

"Yes, he did." I had detained the scout at Danel's camp, awaiting word from Kein. It would have been foolish to send him back to Greve with whatever intel he might have gleaned. "He's with Danel, but I can't hold him for much longer without raising Greve's suspicion."

"The scout's no use to you now," Kein said. "Greve has made his move. Perhaps it was curiosity, or perhaps he's seeking to play you both. Hard to say. The scout's not ignorant. He lied about Greve's location. Better to uncover what he knows before you kill him."

I nodded. I'd been hoping for better from Greve, but had prepared for the worst once I realized Falton was making a play. Still, it left me in a quandary. I wanted Bill, but now with Greve, Falton, and the Jaru to contend with, could I afford to seek Bill out? Could I afford not to?

"Are the rumors about the Jaru true?"

"Yes, a hundred and fifty thousand is our best estimate, with more joining them. A few have crossed the border committing small-scale attacks. The border folk have begun fleeing the region. There will be more refugees. With so many Jaru there's no hope for those who don't leave."

As we reached my horse, I motioned my guards to prepare it.

Kein began stroking his mustache, which snagged my attention. "What?"

"There's something odd about the Jaru movement," Kein said.

"Odd? With so many, how could it be anything *but* odd."

A wolf guard lifted the saddle onto my horse's back while another slipped the bridle over its head.

"This is the farming region, full of supplies as such a vast army requires. If they destroy the farms, they destroy us, and yet they're not heading here, nor to the fortresses, nor the cities."

"Where the hell are they going then? There's nothing else south of the mountains except the wall." I caught myself there. "They're heading for the wall?"

"Yes, I believe so," Kein said.

"Why would they head for the wall?" For a long, stretched moment, I felt nothing, and then tension invaded my limbs and body, and a sense of unease crawled under my skin.

The Jaru were heading for Rymor.

A deep, pervasive sense of protectiveness toward Rymor rose from a corner of my psyche. Knowing I'd sent Hannah there for her safety was undoubtedly part of it, yet the compulsion was so intense I knew there was more to it than that.

I knew about my ancestry and how I'd inherited my father's alpha gene. My mother was a geneticist who'd made studying the people of the planet her lifework. Was this why the Shadowlanders still fought the Jaru with such fierce determination? An endless cycle instigated by the ancients to ensure the colony was safe? It sounded fanciful, and yet questioning it was like questioning the concept of hunger or the need for air.

# The Master of the Switch

Rymor was mine. I could choose to storm it or ignore it, but I wasn't going to leave it to the Jaru.

"Mount up, now," I hollered at my men. "You too, Kein, we need to get back to Danel."

I noted Kein's worried face, but nothing I could say would make sense.

My blind need for action consolidated into a firm decision that my plans to go to Rymor were still sound—so, now it was time to expedite them. The twenty field scientists still in Shadowland had remained with Danel, along with an impressive arsenal of confiscated Rymorian weapons. I was confident Shadowlanders could be trained to use them, only I wanted the Rymorian prisoners on my side before the Jaru arrived, too.

Before the Rymorians could be trusted, I needed to resolve the significant matter of my exile. Doing that would mean returning to Rymor.

It would also mean confronting Bill.

I vaulted into the saddle as my party prepared to leave but had done no more when a scout thundered into the camp and brought his horse alongside mine. He passed a scroll over to me.

What I wouldn't give for instant communication.

The scroll bore Danel's seal, and I opened it to find a brief message from Jon.

> *Scott got in contact. Said the Rymorians want to talk to you. He won't tell me what it is, but it's urgent!*
>
> *Jon*

I rolled it up and shoved it in my saddlebag. "We ride." I urged my horse to a trot, and then into a canter the moment we left the camp.

The rest followed or nudged ahead, and Kein fell in alongside me. I knew he had questions, but I couldn't say with confidence whether my suspicions were valid or the result of poor wording on Jon's part.

The Rymorians wanted to talk to me, not Scott, the *Rymorians*. I hoped that meant what I thought it did, because, one way or another, I was coming to talk to them.

# Chapter 33

## Talin

### Ella

I sat on the little stool in the corner of Bill's office; to my right, the treetops of Shadowland were just visible through the window. I remembered praying for an open window so I could throw myself out. I no longer harbored such dramatic or self-defeatist considerations. Freedom would be mine. No other outcome was acceptable.

Pope sat opposite Bill's desk, where the two men discussed progress on the fortress repairs.

Yesterday had seen the arrival of several thousand people, and this time it wasn't the capsule bringing them, but the Talin gates that opened to allow the arrivals entry. They were workers, skilled or otherwise, and had been set to immediate work on repairs.

This new development worried me and left a bad taste of permanence. Bill also remained at Talin for two full days, which had never happened before. How could such a prominent man not be missed?

"The food stocks are adequate even with the recent arrivals, but we'll need to find an alternative supply now the transportation capsule is gone," Pope said.

Wait? The capsule was gone? Gone how?

In the still of the night, I had constructed detailed plans around using the capsule to make my escape. I'd studied it every time they took me down to meet Bill. Although it was guarded, and I had no idea how to overcome that problem, I had thought I could make it work since it used a standard palm-pressure gate.

Wherever its destination, and whatever or whoever might be waiting at the other end, it was a location inside Rymor and had to be preferable to here.

"—returning tomorrow. I think you have him on the hook. Don't know why Shadowlanders are so fascinated with Rymorian things, but they sell themselves out cheaply."

Pope had continued talking, and I'd lost a valuable chunk of the conversation worrying about the missing capsule. I thought at first he was talking about that abominable man, Falton, but I was certain there had been no mention of his name.

"He's not as easy to influence as the last one," Bill said, "Nor as stupid."

Maybe not Falton, then...

"You think he's playing you? Working for Tanis?" Pope asked.

After a long pause, Bill replied. "No, he's not doing this for Tanis. He was far more interested in my sway with the Jaru, and was cagey when asked about Tanis. Whatever Tanis did that led to Greve's allegiance, he still holds it to some extent."

"That could cause problems later?"

"No, I don't think it will." Bill appeared thoughtful. "He doesn't believe Tanis can defeat the Jaru, a belief I share. An alliance with me offers him protection from them, and it's as uncomplicated as that."

"What about Rymor?" Pope asked.

Something in his tone poked at my concerns again.

## The Master of the Switch

"Rymor?" Bill questioned.

"The fact that there's no wall and masses of Jaru on the move. What if they spill over?"

My chest contracted painfully. Why had he never mentioned this before?

"They've bigger issues there at the moment." Bill's smile was smug.

"What issues?" Pope asked. "Are you still in communication?"

"I need the supplies to keep my new friends happy. I'm expecting a shuttle full of them today, so, yes, I'm still in communication. Rymor will be fine." Bill waved a dismissive hand.

He was lying. I was convinced of it. My family lived there, my husband and my beautiful boys. The thought of them not being safe sent my heart rate and breathing into overdrive, and I fought to get both under control.

"Ella, are you alright?"

My tension spiked. Both men watched me: Bill with concern, Pope with narrow-eyed suspicion.

"I'm sorry, I need to use the bathroom and was afraid to interrupt."

Pope snickered. Bill's indulgent expression disturbed me almost as much as the cold, unfeeling version of him I'd met back at Hannah's apartment.

"I'll send for someone to take you," Bill said.

"I could go on my own. If it would save troubling anyone."

Bill raised an eyebrow. So did Pope.

Then Bill smiled. "Of course, I'm delighted you feel well enough to go on your own. This is a huge milestone."

How was he not seeing through this? Why was he not suspicious of me? I wasn't that good an actor.

Pope smirked. Still, he'd said he would keep my secret, so I decided to plow on. "Can I—can I get some food, too?"

Bill stilled. Had I pushed too far, too fast? His face suddenly broke into a warm smile. "Go ahead, Ella."

I jumped from my stool, knocking it over in my haste. Mumbling an apology, I righted it and fled the room.

As the door clicked behind me, I leaned back against it.

What the fuck was I doing?

Only I knew what I was doing and why. I was strong for now, but how long would it last?

Pope wasn't buying into my act. Maybe he meant it when he said he would keep my secret. Or maybe he was just another monster biding his time.

I couldn't go back to that dark place, and I knew I wouldn't survive it again.

I was intelligent enough to realize that I'd changed and bore scars. Insomnia, the nightmares, on those rare occasions when I managed more than a few hours' sleep, the irrational heart-stopping panic when something triggered me about the past.

Contact, even fleeting, brought me out in a cold sweat.

I wanted to destroy Bill Bremmer for his part in this.

But he had also saved me; he'd been right when he said I liked to be close.

Against all probability, I felt safest when he was near, and I knew what that meant, how unhealthy those feelings were.

Knowing didn't help me while I existed in survival mode.

# Chapter 34

## Rymor

## Sirius

Moiety's base, in the innocuous cleaning bot factory, remained quiet today, and it had taken stealth for me to reach the underground venue for the meet. Serenity was under lockdown, and the people of Rymor were confined to their homes. I had means to move around, as did my companions. Still, it wasn't easy, and the quicker we implemented our plans, the better.

"This is the opportunity we've been waiting for," I said. Sitting across from me were my two most trusted allies, Reece and Mac, the respective leaders of Hope Town's two most notorious gangs.

The walls of the room where we sat were adorned with a mismatched collage of viewers showing images and clips of the underground scene's best fighters. Two security personnel waited on sentry just inside the door. It would be a foolish troublemaker who tried to get inside. "It's time for an uprising here in Hope Town. And I want you to help me to do this."

"An uprising? Like riots and shit?" Reece said. His black hair was cropped tight to his skull, and his dark eyes were set too far apart in a face that, like the man himself, was skeletally thin. The brown retro-leather chair he lounged in was as worn as the room that housed it. Behind him, a window separated us from the chanting crowd cheering on the current fight. "This district is a war zone on a good day, and we're already in control of that shit. You want riots? How does that help us? How's that good for business?"

I detested bad language. It was so unnecessary. "It will be excellent for business." My attention drifted to the cage in the middle of the club, where a fight was taking place. One fighter had his opponent up against the mesh wall. His enthusiastic pummeling splattered the nearby crowd in blood and whipped the spectators into a frenzy.

The numbers were down, apparently, not that I could tell. Still, I did enjoy a good cage fight. It held a certain uncivilized appeal given it was often Shadowlanders taking part. I was happy to supply candidates. For the right reward, the Jaru could be persuaded to capture the occasional child. Those with the alpha gene made an excellent addition.

While some Outliers wallowed in self-righteous pacifist delusions, I suffered no such mental failings. We were people broken in ways beyond what happened to the Jaru all those eons ago. I liked my broken side well enough. It served me and my cause, and the end always justified the means.

The Reeper gang, which Reece headed, was focused on drugs, and he knew his product and its buyers well. It was a position Reece had inherited when the former leader's vision had diverged from mine. Reece owed me for assisting him in the transition, and I was about to collect. I was willing to compensate both men to ensure that my edict progressed according to my wishes. "I realize such an uprising will require the deployment of many resources. You will each receive two full containers of a new drug, Anarchy, along with stun-resistant battle fatigues and pulse beam weapons that have had

## The Master of the Switch

their power limits removed. The drug has unprecedented addictive qualities and interesting side-effects that will further aid in spreading disorder far and wide." My smile was cold. "It's vital that troubles escalate swiftly. I'm already preparing shipments for our operations in each major city." Both men leaned a little further forward in their seats. "The weapons alone have significant value. All I'm asking is for you to use them."

"I'm in." Reece leered and gave Mac a playful nudge, oblivious to the other man's disdain for the contact.

"Rymor has a pitiful number of trained personnel," I continued. "We suspected as much, but the leaked report has confirmed this. Poor government decisions have left their people exposed to attack from within, as well as from without. If we capitalize on this, we can increase our presence beyond Hope Town. More districts under our control equate to more money for all of us. The token military and police force won't have a hope if we hit hard enough, bound as they are to seek a peaceful resolution to violence. They will retreat and Hope Town will degenerate. When we push out, they will retreat again. And so, with each city. Before long, Rymor will be under our control."

"How many weapons are you offering?" Mac asked, the other major player in Hope Town. Where Reece was painfully thin, Mac was built like a cage fighter. He headed up the Loopers gang and, unlike Reece's predecessor, he knew better than to challenge me. His business included weapons, counterfeit goods, the underground fight scene, and associated betting profits. "I'm all in, by the way. This curfew bullshit is killing my profits."

"It's bad for everyone's business. No one is buying outside the underground venues. I need my sellers out on the streets," Reece agreed. "It'll take some planning, though."

"Not that much." Mac nodded toward me. "When will we get the goods?"

Beyond the window, the fight had finished, and the limp remains of the loser were being carried from the cage. "The curfew complicates delivery, but the drugs will be ready for transport tomorrow morning, and the weapons and combat fatigues will be ready tomorrow night."

"Once we have the gear, it won't matter." Mac grinned. "I say we call in our teams now, and get them ready to roll ASAP."

"You think we can do this?" Reece asked, a gleam lighting his dark eyes. "Bring Rymor down?"

My smile was sly. I had been working toward this day my whole life. "Yes," I said. "I believe we can."

# Chapter 35

## Shadowland

### Tanis

"I'm really nervous," Jon said. "Are you nervous? You must be nervous."

"I'm not nervous," I replied, rubbing absently at my chest. Garren had been in here earlier, getting in my face, making demands, and generally being a surly bastard. "Why would I be nervous?"

I sat in my tent at the table. There were two piles of scrolls before me, the ones I'd read and ones I had not. My chest ached all the time. Garren had been with her longer, bonded deeper, and if his attitude was any indication, he was suffering more than me.

It was a hot, sunny morning, and today Rymor's representatives would arrive by shuttle.

I wasn't happy about the shuttle, but I'd specified the model and the number of guests, and would keep Theo close at hand on the off chance they came with weapons.

The tunnels, while far more prevalent than had been suspected, had no access point closer than three days' ride. Rymor didn't have that time to spare. I remained impatient for resolution and to hear what the new powers in Rymor had to say now that Bill had fled—at least, I hoped Bill had fled because, if this was a ruse, I was dead.

"They could put anything on that shuttle, whatever you may or may not have specified."

I glanced up from the scroll to find Jon pacing, like a caged beast, in the limited confines of the tent. "If they want to kill me, they could send a team with weapons, which we may or may not be able to disable. They know where I am," I said, distracted myself by trying to find where I'd gotten to in the scroll.

"Yeah, there is that." Jon sighed. "I'm not sure I'm ready to face Scott Harding."

I tossed the scroll onto the table and contemplated kicking Jon out of the tent. I needed a drink, but given this was my first contact with Rymor after ten years in exile, I recognized it as a bad idea. I intended to set the tone of our interactions from the start. I wasn't about to bow down, apologize, or otherwise be subject to commands or demands the Rymorians might make. I would help them, assuming they asked for my help, nicely. Otherwise, I would crush the Jaru right after I invaded their lands.

Either route would work.

Would I be going at this so hard if it wasn't for Hannah?

Maybe, maybe not.

The bond was stronger than I'd expected and I worried about how it would be affecting her. She was probably going to tell me to go fuck myself when we next met. Not that it would matter, her body would remember and she'd be begging me to fuck her.

Jon halted his obsessive pacing. "That's a disturbing smile," he said.

I forced a blank expression onto my face, but given I still had a pile of scrolls to get through and Jon still wouldn't shut up, it was hard to hide my irritation.

## The Master of the Switch

"I think I preferred the manic grin," Jon said, the corners of his mouth downturned as he resumed his pacing. "Are you going to change?"

"Change?" I frowned down at myself and wondered what the hell Jon was talking about. "I washed yesterday, which is relatively recently given we're camped in the middle of nowhere. I'm sure they'll cope."

Jon nodded at me. "I was thinking about the weapons."

I stared down at myself again, even more puzzled now. "These are my usual weapons? They are both effective and familiar."

"Do you need all of them?" Jon said, ignoring my raised eyebrow. "You'll give the senate members a heart attack. You don't realize what you look like to normal Rymorians."

I grinned. "I'm going exactly as I am. A moment ago you were worried about them launching an attack on me."

Jon let out an exasperated breath. "Yes, sorry, I'm feeling nervous. I want this to work. You didn't deserve to be exiled, but you're not normal anymore." He gestured in my direction without looking. "I spoke to Coco last night, and she assured me it would be fine but still —" He left it hanging and took another deep breath.

Why were people suddenly telling me I wasn't normal?

"Jon, I don't believe any of them are operating under any misconceptions of who or what I am, and I'm not about to pretend to be someone 'normal' by Rymorian standards. If I were normal, they wouldn't want to speak to me. No; better if I appear to be what I am. If they're foolish enough to think they can start bargaining with me, it will be a painfully short conversation. Besides, I did blow up a power station. Maybe not personally, but I made it clear to Joshua that he had no choice. Danel had orders to persuade him if he suffered a change of heart."

The tent flap was thrust open, and Theo poked his head inside. "They'll be at the landing site in five minutes."

Jon had left the tent before I could rise from my seat. Outside, I found my horse was waiting, as were Garren, Javid, Theo, and Kein, ready to accompany me to the shuttle landing site. Finally, and because they had refused otherwise, ten members of my wolf guard.

The camp had been in a state of nervous anticipation since I'd first announced the Rymorians were coming to negotiate. Shadowlanders were deeply fascinated with the elusive world beyond the wall, and were torn between the worry it was a trap, and hope for the greatest day of their lives as the mighty Rymor bowed to Shadowland for help. The much-anticipated rewards of such an alliance were all anyone could talk about.

"Do you think your mother will be there?" Javid asked as we rode out of the camp.

"I hope not. Her absence was one of my stipulations. This isn't the place for a family reunion, and I don't trust you, with or without her there."

When my words sank in a few moments later, Javid chuckled to himself. "You can't blame me, son. Just looking out for you in case you get another foolish notion to hand yourself over. Those tower-dwellers are sneaky bastards. No offense, Jon."

Jon laughed from behind. "None taken," he said.

It took us five minutes to reach the clearing where the shuttle would land. The dozen remaining field scientists sent by Scott Harding were waiting at the site. In addition, Danel and Han were also present and had organized the preparations with another fifty Shadowlanders. Their skills were beyond question, but I'd also included the two brothers because they were individually the most intimidating Shadowlanders I knew, and together they were off the scale.

We brought our horses to a halt at the end of the clearing. Ahead, the shuttle landed with a gentle *whir*. A spacious, open-sided tent sat to the left of the landing area. The open sides were so that those not involved in the discussion could see nothing untoward was going on.

"They bleed just like you do," I said, aware that the sight of the shuttle with its gleaming exterior was confronting for the Shadowlanders, and pleased that none showed their fear.

## The Master of the Switch

We walked the horses over and dismounted to the right where a temporary picket had been erected.

"You must be nervous now," Jon said.

"If I said yes, would it help?" My eyes were on the closed door, but I glanced across when Jon didn't answer.

"No, now that I think about it, I don't think it would. Keep it to yourself."

By prior agreement, we walked into position ready to meet the people of Rymor and whatever fate they brought.

Jon stood to my right, and Theo stood to my left, holding a viewer in his hand that he continued to scrutinize. The rest, including Kein, Javid, and Garren, stood directly behind, while Han, Danel, the wolf guards, and soldiers positioned themselves among the field scientists.

A hiss came from the shuttle, and the door lumbered open.

*Yes*, I admitted to myself. *I am nervous now.*

# Chapter 36

### Richard

I was nervous. The most nervous I'd been in my life. More nervous than the day I entered the facility where Dan was being held and snuck a device to him, and that was saying something. I didn't understand why I was here. I was a senate member, and there were lots of others. Surely one of them could have gone in my place.

I stared out the front window of the shuttle as we came into land. "There are a great many people down there," I said. And by people, I meant Shadowlanders since, although there should be field scientists waiting too, I'd always considered them a curious group. Given they'd ensconced themselves with Shadowlander politics, I felt they offered little reassurance as to my safety.

"What did you expect?" Scott said. He sat to my right. He was an interesting fellow, and while not as odd as Nate, he was closer to that end of the spectrum. Scott wasn't nervous about this momentous meeting. No, Scott was grinning. He grinned a lot. He also succumbed to bouts of intense scowling and possessed no kind of profanity filter.

## The Master of the Switch

Nate had been desperate to be included; but he was one of life's adventurers, unlike me. While I was mentally willing, I was, at best, physically reluctant.

Grace had declined Nate's request, although she'd formed an instant attachment to the young man, partly because of his relationship with Theo, whom she openly admired, and partly due to his entertaining personality. She had offered Nate a position working for her, and a flattered Nate had jumped at the opportunity. Unfortunately, that opportunity would need to wait until the emergency had passed, and no one knew how long that might be.

For reasons I could neither comprehend nor explain, the temporary ruling council viewed my work with the resistance group, as they were now referred to, as an act of bravery. My subsequent disclosure of Bill's corruption elevated their opinion of me further. I was viewed, unwittingly though it was, as key to the survival of Rymor.

I was at a loss about how I had reached these lofty heights.

After much discussion, the final group to visit Shadowland consisted of Grace and me as representatives of the ruling council, Scott Harding and Adam Harris, four other field scientists, and the two mandatory flight observers.

As the leader of the field scientists, Adam's candid and, at times, heartbreaking testimony of the events during his time in Shadowland influenced the subsequent decision by the council to approach John Tanis.

Hannah and Joshua had corroborated Adam's story, except for a minor part around Hannah's personal relationship with a Shadowlander. Joshua mentioned it several times, while neither Hannah nor Adam did so. If there had been any such relationship, she chose to keep it private. Adam was either unaware, felt it was irrelevant, or was simply too polite to mention it.

Whatever Hannah had or hadn't done was inconsequential in the greater scheme of things. They had all behaved out of character. The impossible pressures they'd dealt with and choices they'd made while in Shadowland were why the ruling council had agreed to full pardons for any and all actions taken during the operation. The circumstances had been extenuating, and I knew it was a necessary concession to ensure full disclosure.

Joshua's clumsy attempts to divert attention from his part in destroying the station were evident for what they were. Each of them had succumbed to moral failings, yet Joshua's guilt remained complex. He had destroyed the station, the consequence of which was catastrophic for Rymor.

As the team leader, Adam shouldered much of the responsibility and failure regarding Marcus. Unbeknownst to Adam, Marcus had been working indirectly for Bill when he had killed two fellow members of their party.

Adam blamed himself for not dealing with Marcus earlier and also suffered guilt that he had somehow failed Marcus. He'd done his best during an impossible situation, and that was all anyone could ask.

In the end, I didn't believe any of them gave full disclosure, but it was close enough for the council to seek an alliance with Shadowland.

The shuttle powered down, and my tension rocketed. Scott was out of his seat the moment the flight observer gave the all-clear, and Adam was close behind.

"Such enthusiasm." Grace arched a brow as she gave my arm a gentle squeeze. "It will be fine, Richard. Come, we are about to make history in one way or another."

Reluctantly, I followed Grace to the door where the others were waiting.

"Ready?" Adam asked.

Grace nodded, and the door was released bringing the mysterious Shadowland into view.

My attention shifted left as we walked down the ramp to where John Tanis, I presumed, towered over two men at his side. The warrior, or alpha gene, as Coco had called it, forced a variety of genetic characteristics into play, all of them showcased in the alpha

## The Master of the Switch

who ruled Shadowland. While his mother was Rymorian, no one would mistake where his father was from.

Standing to his immediate left was Theo, who, curiously, held a viewer in his hand. I recognized Jon Sanders standing to Tanis's right. Although I'd never met him, his image had been on news reports and in briefings given to the original action committee.

Three other men stood close, two of similar build to John Tanis and no less intimidating. The final man was short and slight and wore his mustache drooping to either side of his mouth.

Scott and Adam set a brisk pace, Grace and I, and the remaining field scientists doing our best to keep up. We came to a collective stop no more than a pace away from the Shadowlanders, where I regarded the horrifying detail of both the armor and the array of weapons John Tanis wore. He had a presence, despite being younger than I felt anyone ruling an entire country ought to be, and handsome, which surprised me, because I'd drawn a mental image of a great, lumbering monster.

I dragged my gaze from Shadowland's ruler to find Theo grinning at me.

"Tanis!" Scott's grin was broad as he closed the gap and held out his hand. "Always knew you were trouble. Look how you turned out. Even worse than I predicted!"

John Tanis shook Scott's hand, a smile tugging at the corner of his lips. "Glad I exceeded your lofty expectations. I believe you tried to beat my insubordination out of me a time or two under the guise of a training session."

His clear, clipped accent reminded me of Coco Tanis.

"You were smaller back then," Scott said amiably. "I see it didn't work."

John Tanis laughed. It had a pleasant, self-assured sound. "No, it didn't." He turned to take Adam's hand, placing his other hand on Adam's shoulder. "How has everyone been back in Rymor?"

"Good, they're all good," Adam said. "It's over now, and they've been cleared and reunited with their families."

A silent communication passed between them as Tanis retained Adam's hand longer, and there seemed to be genuine affection in their exchange. "Glad to hear it."

His expression cooled as he greeted Grace and me with a formal handshake before turning to introduce his people. "My father, Javid, Lord of Tain. My brother, Garren, and Kein, my advisor."

A brother and his father? I glanced at Grace. If she was surprised, she hid it well. Coco had explained that John Tanis' father was a Shadowlander, hence his stature, but failed to mention he still played a role in his son's life. His meteoric rise seemed a little less meteoric in light of this insight.

"I've arranged a tent." Tanis indicated the open tent to one side.

Jon Sanders and Adam left us. As the head of the Field Reconnaissance section of Global Operations, Adam was doubtless keen to speak with his team stationed out here.

There were guards and soldiers everywhere, armed and deadly looking. Inside the tent were chairs and a table. Food and drinks began arriving as soon as we sat down. My brows drew together as I studied the fare. *We are in the middle of a field, and there are chairs.*

I glanced up to find myself the unwitting object of Tanis' penetrating gaze.

"I enjoy comfort," he said, his face so straight that I couldn't tell if he was serious or joking.

I returned a weak smile.

There were two drinks before me, one was water, and my tentative sip of the other revealed a light, refreshing wine.

I wondered at the turn of events that had led to being seated in a tent in Shadowland with John Tanis, holding a pardon for events during his exile and clearing him of his involvement in the Serenity bombing ten years ago that had led to that exile.

Independent investigators had been tasked with reviewing the bombing case. Even at the early stages of the inquiry, it was clear the charges had no merit. Evidence had been falsified, testimonies had been altered, and not a shred of circumstantial evidence could

## The Master of the Switch

connect John Tanis to either the planning or execution of the terrorist attack.

The case had now been reopened, and the legal team had already filed several corruption charges. John Tanis' absence at the time of the trial had rendered it an open and shut case. His communication implant and access to Rymor had been revoked without him offering a single word of defense.

"If I may." Grace rose from her seat. "Before we begin, Lord Tanis, I would like to present you with a declaration. I hope this will set the tone of our meeting and provide the foundations for openness between us."

"I am happy to take your declaration into consideration, and just Tanis will be fine. It's a long story, but it's my preferred form of address."

"Thank you. Please call me Grace." Opening the folder she had brought, she extracted a letter. "This declaration formally acknowledges your innocence of the crime leading to your exile. I am only sorry its arrival took so long."

"Innocence?" He took it from her, his expression closed.

"We have re-opened the case. Evidence was falsified. Charges have been laid against those involved in the corruption. We expect more to follow as the investigation progresses."

He studied the paper in his hand. "Once, long ago, I wished for this. Not so much anymore, but I appreciate the sentiment in which it is given." He tipped the declaration toward Grace. "It's a comprehensive statement. Do you know about the station? I was blamed for the initial failure, which was a lie. But the second time was all on me. I told Joshua to take the wall down by whatever means was necessary, after learning Rymor had brought weapons into my lands. I admit, Joshua was a little more creative than I expected. And to be clear, I gave him no choice. I may not be guilty of the original bombing, but I am guilty of others."

His polite façade had lulled me into believing Tanis was civilized. Yet those words, cold and hard and without remorse, offered a deeper insight into his character.

"We're aware of what happened at the station," Grace said in a quiet but firm voice. "You had your reasons. The circumstances were extenuating. We declared war on Shadowland without reason and followed a leader unworthy of the title. We have all committed wrongs, Tanis. The declaration is, as you say, broad, for that very reason."

If I'd thought Tanis was formidable, Grace Claridge was his match.

Tanis inclined his head.

"I need to ask about the Rymorian forces sent out here," Scott said. "Kelard Wilder still with us?"

"No, I killed him." Tanis said.

"Did he resist capture?" Scott asked, his brows raising a touch.

"No, we disabled their weapons and overpowered them with ease. Word of Wilder's interview techniques while I was their guest had spread through my army. Shadowlanders have certain expectations of their leader. His death needed to be spectacular. It was."

Grace had gone pale. I swallowed and decided crossing Tanis was a bad idea, not that I intended to.

"Any more incidents?" Scott asked.

"Three men failed to surrender their weapons. I said I would kill anyone found hiding one, and I did. I also said I would kill anyone who attempted to escape. No one tried. I believe they took me at my word. The remainder are my guests. However, they require significant amounts of food, and despite my demonstration, they complain more than is healthy. I'm hoping we can come to an agreement."

"You want to return them?" Scott asked.

"No," Tanis replied. "I want them armed and on my side before the Jaru war tribe gets here."

I blinked several times. Was he offering to help us? And before we had even got to that part.

"Rymor needs a leader, Tanis. A strong one," Grace said. Her

### The Master of the Switch

voice held a slight crackle of age but was laced with her inner strength. "We know the Jaru are heading for Rymor, not Shadowland. Our country is in turmoil. The news of the failure of the wall and the imminent arrival of the Jaru army has been leaked to the public. We are on the brink of collapse. In some sectors, we are already there."

Tanis grunted and picked up his wine glass. "I hope you're not looking at me because that would be really fucked up." He tipped back his glass and drained it. A Shadowland guard was prompt to refill it.

Grace smiled her kind grandmotherly smile. "But we are looking at you."

Javid started chuckling. "You might do alright, after all, son."

"I'm not Rymor's next leader." Tanis gave a pointed look at his father, "but I do intend to halt the Jaru. And I want Bill dead."

Quiet descended on the table. I thought Tanis' admission that he wanted Bill dead too candid for my liking, but I supposed they approached problems in less conventional ways out here.

"I'm afraid we can't give you Bill," I said. It was the first time I'd spoken, and I wondered what had possessed me to open my mouth.

Tanis narrowed his eyes and his penetrating gaze settled on me. "Why not?"

"Because he left." In a striking moment of clarity, I realized I would have handed Bill over to Tanis to do with as he wished, as unethical as that was. "Fled to Talin, we believe. If it were in my power to do so, I would give him to you." I studied the drink in my hand. Feeling awkward, I placed it back on the table before returning my attention to the man who sat opposite. Rymor needed Tanis, and his help was all that mattered now. "I canvassed for the war. Information was subsequently brought to my attention that made me realize my error and I joined a resistance group who worked covertly to stop it. The people of Rymor, Grace and myself included, were lied to. A different threat is coming, one we won't survive without you."

"I'm not Rymor's leader." Tanis shifted his attention between

Grace and me. "You want me to stop the Jaru? You want my men and women to protect you from them? To give their lives? I want any information you have on Bill. I want access to every fancy weapon you have, and I want an integrated future between Rymor and Shadowland. I want the tunnels reopened, and I want the communication resumed. We were never meant to be separate. What I want, I will have or, make no mistake, I will take it anyway. But I'm no leader, temporary or otherwise."

The hairs on the back of my neck rose. The man was *formidable*.

"I am a product of the ancients," Tanis continued, his voice hard and uncompromising. "As many Shadowlanders are. We exist to protect Rymor. It's what we've always done. Rymor cut us off for reasons that were established too long ago to remember, and here we remained in limbo, no longer connected or a part. A missing piece left on the outside... We won't be left on the outside anymore. We deserve our place, and we will have it."

I came to meet a warrior and instead found something more. I'd read his files, understood his unorthodox education and exceptional intelligence, and still I'd come out here bearing prejudice that he would be little more than a savage.

Oh, there was savagery in him and he made no attempt to hide it. Yet so much more lay behind this complex man. The world clicked into place around us. There was such determination in John Tanis and unwavering certainty.

"The people of Shadowland deserve acknowledgement," I said. "I will do all I can to ensure your conditions are met swiftly. We had hoped you would be the one to lead us, but if not, then you may act for us in whatever capacity you decide. As I believe you may have noticed, we are in no position to refuse your terms. I followed William Bremmer blindly. I regret that I did."

"Don't blame yourself." Tanis's smile didn't reach his eyes. "After all, he was once my best friend."

# Chapter 37

## Rymor

### Hannah

My return to Rymor was an emotional experience that had begun with my reunion with Dan and the rather candid conversation with Coco. There had been little respite since.

The interviews had been stressful. Rehashing events in Shadowland had stirred up feelings and thoughts I would much rather have left to settle. Knowing I wouldn't face charges had helped me to speak freely. Yet, parts remained too painful and private to disclose to the temporary ruling council. I'd been honest, though; just circumspect about some details. I had decided that was right, given what I'd been through.

Post-interviews, I'd been free to return to being Hannah Duvaul, the technical master who hoped one day to become a grand master.

My new life felt odd. Shadowland and its people had captivated me, untethering me from societal restraints. Being thrust back into

Rymor now held all the tangibility of a dream. Yet that perspective was quick to shift back again. Rymor was familiar and ingrained in the greater portion of my life. Shadowland and my wild adventure there seemed to be fading too soon.

I knew it was real. I had been there. Yet, it didn't feel like it anymore. It felt like a stranger had invaded my body and taken it on a wild and terrifying ride.

*Here you go,* that other Hannah seemed to say, with a little gesture as if urging trouble away. *You can have her back. I've finished with her.* Like a sleepwalker, I went about my business. I shared comfort with Red, yet every day and every step took me closer to the old version of me, the one I'd come to despise.

Bill was gone, fled to Talin in Shadowland, and that struck a discordant note. I still feared that he would return and tell everyone I was lying. Thankfully, I was too busy to dwell on it, since once the interviews were finally over, we had been enlisted to resolve the power issues.

Anyone with even passing ancient technology skills had been enlisted. The team I was with was now based at a remote research facility in Rymor's semi-wild lake district. Our one goal was to restore power to the wall. We had relocated there four days ago after the interviews were concluded.

I'd learned to put away my grievances with Joshua. It was a pity Joshua hadn't done the same. He seemed to enjoy making snide comments whenever we were alone. As irrational as it was, I felt he blamed me for his actions. I avoided him when I could and ignored him when I couldn't. If my recent life experiences had taught me anything, it was to focus on what was important.

Despite my reluctance to take any personal time, I needed time with my family if I was ever to concentrate on my work. Despite the curfew in place, I was granted special permission to travel to visit my brother-in-law and nephews.

"Let me come with you?" Red urged, his watchful eyes holding mine. "You don't need to do this alone."

# The Master of the Switch

Except, I did, so he relented because he sensed I was determined.

I began by visiting my apartment. My fingers skimmed over familiar surfaces untouched in half a year. My little study nook beckoned me, and I stopped before the wall imager, where the tile still blinked, and the missing picture screamed.

Palm pressed to the blank place where the retro-picture of Ella and I had once sat, I fell to my knees and cried in great body-wracking, stomach-heaving sobs.

I lost time and a part of my soul at that viewer.

After gaining control of my tears, I took the shuttle the government had placed at my disposal to visit Nicholas and my nephews.

There were new lines on Nicholas' face when I saw him and a haunted aspect to his eyes. Guilt consumed me. *I'd* done this; I'd ripped a family apart with my selfish need to let Ella know where I was.

"I'm so sorry, Nicholas." Tears poured down my cheeks, and along with them came words of guilt, shame, and self-recrimination. "I left her a message at my apartment. I made her search for me. I—"

"Hush." Nicholas gathered me into his arms and held me, and we clung together while we both fell apart inside. He kissed my forehead. "None of this is your fault. None of it. You think she would have left it alone, with or without a message?"

He was right, although acknowledging it brought no peace.

"Now, the boys are desperate to see you. When they heard you were back, they talked about nothing else. Will you see them?" he asked. "I asked my mother to take care of them, to give us a little time. It's going to be hard, I know that. Every time I see their beautiful faces, I see Ella." His voice broke a little. "It's even harder looking at you."

I thought I'd run myself dry of tears, but more came, and I clung to his embrace that was filled with our mutual love of Ella. "Please bring them over. I want to see them. I need to see them."

"Okay," he said, kissing my forehead again. "But I'm warning you, I don't think there are enough tissues in the house."

I laughed, the humor short-lived when there was tightness in my throat, and I pulled away, trying to find calm as he placed a call to his mother.

We sat together on the couch in silence as we waited, with the comforting connection of his hand against mine. It felt like forever, and yet only a moment, when the door opened and my nephews barreled in. Two small, wriggling bodies crushed me in a fierce hug. Their faces pressed tight, and I held them, my fingers smoothing their silky hair. I felt Nicholas's arms come around us, pulling us together into a bundle of collective loss.

Over the top of a fair head, Nicholas's mother regarded us with sad eyes. "It's so good to see you, Hannah," she said.

"You too. I thought—" I swallowed hard. "There was a time when I thought I never would."

As the tears eased, we sat and talked about Ella, the woman we all missed. We shared stories and talked of happy moments. We laughed at times and cried more. Nicholas's mother brought us drinks and food we didn't really want.

Time passed too quickly. The boys curled beside me and fell asleep while the adults talked softly.

"I better put them to bed." Nicholas directed a loving smile at his two sons. "It did them good seeing you today."

I helped him carry them to their room. Exhausted, neither boy woke as they were put to bed. I stroked their hair and kissed their heads.

"I know you must be busy, given what's going on," Nicholas said as we returned to the living room. "But please come back and visit us when you can. We missed you. And Ella had missed you." He gave me a mock stern look when my eyes filled once more.

I blinked and drew a shaky breath. "I'll return as soon as I can, I promise." I'd told him earlier about Molly, and his surprise had turned to amusement at my uncensored descriptions of the little girl. "I'll bring Molly with me if she's willing. She would enjoy the garden, I'm sure."

## The Master of the Switch

"Okay, Hannah." Nicholas gave me one last hug. "Ella would be proud of you."

The shuttle whisked me back to Serenity with speed and luxury that I wasn't used to.

It was late, but I put a call through to Red to reassure him I was doing okay. I would see him in the morning, since our mating meant he was based at the research center with me. Today belonged to Ella. Tomorrow, I would pick myself up and get back to helping Dan and Joshua to figure out a way to reestablish power to the wall. It was late and being closer to Serenity than the research facility, I elected to spend the night in my apartment.

I found it quiet, and the surrounding city, which would typically be a hive of activity, was eerily still. I decided to collect my last few essential possessions, as tomorrow the shuttle would take me back to the facility for the foreseeable future. I couldn't see my focus changing until the power was resolved or the Jaru threat was eliminated.

With a tired sigh, I headed straight to bed. I switched the wall viewer on to find the news dominated by rioting in the ever-troubled Hope Town district, which had degenerated into a war zone. With the main armed forces still in Shadowland, no aid was in sight.

*How did we fall so far so fast?*

My apartment complex was secure. No one could leave, and no one could enter. If your home had a printer, and unless there was a medical emergency, that was the way it would stay. Anyone failing to return home after the curfew had either become the predator or the prey. The troubles were growing, and soon, they would spread into the safer areas until those already unraveled began unraveling the rest.

The world's biggest quandary sat over the top of that lawless ravaging. Food, water, air filtration, and shuttles all required power. Diverting power to the wall would leave people trapped without essential supplies and even more vulnerable to the tide of criminals who could tear the country apart from the inside out. If we didn't divert the power, we could be overrun by something even worse than the criminal gangs.

My communicator bleeped and I saw a message from Red.

*Put the live news on!*

I frowned and switched channels.

My communicator started buzzing as Red called me, but I dropped it, numb, in shock.

How was that possible? My brain scrambled to comprehend something that made no sense at all. Why? How?

On the screen, I watched John Tanis exiting a shuttle docked at Serenity's central government district, followed by his wolf guards... and Garren... And was that also Kein? Tanis shook hands with someone official-looking, and they continued to talk as a steady stream of shuttles landed behind them.

My mind blanked out the words, and my attention settled on the timestamp of several hours earlier, before the broadcast cut back to the studio.

I fumbled to answer my communicator.

It had been one hell of a day.

# Chapter 38

## Tanis

I was back in Rymor, with a fancy job title, a luxurious office suite, an even more luxurious apartment that was nothing short of palatial, and an army of willing bureaucrats hanging on my every word.

I was also closer to Hannah and could feel the pull on the bond; a compulsion, animalistic at the core, demanding I seek out and fuck my mate.

Only I couldn't do that yet so, needing something to numb me, I'd reached for alcohol. Her sister was dead by Bill's command, from what I could infer. I already wanted him dead, now I wanted him dead slowly. Only I couldn't go after Bill today, and it was not likely to happen tomorrow.

"This is fucked up," I said to Garren. It was six o'clock in the morning, and I was drinking high-end retro-distilled whiskey. I'd consumed a lot of it in the limited hours since I'd finished talking to Rymor's bureaucrats yesterday evening. As a result, I now needed a couple more shots to shut off the hammering in my skull. I'd only just roused, having passed out about an hour ago, and was supposed to be dealing with... something important that escaped my alcohol-infused brain.

My mind drifted back to the fantasy of strangling Bill with my bare hands, but there was a reason why I couldn't seek him out today, if only my head would stop pounding long enough for me to remember.

Jon Sanders had been sensible and left as soon as I'd ordered the whiskey, professing a desire for his own bed.

"You're not still drinking?" Theo said as he entered the apartment moments later.

The wolf guards did no more than eye him as he approached. Theo was now considered one of my people. Actually, everyone was now my people. How the fuck did that happen?

"A headache." I waved the shot glass in Theo's direction before downing the contents. "Fuck, that's smooth."

Theo made that little harrumphing noise he sometimes did and stalked off... He returned holding a scanner. "This is illegal," he said as if that made the slightest sense. "Do not tell anyone I did this." He tapped a couple of buttons. "Arm out."

I gave Theo a questioning look.

Theo's lips flattened.

"Fine. I'll humor you." I pushed my sleeve back and placed my arm on the table. It stung. I swore. But within seconds, my headache disappeared, and I was sober. A disbelieving snort escaped me. "I didn't know you could use medical scanners to remove alcohol. How did I not know that?"

"You can't," Theo said. "Officially. The feature is part of the standard device, but the manufacturer doesn't make it public knowledge." At my widening grin, his eyes narrowed. "Or everyone would be abusing it."

"I've got a bit of a headache too." Garren gave the scanner a hopeful look.

Theo sighed. "Please don't try to kill it." He pointed at the table and waited for Garren to place his arm out.

## The Master of the Switch

"I'm not stupid," Garren said, the last word coming out on a squeak as Theo activated the scanner. "That metal cleaning rat just surprised me, that's all."

Garren had taken his sword to the cleaning unit—now referred to as the metal cleaning rat—last night when it had tried to deal diligently with a spill.

Garren's eyes widened as the device did its work. "That's amazing. Better use it on the rest of them. Some are in a sorry state."

"Later," Theo said in a no-nonsense way. "Let's get down to business. We need to finalize the plan." He turned to Garren, who had settled back in his seat. "Don't you have some porn to go and watch?"

Garren squared his shoulders before muttering. "If you're planning, I'm staying."

"It's all new and interesting," I said, amused by Theo's disdain for the activities of the Shadowlanders.

"Yes, well, if you really could go blind from it half your guards would be seeking medical assistance today."

The guards and Garren had discovered the delights of the wall viewer and pay-on-demand porn. Several had commandeered the viewer room and got drunk. Garren had quit the room before it escalated. Tay was the only woman present, but they all seemed to have managed fine... And not all of them were only interested in women.

"I'm surprised you didn't join them."

Theo's face turned crimson. "They are extremely liberal and creative!"

Garren snickered, and Theo finally cracked a smile.

"Right, Scott is on his way, and you have a meeting in one hour with the temporary ruling council, followed by the mobilization debrief with your new team," Theo said, launching straight into business. "The ruling council will need an update on your approach to internal conflicts. I recorded what we covered last night... We achieved a surprising amount between escaping the senate members and you passing out."

Theo pressed his palm to the table, and a viewer slid out. Garren jumped back. "The fuck! Some warning would be nice."

"Great work, Theo, but I don't have time for a meeting." Rising, I headed for my room, kicking the nearest unconscious wolf guard, who was sprawled out on the floor. "Get up. And get everyone else up."

The guard grunted and blinked at me with bleary eyes as he dragged himself to his feet. "Theo, start using the scanner on them. I want them functioning by the time I'm ready to leave."

"Where are you going?" Theo asked, following me into my room. He stopped dead in the doorway at seeing me stripping out of my Shadowland clothes.

"I need some decent Rymorian body armor, and so will everyone here. Then I want the Rymorian army and all the Shadowlanders we brought into Rymor loaded onto shuttles." I continued dumping clothing and weapons in a pile on the bed.

"What are you doing... ah... going to do?" Theo asked, his eyes darting between the bed and me.

"Exactly what I said I would, Theo. I believe you documented it. While I'm busy with the riots, you can attend the meetings for me. I'll need someone to work the disabler, so tell your techno-guru twin to get over here, ASAP." I tossed the last of my clothing on the bed, turned around, and tried to ignore Theo's roaming eyes, "But first, I'm taking a shower." I gestured toward the door. "Close it on your way out."

# Chapter 39

**Tanis**

I made my way into the mobile command center, to the drone of shuttles. They filled the sky, ferrying Rymorian soldiers, Shadowlanders, and support personnel to the drop-off point for the beginning of the operation.

"This is going to be one giant cluster-fuck," Scott said in greeting.

"Let's hope not," I said. It had taken two hours to get everyone mobile and to the ironically named Hope Town district, which was the location for the start of the sweep. Ironic, because it was among the poorest suburbs in Serenity, with rumored ties to just about every criminal organization that vied for control of the hopeless population. More notably, perhaps, it was the widely acknowledged base of the Moiety terror organization, which was also rumored to be behind every facet of Rymor's underworld.

I didn't necessarily buy into such rumors—they had been around for enough generations for people to lose sight of where they'd begun—but they provided a convenient target for media and government alike.

The mobile command center, where I waited while the last of the troops arrived, was stuffed with a gleeful array of technology that left me in open awe. I'd always assumed that I relished the more basic allure of Shadowland, but now that I was in the thick of ancient technology again, I found I had missed it. Well, weapons and anything to do with weapons fascinated me, which extended to the command center.

I was definitely sold on the retinal viewer; I had missed those.

"Jordan is going to be pissed he wasn't invited to the party," Scott said, grinning. He had made enough cutting remarks about Jordan for me to get the picture.

"I assume you don't get along?" I asked. My new position, which I'd created myself, included oversight of every government department involved in internal or external security, the most prominent being Homeland Security, under Andrew Jordan, and Global Operations, under Scott Harding.

"You don't have to work with that asshole. I'd say he's not far short of Wilder, but that would be unfair. He's just misguided. Ask Adam, if you want a second opinion."

"We're ready." Nate poked his head into the doorway of mobile command.

"Great. Keep me updated," I called to Scott over my shoulder as I followed Nate into the beautiful, organized chaos of a military operation that'd had little time to prepare or establish common lines of approach.

I was mixing Shadowland and Rymorian forces, who harbored open hatred toward each other. I would need to keep them busy restoring order to the district if I didn't want the Scott-predicted clusterfuck to occur.

I was counting on my familiarity with blending different armies in Shadowland. Shadowlanders were accustomed to playing nicely with others during an operation. Only after did they settle scores.

The Shadowlanders were fiercely loyal to me... and completely out of their depth, while the Rymorians either didn't give a shit about me or potentially harbored hostility after I'd killed three of their

## The Master of the Switch

colleagues. I didn't care much what they thought about me so long as they did the job. Now I just had to restrain myself from killing anyone who stepped out of line and put my operation or troops, be them Rymorian or Shadowlander, in danger.

Yes, Scott was right. This was one giant clusterfuck waiting to happen.

I was comfortable banging heads if people didn't obey me, and I resented that I might need to change. Still, no one realized I couldn't shoot them. I turned to Nate. "It's time for a pre-operation pep-talk. Can you do that thing where you project me to everyone's communicator?"

"How can you not know how to do that?" Nate raised both eyebrows. "That's retinal viewer one-o-one."

I gave him a look.

Nate lifted both hands and offered a placatory and charming smile that I noticed he did a lot. "Do you have a speech?" His eyes skimmed over me as if expecting me to whip a viewer out of my combat gear—I shook my head. "No problem, it's done. Start talking when you're ready."

I walked over to the clearing that marked the front of the forces, and the crowd hushed as they noted my arrival.

"We're about to head into our first combined operation," I said. "For both Rymor and Shadowland, this is a momentous day." *I will personally maim anyone who screws it up.* "I realize there are going to be challenges." *You are going to want to kill each other and me.* "That it will take time to learn about each other and to become the cohesive team I know you can be." *I know you will never integrate, you know you will never integrate, but you will eventually be able to tolerate one another sufficiently to do your job.* "We don't have the luxury of time." *Not enough of it in this lifetime.*

"The people of Rymor don't have that time, either." *Because I blew up your power source, but you don't need to know about that.* "There is a hostile Jaru army coming for us, for you, and for the people you love." *At least I hope some of you have people you give a fuck about.* "But there won't be anyone left to save unless we can restore order within Rymor." *I'm going to let you loose on the general population, don't make me regret it.*

"You've been briefed on the weapon situation. Regulated weapons are disabled, but there could be unregulated weapons here." *The good citizens of Hope Town know how to hack a regulator, print an old-fashioned retro-gun, and, failing that, will come at you with a knife.* "We're here to protect the civilians." *You won't find many innocent civilians here, but if you do, don't shoot them!* "Try to stun first. Killing is a last resort." *The criminals here have better stun-resistant gear than the army—it's fine to shoot them.*

Time to get to the point.

"I have a reputation in Shadowland for dealing harshly with insubordination. This is Rymor, and some of you might be misguided into thinking I will change. I want to assure you that if anyone steps out of line, and puts people or the operation in danger, they will not be killed, but they will soon wish they had."

Nate blanched. *Too much?*

"We have a lot of ground to cover and no time to do it. There are going to be bad days, and days that feel infinitely worse, but by the time we have cleaned up this city and the next one and the one after that, you are going to be better men and women than you are today. We are here to deal with the people who want to rip this country apart, not each other. The bureaucrats don't think we can do it, but I know we can, and I believe in you. Stay focused and stay alert. It is time to make history. Section leaders, get your people to their positions."

A cheer went up, echoing around the surrounding area.

I made a slicing motion across my neck.

"It's off," Nate confirmed.

"That was a terrible speech," Garren said, approaching with a strange, open-legged gait.

"Why are you walking like you've shit yourself?" I eyed Garren's knee-bending antics with a frown.

## The Master of the Switch

"I hate this freakish suit. Why can't I wear my usual clothes?"

"Get used to it," I muttered.

"Other than the threat, I thought the speech was great, highly rousing," Nate said.

"Please tell me you prefer women," I said.

"Women, as opposed to what?" Nate asked, dragging his attention from Garren's continuing antics.

"Men."

"I prefer women." Nate blinked slowly. "Wait. Is this a trick question?"

I frowned. "Why would it be a trick question?"

"Because of who I'm in a relationship with... This *is* a trick question, isn't it?"

"Who are you in a relationship with?" My eyes narrowed as I drew closer to him.

"Our relationship is quite new, and she said she would talk to you about it... You haven't talked yet, have you?"

"Who. The fuck. Is it?"

"Your mother," Nate admitted.

Garren barked out a laugh. "Javid is going to crush him."

"Javid?" Nate asked.

"Our father," I said, with a wry smile.

"Ah, yes. He's not here, is he?" Nate looked over his shoulder as if anticipating the imminent arrival of the man in question.

"No, he's in Shadowland, which is lucky for you." I gave Nate a skeptical look. "My mother has diverse tastes in men." My attention shifted to Garren who was still bending his knees and pulling at the crotch of his combat suit. "Is that a weapon?"

"So, I've been—" Garren's words were cut off as I snatched his micro rifle out of its holster and shoved it at Nate.

"Who the hell gave Shadowlanders micro rifles?"

Nate gaped at it in horror and then sent a scowl my way. "Do I look like a military grunt?"

Garren chuckled. "Genius doesn't want to get his hands dirty."

He took back the weapon. "And you said we should have Rymorian weapons."

"I meant something smaller and less deadly." My cursory glance had followed the rifle as it transitioned back to Garren so I snatched it from him. *Now we're playing pass the bloody parcel!* "You've been messing with the settings, haven't you?" I turned accusing eyes toward Garren.

Garren shrugged.

"Get back to the mobile command center, we're moving out," I said to Nate. "And I want a full feed of everything that's going on."

Nate headed off, leaving me with Garren. "I know how to shoot it." Garren gave me an indignant glare. "Same as a crossbow, but more effective. Point, click, and the body explodes." He made a little motion with his fingers spreading outward while a gleeful expression lit his face.

"Nice description," I said, adjusting the setting. "It's on stun, now. Do not touch it again or I will shoot you with it myself." I reluctantly gave it back to Garren. "Don't fuck this up, Garren."

"I won't," Garren replied, appearing contrite.

"Right, let's move out."

I joined my waiting division: Garren, half of Garren's section, the same number of Rymorians, and my personal guards, who I was alarmed to note, also had Rymorian weapons. I shoved my helmet on.

"Nate," I said into my communicator, *"override all Shadowlander weapons so they're on stun. I don't trust them not to fuck around with the settings."*

*"Already done."*

Ah, communication.

*"By the way, Tanis, you, ah, broadcast that request to all the Shadowlanders."*

"Fuck!"

*"Yes, and you did it again... I've locked it. Just tell me if you want to speak to anyone else. I'm going to project the map now."*

The street view of the district superimposed itself over the real

## The Master of the Switch

street in front of me, giving the positions of my troops. I tried the hand gestures, and the image zoomed in and out. I grinned. At least I could manage that.

We moved out into Hope Town. It was going to be a trying day for everyone, and a tense one on my part. There were going to be bumps and screw-ups, but every day we delayed, thousands of people would die in the violence. It was a numbers game, except the numbers were real people. The violence wouldn't stay here, and if we didn't bring swift resolution, it would spill out into the denser city centers, and those numbers would rise.

I'd made this mess. Not the violence here, and not the Jaru. But with the wall, I'd left them vulnerable, which was ultimately the trigger.

How the fuck had I ended up here? This had to be some sort of fucked up karma.

Somewhere, far away, in a distant research base, Hannah was working to restore the power.

A shot cracked the air, followed by a barrage of PB blasts that pounded into the street and sent dust and debris raining.

It had begun.

# Chapter 40

**Talin**

**Ella**

Bill was still at Talin and had been for almost a week.
It was the longest he'd ever been here.
The grunt, as Bill referred to any of the essential workers here, had collected me first thing, and I now sat on my stool before the window while Bill continued his work overseeing the fortress transformation.

More workers had arrived yesterday morning, while this afternoon had seen the arrival of an astonishing array of supplies, which had included sacks of grains and vegetables, building supplies such as cut timber, stone, and grit and, finally, two wagons loaded with pigs.

The pigs had alarmed me, and I'd become a little queasy. No one should ever need to eat real animals; yet what else could they be for?

Damien was also back. I didn't think he'd been absent long enough to reach wherever he had been going. A location deep in the

## The Master of the Switch

Jaru plains was as much as I'd gleaned from listening to the discussions Bill had.

My memories of Damien were vague, but I thought he might have met Bill while I was still under my mindless cloud. The only meeting I recalled with clarity was to do with the final plans for a trip. Then Bill had referred to the investigative archeologist several times in conversations with Pope.

A knock on the door brought me out of my reverie and, at Bill's call to enter, Pope brought Damien into the room. At Bill's indication, they took the seats opposite his desk.

Seeing Damien again instilled a tremble in my hands. There was something about him that worried me, a dark, terrible unknown thing he had discussed with Bill long ago that I knew would terrify me if only I could remember it. I pressed my fingers together on my lap and forced my attention toward a notch on the floor. Whatever they were about to discuss, I must show no reaction.

"Nice to have you back, Damien," Bill said.

Pope, I noticed, had seated himself in such a way that I would be on the periphery of his vision. He was acting odd and had taken to locking me into my room at night, or even during the day if Bill was absent, ever since that day when I'd let my mask slip.

"The shuttle made the return journey swift, and I must say with everything that's been going on, I was quite surprised about that," Damien said.

His tone was a little sharp, and I sent a surreptitious glance Bill's way to check for a reaction.

"Precisely why we decided to escalate the matter," Bill replied. I'd spent enough time around Rymor's chancellor to know Damien had pissed him off. "You had contact with a Jaru tribe? An Outlier?"

"Yes." Damien fidgeted, as though sensing Bill's underlying mood. "It was after we entered the ship. We were able to access the main sections and now we have a full plan of the structure. Several chambers remain locked, but we did restore limited power and were able to find its identification. I've collaborated on each reference and

I can confirm it's one of the three sister ships that brought the first Rymorians here…"

Damien's words trailed off, and I glanced up to find Bill staring at Damien with tight-lipped, simmering anger. The room became deathly quiet. "The master switch?" Bill asked.

My body flooded with adrenaline. The master switch? He had talked of that before. I was sure of it. There must be lots of master switches. Yet my thoughts went straight to *the* master switch that the doomsday theorists touted would bring about the end of days.

A chair creaked as someone shifted. My heart began pounding as a sense of apprehension washed through me.

"It wasn't there on the ship," Damien continued, "but, while we were searching, the Outliers arrived." His laugh was a little high and nervous. "We thought they were going to kill us. Then they said they had the device we were seeking and wanted to exchange for it."

"I'm guessing you didn't simply kill them and take it," Bill said dryly. "What did you give them?"

Damien's chair creaked again. "None of us were comfortable killing innocent people, nor leaving them with the switch, assuming it was real. They asked for a transmitter. It seemed like a harmless compromise."

"And *did* they?" Bill asked. "Did they have it?"

There was a long pause during which my nerves rose.

"Yes, we brought it back, as you asked. But I'm uncomfortable with this. This isn't Rymor. It needs to be secured. It could destroy us all!" Damien's voice rose high and hysterical. "You're talking about the Armageddon switch. The end of days!"

A chair thumped to the floor, and I looked up. Pope's sword flashed, blood sprayed, and Damien crumpled to the floor.

I screamed, a long terrible sound that continued until someone slapped my face. It shocked the scream from me, but I shook so violently that my teeth rattled, and my bones felt like they would break apart. Pope stood over me, a bloody sword in one hand, the other palm open from where he had struck me.

## The Master of the Switch

My ears rang from the blow, and I panted for breath.

"What a mess," Bill said. "Could you not have just strangled him or snapped his neck?"

Pope glanced over his shoulder at Bill, his body still blocking my view. "You told me to kill him. If you wanted specifics, you should've said how."

I started rocking back and forth, shivering and rubbing my arms.

"Take her back to her room, get someone in here to clean this up, and find out where the fuck he put it before someone stumbles upon it."

I flinched back as Pope wrapped his fingers around my arm, but his grip was tight, and he hauled me off the stool.

"His team?" Pope asked, his body blocking my view of the dead man.

There was a lengthy pause.

"Yes," Bill said, wearily. "You'll need to get rid of them too."

Pope dragged me out of the room, barking orders to the men who stood outside that sent them scurrying. He hustled me down the corridors to my room. "I wish you hadn't seen that, but when Bill gives an order, you do it, if you don't want to end up dead yourself. You already knew that, though, didn't you, Ella?"

Confused, shaking, and barely able to grasp what was being said and what had been done, I blinked up at him. Pope was a monster. I'd suspected as much. He was just like Bill, and now he had killed someone.

"I can't let you do something stupid, Ella." He opened the door and shoved me inside. It slammed shut on me a moment later, and the key turned in the lock.

# Chapter 41

## Rymor

### Tanis

It had been a day of successes and failures, but we were close to completing the Hope Town operation. Given the late start and newness of collaboration, it went as well as expected.

It was late, and we were about to sweep the last building for the day. Farther down the street, supplies were being organized for those homes without printer connections. It amazed me that, despite Rymor's advancement, people lived without basic amenities. Hope Town was a desperate place.

Most teams had returned to the base where the Shadowland and Rymor forces would stay until order was established. There were dangers in keeping them together during the day and then again for rest periods, but there was also an opportunity for them to bond. Hopefully, they were too tired to brawl.

On the whole, while there had been plenty of casualties, no

## The Master of the Switch

serious incidents had occurred. I considered it a success and was proud of what we had achieved.

"It's a bit tight, still," Garren muttered, under his breath. He stood on my left, still tugging at the crotch of his armor. "Is Danel on point with you tomorrow?"

"No, it's you," I replied, coming to the realization that, after our many years of altercations, I enjoyed having him around. Han, while effective, was conventional, and Danel could be downright depressing when he was in one of his doom and gloom moods. Garren, in all his crotch-adjusting glory, was never boring to be around. And we were tied together now, in ways that went beyond being brothers. I could have done a lot worse.

With hindsight, it had turned out well.

"We're ready to take the last building, sir. The south entrance teams are in place."

I nodded my thanks to the Rymorian man by the unfortunate name of Godfrey. Unfortunate, because his subordinates referred to him playfully as Captain God. Godfrey had clearly reached an impasse about dealing with it, yet suffered poorly disguised irritation every time one of his team said it.

Standing beside Captain God was a tall Rymorian woman who was God's second in command. She had the kind of muscular, curvy figure that made the form-fitting Rymorian battle fatigues appear borderline obscene. Garren's second in command, Alid, had been staring at her ass most of the day in uncensored admiration. From the heated looks she was sending his way, I got the impression that she would either thump him or jump him.

The doors of the building we were about to sweep had been hacked and hung open, emitting the sounds of gunfire, PB fire, screams, and general chaos.

The only good thing about Hope Town was the small stature of its buildings. The elevators were disabled as part of the curfew, meaning stairs were the only way up or down. Not that an elevator was practical for sweeping a building, but it might have helped for the return. This building was a snip at thirty stories. I'd spent most of the day running up and down stairs with the occasional burst of action between. I was well-practiced at riding, walking, and even running, when necessary and could handle the six flights of stairs to my room at the fortress at Thale. This many, I could not.

My thighs and calves had gone numb hours ago, and I wasn't alone in dosing myself with stimulants.

"I hate stairs," Garren grouched as he entered the building. The rest of us followed behind.

We started at the bottom, clearing each room on each floor on our way to the top. We dealt with trouble as it unfolded. Perpetrators, whether conscious, unconscious, or dead, were dragged back down.

Garren had suggested throwing the dead ones out the window to save time.

Yeah, I liked Garren more every day.

We covered the first dozen floors without incident. From there on, it was a hard slog.

The door on our right thrust open, and a man emerged, ranting at us about a myriad of government failings that stretched from now back to his birth, which distracted me as a door on our left burst open, and all hell broke loose.

A pulse beam blast slammed me into the corridor wall, and while my suit soaked up much of the explosion, it was still a skull-rattling blow.

"Nice timing," I grunted between gasps for breath.

As I staggered to my feet, Garren shot the man with his micro rifle. The perpetrator must have been wearing stun resistant wear because all it did was slow him. In true Garren style, he drew his sword and hacked the attacker down. The two Rymorians with us dived back as blood arced across the walls.

More people spilled out like ants from a disturbed colony. I called for backup to the floor we were on, just as two thugs rushed me. I fired. One man went down, but another rammed me, and we grappled before I got a lock on his neck sufficient to snap it. Another of

## The Master of the Switch

the thugs had grabbed the discarded PB rifle, and used it to blast Garren to the floor. I shot the man and snatched up his weapon before anyone else could.

Garren, meanwhile, lay sprawled out and winded on the floor. A thug had knocked Garren's helmet off and was smashing his elbow into his face.

I yanked the thug off, put my gun to the side of his head, and pressed, splattering the corridor and Garren in an unwholesome soup of brain, blood, and bone.

Garren grunted in disgust as he heaved himself from the floor. "You took your fucking time." He wiped his fingers over his face, spreading the gore, snatched his helmet from the floor, and shoved it back on.

The support units arrived, so I stood back as they surged in to take the room in a heady rush of PB fire and screams of terror.

I glanced at Garren, still winded, propped myself against the wall beside him, and burst out laughing.

"What?" Garren demanded.

"The zombie apocalypse has arrived," I quipped.

"What's a zombie apocalypse?" Garren asked.

"I'll show you on the wall viewer you're so enamored with later," I said. A thug tried to flee the room. I shot him. He exploded. I inspected my rifle. "Hmm, I think the setting is too high."

"Zombies? That a porn thing?"

"No." I laughed. "Although, now you mention it, I'm pretty sure someone will have broached that cross-genre abomination." I patted Garren's shoulder. "Stick with the porn."

Captain God hurried over. "We've cleared the room, sir!" He did a double-take at Garren before taking a rapid step back. "Does he need medical assistance?" he asked me.

"Weapon malfunction," I said.

"Operator malfunction," Garren corrected.

"Right, let's finish the building and call it a day," I said. Thugs, now subdued and in restraints, began filing out of the room under escort.

We covered the remaining floors, meeting the occasional scuffle, until we were done.

I made the official announcement that Hope Town was back under control.

Weary feet took us back to where the shuttles waited. Relief forces jogged past us, heading in to patrol and maintain the hard-won peace. Ahead, a shuttle took to the sky, and Captain Godfrey and our team loaded up into the next.

*"The council of twelve, as they have now been named by the media, have arranged a meeting so you can debrief them,"* Theo communicated. He was in my fancy office, and his image was displayed directly through my retinal viewer. His face was flushed, and his hair in disarray.

"Had a bad day?" I asked dryly.

*"They're waiting for you to get here,"* Theo said. *"Eager to find out how today progressed."*

"I bet they are," I muttered, as happy thoughts of collapsing into bed with a bottle of retro-distilled whiskey slipped away. I should have taken the job they'd offered me. I really wasn't cut out for following orders or explaining myself.

On second thoughts, what were they going to do? I grinned as I joined Garren and my guards, who were piling into a shuttle. *"Tell Harding to give them an update. I'll talk to them in the morning,"* I replied to Theo. Then added, *"If I get the time."*

*"They were specifically asking for you."* Theo raked his fingers through his messy hair.

*"I know, but better if we set precedents right from the start. I'll see you in the morning."* I closed the communication and took my helmet off.

Garren cast a baleful look around the shuttle as he sat down. "What's with the grin?" he asked.

## The Master of the Switch

I sat beside Garren. "The leaders here were asking me for an update."

Garren grinned. "That's not going to work out too well for them then."

"No," I said, and my grin became all teeth. I'd just had an excellent idea about how to solve the problem of the temporary ruling council.

# Chapter 42

**Richard**

I wasn't a morning person by any stretch of the imagination. It was early, a time when I should have still been asleep. But much to my irritation, I was up and about.

Yesterday, my fourth wife had filed for divorce. It hadn't been the best of days.

She had left last night under a cloud of drama, taking off to stay with her sister, who lived on the outskirts of Tranquility. I couldn't say I was sorry to see her leave. Our relationship had been troubled for months, and my mind had been elsewhere for most of that time. When I had been present, mentally, I'd been cognizant that our lives had been drifting apart in a way that felt like I'd been slowly waking up.

I was awake now to the discord in my personal relationship and the troubles at large.

The council of twelve, which I was part of, were demanding answers, and Scott Harding was a poor substitute for the man they wanted. So far, Scott was all they had got.

My shuttle set down on the landing pad of Serenity Tower, one

## The Master of the Switch

of the most prestigious addresses in Rymor, and, under escort, I made my way to the apartment where John Tanis resided.

There were two guards standing shoulder to shoulder outside the door. They were wearing Shadowland armor—and swords! I was so confronted by this that I stopped dead, and one of my escorts plowed into my back.

I squared my shoulders and approached the door as confidently as I could. The guards regarded me through narrowed eyes, then the one on the left turned to rap his knuckles against the door.

What was the significance of knocking on the door?

The right-hand guard nudged the one on the left, who scowled back before turning and pressing the door communicator plate. The door opened a second later.

"You can't leave a senator waiting out here!" Theo said.

The two guards shuffled apart far enough to allow me to squeeze between them into the doorway, before they closed the gap on my escorts.

"Perhaps wait out here," I said, fearing a physical altercation would ensue. "Maybe return to the shuttle." The two opposing sides continued to glare at one another. "I will send a message when I'm ready to leave."

My escorts left with poorly disguised reluctance, while Tanis' men puffed up. The door closed behind me, and I turned back to the room... and nearly walked into a blond giant I recognized as John Tanis' brother.

"Everything alright out there?" Garren asked Theo.

"Yeah, they're fine," Theo replied. For an average sized man, Theo appeared child-like next to Garren, who wore full-body Rymorian combat gear, incongruously matched with a sword. "They're still a little enthusiastic."

The suite was bustling with Shadowlanders. I estimated a dozen people in various degrees of readiness; either eating, drinking, or loading up with weapons.

From the other side of the room, Tanis, as he preferred to be called, stepped out of a bedroom.

"Please get dressed," Theo said.

He sounded a little panicky.

Garren chuckled.

Why did Garren chuckle?

"I wasn't expecting visitors." Tanis glanced between Theo and me.

He wasn't actually undressed but only wore the bottom half of his combat suit, leaving the top hanging from his waist. He boasted an impressive physique, but I still felt like I was missing something.

"Richard, Theo, to what do I owe this pleasure?" Tanis held a microfiber under-vest in his hand, which he pulled over his head.

"I came to warn you that Richard was coming." Theo's eyes softened in apology. "Which didn't work, obviously, and Garren wouldn't wake you for me."

Garren grinned. "I told Theo to do it himself."

He found the oddest things amusing.

"Ah." Tanis also grinned before he turned back to me. "Richard, how can I help you?"

"The council wished to talk to you." I decided on a direct approach. "They convened this morning."

"I'm aware they want to talk to me," Tanis replied, tiredly, approaching a table littered with a frightening array of weapons. "Constantly." He shrugged into the top half of his suit and began clipping it shut. "That's why I've decided to activate martial law."

Garren frowned. "What's martial law?"

"It's similar to the way I took over Shadowland except I don't need to kill anyone and it happens a lot quicker."

"The council won't agree to that," I said, frowning while trying to ignore the many weapons Tanis was strapping onto, and plugging into, his clothing.

"Richard, yesterday was a long, hellish experience. I collapsed into bed late, exhausted after ascending and descending the equiva-

## The Master of the Switch

lent of a small mountain's worth of stairs, being shot at point-blank range by PB rifles, and slugged by an inventive array of home furnishings and fists." Tanis selected a couple of smaller knives, weighed them up, and then slotted them into his ever-growing arsenal. "Today will be more of the same in a new district. I'm not looking forward to the inevitable death by stairs or coffee table. I relish the prospect of the council of twelve grilling me even less."

"They just want to be consulted." I felt terrible now.

"I guess the quicker I set expectations, the quicker I can get on with the minor matter of quelling the rioting."

"You're going to talk to them?" I was torn between hope that I'd achieved my goal and concern that Tanis wasn't joking about declaring martial law.

"Yes, let's get this over with." He turned to Garren. "Take this lot to the next drop point and I'll meet you there." He turned to Theo. "I'll update you later."

With that, he marched over to the door. I hurried to follow.

His guards stepped back as the door opened and they made to follow him. "I'm fine!" Tanis snapped.

Disapproving grumbles could be heard as the men returned to their posts.

We made our way to the roof with disconcerting speed, startling my escorts, who scurried to prepare. Within minutes, we had landed again at State Tower, where a forewarned temporary ruling council had assembled to greet us.

"You can't go in there with weapons!" I exclaimed, still hurrying to keep pace.

Tanis didn't pause to acknowledge the words, nor did the security personnel outside the council room offer more than a cursory suggestion that they might impede his progress. If there was an art to looking like you owned the world, Tanis was the master.

Inside, the council members sat in a neat row of eleven. I hurried over to join them, my breathing elevated, feeling like I had just completed a speed-walking challenge.

Tanis was dressed for the day ahead in Rymorian battle fatigues, with weapons strapped to every possible location on his person. My fellow councilors were already regarding him warily when his opening line, "I'm declaring martial law," produced mutters of dismay.

I cringed.

"Who gave you the right to come in here and make declarations about obscure ancient laws?" one member demanded.

"You did," Tanis replied. "I'm the highest-ranking military officer, every major city is on the brink of collapse, and I don't have the time to pop over here to explain myself to a bunch of egotistical bureaucrats out of touch with reality."

I thought the 'egotistical' comment was going too far, but Grace Claridge quickly recovered.

"Two days ago, you refused the leadership position," Grace said mildly. "And now you are proposing to claim it via martial law. This doesn't make any sense."

"This isn't working." He gestured toward us. "I'm not well-versed in answering to people, and you have the whole committee thing going on. Twelve people cannot make effective decisions at the best of times, and this isn't the best of times."

"Everyone has to be accountable to someone, Tanis," Grace continued, unfazed. "You are accountable to us, and we are accountable to the people of Rymor."

He shrugged. "Not anymore. Not today. You're not in a position to negotiate this—or indeed to negotiate anything. Our situation is desperate. We don't have time to play nicely with criminals or give them a stern talking to about their nefarious ways. If they offer anything but compliance, they are going to die."

Mutters of outrage followed, but none of them were loud.

"I know what I'm doing. We need to park Rymorian ethics until we bring the lawless few to order. It worked well yesterday, but we have many days ahead before Rymor can claim stability. I shouldn't be here now. The teams have begun moving out for today's operation,

## The Master of the Switch

and I am better placed there where I can manage things on the ground. Once we have a few days behind us, perhaps I can afford to step back and leave it to the section leaders. We've mashed two opposing forces together. Expecting them to work seamlessly is a stretch. There will be the occasional bump."

"We do need a method of communication," I said. My fellow council members showed differing degrees of acceptance that stretched from outright disdain to reluctant agreement when no alternative was available.

"I'll give an update through Theo Gilmore."

"Who is not yet a recognized human," I said with a small smile.

"Who is soon to be recognized as human," Tanis countered.

"Who is soon to be recognized as human," I agreed. "On the condition that Dan Gilmore does not create any more!"

"That's between you and Dan, but I'm glad we're all in agreement." Tanis smiled without much warmth. "Soon, this will be over, and Rymor will be safe once more."

And with that said, he turned and left.

# Chapter 43

**Sirius**

It hadn't gone to plan.

"Well, that was a fucking disaster," Mac said, pacing.

The stark, windowless room held only a single desk, a few battered chairs, and a cot against one wall. The labyrinth beneath Rymor ran far and deep. It had been used on many occasions over the eons of Moiety operations. We had often retreated here during the ebbs and flows of our struggle. I hadn't envisioned us fleeing here, though, not on my watch.

I'd thought this was our time, but perhaps I'd been wrong. Reece was dead, and most of his former gang were also dead or had been taken into custody. Reece hadn't been a man blessed with intellect, but still, his loss was inconvenient. There was no second in command to take over since that man was also dead, and the remnants of the Reeper gang had imploded into anarchy.

"I thought you said they would fold?" Mac continued to pace. "This isn't folding. This is them grabbing us by the balls and twisting."

I sighed. "These are unprecedented circumstances. No one

## The Master of the Switch

suspected the Shadowlanders might unite with Rymor. That you resisted as well as you did is testament to the weapons I provided. Without them, you would likely be dead by now. You know this to be true."

Mac sneered but offered no dispute.

"The Shadowlanders have been pragmatic in dealing with resistance." I wondered if the members of the government were even aware of the unethical actions of those enlisted to restore order. They must do, I decided. After all, the Shadowlanders had Rymorian soldiers with them. "Rymor's new temporary ruling council has made some bold moves. The sudden absence of the former leader and the arrival of the Jaru has led to these interesting developments."

"Interesting? Sons of bitches aren't afraid to take a hit. Most Rymorians run for cover at the sight of a pulse beam rifle, but blasting a Shadowlander just gets the bastards all riled up."

Yes, it was all very inconvenient.

Mac brought his pacing to a halt, snatched up a dilapidated metal chair resting beside the wall, and set it down opposite me. "So, what're we gonna to do about it?" The chair creaked as he lowered his big body into it.

"They have opened up the district again, so we'll need to regroup. Their continuing presence here is a concern, and we should do nothing to raise suspicion. Other troubles are brewing. The Jaru are on their way and Rymor still has no wall. There will be more opportunities."

Mac produced a crooked smile and shrugged. "With Reece gone it opens an opportunity for me. Someone needs to pick up his slack or they'll turn Hope Town into a war zone worse than it already is. His existing service is folding, and his dealers are turning on each other. I've had a few approach me. Can you get me supplies?"

I nodded. "It will take a little adjustment, but yes, I can get you drugs. I've had to relocate a few labs underground, but once I can get the raw material, they will begin producing again. No one has interfered in Hope Town for many years. I'd become complacent; we all had... I'll need some help with the supplies."

Mac ghosted a smile. "I think we should renegotiate our partnership."

"We don't have a partnership," I said resignedly, aware of the direction this was going.

"No, we don't, but we should." Mac sat back in his chair, looking steadily at me.

I reluctantly conceded. "Perhaps it's time we did." I was out of options for now. If life had taught me anything, it was to be patient. "There's someone I need you to acquire for me."

"Someone?" Mac raised an eyebrow.

"Yes, a young woman, girl really; she's thirteen. She's important to the Jaru leader. I've been watching her for a while. If we have her, we potentially have control of the Jaru."

Mac's chair screeched as he shifted. "That's pretty fucking big. Where is she?"

"A guest of your counterpart in Tranquility. Originally, she was held in a less questionable environment, but it would seem she is an unusual type of girl."

"Yeah? Unusual how?"

"She's part Shadowlander and has the warrior gene."

Mac burst out laughing.

"Yes, she's quite the star in the making. I was satisfied to leave her there, but much of Tranquility's underworld has been compromised by Shadowland's arrival. I've not heard anything from my contacts there. Rumors suggest his employees are in disarray and infighting has prevailed. It's good you're picking up from Reece's demise. We can't afford that kind of disruption here."

Mac shook his head and gave a disparaging huff. "Never saw myself becoming a drug kingpin. Don't touch that shit myself, and I don't tolerate it from my employees. But you're right, we can't leave a vacuum. Never know who's going to step up. And as much as Reece pissed me off, he played it straight."

## The Master of the Switch

"He did," I agreed.

"There are other drug suppliers, but their product is poor compared to yours. If we flood the market they'll fold," Mac said.

"You've suddenly become an expert?" I raised a brow.

"I've watched Reece make that move a time or two. And cheap drugs encourage new business. It's a win-win. If I'm going to take over his operation, I'm going to do it right." Mac stood. "I've got to go. Send me the details of that girl you're looking for. I've still got a few contacts in Tranquility. Not sure for how much longer—that city's in a worse state than us—but I'll see what I can do."

We left the meeting at that; Mac, to head back to the Loopers' base in Hope Town's southern slums, and me to update my people within our base in the tunnels. Out in Shadowland, the master was closing in on Ailey, and that meeting might change the dynamics of the war yet again.

# Chapter 44

**Hannah**

The research facility where the ancient technology experts now resided was located in the middle of nowhere. Given the unrest in Rymor and the essential nature of our work, the council of twelve had elected to relocate everyone with ancient technology knowledge, along with our immediate families, to the site.

I was grateful to receive leeway for Nicholas and my nephews. Nicholas had been reluctant to leave his home and disrupt the boys further, but I'd convinced him that it was temporary. I could focus on my work more easily knowing they were here. Until we resolved the immediate power situation or the Jaru returned to the plains, my concerns for their safety remained.

The main work area was buried in a sprawling basement complex. Above ground was a similarly spread out collection of apartments, facilities, and supporting research labs. Since its original purpose was to house researchers and their families, it handled the influx of people and soon resembled a small community.

"What am I going to do with you, hmm?"

### The Master of the Switch

"I was just resting my eyes," I mumbled as Red lifted me into his arms. I had fallen asleep at my workstation, not for the first time.

"Yeah?" He chuckled. "Nate called me, said your snoring was getting on his nerves."

"I did say that," Nate offered helpfully.

I pried one eye open to glare at him. Nate didn't need to sleep, which I discovered was because he wasn't human.

Theo also wasn't human.

Yes, it had been one big barrage of revelations since I'd returned.

"I can walk!" Thank goodness it was empty here, so no one could see me being carried out like some fay princess.

"That was a weak protest at best," Nate said, smirking. "She wants to be carried."

"Fine, carry me." I could admit this was nice. "See you tomorrow, Nate."

"See you tomorrow," he called after us.

"Where's Molly?" I asked as we entered the elevator.

"With Coco." Red dipped me so I could press the button, and the elevator rose. "I think she secretly likes looking after Molly. Like a personal challenge."

I snickered. "She's not that bad."

"She really is," Red countered. The elevator opened, and he carried me out into the corridor of the personnel quarters. "But she's also a wonder, and fun, and life is never dull when she's around... hit the door plate for me."

The door swished open and shut on us.

"Wanna eat?"

I shook my head. "No, I ate at my desk. Take me to bed, please."

He did, lowering me onto the bed and undressing us both before slipping in beside me.

I sighed.

This was nice, wrapped up in his arms, where I could breathe and forget the world was still turning.

"Stop thinking," Red said, nuzzling the side of my throat. "Just be in the moment with me."

A knock sounded on the door.

"Is someone knocking on the door?" I asked, confused.

Red's head lifted. "It's a..."

He scrambled off the bed with more energy than I could begin to muster.

I frowned after him, then set my head back down on the pillow.

I was about to try to sleep when I heard voices, and something prickled under my skin, a soul-deep awareness blooming, setting goosebumps across my skin. Pushing the covers aside, I stumbled out of bed and ran, only to collide with a wall in the form of human flesh.

"Uff!"

"Steady!" He purred.

I tried to climb him, purring manically in turn, wanting to smother myself in Garren's scent. He picked me up, and I wrapped my arms and legs around him and buried my nose against his throat.

Was he wearing a t-shirt? Why was the thought of Garren wearing Rymorian clothes so hot?

Red chuckled. "I think she's pleased to see you."

I was nuzzling the side of Garren's throat, but my head popped up. I glared between Red and Garren. "I am not pleased to see him," I lied.

∼

## Garren

"Yeah, you are."

As my eyes locked with Hannah's, I thought she was going to argue with me. Instead, she buried her nose in the crook of my neck and bit.

"Fuck!" That fast, blood pounded into my already hard dick. I

# The Master of the Switch

didn't care about the consequences of anything besides knotting her and reminding her she was mine.

"Bed?" I barked out.

Red snickered. "Though there."

I stalked past him with my naked mate in my arms. She was getting needy, peppering kisses all over my throat and across my jaw, trying to hump herself against me.

I came to a stop. "Fuck! I'm going to bust that bed." Not that I cared about the bed, but it might interfere with the fucking, which I *did* care about.

"Rymor makes things sturdier than they look," Red said.

When I glanced over my shoulder, he was standing in the doorway naked. My eyes lowered to where his cock bobbed before lifting to meet his gaze. Things had gotten a little wild at one point during her heat.

Was he thinking about that?

He swallowed.

My lips tugged up. Yeah, he was thinking about that.

"Better find some oil. This is going to be a two-man job."

"*Fuck!* It's called lube here." He stalked off, I presumed to get some oil or lube, whatever the fuck they called it.

My attention remained focused on the omega in my arms, who shamelessly rubbed her wet pussy all over my t-shirt as she nipped at my throat.

"God, please, Garren. I need to feel you inside me, right now."

I took her down on the bed, fisted her hair, and closed my mouth over hers. Our tongues tangled. Her manic purr turned to a moan and she tugged at my t-shirt.

I dragged my lips from hers long enough to rip the t-shirt over my head and toss it to the floor. Boots were kicked off as I dived in for another kiss. I fumbled with my belt buckle, managing to free it, and shucked my pants down far enough for my aching cock to spring free.

"Please!"

Her small hands were on my ass, pulling me in, her legs spread wide around me. Her little whimpering sounds shifted to a deep, guttural cry as I snagged her pussy entrance and sank deep.

I heaved a breath, my vision narrowing as though coming through a tunnel.

Bracing my arm under her ass for leverage, I pounded into her. It took a dozen strokes for me to reach the point of no return. She came, squeezing lovingly over me, her head tipped back on a squeal. I followed her over, hot seed jetting into her silken cunt, filling her deeply as she spasmed over me.

Her arms and legs wrapped around me, holding me close like there was a chance I would disappear, as my lips sought the junction of her shoulder and throat. I bit over the claiming mark and sucked hard, and her pussy clamped down over me, sucking another hot splash of seed from me.

Perfect. Every single thing about her was perfect. This tiny omega clinging to me was my beginning and end.

When I could find my wits, I realized Red was standing in the doorway staring at us.

"Sorry," I said. "It got a bit out of hand."

"At least I didn't embarrass myself and come," he said dryly.

I chuckled.

"Do you, ah, still want the lube?"

Her pussy fisted my cock.

"Hannah says yes."

"She didn't say a word," he said, closing in on us. As I rolled onto my side, he settled behind Hannah. She turned to share a lusty kiss with him, her pussy fluttering all over my cock in a way that set a weak jet of cum gushing.

"Her pussy did the talking."

He chuckled against her lips. "Thank fuck. I've been dreaming about this."

He slathered up his cock to be ready and fingered her ass while we waited for my knot to soften. We took her slow and easy, getting her used to being with both of us again, to the fullness. The feeling of

## The Master of the Switch

her tight pussy around my dick as Red fucked her ass had me gritting my teeth long before she started clawing at my back and urging us for more.

"This feels so good," Red said. "Come for us, Hannah. Come, baby, I'm not going to last."

She did, her pussy fisting me in a way that had me seeing stars. I kept my knot outside, squeezing it roughly as I shot cum into her pussy as Red filled her ass.

Red eased out with a grunt, staggered from the bed, and went to get a cloth to clean her up before taking a quick shower.

I felt the instant her mood changed. The light and bright happiness that had surged to my side of the bond suddenly went quiet. I tipped her chin and her solemn eyes met mine.

"Did you hear about my sister?"

"Yeah." I pulled her close and purred. "I did, and I'm so sorry." Tanis had already wanted Bill dead. Now, I wanted him dead, too, slowly.

"Where's Tanis?" she asked quietly.

"He has a lot of important people vying for his time."

Her lips trembled.

"You worried about him or you think he doesn't care?"

"Both."

"He's just overseeing the operation," I lied. He was probably in the thick of it, but he could handle himself, and she didn't need the details. She blinked back tears, and I wanted to thump the stupid fuck all over again. He'd been right to send her away. The way he'd gone about it, not so much. Even as I tried to blame him, I knew deep down that Hannah wouldn't have gone without a fight. "He cares, Hannah. He just fucked up. We all do, sometimes."

I purred, and she settled some. I couldn't allay her fears, that was down to Tanis getting his head out of his ass. I hadn't told him I was coming here tonight. Instead, I'd gone behind his back and spoken to Theo. As I'd sat on the couch of his fancy apartment with a beer in my hand, I'd asked myself what the fuck I was doing. I hadn't slept properly even one night since Hannah had left. All I did was fight, drink, pass out, wake up and repeat.

A part of me hoped that when Tanis came back, he would find out, and be pissed enough to finally do what he should have done the moment he first stepped foot in Rymor—acknowledge Hannah as his mate. That was Tanis, though, always trying to do the right thing. I wasn't a leader, suffered no pressure or expectations, and was free to fuck up and make mistakes.

Well, fuck leadership. Who wanted it anyway? Being a leader took him elsewhere while I was here with Hannah.

Pulling back from responsibility wasn't easy, I got that. He was locked on a path without sign of escape. If he did, her country and ours would be even worse. They needed someone, and Tanis was that someone. Only the reality was that he'd paid his dues a thousand times over and didn't owe Rymor or Shadowland a damn thing.

I was twenty-five and had never once thought about a mate. I definitely hadn't expected the complex situation I found with Tanis, Red, and Hannah. But here we were, and none of us were about to quit. I'd been fifteen and full of attitude when Tanis had turned up at the gates of Luka with an army, after clashes with our men. I'd thought him an arrogant bastard at the time and had wanted to run him through. Later, when we'd found ourselves on the brink of war, I discovered he was my half-brother and over time realized he was more self-assured than arrogant.

My older brothers had all been maniacs. Tanis, while ruthless, was also calm. I gravitated toward him once I'd gotten over my jealousy, because it was fucking obvious that Javid loved him. Javid clashed with Tanis. I clashed with Tanis too. But I still wanted to be near him and the crazy shit he was doing as he took control of Shadowland.

I purred deeper, drawing Hannah closer to me.

It had hurt so fucking much when he'd drawn his sword on me, ready to fucking kill me after rutting Hannah behind my back.

I'd asked myself if he would have followed through, and the truth

## The Master of the Switch

was, I didn't know. Yet how could I judge him when I'd been ready to kill him, too? Yeah, I loved him and all his fucking faults, which was why I'd sheathed my sword.

The bathroom door opened, and Red stood with a towel at his waist, all uncertainty. He was an easy man to like, even-tempered for the most part, although he'd fucked up with Hannah, like we all had. He also had a tight fucking ass and got off on being dominated. My dick was already in love. I smirked.

"We need to distract her." I shifted out of bed and stalked over to Red. "And I'm going to need some of that lube stuff."

Red's face darkened as I collared the back of his neck and ripped the towel away.

"Open your legs, Hannah. Red's going to clean your filthy pussy all up."

"I don't have a cloth," Red muttered, making like he was going back into the bathroom.

"I know. You're going to use your tongue."

He wasn't fighting as I pushed him forward. Hannah was panting, and the bond buzzed with her arousal.

"You've come in her." He glared over his shoulder at me.

"That a problem?"

He swallowed. His dick was bobbing wildly, so I would call bullshit if he said yes.

"No."

"Good, get to it." I slapped his ass.

Hannah giggled—distraction from Tanis' bullshit achieved—then gasped as Red buried his head between her thighs.

Now, wasn't that a pretty sight. Sweet, filthy little omega spread out, fisting Red's hair as he licked up all our mess. I guessed Hannah wasn't the only cum junkie.

I grabbed the lube, squirted out a generous amount, and slathered my dick. Squeezed some more over my fingers and stuffed two of them into his ass.

He huffed against her pussy. Hannah tightened her grip on his hair, not liking me distracting him from tending to her. I was a little rough about it because his muffled groans and squeezing ass said he liked it, a lot. "You're going to take my dick in here soon, get used to it."

His fingers turned white where he had closed them over her thighs. He grunted as I lined up and sank my cock head into his tight ass, setting him clenching over me like he was trying to snatch me in.

"Relax."

I palmed his ass and spread him. The lube made it a sweet glide home into his hot, tight ass. He shuddered and twitched when I hit the sweet spot.

"Keep eating her out," I grunted. My dick bottomed out at the knot. Reaching around, I closed my fingers over his dick. He jerked and muttered a curse as his ass crushed my dick.

"I don't need to be gentle with you, so I won't. Make sure she gets off."

I fucked him, hard, deep strokes, while he grunted, huffed, and ate her out like he was starving. I liked this, being in control, dominating them and watching as they enjoyed it. The bond pulsed with pleasure, theirs and mine, lifting all of us higher, letting me know when I found that rhythm that sent Red twitching. It all felt like heaven to me, the image of Hannah spread and tended, the beta male stuffed full of my cock, and the silken, tight on the cusp of pain pleasure as I reamed his ass.

I had him stick his dick in her before he blew his load, and I filled up his ass as he filled Hannah and she squealed out her release.

As the two of them collapsed together, barely conscious, I went and cleaned up. She clung to me when I returned and told her I needed to leave. Everything inside me went fucking haywire. The bond, which had been sparking with pleasure while we fucked, now grew cold and sharp. "I'll be back, Hannah, I promise. And when Tanis finds out, he won't be able to stop himself from coming over too."

Red looked forlorn as he drew her against his chest.

That was the image I took with me as I walked out the door.

## Hannah

It was still dark outside when my alarm woke me up. The bond thrummed after Garren's visit, contented, yet also bruised that he'd left and sore at Tanis' absence.

Red groaned and tightened his arm around me. "You're not getting enough sleep."

I snorted a laugh. "Neither of us got enough sleep last night."

"True," he muttered. "I've got patrol today and I'm not going to be walking straight."

I wriggled over to face him. "Have you ever been with a man before?" Dawn was breaking beyond the window; it was just light enough to see his face flush.

"Before Garren?"—I nodded—"No."

I bit my lip to hide my smile. "But you like it?"

"Hannah, can we not have this conversation early in the morning when my mental vigilance is weak?"

"You like it," I said confidently, feeling his dick kick against my thigh.

"Fine, I like it," he groaned against my throat. "Just not all the time because while it seriously feels amazing, it's also like he's rearranging my innards. Now, I need to get ready."

He pecked a kiss against my forehead and climbed out of bed.

"Red."

He looked back from the door to the bathroom.

"I like that you like it."

"Filthy omega," he said, wiggling his eyebrows.

I left my apartment with a large coffee in my hand after visiting with Coco and Molly.

Nate and Dan were already busy when the elevator door opened onto the basement. The days since returning to Rymor had been a constant bombardment of revelations. None of these revelations had been quite as meteoric as Tanis' return from exile.

Once upon a time, I'd loved watching the news. Now I avoided it, partly because I had been in the news since the story of our return broke, but mainly because of Tanis.

He was the most interesting thing to happen to Rymor since we'd lost the station. Everyone in the research center was gossiping about it or, worse, asking me for the insider scoop.

After those terrifying weeks as Karry's prisoner, the admission I barely knew Tanis rolled off my tongue. I was pretty sure that this time people believed me. After all, who wouldn't take the opportunity to offer insights on the now famous man?

I dropped into the seat at my workstation with the coffee close at hand and pulled yesterday's work to my desk viewer.

"Coffee," Nate said, his face brightening. "Where is mine?"

I used to miss the little vendor in the foyer of Serenity's Technology Center, but after six months in Shadowland, the printed version in my hand served my needs just fine. "You should have messaged me," I said, sounding a little defensive.

I'd spent several guilty minutes calibrating the printer in my rooms here to produce coffee to my liking. Nate and Dan agreed it was impressively close to the retro-barista version.

"He's teasing you, Hannah. He finished one no more than five minutes ago," Dan said. "How is Molly?"

"Driving Coco crazy."

Dan chuckled and returned to his work.

Coco and Molly had accompanied us to the research facility complex and they were given an apartment next to mine. I didn't get much free time, but those brief moments of downtime in their company had become an essential part of my day. Molly was some-

## The Master of the Switch

thing special, a strange, forthright presence. Despite her incessant chatter, she had wormed her way into my heart with surprising ease.

"Any luck with the boost from Station thirty-seven?" I asked.

"Three percent," Dan replied.

I sighed. "That's nowhere near enough." I tried to keep my worries at bay. Station fifty-four had been the most powerful, producing more energy than the rest collectively. Its one and only job was to power the wall. Dan had been scraping percentages out of the other stations. Still, it would take an extraordinary effort to find the power we needed to re-energize the wall without shutting Rymor down.

One of Nate's team members joined him, and they began a lively discussion. Dan, like me, lapsed into silence. Given the desperate need to find more power, Dan had the assistance of Joshua, me, and most of the accompanying experts.

Nate and a small team of encryption specialists were working with an AI conglomeration named 'George' to decode Bill's communications. It was unusual for an AI to get involved but, apparently, George liked puzzles, and since it was George's nemesis AI counterpart that had created the encryption, credibility was at stake.

The nuances of this cybernetic duel passed me by, but suffice to say, George had deployed all of his considerable capacity to the task. Unfortunately, this meant George gave us nothing in the way of updates other than support demands he made of Nate and his team.

"I don't believe it!" Nate's excited whisper snagged my attention. His hands blurred as he tapped and pinched the screen in a complex series of commands. "Sure looks like communication to me."

I stood up, as did others, as we noticed their excitement, and within moments, a crowd had gathered at Nate's desk.

"How much have we got?" Dan cut a glance between Nate and the encryption expert at his side.

"It's only a twenty-day block, but it's the most recent communication." Nate nodded at his viewer. "Plenty to get the analytics working on it." The buzz settled, and the room returned to quiet industry as people drifted back to their tasks, encouraged by the news. I sat down, pulled up the blueprint for Station twenty-three, and reached for my coffee.

I lost myself in my work. When I lifted my head sometime later, I found Nate at the side of my desk with a solemn expression on his face.

Dan stood to Nate's right, and then Coco came and placed a gentle arm around my shoulder.

"What is it?" My gaze shifted between them, a sense of misgiving rising.

"It's Ella," Nate said. "She's alive, and she's with Bill."

# Chapter 45

## Shadowland

### Tanis

Ten days had passed since I'd first returned to Rymor, and the combined Shadowland and Rymorian forces had reached an uneasy truce that might, in many years' time, lead to a relationship nearing true camaraderie. While such heady days were far off, it was enough of a start to allow them to work together under less intensive supervision.

The progress in restoring order within Rymor had allowed the curfew to be lifted in several cities, including Serenity, and life was returning to a semblance of normality. Businesses and services couldn't close indefinitely without economic consequences. The swift return to semi-stability buoyed both people and stock markets.

There was still a significant amount of internal conflict to resolve before we tackled the estimated two hundred thousand strong Jaru army.

I'd taken a shuttle back to Shadowland to meet with Han, Javid, and Adro, who had continued to manage my forces here. Kein had also just joined us, but Adro had yet to arrive. As the furthest north of the three groups, this was the first holding place for those fleeing the Jaru.

It was odd being back out here and while it'd only been ten days, there was a comfort in being in a tent and surrounded by my personal things.

Kein, in his usual way, launched straight into an update. "The Jaru have crossed the border and, while there are few Shadowland villages in their path, the refugees bring rumors of safety from the Jaru within Talin. Many have gone over to the new lord there."

"In other words, they've gone to Bill," I said.

Kein nodded. "It appears so."

I'd arranged for Kein to be fitted with a communicator, but it was still good to see him in person. It was also important my Shadowland forces saw I hadn't abandoned them. Kein took the myriad of changes in his stride. He had studied me with speculative eyes that encompassed my Rymorian battle fatigues and weapons the moment I arrived. "How much trouble has the Jaru caused so far?"

"The occasional scouting party, but in the last week we've seen a couple of larger scale assaults," Han said.

I nodded. "We're making progress on the conflict inside Rymor, but it will be a week, maybe more, before my return can be permanent."

"You're coming back then?" Javid asked. "I was worried you'd turn into a soft tower-dweller and would leave the Jaru to us."

"I've been gone for ten days," I said dryly. "And I am curious as to why you think we should stop them. They're not coming for us. They're heading for the wall."

"We stop the Jaru," Han said gruffly. "It's what we do."

"But if they don't attack Shadowland?" I pushed, knowing I was seeking answers to a question I didn't understand myself.

"It's what we do," Han repeated. "How can you ask us this?"

"There is a mysteriousness to tower-dwellers and their technolo-

## The Master of the Switch

gy," Kein said. "Superstition is a powerful driver, but in Shadowland, less tangible notions underpin it. The Shadowlanders, in particular those of the warrior caste, have a strong compulsion to fight the Jaru. They have followed you by choice this far, but even without you, they wouldn't let the Jaru pass."

"What about Greve and Falton?" I asked. "They seem to have slipped the fold."

"They don't have it so good." Kein shrugged. "Greve is torn and his men confused. There is talk of deserters. Falton is reckless, and already bragging about the tower-dweller riches. It's important for your people to see the shuttles and the weapons you bring. The people of Shadowland had to pick a side, but neither side would be for the Jaru."

"I itch thinking about them being in our lands," Javid said, "but perhaps you don't suffer the same, being a half-breed?"

"I feel it," I said. "I merely wondered if I was alone in doing so."

Javid grinned and slapped me on the shoulder. "That's a relief. Thought I would have to disown you."

"You are a strange father," Han muttered seriously.

The tent flap was thrust open to admit Tay. "There has been an attack on Adro and his party. Adro is dead."

∽

Despite his many altercations with Javid, I had considered Adro a loyal and capable leader. His son had taken over, but at only nineteen, he lacked experience and had the added burden of picking up the mantle amid Shadowland's greatest test. Despite this, Arand impressed me with his calm acceptance and the way he lifted to meet the challenge. His men appeared to be backing him for now.

I found returning to my plush office odd after a day in Shadowland. My suite was beyond opulence. I'd initially been suspicious that it might have once belonged to Bill. Theo assured me it hadn't, which was good because if it had, I would have taken my sword to the rosewood desk, no matter how deplorable the act of destroying such craftsmanship and the consequence of blunting my sword.

Since our first meeting two months ago in that fateful tent, Theo had become indispensable to me. I still found his open admiration disconcerting, but more often, it was amusing. Personal feelings aside, nothing hindered his machine-like capability. I'd never met anyone who could remember and disseminate information the way Theo could. Still, he wasn't a normal human, so it made sense that his skills were unique.

The door opened, and my overzealous guards allowed Richard and Theo into my office. One look at their faces told me I wouldn't like the news.

I pointed at the seats in front of me. "What's happened?"

"A recently decrypted message." Richard lowered himself into the chair. "Bill found one of the colony's founding ships and sent a team out to search for the master switch."

"You mean the fabled Armageddon switch?" I asked, needing to be absolutely clear.

"Yes, exactly," Richard said. "He enlisted the aid of an investigative archeologist named Damien Moore. The Armageddon switch has been Damien's life's work. No one would give credence to such work under normal circumstances, nor would they fund an exploration into the Jaru plains. Except Bill did."

"Finding the ship doesn't mean anything." I countered. "The switch could still be a myth?"

"The ship was also a myth," Richard said.

I huffed out a breath. "We really needed another problem. Why would the ancients create such a device? The ship, myth or not, makes sense. We know we got here somehow. But to render technology obsolete permanently? That makes no sense."

"It was a safety mechanism in case the colony failed," Theo said. "To return the planet to its natural technology-free state. At least, that's what the records show."

Why would a culture as advanced as the that of the ancients be

## The Master of the Switch

reckless enough to create the instrument of their own destruction and then leave it in a ship that would be abandoned? Still, the ancients had built a wall with a single point of failure. I guessed anything was possible.

"What are we doing about it?" I asked. "I'm afraid my knowledge of ancient technology is limited to how it helps me to kill. I assume someone is looking into this: how it might work and how to mitigate it?"

"Hannah," Richard confirmed. "The power situation remains the most pressing, and everyone else is focused on that."

My chest squeezed at the mention of her name, and I rubbed absently at my chest. "We can hack technology, though? Our criminal fraternity can manage to take weapons off the network when they need to. Can we do the same for everything?"

"The records imply the master switch is all encompassing," Theo said. "We assume there is a reference somewhere explaining how it works, and if we can discover that, we can prevent it from activating, theoretically. We need to plan for the worst. We can't assume we'll have a weapon advantage over the Jaru. Then there are broader impacts for the population if we lose everything."

"Without technology we're dead," I said. "There's no getting around it. The recent riots will be trivial by comparison. No food, no water, but that would be the least of our concerns in a country where it is integral to survival."

"That's why we're here. You did declare martial law," Theo pointed out.

"So I did. Let's hope I live long enough to regret it... Whoever you have working on contingency plans, ensure the information is secure. We can't afford to have this leaked. If word of this gets out, we won't need the switch to finish us off." I stared out the window to my left, where Shadowland sprawled out into the distance.

"What are you thinking?" Theo asked, drawing my gaze back to him.

"That I need to get someone into Talin," I said softly. "I've been thinking about it for a while, but it's becoming urgent."

"He'll be expecting you to try," Richard said.

"I know, and I'd hate to disappoint him. We can't stop plans already in motion because of a possibility, but I agree we need to prepare."

We talked at length, and when Richard took his leave, I found myself the subject of Theo's troubled gaze. "We have about five minutes before the meeting. So, whatever it is, make it quick."

Theo drew a deep breath and let it out in a long sigh. "It's Hannah's sister, the one we thought was dead. She's not."

The sudden sharp pain I experienced was akin to a knife stabbing the center of my chest.

"We think she's with Bill in Talin." Theo continued.

"Does Hannah know?"

"Yes."

"And how is she?"

"Distraught. She thought her sister was dead. Now she's found out that Ella's alive and with Bill and, well, after what Karry did, Hannah wants her sister out."

"What would you have me do about it?" I asked, conscious that I'd been avoiding Hannah, that deep down I was terrified that I had fucked things up by sending her away. While I stayed away, I could convince myself she didn't hate me, that she might not tell me to fuck off. Garren had been to see her, and his smug message on returning had been enough to have me seeing red.

"Talk to her, reassure her."

"You mean lie to her," I said. I'd done enough of that, told her to leave, told her I didn't care, in not so many words. Whatever Bill was doing with Ella, the results wouldn't be pretty. He'd had Hannah and me within his grasp and lost us both. Her sister would be paying the price.

"It's not lying to give her hope. You said yourself, you need to

## The Master of the Switch

send someone to Talin. Locating Hannah's sister could be part of that."

"I've no idea how or when that is going to happen. He could have her anywhere inside or outside Rymor. If and when we do find her, she might not be the woman Hannah knows and loves."

"I know," Theo said, his voice soft. "She just needs something."

"You want me to talk to her?" Here it was, the excuse I'd been waiting for, a reason to see her, and I was fucking terrified. If she rejected me, I didn't know what the fuck I would do, but it would be likely to escalate swiftly. I was back in Rymor with access to technology... and medical procedures. One in particular, I'd reversed. Without asking her, without remorse, because whatever civilization dictated, I was still an alpha, and I was going to breed my mate the first chance I got. "I'm not convinced she would want me to."

"I think you would be surprised." Theo said softly, only his eyes settled on me in a way that said he wanted to say more.

"What?" I demanded.

"It's about her parents. About their deaths and about Hannah," he said. "She told me something back in Shadowland when she first learned of Ella's death. I didn't want to mention it at first, not until I'd had a chance to look into it."

My brows drew together.

"They were Moiety, and from the looks of it, they were killed by one of their own."

*Well*, I thought. *That's got to fuck you up.*

# Chapter 46

**Rymor**

**Tanis**

I forced aside thoughts of Armageddon switches, Talin, and Hannah-related revelations as I headed into the adjoining conference room, followed by Theo and the two guards on duty.

An ensemble of people waited within, including Gaia representatives, various subject matter experts, Richard, and Andrew Jordan. Sticking Jordan and Harding in the same room was a confrontation waiting to happen, so I was glad Scott was occupied with the day's operation.

Having met Jordan a few times, I sided with Scott. Jordan was abrasive, arrogant, and borderline incompetent. Abrasive and arrogant I could handle, the incompetence not so much, but Jordan had extensive knowledge of the wall and homeland security, so I suffered the rest.

# The Master of the Switch

A lively discussion on internal conflict soon shifted to a geographical assessment of locations to make a stand against the Jaru.

"We should use missiles," Jordan said.

"Missiles?" I asked, frowning. "Rymor has no active missiles. We have limited time. How would something we need to investigate, design, and test help us?"

A few people shifted about the table, but my attention remained fixed on Jordan.

"We only need one decimation-level or bio-chemical warhead to do the trick. There might be a bit of fall out in the area, but it's only Shadowland."

I ground my molars so tightly they ached. "Only Shadowland. You've investigated this, I assume? How large an area are we talking about?"

"Thirty to fifty percent," Jordan said, warming up. "The longer we leave it, the worse the contamination of the indigenous lands. Leave it too late and there could be impacts on Rymor. It would be quick, and effective, and better a few Shadowlanders die than the whole of Rymor."

A Gaia member, two down from me, opened his mouth to speak. I lifted my hand, and whatever the man had been about to say died on his lips.

Oblivious to the room's undercurrents, Jordan continued to list the various merits of thermonuclear versus biochemical warheads.

His words trailed off as his gaze settled on the tic thumping in my jaw.

He swallowed.

"Everyone out," I said in a low, dangerous tone.

There was a pregnant pause before chairs creaked and feet pattered against the floor. I pinned Jordan with a look. "Not you."

I waited until the room was empty of everyone but my guards and Jordan.

"Close the door," I said to my wolf guard. As usual, they were in full Shadowland armor, complete with swords.

Jordan made a bolt for it. I closed the gap. He managed a couple of backward steps before I punched him. It was more of a tap, but there was a satisfying gush of blood.

"What the hell!" Jordan closed his hand over his nose. "What did I say?"

I fisted his throat and leveled the muzzle of my gun at the center of his forehead. "I'm half Shadowlander, asshole. If you ever suggest decimating it to save your own ass again, I will shoot you in the head. Now, any further suggestions that involve massacring half the planet's population?"

Jordan gave his head the barest shake.

"Excellent," I released him and returned to my seat, nodding in indication for Jordan to do the same. "You can come back in now," I called, knowing Theo would be monitoring.

The doors opened, and everyone returned. The subsequent conversations were focused. Jordan didn't offer further stupid suggestions. After several hours of debate, during which Jordan wheezed and fidgeted, we reached a consensus on the best location to stem the Jaru attack.

Afterward, I visited a team of experts to discuss the production of simplified versions of the weapons. I wanted the Shadowlanders armed but wasn't deluded about their capability of using such elaborate equipment. Inside Rymor, we could limit it to stun. No one wanted a Jaru to wake up when they outnumbered us by a significant margin. We needed every advantage we could get.

Finally, another meeting after trouble flared again in Hope Town.

By the time I'd met with Theo again for another recap of the rest of the day's events, it was late. I took the shuttle back to my suite, accompanied by Theo and my ever-present guards.

Unlike the troop carrier transports that rose and landed with bone-crunching g-force, the diplomatic glider gave little indication of flight. The plush, luxurious retro-leather seating and fixtures inlaid with rosewood were also a stark contrast to the troop transports, which were little more than metallic shells. Within minutes of

## The Master of the Switch

leaving State Tower, I was back at my apartment, to where Garren, Scott, and the rest of my guards returned not long after, casting the accommodation into a state of bedlam.

I needed to do something about the number of wolf guards here. The two standing outside were overkill, and the others invading my personal space were worse. I'd occupied half of them in Shadowland. My suite may have a dozen rooms, but that didn't mean I needed to fill them.

"Is that necessary?" Scott said, gesturing toward the door where the guards stood at attention. "I think they're scaring the neighbors."

"Old habits die hard," I said, collapsing onto the couch. I rubbed my tired eyes. It was late, my day had been busy, but there was a restlessness building inside me, a frustration that I couldn't do what I wanted. If I could, I would be with Hannah now. It was late. She was probably in bed... with Red, who was comforting her. Red, who hadn't sent her away. Never had the mantle of leadership chafed as it did now. "How did the operation go today?"

"Fine, mostly. Hope Town has been flaring up in little pockets most of the day. We've had to leave additional forces there," Scott said, flopping down into the seat opposite. "It took them a while to get focused. It would be good if you show your face tomorrow."

I nodded.

Scott grinned suddenly. "I heard you had a run-in with Jordan today. Nicely handled, so Theo reckons." He nodded his chin toward Theo, who had joined us.

"It was not nicely handled," Theo said, scowling. "I'm confident he couldn't have handled it worse if he tried."

I gave Theo a lop-sided grin.

"I take it back," Theo said, rolling his eyes. "I have no idea how you're going to get through the interview."

"Interview?" I frowned.

Garren joined us with beers for everyone. Garren was much enamored with printing and delighted by any opportunity to print more. He was also still walking with a fucking swagger after visiting Hannah and I wanted to punch him in the face.

"The one you have scheduled for tomorrow," Theo said.

"Tomorrow?" Talk of interviews distracted me from a Garren-thumping fantasy. "When was this decided?"

"I did tell you." Theo threw his hands up. "Do you listen to anything I say?"

Scott laughed. "Like an old married couple."

Garren chuckled.

I glared between Garren and Scott. "I'm not doing an interview," I shifted my attention to Theo. "Cancel it."

"I can't." Theo did that steely-eyed thing he sometimes did. "The council believes this will improve your image. Let the people see the real you. Interest was high while the curfew was in place, but now life is returning to normal, the press are demanding more information on the savior of Rymor."

"Ha! Let them see the real you," Scott encouraged, still chortling. "Theo, do you have the footage of him punching Jordan in the face?"

"The punching part was relatively mild," Theo said. "Afterward, he put his gun to Andrew's forehead and threatened to shoot him in the head. I believe it would be an exceptionally bad idea for Rymorians to know anything about the real Tanis, but I trust he can fake it for the duration of the interview."

"Don't count on it." Scott grinned.

"I'm not," Theo said. "The government retains editing rights before it goes near the public."

"Good call." Scott turned to me. "I can't believe you bombed our only defense against the Jaru, and they fucking love you. Women want your baby. Men want to shake your hand."

"It was the same in Shadowland," Garren said.

"Which part?" Scott asked, all curious interest.

"He decimated five fortresses and sired a dozen bastards, which he claims tower-dwellers cannot." Garren gave me a look. "The handshaking does not make sense, though. Unless that's a tower-dweller

## The Master of the Switch

term for stab. Many men tried that, and a few women too." He shrugged. "It makes life interesting."

I drank some beer and said, "Well, don't look at me for answers. I don't understand it either. I'm not delusional about my personal virtue, and as for fathering children, I hadn't been in the same room as some of them."

"So, you say," Garren grinned.

We continued talking for a while, mostly Garren amusing them with tales of misadventures. The conversation soothed me, but the restlessness remained. Elsewhere, people were desperately trying to find power and decrypt messages. Hannah was once more looking for a way to save our world. Then there was the council, the troops, and the people I now thought of as my own, both Rymorian and Shadowlander, and a terrible Jaru army killing everything in their way.

On top of all this, I still hadn't seen my mother, and I was strangely afraid that I might not know her when I did. She was with Hannah, I'd heard. I had a thousand and one things to do tomorrow and not enough time for sleep. Yet the thread was pulling me, demanding I get on a shuttle and race over there.

"Damn it!" Scott's curse dragged me from his rumination. "Hope Town just kicked off again." He heaved out of the seat.

*If I see one more set of stairs,* I thought despondently as I rose too. "I'll lead from the ground. I missed my exercise today."

# Chapter 47

**Talin**

**Ella**

I was supposed to be in the kitchen getting some dinner, but instead, I was in the dark underground tunnels of Talin, searching for the transport capsule. The nightmares had returned in full force after Pope killed Damien, and I could feel the blankness tugging at my mind. I refused to lose myself to mindless compliance or accept my life here again.

I tried to hold onto the image of my family, but the wound was raw and brought both pain and resolve. The firmer the resolve, the greater the pain. It was a vicious circle, leading me to the firm determination I had to get out.

News had arrived along with a shuttle full of Rymorian goods a few days ago, which had left Bill furious. I didn't know what that news was, but Bill had been in such a dark mood that even Pope, who didn't shy away from challenging him, had been unusually circumspect.

## The Master of the Switch

On top of Bill's unmasked fury was Pope's propensity to hound my every move. He was always watching and following, and he locked me in my room when Bill dismissed me at the end of the day. I assumed Pope was out on reconnaissance today as I hadn't seen him yet. One of the grunts had collected me from my room in his place.

I had sat in Bill's room earlier this morning, as I did every day, and tried to ignore the blood stains on the wooden floor, the escalating nature of his foul mood, and the knowledge that he had the fabled Armageddon switch.

I had tried convincing myself that it wasn't the real one; that it wouldn't do what I feared; that even if it was, Bill would never use it. What could he possibly gain?

On top of all this, he was still here in Talin and showed no signs of leaving, and I was reluctant to acknowledge what that meant because, if Bill was here, how much did he care about Rymor?

Ahead, the corridor branched, and I paused to shine my flashlight left and right. A Rymorian grunt always took me to the capsule. Although I was sure I knew the way, my earlier surety waned.

No, it was definitely to the right. Mindful of my extended absence, I hurried the last stretch until I reached the capsule cavern.

I stopped dead, casting my flashlight over the space where the capsule had once been and finding nothing but piles of rocks and debris.

Where had it gone?

Dropping the flashlight with a clatter, I clawed at the rocks, rolling them away in a sobbing frenzy like I might unearth it.

It was gone.

I was desolate, inconsolable, my escape plan lost under a pile of rubble. They had said it was gone, but I hadn't believed it, but now I knew.

"What are you doing down here, Ella?"

I jumped at the voice, so focused on my lost hope that I failed to hear Pope's approach.

With my back to him, I rose and quickly wiped tears from my

cheeks with the back of my hand. It was a lost cause. I must look wretched and ridiculous.

"I just—" I floundered for a plausible excuse, "—I got lost."

I retrieved my flashlight, aware that Pope, while a monster, wasn't stupid. I just happened to get lost while carrying a flashlight in the capsule chamber—no one would buy into that.

I finally found the strength to meet his eyes, only I couldn't read anything in the gloom.

He stalked over, plucked the flashlight from my fingers, and snapped it off. "Come on. He was wondering where you were."

I trailed after him, my heart hammering, wondering what he would do. I didn't trust Pope, but after he had killed Damien, I'd understood he was scum, like everyone here. He would sell me out to Bill or keep it a secret if he thought it useful.

My breathing turned choppy. Should I run?

He drew a slow breath and let it out in an exasperated puff before turning to face me. "I've got your flashlight, Ella. Please tell me you're not that stupid."

No, I was something far worse. I was desperate, and desperate manifested a lot like stupid. I followed him into the bustling section of the keep as my mind continued whirling, wondering what had happened to the capsule. Was it an accident? This must be why Bill was still here.

Was he trapped?

I tried to find answers in Pope's eyes, but the man was impossible to read.

When he started walking, I fell in step beside him, resigned, knowing my fate was in his hands and that there was not a damn thing I could do about it. I felt numb, only it wasn't the same numb as before, more exhaustion with my fear.

He dropped both flashlights off at the rack at the edge of the labyrinth, and we made our way to the kitchen, where he dumped food onto a plate before shoving it into my hand. Then we continued to Bill's office.

## The Master of the Switch

He pushed the door open and stood back to let me enter. Inside, I found Bill sitting at his desk.

"Your door was shut. She got worried and returned to her room," Pope said.

Bill frowned. "Where's the grunt outside? Why didn't he tell me?"

"Left his post. I'll deal with it," Pope said, leaving without a backward glance.

"I'm sorry." I was shaking. The plate in my hand was shaking. I hated Pope and his suspicious, creeping presence, but I feared Bill's wrath more, Bill who had beaten a man's face to a bloody pulp for raping me.

My protector and my jailer.

The man keeping me from my family, and the man keeping me safe.

Bill pointed at the stool, and I dutifully sat and tried to force some food down.

"What am I going to do with you, Ella?" he said softly. "I thought you were getting better, but perhaps not. You're so dependent on me. I only want to keep you safe, but I can't do that if I don't know where you are."

I couldn't swallow any food down, and instead, I sat in silence, staring at my plate.

"We'll have to make some changes," he said. His sigh was heavy. As he rose and rounded the desk, my heart rate kicked up. Crouching down before me, he rested his palm against my cheek. "Was it Pope? Did he scare you?"

I shook my head. "No, not Pope. He brought me back. I trust him." I didn't trust that killer, but he lied for me, and I thought Bill's charity toward me would dry up if he knew.

He studied me, his expression thoughtful while I fought a silent battle to control my runaway thoughts.

"You don't need to worry about the Rymorians here. I took precautions."

"Precautions?"

His lips formed a tight line. "I can see you're still unsettled. Would you rather go back to your room?"

I nodded.

He opened the door and spoke to the grunt on duty outside.

A few minutes later, Pope returned and escorted me to my room. Once inside, I heard the familiar turning of the key.

∽

The rest of the day was lost to hazy thoughts that scattered and gripped me. The fading sun told me it was late, but I was sinking into depression.

I went to bed. I thought sleep wouldn't find me, but I was roused later by a fierce pounding on the door. Raised voices were muffled by the solid wood barrier. Disorientated by the darkness and the violence of the noise, I stilled, my ears straining to listen.

Deathly silence followed, filled only by the thudding of my heart.

The disturbance returned, louder. God help me. What was happening now?

My fingers gripped the covers so tight my knuckles ached, and my eyes shifted feverishly about the room. I needed to hide!

There was nowhere to hide.

Raised, angry voices drew closer again. The door was thrust open with a thud, and I clamped my hands over my mouth, stifling my scream when I realized Bill and Pope were standing there.

"Is that the only key?" Bill demanded.

"Yeah, that's the only one." Pope's eyes were in the shadows, but I could see his jaw locked tight, and he hesitated before he passed the key to Bill. "She's not fucking well."

"If I want your opinion, I'll let you know. Don't ever argue with me again," Bill said coldly. "Now, get the fuck out."

Pope's fists clenched at his side.

## The Master of the Switch

He wasn't locking me in because he didn't trust me; he was trying to protect me from Bill.

I watched Pope's face empty before he turned to walk away. The door closed, and this time it was Bill who turned the lock… from the inside.

My chest heaved as I drew a sharp breath in. Why did Pope leave? Why didn't he stop Bill?

"Hush, Ella." The bed dipped beside me, and a clank followed as Bill put the heavy key down on the table. "Hush." His fingers stroked my hair back from my hot cheeks.

I closed my eyes. Why now? Did I do this? Did I bring this on myself because I went wandering? Was this what Pope has been trying to tell me?

I felt Bill's lips brush my cheek, and although my whole body trembled, Bill didn't seem to notice or care.

Pope was one of the good ones. I was so certain of this that it made me want to cry. I prayed Pope would return, force the door open, and take his sword to Bill, as he had done to Damien.

He never came.

Was he afraid of Bill? Did Bill have something over him?

It was likely he did.

"You don't need to worry, Ella, I'll take care of you," Bill said, oblivious to the spell my body was under. "When I first arrived and discovered what had been happening to you, I decided to take action to ensure you were safe. I know you're not the same person, Ella, that you might not understand this, but I took precautions. All Rymorian here have been infected with a genetic level inhibitor… Think of it as a safety mechanism. Our ancestors had quite a propensity for biological warfare. None of the people I brought out here knew what had been done to them at the time. They're not criminals and would never have signed up for this. They can't kill me, it won't let them, even to contemplate it would make them unwell." He stroked my cheek. "If they pushed past it and ignored the warnings, their body would generate a toxin. It's swift and painful and leads to temporary paralysis. A few tried to go against me. Word of the results quickly spread. Does that reassure you?"

"Yes," I said. And it was then everything clicked into place. "Do-do I have one? A device like Pope?"

"It's a biological implant, not a device, and no, of course not. Why would I need to use that on you?"

"You don't."

I settled my hand against his chest. It was harder than I thought, but I felt like I had clawed back some control by doing it. In a strange, warped world, I thought that Bill might even love me. I had hated him once. What I felt for him now, while not love, was certainly compelling.

He was keeping good on a promise he'd made earlier.

He was keeping me safe.

Safe from everyone but him.

# Chapter 48

**Rymor**

**Tanis**

After a night of fighting with rioters in the Hope Town district, I visited the location of the next troop deployment. Per Scott's instructions, I made a brief speech calling out a few incidents of poor behavior before praising their hard work and reminding them that their efforts were making a real difference. We were dealing with the tail end of the troubles, which were scrappy and scattered and much harder to resolve than the riots of the lowest socio-demographic suburbs. Hope Town was quiet for the time being, but I suspected trouble would start there again soon.

Afterward, I returned to my office, where the dreaded interview would occur. I wanted to cancel it, had tried to, but as Theo had pointed out, it was a mere hour of interruption, and then I could get right back to killing thugs. Too tired to offer a credible argument, I had been in my office only minutes when Theo entered and approached my desk in an odd, cloak-and-dagger sort of way.

I glanced up with a frown. "What is it?"

"Ah, your interviewer is here."

"Yes," I said, wondering why Theo hadn't used the communicator. "Show her in so I can get this over with."

"Yes, but she's, ah, do you want me to sit in... In case there are any awkward questions?"

My frown deepened. "I'm sure I can handle it."

Theo didn't move. I'd seen the weird, wonderful, and grotesque in my life. I'd also dealt with assholes and abrasive personalities of every kind. I struggled to determine why he felt I needed my hand held. "Is there something wrong with her I should know about?"

"No, no, not at all!"

I got out of my chair and joined him. "Theo, you're acting odd. More so than usual, and that's saying something. Bring her in. If I need you, I will call you."

Theo left the room with thinned lips and reluctance radiating from every fiber of his being. Shortly after, he escorted a woman in. She benefited me with a warm smile and reached out her hand for a formal greeting. Behind her, Theo fidgeted from one foot to the other.

I managed not to laugh. Okay, now this was starting to make sense.

Did he know nothing about alphas and omegas?

"A pleasure to meet you."

I shook her proffered hand, indicated the seating in the less formal part of my room, and watched her ass as she passed. There was no doubt the woman was stunning... yet my body didn't so much as stir with interest. *So, this was what being mated was like.*

"Thanks, Theo. I'll let you know if I need you." I flashed an innocent smile.

Theo glared back, went to speak, and then left in a huff.

I joined my guest as she relaxed into the seat. As she crossed her legs, her jacket fell apart in what I suspected was a well-practiced maneuver to place her cleavage on display.

## The Master of the Switch

I let my eyes lower before I returned my leisurely attention to her face. If she wanted games, I could give her games.

"Not the average Rymorian, John Tanis?" She raised one delicate eyebrow.

"No need to be coy. I'm confident you wanted me to look." I let my attention drift again, past those perfect perky tits, onto her flat stomach where the jacket was cinched in, and then to those long-toned thighs displayed in her fitted pants. She was tall, and I liked tall women; at least I used to. Her shoes were business with a hint of stripper. Yes, I definitely liked the shoes. They had emphasized her endless legs when she walked in, legs that were topped by an ass with the perfect level of plumpness.

"Showcased to perfection, and doubtless intended to distract me from the probing questions you're about to ask. Living among savages, civilization-starved, and fair game." I sighed and raised my eyes to meet hers, and mine didn't stray this time. "Perhaps we could begin the interview now."

Her face sank the tiniest amount before she plastered on a killer smile. "It was worth a try."

"No offense taken," I replied. "I wasn't joking about the civilization-starved part. I rarely see women with legs that good in pants who aren't also carrying a sword."

She chuckled. "I dare say Rymorian women are a little different."

"Not that different, as the last six months has reminded me."

"You're referring to Hannah Duvaul?" she asked. "Is the speculation about your relationship true?"

"There is nothing to speculate on." *Not after I fucked up. But I'm not going to let that stop me.*

"Well, your comment will close the matter, I'm sure." Her words dripped with sweetness and a touch of condescending.

*As if!*

"So, onto the infamous Station fifty-four. Is it true you ordered its destruction?"

"I did."

"Yet the government still offered you a job as the leader of Rymor?"

"Yes, they did. Maybe they were worried I would blow up another vital piece of infrastructure if they didn't pander to my ego?"

"Or perhaps you are just the lesser of two evils?" she inquired, her face serious.

I laughed. "I believe you've got the measure of me, Ms. Fielding."

"John, I doubt I will ever get the measure of you, but I intend to do the best I can within the bounds of this interview. Assuming the government doesn't edit all the controversial parts out." She gave a rueful smile. "Did you ever envision conquering both the civilized and uncivilized parts of our world?"

"Not in my wildest dreams."

"But isn't your meteoric rise all part of the John Tanis master plan?"

She certainly wasn't afraid to unleash those probing questions. "There is no master plan. My life has been nothing more than a battle to survive that got a bit out of hand."

"Survival?" She countered without pause. "Some would see it as thriving in an environment you were genetically designed for."

I realized I'd more than met my match. "I've been too close to death too many times, and have become too hardened to the consequences of killing, to be enamored with the process or its conclusion. There are two hundred thousand Jaru coming, and I'm charged with stopping them with fifty thousand Shadowlanders. The probability of us engaging in a second interview is unlikely. Death is rarely glorious. More often, it is messy, ugly and is preceded by excruciating pain. The savage side of life is something many Rymorians know little about."

"So, you don't covet power."

I laughed, because I definitely did. "As you just mentioned, I'm a genetically designed killer. That's about as uncomplicated and base as it gets."

The remainder of the interview passed pleasantly. Her reputation as the best reporter in Serenity wasn't based on her looks, although I was certain they didn't hurt.

"I was worried about you for a while in there," Theo confessed the moment she left.

"Worried about what? That I would take her up on her offer, or that I wouldn't."

Theo gave me a steely-eyed glare. "I care about Hannah."

"And I haven't seen Hannah for over a month." A point I intended to rectify imminently.

Theo folded his arms and returned an even more censorious glare.

I laughed.

"Theo, don't ever fall in love or find yourself mated. It allows you to admire other women's tits, even as your balls are in a vise."

Theo bit back a laugh. "So, you do love Hannah, then?"

"I feel an overwhelming urge to kill anyone who hurts, upsets, or shows more than a passing level of interest in her. It's close enough."

"That's not love!"

"And you would have vast experience in such matters?" I raised a brow. "Besides, isn't Hannah another Theo fixation?"

"Ah, no, I'm more interested in the package."

"Package?" I asked, baffled.

"I have this fantasy about being sandwiched—"

"Theo, if you finish that sentence you will regret it."

"Sorry." Theo looked everywhere but at me. "But everyone knows, thanks to the show last night, that you have had sexual experiences with more than one person at the same time, which brings me to whatever is happening between Hannah, you, Garren and Red. And ever since, I've been distracted."

"Show?" What the actual fuck? "When the fuck was this?"

"Last night. You know I don't need much sleep, so I decided to visit Dan and Nate. It was showing in the community room. Your mother said she remembered the woman on the program."

"How could the government let this happen? No wonder Ms.

Fielding was giving me an eyeful." I lapsed into cursing and pacing. "As if I don't have enough problems. What is wrong with Rymor? We're about to have the mother of all wars, and they're gossiping about my pre-majority sex life."

"Panem et circenses," Theo said with a shrug.

"Which means?"

"You're a distraction," Theo said, his smile wry. "Of the most comprehensive kind."

# Chapter 49

**Coco**

For the second time in a matter of weeks, I had moved home. This time, a remote research center had become my home. Molly was outside, helping the army of support staff in the organic garden. It was her favorite activity, and it gave me a break from her monologue enough to get a little research done.

If anyone had told me I would be caring for a young child and enjoying it, I would have called them a fool. Yet here I was.

The common room was quiet when I entered. A small group of people sat in a cluster on the far side, talking, while a few individuals were scattered around the room with viewers in their hands.

I dropped mine on a seat near the window and headed to prepare a cup of tea in the adjoining printing area. Unlike my personal printer, it wasn't configured for chamomile, and it took me a little time to select the flavor and temperature I required.

"I can't believe you're still drinking that stuff."

I had expected him to visit me at some point, but it was still a shock. I drew a ragged breath and turned around to find my son leaning against the wall behind me.

Time contracted around us. The eleven years of absence were sharp and painful, yet the pang soothed now he was back. My eyes clouded over, and I clamped my hand over my mouth. My baby was home. Only he wasn't so much a baby anymore.

His laugh was warm as he drew me into a hug. I hugged him back, and really, there was so much of him to hug.

"I'm so glad I don't need to feed you." I pressed my palm to his cheek. "Oh, John, it's so good to see you."

I leaned back and looked him up and down. *How in the world did I produce that?* I smiled.

"How have you been?" he asked.

I dashed the happy tears from my cheeks. "Fine, mostly, until a few months ago when I found myself part of a resistance group and went into hiding." My guilt rose. "I have so much I want to say to you, and now you're here, I don't have the faintest idea where to begin." I fought to get my emotions under control. *I don't do emotions,* I admonished. "I didn't accept you were gone at first." The crushing weight of guilt returned. "After, I fell into denial. Unable to acknowledge it for fear doing so would make the nightmare real. I forbade Jon from talking about you, and eventually, he gave up trying."

"It's okay," he said. "I don't think there's a right way to handle what happened. As reactions go, I think my subsequent life choices would be viewed as extreme."

"Yes." I smiled again. "They certainly were, and still are, as I found out from Jon last week. He's gone back out there, hasn't he?"

He nodded. "The field scientists are an easy way to relay information to Shadowland, and he's one of the best."

"I was so worried about him. He's been a true friend to me over the years."

"A friend?" He smirked. "Is Nate also a friend?"

"Well, a little more than a friend." How had we gotten on to this? "But you know how Jon is, and how he takes nothing seriously. Not even nearly dying in Shadowland. I have always loved him, but he

## The Master of the Switch

does drive me crazy." I noted his raised eyebrows. "He must drive you crazy sometimes, too?"

"Yes, but for very different reasons, I expect. It's bad enough having one father, but two provide an interesting challenge. They get along well enough, by the way, which is surprising given Jon helped you to escape Javid."

"Ah yes." I wasn't comfortable broaching the subject of Javid. "Jon mentioned you had met Javid." My conversation with Jon Sanders a week ago had been a tsunami of information that I was still getting to grips with. "You look so much like him." Hearing the wistful note in my voice, I was determined to change the subject. "Have you grown since you left?"

He laughed. "No idea. Maybe." He sent a cursory glance down at himself before directing his gaze at me. "You look smaller. Maybe you shrank?"

A sudden ear-piercing squeal snagged our attention as the tiny, disheveled form of Molly hurtled through the door. "Tanis!"

She launched herself into his arms, where she clung and began to chatter about seedlings, chocolate, and drawings of pigs.

I burst out laughing. "Molly seems to like you."

There was a smudge on Molly's cheek, her hands were covered in soil and her shoes were filthy. How the child acquired so much dirt so quickly was beyond me.

"Yes, and she is now killing my reputation on both sides of the wall," he said dryly.

"Tanis got the bad Jaru who killed my family," Molly chirped. "They can't hurt anyone else now."

My face softened as Molly pressed her little cheek against John's and wrapped her arms around his neck.

A second later, Molly's head popped up, and she pressed her fingers against his cheek to ensure he was giving her his full attention. "Are you going to give Hannah a spanking again?" she asked earnestly.

"I wasn't planning to." His lips twitched. "Why, has she been naughty?"

I choked out a laugh, while also being slightly outraged on Hannah's behalf.

Molly chewed on the ends of her hair while she thought it over. "Yes, I think she has."

"Molly!" I shook my head. "Hannah has not been naughty. How can you tell such fibs!"

John pulled the tiny hand away from his cheek and gave it a critical inspection. "What have you been doing?"

"Planting!" Molly stated proudly.

The room had become busy, I realized. News of his arrival at the research facility must have spread. After the media attention he'd garnered, I wasn't surprised.

"I guess I'll be in the news again," he muttered. "In Shadowland my exploits take longer to reach the masses."

"They do still reach the masses, though?" I teased.

"Yes, unfortunately," he said.

"I assume you're going to talk to Hannah while you're here?"

His eyes met mine. "I was advised to." His expression was guarded, giving little indication of his involvement in the maelstrom of events Hannah had offloaded the first night I met her.

"Advised to?" I said, one eyebrow rising in a subtle question. He may have been my son, and I may not have seen him for eleven years, but I wasn't about to let this pass unaddressed. "The woman is smitten with you, has been through more trauma than I would wish on my worst enemy, and the best you can do is 'advised to'?"

He flinched. "I'm not sure smitten is the word you're looking for. She has a history of stabbing people who piss her off, and the last time I spoke to her, she was pretty pissed."

"Don't be ridiculous." I waved a dismissive hand. "I contemplated stabbing Javid on many occasions. It doesn't preclude love."

"I'll be sure to let him know," he said.

"Please don't," I muttered. How had that slipped out?

### The Master of the Switch

His eyes tracked across the packed room, then stilled. His smirk turned downright predatory.

I followed his line of sight. Hannah had entered the far side of the room, and from the state of her slack jaw and wide eyes, it was clear she'd been unaware of the visitor until now. "She's been distraught since she found out about her sister; please bear that in mind."

His expression softened as he placed Molly down on the floor. "Given your past and recent relationship forays, I'm not sure you're qualified to give advice. But I will bear it in mind, assuming there are no sharp implements nearby." He winked and smiled. "It's good to see you. I wish there was more time." He glanced down at Molly, who clutched at his hand. "Stay with Coco, Molly. It's spanking time... Unfortunately, this one's for me."

# Chapter 50

**Hannah**

After another fraught discussion with Joshua, where he'd sent poorly disguised insults my way, I needed a break. I didn't understand his desire to rehash the past, but after Tanis' infamous interview, Joshua seemed determined to dig into the sorry mess, in particular, my relationship with Tanis—if you could call such a disaster a relationship.

Joshua hated Tanis, which I suspected was because he still suffered guilt and blamed Tanis for his guilt. He had accused me of jumping into Tanis' bed in an attempt to better my options. "I don't blame you," he said. "We all did what we had to."

I'd never hit anyone (stabbed, sure), but I thought Joshua was riding the line that might break me. My tolerance levels were at an all-time low after discovering Ella was still alive and now reputedly in Talin. I couldn't care less about petty games, yet if I had told Joshua what I felt, it would open a floodgate. So I ignored him, hoping he would tire of the snipes, and instead left the room.

The hub room, typically quiet at this time of day, was so packed it

## The Master of the Switch

appeared the whole base had converged on the area. I nudged my way inside, wondering if I'd missed an announcement.

I stopped at the edge, as far as I needed to go, since he stood a good head and shoulders above everyone else. It was clear the announcement had been the unofficial kind. He was holding Molly, who clung to him like a little monkey, her hand pressed against his cheek, making sure he paid attention to whatever she was telling him so earnestly.

His mother, Coco, was standing beside him. There was so much love in her expression that I felt like an intruder in a private family moment.

Still, I wasn't the only intruder, and from the looks of it, everyone had piled in to have a gawk, which was abhorrent, really. *Yes, now I'm here gawking too!*

I felt like I should leave —this was too much after Joshua's last dig —except my feet remained rooted then as was inevitable, he turned his head and caught me in the midst of my indecision.

He grinned at me, a lazy kind of smile that made me feel a little breathless, and then irritated with myself for feeling like that, since our last meeting had hurt so much.

He leaned down and spoke to his mother, putting Molly on the floor, which gave me the perfect escape opportunity. Except as I tried to move back to the door, I found I was stuck since more people had arrived, which was amazing given I couldn't believe there were any more people left in the building.

I was side-stepping the blockers when I had the uncomfortable awareness of everyone looking at something over my shoulder. My internal battle continued, during which I tried to convince myself I should ignore the funny looks and get the hell out of the room, but my body wasn't listening, and I glanced back anyway.

"Going somewhere?"

The silent notion of 'being busted' accompanied those two words. Against my better judgment, I turned around. "I told everyone I didn't know you." I became aware that people were standing close enough to hear this confession. Joshua hadn't enlightened the base personnel about my relationship with Tanis. His snide threats had made it clear he enjoyed holding it over me like our shared dirty little secret, leverage in case I told them he'd destroyed Station fifty-four.

Tanis had the audacity to laugh. "And how is that working out?"

I gestured toward him. "Well, terrible now, obviously." All I needed was for Joshua to arrive and make some snide remarks to complete my public humiliation.

"I need to talk to you," he said after a pause sufficient for yet more people to force their way into the room. "Privately."

My eyes settled everywhere but on Tanis. "I don't want to talk to you."

"Yes, you do," he said softly.

I let out another ragged breath and looked up at him.

"You know there is a certain cyclic familiarity to our conversations," he said. "I will give you two options. Option A, we go to your room to talk. Option B, I order everyone out of this room so we can talk."

"I don't like those options." I leaned in closer, with a furtive glance at the people trying to listen in, and whispered, "And you can't order people out of the room; we're not in Shadowland anymore."

He grinned, which did nothing to put me at ease. "There's option C, in case you can't decide But you won't like option C."

My heart gave a little *ba-dump*, and my brows drew together. "What's option C?"

He put his hands on his hips in a way that suggested he meant business. "Are you picking option C?"

"Pick option C!" Someone called out enthusiastically—it sounded like Nate.

"I'll take option A," I said.

He gestured for me to precede him, and because I had a genuine desire to escape the interested stares, I left the room with him.

The elevator ride was uncomfortable. I was aware of Tanis' looming presence beside me, which I tried and failed to ignore.

## The Master of the Switch

"So, I guess you've been busy," he said conversationally. "Not much time to watch the home viewer?"

"You mean have I watched the interview and the other thing? No, I haven't, but everyone else has talked about it obsessively and I'm confident I know all the details. I don't think Rymor knows what to make of you." I gave him a flat judgmental stare, and he shifted about in a very un-Tanis-like way that I found amusing.

The elevator opened on my floor, and we stepped out.

"What?!" His feigned outrage was comical, given what he was affronted about. "It hasn't happened recently."

"How recently was it?" I halted at my door, feeling my fingers turn into claws. Somehow, I uncurled them, pressed the door scanner and stalked inside.

"Well, not since I met you."

The door swished shut, closing us in, and I did a double-take when I found him grinning.

He shrugged, dropping any pretense of innocence. "I am the leader of Shadowland. I think you mentioned the power had gone to my—"

I punched him half-heartedly in the stomach.

"I'm pretty sure that means you care about me," he said.

I could see he was fighting his laughter. "Me punching you in the stomach?"

"No, you not punching me in the balls."

"I'm pretty sure that's optimism on your part."

I tried to walk away, but he caught both my wrists. A silent tug of war ensued, and he pulled me against him without seeming to apply any effort. "Your bed isn't going to be big enough, by the way."

"Not big enough for what, asshole?" I gave up the fight. "How do you know about my bed? Have you been in here?"

"Did you just call me an asshole?"

"Have you been in my apartment?"

"I may have."

"Yes or no?"

"I was trying to speak to you without the crowd... And I can rig a locked door pad if I have to."

I tried to stifle a laugh, but it came out as an inelegant snort. I heard his answering chuckle and, defeated, let my head fall against his chest. *This is not going how I expected.*

His arms drew me against him in a way that felt just right. Memories surfaced. When I'd been locked in Station fifty-four, my fate precarious, and my opinion of him confused. (My opinion of him was still confused.) At the time, I'd believed returning home was an impossible dream. The idea that one day he might be standing here in Rymor, stating those very words, had seemed equally impossible. But here he was.

I sighed. "What are you doing here?"

"What do you think I'm doing here?"

"Can you please answer my question?" I was exasperated, yet I didn't try to pull away.

He stroked my hair and said, "I thought it might be a little less wild now you're back in Rymor."

"You came over to critique my hair?"

"Well, no, but it *is* distracting. I'm amazed anyone gets any work done."

This entire conversation baffled me, and I pulled away from him. This time he gave me space. "Don't you have more important things to do than discuss my hair; like riots to manage or Jaru to kill?"

His face turned serious. "Yes, but tomorrow, not today."

"You sent me away." The separation had broken me.

"I know, I'm sorry. You know I love you, Hannah."

I turned my back as my lips trembled and the bond sparked to life. I shook my head, feeling the sting of tears behind my eyes: because we were bonded, I *felt* his truth.

"I'd kill every fucking Jaru single-handedly. I'd level cities, and I wouldn't lose any sleep about it, if I thought it was necessary to keep you safe."

I wasn't sure where this admission had sprung from, nor did I feel

## The Master of the Switch

worthy of its sentiments. I was just Hannah, whereas Tanis was something else, and the two things didn't seem compatible. Yet he had said it, and I believed him. There was no hint of duality or fraud nor any trace of deceit.

"I'm frightened." It wasn't until I spoke that I recognized this unequivocal truth. It felt like being afraid had become so ingrained that I no longer knew how to be anything else. "I'm afraid for Ella. I... I can't leave her with Bill."

"I'm not going to let anyone hurt you, and if there is any way I can help your sister, then I will." I hadn't noticed his approach, but I'd been so inwardly focused that a tornado could have descended, and I would have stayed in its path, unaware. I let him pull me into his arms and, for a moment, I felt safe. But I knew that it was a false safety, because a Jaru army was heading for Rymor, two of the fortresses had deserted Tanis to support Bill, and the wall had no power. The odds were impossible. Our downfall felt inevitable. Our civilization would be laid to waste, and even Tanis, with all his formidable skills, couldn't prevent it.

Only... his words rang with truth and certainty, and it was hard not to believe him. I wished I could believe him.

"I'm designed for war and to protect the colony. It's what the ancients created people like me for. I could no more fail at this than fail to breathe."

"There are so many of them."

"That doesn't matter," he said. "It didn't matter in the past. It won't matter now. The colony survived here before the wall, and it will survive here now the wall is gone."

He led me to the bedroom, where he undressed me and then himself and settled beside me on the bed. He purred, drawing me into his arms, and for the first time in forever, it felt like the world was shifting back into place.

"Red?" I mumbled into his chest.

"Giving us some space, at my request."

Bless Red for being Red. He would be worrying about how I was handling Tanis' return.

I'd spent so long angry at Tanis. Now that he was here, pressed against me, my prior fears felt foolish.

*I love you,* he'd said. That was all I'd needed.

It had been so long since I'd taken more than a few hours of rest. Now, the underlying tension I'd suffered in his absence lifted, and I slept, first fitfully and then deeply. Yet the long work hours had pushed my body clock out of whack, and I woke to find it still dark. I didn't know if my movement woke him or if he'd spent the night awake, but I felt his eyes on me, studying me for a long moment before he kissed me.

It was a slow, tender kind of kiss, the sort we didn't usually share, and we made love in its echo. It wasn't the intense passion that I wanted, yet I knew I needed his gentler side tonight. We both did. His gentle kisses and caresses, the passage of his big, calloused hand over my hip, waist, and breast, were sublime. Enveloped in darkness, the only option was to feel. And how I did.

"It drove me fucking crazy when Garren said he had visited you," he said, nipping at my throat. His big hand skimmed over my belly to cup me intimately. I was drenched with need, his scent and his proximity, enough to trigger my body to respond even without his feather-light caresses.

His mouth lowered to my breast, and he sucked on one nipple, drawing it into his mouth and lashing it with his tongue. Lips popping off it, he angled his head and slanted his mouth over mine. The kiss was hungry. I spread my thighs wider and rocked my hips, encouraging him to move his fingers against my pussy.

He slipped a single finger inside and brushed his thumb over my clit.

"Come for me, Hannah," he mumbled against my lips. "I want to feel you gushing all over me."

My chest heaved. I reached between us and snagged his cock,

## The Master of the Switch

pumping it erratically as we shared sweet, hot kisses and renewed our bond.

"I need to taste you," I whispered. "Please."

"Fuck," he muttered gruffly. He rolled onto his back, picked me up like a doll, spun me around, and dropped me over him. I lay sprawled over him, my thighs spread wide over his shoulders and mouth inches from his cock.

I grabbed my prize and sucked. He dragged me back and buried his face against my pussy with a groan of pleasure that sent me spinning. Then he licked and growled, and every nerve in my pussy flared to life. I was so close, fluttering with every lap of his tongue. When he began to suck on my clit, I felt my breath stutter as the sweet climax tipped me over. I sucked harder, rewarded with a heavy gush as he came down my throat.

I had barely come down when he was lifting me off, putting my back against the bed, and sliding his cock into me. I squeezed over his silken length, wrapping my arms and legs around him, feeling the emotion well in my chest spilling out as tears trickled down my cheeks and into my hair.

"Hush. I'm here now. I love you. It will get better, I promise."

He fucked me slow and considerate, kissing up my tears, and lifting my pleasure, reminding me of how perfect it felt when he was inside, his knot swelling and making all the sweet nerves within me sing. I would come again soon, yet I tried to hold it because this was perfect, and I wanted it to go on forever. Only nothing lasted forever, and sublime pleasure built into a pressure until it could not be denied.

We tumbled over together, his knot locking us and my pussy squeezing over him as he filled me with come.

I slept peacefully afterward, and when I woke, I was sprawled over his chest, and he was stroking my hair, watching over me in the semi-gloom of early morning.

Had he taken any rest at all?

He fisted my hair and kissed me in his usual hard, relentless way, the way I'd come to crave, moving me to where he wanted me as his tongue plundered my mouth. When he rolled, taking me under him, he nudged my thighs apart then buried himself inside me and it was pure heaven. He caught my wrists, dragged them above my head, and set a pace that was as hard and relentless as our kiss. It shut down my internal agitation, making all considerations and worries disappear. There was only the connection between us, the moment, and the pleasure. The war, tomorrow, and yesterday faded away. It was the only time I was free from myself and the endless cycles of consideration.

I came hard and unexpectedly. Whether Tanis noticed or cared, he didn't stop, either way. This, too, I needed, in order to escape everything in the blessed oblivion that only my last and final mate could provide.

# Chapter 51

**Shadowland**

**Ailey**

It had become cooler since we'd crossed into Shadowland, but today was a throwback, a hot and sweaty stinker, and the shade of my tent offered little respite from the heat.

I was guiding the Jaru in a steady south-easterly direction, cutting the corner of Shadowland, on a route that would take us toward the wall. As we had crossed the border, the vast group had stretched, leaving the elderly and those with young children lagging toward the back in what might be considered a protective move. The Jaru suffered no such sentimentality. A simple lack of speed and endurance during the rapid pace left the weaker at the back, and the younger, more capable warriors who desired glory at the front.

Yesterday, we'd sighted Talin in the distance where a gap in the trees at the top of a rocky escarpment offered a view. I'd seen a couple of fortresses during my time raiding Shadowland. There was little to distinguish between their glistening black stone structures, all sharp, unnatural angles with strange glass openings at the very top and the hulking gates made of metal that sat like the jaws of a beast. Thale was the biggest fortress, so I'd heard, but I'd never seen it in person. Talin was similar to Luka in size, but the two west towers were crumbling. The facing wall was covered in a patchwork of wooden lattice walkways where repairs were underway.

In front of Talin, on the broad plain leading to its gates, had been thousands upon thousands of white tents glistening in the sun. The little plumes of smoke rising from the surrounding forest indicated more. A fortress had pledged allegiance to Bill, or so a scout told me. I had no interest in Talin or the Shadowlanders there, so long as they stayed out of my way. I had killed every scout Bill had sent to talk to me. If he sent more, I'd kill them too.

I didn't want the Shadowlanders, or Bill, to have another presence here, not unless I was part of it. I hated the Shadowlanders, but the Jaru were stupid animals, and I was coming to realize that I didn't belong with them either. This quest to unite the Jaru, to gain their reverence, had lost meaning with my daughter gone. She didn't belong with the Jaru anymore than I did, nor did we belong with Bremmer's people.

Doubts festered like a puss-filled sore in my mind, rancid and awash with failure.

I wanted her back where I could protect her. I would do anything toward that aim.

Even if it meant destroying Bill, the Shadowlanders, the towerdwellers, or all three—I'd kill every bastard in my way.

Talin was the closest fortress to the wall and not far north of the place where we would cross the mighty Yandue River. From there, and even with this vast procession, we would reach Rymor in two weeks.

"There's one here insisting he speak to you," a guard said from the entrance to my tent. He shifted, uncomfortable under my scrutiny. "They call him the master. He's from one of the Outlier tribes."

My grunt was noncommittal. I had been on a bit of a killing spree

## The Master of the Switch

over the last couple of weeks. The weather made me irritable, and when my temper flared it inevitably led to someone suffering. Given the blistering temperature, pissing me off was in no one's best interest.

"Bring him here. We're not moving today. Too bloody hot."

The man left, and I scratched at my damp chest. Nemi lay on the furs, fast asleep, arms splayed. It had been too hot to fuck her last night, and I was too hot to find motivation now, either. I nudged her with my foot. Not quite awake, she blinked up at me.

"Out," I grunted.

She remained disorientated until I nudged her a little firmer. She jerked upright.

"Out!"

Snatching her clothes from the floor, she threw them on and left.

A few minutes later, the tent flap parted, and a man was shown inside. He wore a simple tunic with trousers, unlike the hide pants and naked chest most Jaru favored. His lack of weapons was notable. The flesh at his wrists and neck revealed intricate, swirling tattoos, while his face was lined by the sun, and his head was shaved other than for a single topknot bound with a strip of leather.

"I have been traveling long, from the far reaches of the plains, to join you here." The Outlier man spoke in a melodious voice that was soothing and briefly distracted me from the oppressive heat.

"From an Outlier tribe?" I asked. "You're the master?"

The man inclined his head and sat opposite at my indication.

Many were still joining us, even at this late stage. Word took time to reach the distant plains and longer for those who made their homes on the slopes of the mountain range beyond.

I didn't know a lot about the Outlier tribes. Not many did, but they were revered by the other Jaru tribes. Killing an elder was taboo, but that hadn't stopped me before. He dared to call himself the master like he was important. Maybe I needed to make an example of an Outlier?

"I have a gift for the harbinger who unites us." The master bowed his head and reached into the bag at his side.

A few tribes had brought me gifts, and although most of it was junk, the occasional item stirred my interest. He fumbled beneath the flap of his bag before pulling out a cloth-bound item that was flat but wide enough to require both his hands. He passed it to me with another bow of his head.

I parted the cloth to find a golden torque, the metal twisted into a pattern that matched the tattoos on the man's wrists. My nod was one of satisfaction. It was a delicate item, perhaps the finest gift I'd received yet. I thought the Outliers paying homage to me would keep the other Jaru in line.

I'd been gifted a pair of gold cuffs a few days ago. Lifting my wrist I compared and noted that the torque was of similar quality. The cuffs fitted me perfectly. The man who'd brought them had twisted them apart to enable me to put them on. They had closed around my wrists with a snap. They wouldn't come off again, but they were beautiful, and I hadn't been too bothered about it.

"I see you now have the full set. It is a good sign." The master bobbed his head.

They were always muttering about signs. I didn't give a shit about signs, but the cuffs and torque were quality, and I enjoyed both the Jaru's fear and adulation.

"Our tribe would be honored if you would wear it." He indicated the torque.

I inspected it, trying to find the hidden catch mechanism.

"Please allow me?" He held out his hands and waited for my approval before twisting the torque open. "A great honor," he muttered, bowing his head again as he returned it to my waiting hands.

The Outlier master was respectful. I appreciated that.

"Is this Rymorian?" I asked, brows drawing together as I tried to discern how it closed and opened. The craftsmanship was too fine to

## The Master of the Switch

be Jaru. Stolen Rymorian goods should have been brought to me immediately and not presented as a gift.

The Outlier looked at me questioningly.

"Tower-dweller?" I said. "Is it from the tower-dwellers?"

"Ah, no." The master bobbed his head. "The Outliers have skills. Much time was dedicated to its making."

Better not kill any yet if they had more treasures stashed away. I lifted it toward my neck, concerned it wouldn't fit. I eased the two halves together cautiously, and as had happened with the cuffs, there was a click as it closed.

It felt heavy and pleasant against my neck, and I ran my fingers over it.

"I have one more gift for you." The master inclined his head again.

I nodded, intrigued.

This time he pulled a tiny gold box from his bag with the same intricate markings on the side, and a single blue jewel on the top. I wasn't a discerning man, but it looked valuable, and together with the torque and the cuffs, I thought I could sell it for enough to live a comfortable life with my daughter when this was over.

I reached to grab it. The master snatched it away.

I growled, ready to beat the insolent fucker.

"Allow me to demonstrate." He pressed his thumb against the blue stone.

There was another click.

*Pain.*

I screamed, maddened as thousands of tiny blades pierced my neck and wrists.

I thrashed, clawing and raking my nails over my skin to get it off.

It ceased abruptly, and I blinked, rousing myself from the floor and staring at my bloody fingers.

What the fuck had just happened?

The Outlier watched me, a serene smile on his face. "I'm sorry, there is often a little discomfort when it hosts."

I gaped at him, my gaze lowered to where bloody rivulets trickled down my chest and from my wrists. "What the fuck have you done to me?"

I intended for my fingers to close around the master's throat and snap his neck, but instead, I was again writhing on the floor, consumed by an agony so great I wanted to tear the skin from my flesh.

When it ceased, I lay panting, sweating, and blinking at the Outlier bastard.

"Who are you?" I croaked.

He smiled. "I am the master, and now I am your master. Let's see how quickly you learn."

# Chapter 52

**Talin**

**Bill**

Dawn had broken an hour ago on what promised to be another warm day at Talin as I walked along the battlements with Pope at my side. Falton's camp was visible through the nearby forest, the smoke from campfires indicating the vast area it covered. A trail of a dozen caravans with goods and food trundled toward the fortress from the south.

I studied the view that provided a source of satisfaction and failure. I was back in Shadowland but could no longer return to Rymor.

I could not have both—I still wanted both.

I pulled out of my pocket the device Damien Moore had discovered and studied it in the light. A tiny gold box covered in an intricate scrolling pattern with a single red jewel on the top.

"You gonna use it?" Pope asked.

Pope had been surly since I'd entered Ella's room, in a mood reminiscent of the day he discovered I'd used underhanded means to ensure his compliance.

I regretted taking that personal step with Ella. Still, it was done, and I preferred not to get Pope further offside than he already was.

"Probably," I said. "I was hoping to be in a position of greater stability before I needed to. Tanis' return to Rymor is an unfortunate development."

I didn't want to disable technology permanently, just for long enough to bring Rymor down, but the kind of anarchy this innocuous-looking little box would produce wasn't the temporary variety—assuming it worked—and whether or not to engage it was proving a weightier decision than I'd anticipated.

I slipped the device into my pocket and continued along the battlements.

The Jaru under Ailey were still moving south and were not far from Talin, along with the nearby camp of the fifty thousand Shadowlanders I'd persuaded to follow me instead of Tanis.

"The Jaru should have been enough to obliterate Tanis' Shadowland forces. He'll have weapons now, though," Pope said.

"He will," I agreed with ill temper. "Why Rymor would consider asking a man convicted of terrorism to save them from the Jaru, who are not even interested in Rymor, is beyond me."

"The Jaru are taking an odd path according to the scouts Ailey hasn't killed, which does take them on a trajectory toward the wall," Pope said. "And funny how the Rymorian government overturned the terrorism charges so quickly."

"Panicked by the lack of wall with a battle about to take place so close," I replied evenly.

"You set him up, didn't you?" Pope had a nasty smirk on his lips. "He was never involved in that bombing ten years ago, was he?"

I stopped walking and regarded the other man steadily. "You should learn when to keep opinions to yourself, Pope."

Pope's grin faded, and he shrugged. "Not much point. You've got me here. Got my guaranteed obedience thanks to your clever bit of

# The Master of the Switch

human rights abuse when you fitted me and everyone else here with a personal off switch. The least you can do is not treat me like an idiot."

I inclined my head and continued walking.

"The Jaru could be heading toward Rymor," Pope continued. "Ailey was little help with Damien, and we've had no communication from him for weeks. They could also be coming for us. You sure he's going to pass straight through?"

"I have Ailey's daughter. He'll follow orders." Considering Pope's declaration, I saw little value in hiding the details. He was part of this now, and his future depended on my survival.

Pope laughed. A low, wicked sound that I liked.

"I'm not a man who leaves things to chance," I said, smiling. I also didn't tolerate demanding guests, and Ailey's daughter had become increasingly difficult to control as her alpha genes had kicked in. I'd given her over to the leader of the underground cage-fighting scene in Tranquility a year ago. Ailey would eventually work out that I'd screwed him over. But, according to reports, his daughter was thriving in her new situation, so perhaps I'd done them a favor.

"Still, that many Shadowlanders armed with weapons could destroy the Jaru army," Pope replied. "And they could also destroy us."

I paused to stare pensively down at Shadowland. The supply wagons were nearing the gates, and I could hear the clank of the portcullis rising.

"I need to press the button," I said, "But pressing the button destroys my weapons, too, along with my shuttle access to supplies from Rymor. It is a quandary. Pressing the button would give advantage to the Jaru. Not pressing leaves the advantage with Tanis and Rymor."

"Greve doesn't need more than protection from the Jaru. Falton is going to be the tricky one. He wants to be wooed by Rymorian things. You press the button and it's goodbye to Rymorian things and Falton."

I wondered what Pope thought about Rymor's imminent demise,

should I follow through. I'd done a thorough background check, and the people I'd selected to work out here were loners with no family ties. It would be presumptuous, though, to presume Pope had no feeling toward the destruction of his former home. "How do you feel about me obliterating all technology? Assuming it works and assuming it does what we think it does." I'd had the switch scanned, but all the experts could tell me was that it contained complex ancient technology.

"As if I have any say in this?" Pope barked out a laugh. "There's no one back in Rymor I care about, but destroying a civilization for... whatever this is... revenge? Survival? That would be crazy."

"I agree. Using it is a last resort." I was damned whatever I did. My place was at risk without adequate forces to protect me. I had very few, and those I did were reliant on technology. I also needed something to trade for food and other essential supplies since the farms owed me no loyalty.

The Jaru offered no long-term protection. Holding them together was complex, and relied on Ailey, who was increasingly frustrated. The warlord wouldn't remain in my service for much longer, assuming the Jaru didn't implode once they destroyed Shadowland.

We made our way down the stairs and into the courtyard as the wagons arrived and the workers began unloading the supplies. We were returning to the office when one of my men hurried over.

"I have news from Rymor, sir. There's a message for you." The man held out a viewer.

I activated it and read the message. Tanis had left Rymor and was on his way to Shadowland with an army bearing Rymorian weapons. He was worryingly close to Talin and had set up a base south of the Yandue river. Doubtless intended to cut off the Jaru. With tech-based weapons, and such numbers, they could obliterate the Jaru and come straight here for me.

I felt the bite of inevitability. I passed the viewer to Pope, who read it with a grim expression and then passed it back. "He doesn't have an implant. Get rid of him."

### The Master of the Switch

Pope swore but immediately drew his sword and ran the man through.

The messenger's startled expression went slack as he slipped lifeless to the ground.

"Get on with your work!" Pope hollered when the unloading of the wagons came to a halt. He turned back toward me. "Shit! Don't."

Pope froze, his hand stretched toward the device in my hand.

The red button flashed where I'd just depressed it.

Seconds later, a thunderous boom reverberated within and without the fortress. The heavyset draft horses reared, and people ducked or scattered, seeking escape from the invisible threat. A sharp pain stabbed behind my eye—the retinal viewer was likely dead. Not that I have been able to use it for weeks.

Pope pressed fingers to the back of his ear. "Fuck!"

It was too late, though. It was done. For better or worse, it was done.

∼

## Kein

Arriving with the wagons, I was helping unload the goods when two men approached.

People of importance had an air to them that I'd learned to recognize. I would have marked the shorter of the two even had he not worn tower-dweller clothes. The local soldier with him was tall and lean with cropped gray hair.

The wagon drivers muttered at the men's arrival. Word had spread to the surrounding farms and villages that the lord here was a tower-dweller, and there had been much speculation. I wasn't the only person watching the man I suspected to be Tanis' enemy, William Bremmer.

Another man arrived dressed in tower-dweller clothes and gave something to Bremmer.

The next time I looked up, the newcomer lay dead on the floor, killed by the gray-haired one.

The traders cowered back.

"Get back to work!" the gray-haired one hollered.

Before we could respond, a great boom reverberated around the courtyard.

Pain lanced my head at the back of my eye. My reaction was covered by the rearing carthorse, but I noted others, including the gray-haired one, holding their heads, marking them tower-dwellers.

Was it the switch Tanis had talked of? Had William Bremmer just leveled the field? And if he had, what would that mean for Shadowland?

What would it mean for my mission here?

One thing was certain. If Ella was here, I needed to find her fast.

# Chapter 53

**Rymor**

**Richard**

It was morning, and I was standing before the windowed wall of my apartment.

Tanis had left today and would be in Shadowland by now, along with the Rymorian forces, the Shadowlanders he'd brought here to help with the riots, medical personnel, and a terrifying array of weapons that I prayed would be sufficient to stop a Jaru hoard and the fifty thousand Shadowlanders who had turned against Tanis.

A few troops remained, enough to patrol the trouble hotspots that remained, but that was all. With no wall and little internal protection, this was the most exposed Rymor had ever been.

I sipped my coffee and watched the shuttles zipping about. It was dull, with the promise of rain and lights from the skyscrapers and shuttles blinked and twinkled in the washed-out sky. The country was buoyant and hopeful.

Today, I was leaving, along with the council members and anyone considered critical. Our destination was a secure base in northern Rymor.

Was I abandoning the population?

I turned away, intent on finalizing my travel bags, when a series of booms cracked like thunder, snapping my focus to the window. My chest heaved, and my cup dropped to the floor with a thud. A flash lit the sky, needles of lightning too numerous to be real. I winced as a sharp sting pierced my ear and right eye. Outside, the unnatural lightning pulsed up from the ground, arcing and dancing destruction over the city. Windows shattered in random pockets, accompanied by more explosions and fire.

Inside the buildings, electronics popped and emitted blackened smoke.

The wrath of God felt appropriate, only this was no god but the work of the ancients.

The lightning fizzled out, plunging the city and my room into darkness... My last fleeting sight was of shuttles plunging eerily toward the ground.

Shakes overcome me. It had really happened.

I was powerless to help anyone. All the research, all the planning, and we still had little to show besides a start on stockpiling food, water, and medical supplies. We weren't far enough through the process, and there was nowhere near enough of anything and no one to manage the distribution, let alone deal with the carnage in the streets below.

The sounds of footsteps came from behind—the apartment door lay open, and people were fleeing.

I stood immobilized, grappling with the impossible, when there was an itching sensation behind my right ear. Was my technology about to kill me?

*"Richard? Are you receiving this?"*

"Nate! Is everyone okay there?"

*"We're okay. Shaken but okay. Are you at home? I can't see your location data."*

# The Master of the Switch

"Yes, I'm at home."

*"Get to the sky port and wait for me there. I'm coming to get—"*

The communication closed abruptly. The tumult continued beyond my window like a movie playing on mute. Only this was no movie. It was horrifyingly real.

I fled my apartment, taking the stairs up when everyone else was heading down. If Nate didn't make it here... no, he said he was coming. If he didn't, I would worry about it then.

The ground beneath me shuddered, and I pitched into the wall, my arms flying out to steady me. Screams erupted from the stairwell as I staggered into the skyport.

The glass canopy had shattered, leaving debris scattered over the landing pad. The world beyond was dazzled by eruptions of flame and smoke. Shock took me. I collapsed against the wall, put my head in my hands, and cried.

I lost track of time. The biting wind didn't penetrate the stupor into which I sank. Should I leave? Should I wait for Nate?

A deafening cracking sound tore me from my daze, a metallic screeching... the sound of rupturing, as if of the planet breaking apart.

I blinked. The tower complex opposite was collapsing, gaining momentum as gravity worked on the crumbling structure, dragging it down into a billowing shower of dust and debris.

The floor shook again, stronger this time.

The buildings were moving, all of them sliding from my view.

I started to slide.

Only it wasn't other buildings... It was my building.

I fell backward, tumbling against the wall behind me. Around me came a screeching, so loud I felt it reverberate through my bones. I went tumbling again, only this time, the tumbling didn't stop.

# Chapter 54

**Shadowland**

**Tanis**

With so many new arrivals and supplies pouring in, the Shadowlander camp was borderline chaotic when I stepped into the mobile command center.

When I exited half an hour later it had progressed to full chaos.

I squinted across the camp. Behind me, Scott Harding muttered and cursed to himself in a now familiar way. The adopted shuttle, which had been used throughout the internal Rymorian struggles, had been cool, but outside it was blisteringly hot.

Someone, in their infinite wisdom, had scorched an area vast enough to hold the accompanying fifteen thousand troops and still leave room for the landing shuttles and endless stacks of supplies. Obliterating the trees and vegetation down to ground level, while vital for shuttle landing, let the harsh Shadowland sun through.

# The Master of the Switch

Directly ahead, Theo was inducting a group of new arrivals. Supplies had been arriving from Rymor in a steady stream over the last week putting Theo's impressive organizational skills to the test. Much of the supplies had been distributed, but a huge amount still remained. Everything and everyone useful to halting the Jaru had been, or were being, brought out here, too. The sky had been buzzing with shuttles earlier, but I thought the influx was slowing.

I hoped they were tapering off.

This morning would complete the last personnel drop before we would move out.

Not that it was peaceful now. There had been constant attacks, and although they were more of a nuisance than a threat, it kept my forces on high alert. Stepping outside the camp was a sure way to end up dead.

The north-east of Shadowland had been decimated by the Jaru approach. For a country so alive with life, where you could barely travel more than a few hours without coming across a farm or village, it twisted my gut to think of the people displaced or dead as a result of the invasion. Assuming we achieved success, some would drift back, but with so many losses it may be impossible to rebuild some of the smaller communities.

The closer ties with Rymor would help yet, despite our weapons advantage, there were still too many Jaru. There was also the possibility that the Jaru would have weapons. They'd had weapons before and it was reasonable to assume they still had them.

Garren approached from my left. "Can't be many more?" Like me, he was wearing his Rymorian battle fatigues, along with a curious mix of Rymorian and Shadowlander weapons.

"Twenty-seven shuttles left to land," Theo said, arriving on my right with a viewer in his hand. "Twenty-six."

I laughed. "I don't think Garren was seeking a precise figure, Theo."

"Well, he got one." Theo narrowed his eyes on Garren who grinned back. "The last of the Rymorian medical team have arrived.

We'll need to decide how best to distribute them... Oh and Kein should be in Talin by now."

"Talin?" I said, frowning. "Why didn't he message me?"

"Because everything comes through me," Theo stated. "Unless you want an information overload. He used the cover of a supply wagon and intends to slip away while they're unloading. Supplies are heading into Talin regularly. Kein accompanied a twelve-wagon team. We should consider how to cut that off at some point when we're less busy."

"Who the fuck is sending supplies to Talin?" I bit out.

"Plenty of local farms in that area," Garren said. "Or it could be Greve or Falton."

"Bremmer has assimilated himself into Shadowland with alarming ease," I said. "I look forward to finishing with the Jaru."

"Sixteen," Theo said to himself. "I need to get back." With his eyes still fixed on the information he hastened off to where another shuttle was landing.

"So, you and Hannah are all made up?" he asked casually.

"She didn't kick me out of her apartment." I side eyed him, wondering where this was going.

"Did you tell her about—" He gestured toward my crotch. "—fixing your defective junk?"

"It wasn't defective. It simply didn't—" I shut up on seeing Garren's shit-eating grin.

He cracked his knuckled dramatically and wiggled his eyebrows.

"How do you even know?" How had we gotten on to discussing my junk?

"Theo," Garren said. "I swear he's a worse gossip than Kein. Admit it, you were thinking about the possibility of breeding Hannah when those fancy Rymorian officials first approached you?"

"I was thinking about a lot of things."

"Yeah, and none of them were related to sowing seed."

I laughed. "You are so full of bullshit, it's wonder you can walk."

"Tell me you didn't think about it once?"

## The Master of the Switch

"Fine," I admitted. "I thought about it once."

Garren emitted a deep guffaw.

I *was* an alpha.

"Now, let's ride out. I want to speak with Arand and Javid. We'll take the wolf guard." Our camp was located on the predicted Jaru trajectory toward the wall. Javid and Arand had camped an hour ahead. The brunt of the Jaru frontrunners were hitting them, but plenty had scouted the edges. "Or we could use a shuttle?" I said casually.

"Horse." Garren gave the nearby shuttle a baleful look. "I like their weapons. The shuttles and the metal cleaning rats, not so much." He patted the PB rifle strapped to his leg affectionately. "My personal favorite," he said before calling out instructions to a nearby wolf guard to prepare for my departure.

"That's because you have the setting so high it can blow a hole in a building," I muttered.

Agregor hurried to join us as he noticed us preparing to leave. "Where are you going?"

"To see Javid and Arand," I replied.

"Oh." Agregor's face fell. "Are the wolf guard going?"

"Yes, and so are you. I want you where I can see you."

A sudden boom reverberated around the camp. People ducked, horses reared. A sharp sting to the back of my right eye and behind my ear—the retinal viewer and personal communicator were dead. Hearing the dull pop from the PB rifle strapped to my thigh, I ripped it out and then stared at the lifeless device.

Scott stumbled out of the command center to my left, surrounded by clouds of smoke.

"What the fuck?" Garren muttered.

I looked up in time to see the airborne shuttles plummeting toward the ground.

The world felt like it stopped moving. A sense of dread enveloped me, followed directly by hopelessness as the first shuttle plowed into the ground with a thud that reverberated through the soles of my feet. It exploded into a fountain of sparks and flames.

Fires sprang up and mini explosions continued to boom throughout the camp.

Closing my eyes briefly, I heaved a breath.

"Stay there." I pinned Agregor with a look, lest he start arguing, and pointed in the direction of the medical tent.

Then I started toward the shuttle landing zone where the worst of the decimation had occurred.

Theo had been over by the shuttles, an area now engulfed by flames, I realized, and he had been fitted with an array of cybernetics far more comprehensive than the retinal viewer and communicator.

*Theo?* Panic gripped me.

I picked up my pace to jog.

The nearest crashed shuttle exploded, blasting shrapnel into the surrounding area, screams added to the cacophony.

I started to run.

# Chapter 55

**Rymor**

**Nate**

Hannah lay on the floor of the shuttle with a jumble of blackened ancient technology plasma plates, connectors, and switches strewn around her. Her head and shoulders were jammed inside the control slot, and her fingers were busy yanking out plates and tossing them aside. "What are you going to do?" she asked.

"Find the council members. We're going to need their direction."

She sent another plate clattering to the shuttle floor.

"Are you sure we don't need all of them?" I hated to interrupt her while she was working, but she had ripped several important looking pieces of technology out and they had to be there for a reason.

"They're fried, literally. We can't start it until they're out. Besides, I don't think we need to worry about crashing into other shuttles or orchestrating flight paths when this is the only shuttle in the sky." Three more switches were tossed out in quick succession, amid mutters and cursing—I had never heard her swear.

She shimmied out and ran over to the front console.

I followed close behind her, watching as she pressed her palm to the plate.

Nothing, not so much as a flicker.

Pivoting, she smacked into me. "Damn it, Nate!"

Darting around me, she ran back to the open panel and threw herself half in on her hands and knees. More muttering followed. Another two plates were sent skittering across the floor before she rushed back to the console.

The lights popped on and it stuttered to life. We both let out a shaky breath.

"Load up!" I hollered out the open door, and a dozen soldiers stomped in, crushing the discarded plates under their boots.

Hannah winced, then frowned at the plate in her hand. "The takeoff and landing might be a little abrupt," she said before adding earnestly, "Are you going to be okay on manual?"

"Yeah, I'll work it out." Hopefully they were not my famous last words.

"Take care, Nate!" She threw her arms around my neck and hugged me before dashing down the ramp.

Does she think I'm about to die?

*"I've not been able to reestablish communication with the Shadowland forces yet,"* Dan messaged me through the communicator.

"What about Theo?"

*"Nothing yet,"* Dan replied.

"Okay, I'm up and running here. Hannah is on her way back," I replied. "Let me know as soon as you hear."

Dan's confirmation came through the communicator.

"Buckle up," I called, sliding into the flight observer seat and placing my palm against the control plate. The manual flight interface popped up on the front viewer.

## The Master of the Switch

"You ever piloted a shuttle on manual before?" someone called out.

"You want me to answer that?" I asked as I initiated the takeoff.

"No, we're good," another man called.

The shuttle juddered with the screech of metal against metal before I remembered to release the anchor, and we lurched into the sky. It rocked and bounced as a down draft buffeted us before it surged upward with bone-crushing g-force. Muttered curses and a noise that sounded a lot like a scream came from the back of the craft.

Controlling the flight took all my concentration, but finally we rose above the weather and leveled out.

A round of applause and a couple of whoops came from the back.

I raised my spare hand in acknowledgment. "I think you pulled something vital out, Hannah," I muttered. "I can't wait to try and land!"

It was a two hour flight to Serenity where we would collect Grace Claridge and the other members of the council of twelve. The flight passed without incident, until we reached the outskirts of the city and the scale of the destruction was revealed.

Although we had been in contact with some of the council members, after the tech failure, we'd had no contact with several others, and yet more had lost contact in the interim, including Richard, which worried me. The retinal viewers and personal communicators were broken in fifty percent of cases and one or both components needed to be replaced. My cybernetic implants had also taken a hit. After the initial burst of pain, several hadn't worked.

Outside the window, the world was afire and sluggish smoke drifted in a dull gray sky that was more smoke than genuine cloud. The soldiers in the back of the shuttle had gone quiet. It was possible they knew people in Serenity.

"Are all the cities this bad?" one man asked.

"It depends how densely populated... And how much technology there is. I expect every major city has suffered the same," I replied.

The EMP blast had a compound effect. The denser the presence of technology, the greater the destruction.

Far below, buildings had collapsed in the heavy commercial districts. As we swept into the first pick up, we glimpsed people scurrying like ants through the decimation. Further on, the Serenity Technology Center had been reduced to rubble, taking down most of the surrounding buildings.

I swallowed hard, but the ache in my throat remained.

"How are we going to get over this?" someone asked.

"A day at a time," someone else replied.

# Chapter 56

**Shadowland**

**Ailey**

"I see I have your attention," the master said amiably.

I wasn't fucking stupid and made no further move against the master.

"This is all very confusing, I'm sure." The master's soft, lyrical voice continued. "But I'm delighted you are learning. It won't let you harm me, and the result, as you have just discovered, is exceptionally painful."

"What have you done to me?" My throat felt raw. I wanted to wrap my hands around his throat and squeeze until his face turned blue and his eyeballs popped out.

"A little device I created especially for you. I've had to apply some ingenuity to the design to protect it from other events, but I expect such subtleties are beyond you." He chuckled to himself. "You can't remove it, but I dare say you will try. You can't kill me either, but I dare say you'll try that, too. You've had enough fun, but no more. Not that they need any help. They don't know better since the age of regression." He sighed. "I realize your behavior is not your fault. You can no more help your desire to kill than the children can, albeit for different reasons. Your ancestors have much to answer for."

"I don't give a shit about my ancestors or these children. What do you want from me? What do I have to do for you to take this off?" They always wanted something from me. My life was one long, endless battle to be free.

"I want you to take the Jaru to Rymor," he said. "Without slaughtering them along the way. I don't underestimate the Shadowlanders, and neither should you. No more wasting Jaru lives before their time."

My fingers twitched at my side. I would be in great pain if I tried to touch the torque or attempted to kill the master, so I restrained myself. "Why do you want Rymor?"

The master smiled. "Because it's ours."

"Not the end of the world then?" I sneered.

"Hmm, yes... Uncertainty often gives birth to such tales. They are echoes of the truth but never the whole truth. The Outliers alone know the truth. Your ancestors covered up their shame. One does not advertise that one is a thief, among other things."

"Thief?" I spat out, made reckless by my rage. "You think the Rymorians stole Jaru land? I've heard that before. Maybe they did, but nobody gives a fuck."

"That's where you're wrong."

"Wrong? You're not making any fucking sense."

"Let us keep it simple." The master's condescending air riled me further. "We want Rymor back and, as you know, the Jaru are not so easy to control or to unite. That was always the problem: until you came along. I can't let you deviate from this goal. I know your other master wants you to destroy the Shadowlanders, and that's why I acted."

"You want me to lead the Jaru to Rymor?" I demanded, impatient with the convoluted conversation. "I was going there anyway. I don't

## The Master of the Switch

give a fuck about Bremmer's plans, haven't for a long while. He's got my daughter. The bastard has been threatening to sell her to a skin trader for the last five years to keep me in line. Bremmer will never give me up, and I'll never see my daughter again. That's why I'm going to Rymor, now he's trapped out here."

"A fascinating development." The master indicated the gold box with the blue switch on the top in his hand. "As you can see, I'm familiar with ancient technology. If it's possible to find your daughter, I will. Once we're back in Rymor."

"I knew that was Rymorian," I growled, angry my vanity had allowed me to be tricked.

"Ancient does not equal Rymorian." The master returned the delicate gold box to his bag. "If you follow my directions, the torque will give you no further pain."

I grunted.

"Hmm," the man said, a light smile on his lips. "For a start, you can instruct everyone to begin today's travel."

I grunted again and stood. Outside, I kicked the Rymorians sitting outside the tent. The master had made no reference to the Rymorians being off-limits. "We're moving out."

"What?" the man asked as he scrambled to his feet. "We just told everyone to stay here today."

I punched him. A satisfying crack accompanied the blood splatter, and my excitement rose when there was no torque-induced pain. "Give the order! We're moving out."

As the Rymorian men hurried to do my bidding, I turned to find the master watching me.

"You don't care how I treat the Rymorians?"

The master shook his head.

"What about Jaru who step out of line?"

"Most are suitably cowed, but if necessary, you may discipline them. So long as they are still functioning, and all their usual body parts are attached."

"Can I still have Nemi?"

"For a man without any apparent bargaining power, you like to test the boundaries." The master's lips twitched with humor. "But you do adjust to your circumstances remarkably well."

I stared back. "Is that a yes?"

"As long as she is well and the usual body parts remain attached after you have finished with her, then yes."

I grinned.

"Oh, I'll need your Rymorian weapons and any other technology you have," the master added as I was about to walk away.

"What for?" I asked, instantly suspicious.

"Because your other master has destroyed them, and I believe I can fix them again."

# Chapter 57

**Rymor**

**Hannah**

The research facility had been restored to a semblance of normality, with no fatalities, and only minor injuries. The equipment failure was comprehensive, but the building at least was largely undamaged.

After the EMP obliterated the technology, there was a mad scramble to return the base to operation. I hadn't seen Red since this morning. His time as a field scientist had given him many practical skills and he had been treating the injured before helping reconnect the solar power. After immediate injuries and hazards had been dealt with, we'd worked on communication, workstations, and printers, which were invaluable for replacing any plasma plates or circuits needed to get other vital technology working.

The research facility was being restored piece by painful piece.

Nate was out on a shuttle and had located several council members, including Grace Claridge. Many remained missing. Given the extent of the destruction, I feared they might be dead. He was continuing to spend the remaining daylight hours searching.

I tried not to dwell on how bad it must be throughout Rymor. We'd had no contact with the forces in Shadowland either. For selfish reasons, this worried me more.

*They will be alright—they have to be.*

I understood how EMP worked and had seen firsthand the impact at this facility. Most of the workstations had been destroyed due to the compound impact of the destruction. Only the isolated nature of our base had saved us from worse.

"What's the tech we should get up and running next? Medical scanners? Or weapons? Or something else?" I asked. I'd just repaired the third workstation following Dan's instructions and now I was ready to put it to use.

"Scanners," Coco said.

"Weapons," Dan said.

"The Jaru army is still a few days away," Coco said. "The medical scanners will be more useful to us at first." She had Molly on her lap, who was unusually subdued. The little girl wanted to cuddle with me, but Coco had explained how I was busy repairing equipment the bad people had damaged, and Molly had settled to watch.

Dan nodded in agreement. Grabbing a scanner from the box the base personnel had gathered, I plugged it into the workstation and brought the schematic up to the viewer.

With my fingers against the interactive work surface, I shifted through the plasma circuitry revealed in the schematic. I'd never dedicated any time to medical scanners before, but all ancient technology had a pattern, and that pattern had symmetry and logic. The EMP had targeted either the power source or the microcircuits connecting it to the master network, these being the most vulnerable to the blast. It was a clever means of attack.

I had to find a pattern that could bypass the degraded cells to restore it.

## The Master of the Switch

Time drifted, and the other occupants of the room faded from my mind as I studied the intricate details of the scanner.

"Nate!"

I snapped my head up and turned to find Nate standing in the doorway.

"I wanted to tell you in person, Dan," Nate said.

Coco rose from where she had been tucking Molly down for a nap on the nearby seat and came over to join them.

"It's Richard," Nate continued. "He's—well, he's—"

"What in the blazes? Spit it out," Dan said gruffly.

"About to start a secondary career in action and adventure after jumping onto the shuttle from a moving landing pad."

"It sounds more exciting than it actually was," Richard interrupted. He had a huge bandage around his head. "Also, I have concussion and there are two of everyone. There were two shuttles. Just glad I picked the right one!"

Dan burst out laughing.

"Woah!" Nate said making a grab for Richard when he teetered a little, helping him to a seat. "Do we have any scanners working?"

"Not yet," I said. "I'm working on them now."

"What is it like out there?" Coco asked, her concerned eyes on Nate.

"Yeah, as we expected, possibly worse. I don't know where or how we begin to make this right."

"How many council members did you find?" Dan asked.

"Four," Nate said tiredly. "I only found four."

"Four grateful people, Nate." Grace entered the room behind him, followed by the other council members. "Four people who share your grief for Rymor." The room began to fill as the facility personnel arrived to hear the news.

"We are the fortunate ones," Grace said, and the room settled to a hush as all eyes turned to our leader. "We are also the ones with the hardest burden, who must maintain our focus and discipline when we want nothing more than to grieve. We must continue, even knowing how gravely our fellow Rymorians suffer." She looked toward Nate before she scanned the crowded room. "There is no precedent for this, and we are certain to make mistakes. But please, whatever you were doing before we brought this sad news to you, keep working. Take a rest when you need to, and then keep going, even when it seems impossible, because Rymor is counting on you."

The weight of unshed tears gathered behind my eyes as people began dispersing and, urged by Grace's words, returning to their designated tasks. My stomach was in knots thinking about what might be happening in Shadowland with Tanis and Garren.

My focus returned to the workstation, where the viewer had paused on a section of the schematic. I blinked, realizing I could see a solution. Would it work for the rest, though?

Fingers fast against the interactive surface, I manipulated the plasma through the interface, shifting properties, moving cells, and reassigning functionality.

Then, with bated breath, I pressed the thumb plate, delighted when it sprang to life. I grabbed another and quickly checked it to find the same issue.

"How are the scanners going?" Nate said. "Grace wants us to head out to the Shadowland forces as soon as possible. We've had limited contact and most of it's confusing. Scanners are great, but we'll need weapons too.

"I think I've worked out how to fix them," I said, offering up the scanner.

"It's not going to kill anyone, is it?" he asked with a raised brow.

"No," I said defensively. "I haven't touched the medical programming. The power link was damaged. I think it might be a common failure."

"Someone has to try it." He took the scanner and disappeared out of the room.

I followed. Was he looking for someone with an injury?

I stopped dead, finding Nate with his sleeve pushed up and blood dripping from a cut on his arm. "Nate! What the hell?!"

### The Master of the Switch

A scowling Red took his knife back from Nate. He sheathed it, and looked at me askance.

"It's a scratch," Nate said, "and no offense, but I nearly crashed the shuttle twice."

"I did tell you the landing would be abrupt."

Red snickered.

"Abrupt and crash-landing are not interchangeable terms," Nate said, his smile taking the sting out of his words. He pressed the scanner against the wound, sighing as it healed into a neat pink line.

"Will the same principle work for the weapons? How soon can we fix the rest?" he asked. "I'd like to get these scanners and any weapons out into Shadowland at first light."

"I think I have the pattern. I need to try it on a weapon, but if I'm correct, we should be able to replicate the technique on any handheld device. If we can get a couple of the portable workstations ready, and maybe a printer too, then it might be possible to repair on-site."

"I'll get some weapons brought to you, but meanwhile, see if you can fix another scanner," Nate said, before he hurried off with intent.

"How long do you need? I'll get the shuttle and a team ready," Red said.

"Only if I'm coming with you." I folded my arms to let him know I meant business.

"Only if Nate is confident the shuttle is not about to crash," he countered, folding his arms, and looking surprisingly stern.

# Chapter 58

### Shadowland

### Tanis

The Shadowland operational base looked like someone had dropped a bomb. Given the stacks of weapons that had randomly exploded and the debris from the crashed shuttles, it was a fair comparison.

I ferried the wounded to the medical tent throughout the evening and into the night. By the time the sun started to rise, most of the fires had died out. The destruction was comprehensive. Smoke rose in drifting plumes, and people stood or sat in exhausted clusters. Most of those we found now were dead, so it was a case of helping the injured as best as we could.

Some people were not going to make it without a scanner.

Had this been the Armageddon switch? It'd certainly felt like it.

Scott had organized a search for the closest crashed shuttle. Some people might have survived, but it was unlikely. The rest of the shuttles were too far away to do anything about.

# The Master of the Switch

We'd heard from Red at the base that Hannah was okay and the base mostly intact, although the equipment was severely damaged, and they were piecing it back together.

I still hadn't found Theo. I cold, empty space was opening up inside me the longer he remained missing.

To my right, two men carried another to medical. A bloody bandage was wrapped around his leg, but it didn't appear to be life-threatening. A medic hurried over to make an assessment. I was grateful that basic response training meant the Rymorians could manage medical emergencies without a scanner.

The warning of a Jaru attack roused me from considering where the fuck to look for Theo next. I drew my sword and ran toward the attack before the warning call finished. My guards converged on me in support; not only my wolf guard but the whole camp. Han was organizing those around the temporary medical tent, and all of those injured or incapable of assisting in the fight were gathered together for protection. Garren and his section followed me to meet the Jaru from the north, and Danel and his section met the Jaru surging from the south.

"Just when I was getting used to my new favorite kill toy," Garren quipped. Sword drawn, he cut down a Jaru warrior, turning his battle cry to a gurgling shriek and his pale tattooed skin red. "Nice to get back to the basics."

"You would be much more efficient if you didn't talk so much." I killed the approaching Jaru in a steady stream, evading the slash and stab of their stubby axes.

Only we were being pushed back. The vast camp was on flat ground, making it impossible to know how the rest were faring. Bodies began piling at the edges of the clearing. The fighting continued but soon, Shadowlanders were falling along with Jaru as more of the enemy arrived in relentless waves.

We fought on, trapped and without the option to retreat except toward the center of the camp.

Out of the corner of my eye, I spotted Agregor about to be cut off as Jaru swarmed.

"Fuck!"

My curse snagged Garren's attention. "Fuck!"

Letting out a cry, I raised my sword and barreled through the nearby Jaru, shouldering them out of the way. Most fled in the wake of my sudden and violent assault, but a few remained. I cut down one and leaped over the fallen remains of one before pivoting and driving my sword deep into the chest of another.

Garren and my wolf guards charged, pushing the Jaru back and creating some space as I yanked my sword out, breathing hard.

"That was, um, impressive," Agregor said, his voice shaking.

"You're a bloody idiot." I grabbed the back of his neck and dragged him against me for a swift hug. "Don't die on me, alright? You're fourteen, you're not ready for this shit."

His face flushed. "There were a lot, and they came quickly!"

"Yes, they do that," I agreed, relieved that the Jaru were fleeing.

Garren stalked back toward us, wearing a thunderous expression. I shook my head. Agregor was subdued now that the excitement was over, but hopefully he would learn from his fright.

Garren gave me his best innocent questioning look, which I wasn't falling for. "Idiot," he muttered as he cuffed the back of his brother's head.

Hearing a drone coming from behind me, I turned and frowned at finding a shuttle landing. "Red didn't mention they had a shuttle working."

"Shuttle must have scared the Jaru off." Garren lifted a hand to shield his eyes from the glare of the sun as the ramp began to lumber down. "I thought it was the master switch you mentioned?"

"Maybe not." I checked the PB holstered at my thigh. No, still dead. I squinted at the shuttle, distantly aware of soldiers moving around me, dealing with the wounded and ensuring the fallen Jaru were dead.

I rubbed absently at my chest, feeling that strange tingle associ-

## The Master of the Switch

ated with the bond. "Let's find out what has happened," I said, walking toward the shuttle as Garren, Agregor, and the wolf guard fell in beside me.

As the ramp touched down, I noticed a disheveled Theo waiting to the right with a Kelo bandage around his head and a Rymorian medic at his side.

Thank fuck!

He offered me a weak smile when I joined him before returning his attention to the craft.

Nate, Red... and Hannah stepped out.

"Were things too boring at the research facility?" I asked bluntly.

Hannah rolled her eyes—I smiled. There was a bulky container in her arms, which Garren grabbed from her and dumped in my arms. Nice move, the bastard.

I peered into the container, catching a glimpse of medical scanners before a medic snatched it from me and hurried off.

"You have no idea how many bodies I dragged out of the carnage searching for you," I said to Theo.

"I, ah, my cybernetics caused me to black out." Theo fingered his bandage. "I hit my head on the way down. I woke up in the tent." He grinned. "You were worried about me."

"Yes, Theo, I was worried about you. Was it the Armageddon switch?" I looked between Theo, Nate, Red, and Hannah... who was still plastered against Garren. I stalked over and snagged Hannah for myself.

Garren growled. I smirked. Then Hannah buried her head against my chest and emitted a needy whimper.

"We've restored some basic functionality at the research facility," Nate said, interrupting me from thoughts of dragging Hannah somewhere and wasting time we didn't have on a quick hot fuck. He thumbed over his shoulder. "We've got another couple of batches of medical scanners working, and some weapons. It will be a slow process, but we're here to fix as many as we can."

"What about Rymor?" I asked.

349

Nate shook his head. "We don't have a global solution to the technology failure, nor enough people to help with even a piecemeal type of aid. We can only rebuild one device or system at a time. It's laborious, but it works."

"Is there much damage?" I asked, thinking about how the shuttles had crashed and the damage we had suffered.

"Catastrophic," Nate said gravely. "Rymor, as you know it, is gone."

# Chapter 59

**Talin**

**Ella**

"What are you up to, Ella?" Pope stood in the kitchen doorway. He was watching me and what I was surreptitiously doing. *Not doing anymore,* I reflected. "Nothing," I said wearily. And that was the pity of it.

I was trying to steal a knife, which was harder than I'd first presumed. In my plan, I'd wandered down to the kitchen, hung around on the pretense of getting food... and pilfered a knife. Unfortunately, knives were not left lying around, and I'd yet to discover where the kitchen workers kept them. One good knife was on the table beside the head cook, and she rarely left her station. Even if I managed to take it, I would be the prime suspect.

Getting past the kitchen staff was hard enough, but it was going to be impossible with Pope shadowing my every move.

"Come on. I'll take you back," he said.

My shoulders slumped as I followed him out of the room. This was my hope. It kept me sane and occupied my mind when Bill came to my room and put his hands one me.

We wound our way along the now familiar maze of corridors toward the living areas and the office Bill used.

More wagons had arrived yesterday, bringing food and supplies to help with the repairs. Word must have spread to the surrounding communities, and a steady stream of people arrived seeking work. Many had been displaced by the troubles, Bill had told me. Troubles that Bill had instigated, which was about as ironic as it could get.

"He used it yesterday, didn't he?"

Pope gave no reaction in either his expression or his pace.

"Didn't he?" I persisted. I was no longer angry or suspicious toward Pope after that terrible night. He was trapped here the same as me. He'd tried to protect me. An act that brought him all my loyalty.

"Yeah, he did." Pope's tone was tired, and the knowledge crushed a part of my soul.

Was my family still safe? I shuddered, cold inside at the news yet grateful for Pope's honesty. This was the first time we had engaged in an authentic conversation. For so long, I'd been caught up in my fears that he would betray me to Bill.

I no longer worried he would tell Bill about my plans, but I did worry that he would stop me from following through.

"Well, what are you going to do about it?"

He stopped abruptly, and I stopped too, looking at him unflinchingly as he stared down at me.

"What do you think I can do about it?" he bit out. "The inhibitor still works if that's what you're asking. Some poor bastard tried to take him out yesterday. It wasn't a pretty sight."

"I don't have the implant," I said and started walking. A few strides later, Pope caught up. I watched him and said, "I don't have any implant and I'm going to kill him."

### The Master of the Switch

He made a noise that was a cross between choking and a laugh.

"I'm the only person here who can. He orders you to kill anyone without an implant the moment they offer a threat. He doesn't see me as a threat and that's the only advantage we have."

"That's because you're not a threat, and you're not going to do anything stupid that makes him see you as one."

We both lapsed into silence as we passed two grunts heading in the opposite direction. They nodded to Pope.

He slowed his pace once the men were out of hearing. "If you screw up, he's going to kill you. Or tell me to kill you. Don't put me in that situation, because you know I will have to kill you if I he tells me to. I would rather it was me doing it than some other sick bastard who'll take their time." He shook his head. "It was bad enough the last time you tried something stupid."

There it was, the guilt, the anguish, and the confirmation I'd brought Bill's attention to myself. *Perhaps I had?*

"It would have happened eventually, with or without my provocation. I'm Hannah Duvaul's sister. She was in a relationship with Bill for months. The station suddenly went down and she disappeared, so I went looking. I knew Bill would have me followed. I thought I'd been clever, slipping away, but I wasn't, and they found me. Only I never imagined he would have me taken out of Rymor. Arrested on some fake charges to keep me out of the way for a while, maybe at worst."

Pope smoothed a hand over his face.

"It was worse before he came here." My voice broke, and for a terrifying moment, I thought I might break down.

"I know," he said softly. "I asked around."

"You think I enjoy this? You think this is living?" I stopped talking, concerned my distress had shifted toward anger and that, if Bill caught us, it would draw his attention. I drew a shaky breath. "I know the risks. I'm going to do it anyway. Will you help me?"

He grumbled. "Yeah, I'll help you."

"Good, I need a knife."

"Fuck me. Have you ever killed someone before?" He side-eyed me.

"No, of course not."

"It's one thing to talk about it. To contemplate it, even. Most people, even those who have trained, still balk. You fuck up, Ella, you're not getting another chance."

"I'm not going to balk. I'm not going to hesitate or freeze, and I won't spend the rest of my life regretting it. He needs to die. He needed to die back in Rymor when this was no more than a twisted seed in that abomination he calls a mind. Get me a knife, and I will kill him."

"You've already planned this, I assume?"

"In the bedroom. I will leave it under the pillow."

"Like hell I'm going to put a knife in the bedroom where the door's locked and I can't get in if your plan goes wrong."

"And what would you do if you could get in? Try and save me? How are you going to do that? You can't kill him. The best you could offer is to put me out of my misery. There are no scanners now, not after he used the master switch. All I need is one good stab."

"This is insane. Listen to yourself talking about one good stab."

"My plan is going to work."

"Like your plan to stow out on the capsule? Like your plan to steal a fucking knife? How did those work out?"

"They would have worked fine if you had been helping me instead of getting in my way. You promised you would help me."

"I said I would help you. There was no pinkie promise involved, and I didn't know what you had planned when I said it."

"Do you have a better idea?" I asked. We had arrived at the door to Bill's office, and our conversation was about to end. "I need this. Please, Pope. I need this."

His lips tightened, but he nodded. "I'll get you a knife."

Then he opened the door, and I walked in to join Bill.

# The Master of the Switch

## Kein

Normally I enjoyed the thrill of infiltration, but my failure in the Jaru camp beside the station was a fresh memory and reminded me of my fallibility.

Was I getting old? Losing my edge?

Someone had needed to go into Talin, and I'd made that someone me, wanted to play my part in the great schemes breaking the world apart. The Jaru had left their homelands under the banner of a single warlord, something that had never happened before. Shadowland had been ripped down the middle with nearly half of its army turning their back on Tanis for his enemy, Bremmer.

So here I was, seeking information on Bill and Ella, and so far failing in the task.

My communication device didn't work after the big boom in the courtyard as we unloaded the cart, but today it started working again, first with a buzz then a voice belonging to Theo that sounded like he was beside me although I knew he was far away. That was when I found out that what had happened was the master switch had been activated, and that the man who had held it was definitely Bremmer.

I could have killed him, had I been sure. I was swift, could have snatched the gray one's sword and killed Tanis' enemy before anyone realized. It would have meant my death, but that felt a small sacrifice for all the terrible things he had done.

The opportunity had passed. Besides, it was not my place, nor what Tanis had sent me here to do. My task was to find Hannah's sister and learn whatever I could about Bremmer. If he died, that belonged to Tanis.

Despite my best efforts, I was no closer to finding out anything useful. The excessive security inside the fortress meant a large section was guarded, and I was soon convinced Hannah's sister would be found there.

My initial plans for a swift infiltration were over, so I plotted, and kept myself busy with the menial task of lumbering sacks of grit from the store to the construction area. The work was hard, the hours long, and the food foul.

Despite my exhaustion, I decided tonight was the night to investigate the forbidden part of the fortress. The air was still warm when I slipped out of the rough outbuilding allocated to the workers for sleep.

"Where are you going, little man?"

I froze, and cursed my lack of weapons, as the gray haired man I'd recently learned was called Pope stepped out of the shadows.

"I saw you crossing the courtyard," he continued, "but don't feel bad about that. I expect you know little about tower-dweller technology, but it can do some magical things."

"I was looking for food," I said. My lithe frame often gave the impression I was half starved. It wasn't an unreasonable lie.

"You do look in need of food," Pope said dryly.

"They have me lugging bags of grit." I gestured toward myself. "Not the best use of my skills."

Pope chuckled as he stepped out of the shadows. "And what would be the best use of your skills?"

His hand remained on the hilt of his sword, one I'd witnessed him use confidently. He was a tower-dweller; the way his hand shot to his head the day Bremmer used the switch marked him as such. But perhaps, like me, he'd had it fitted, or maybe he was a former field scientist?

"I farmed before the Jaru destroyed my home and killed my family." Which was the truth in a way.

"A farmer, hmm?" Pope said. "Any skill at managing food stocks? The current man in charge is an idiot and we are throwing much away."

I grinned. "I can manage food stocks. A farmer never wastes goods."

"Alright," Pope said. "You've got a new job. Let's see how you do."

# Chapter 60

### Shadowland

### Tanis

All our weapons were being ferried to the shuttle, where Hannah and Nate worked through them systematically. Any Rymorian personnel with sufficient technical knowledge assisted in the task. Theo helped with the logistics of dispersing the working ones back to Javid, Arand, and my forces. My communicator had been destroyed by the blast, but they had managed to repair that too. There wasn't time to fix everyone's communicators, but enough worked now for good coverage across the forces.

Scott's search for shuttle survivors had found only dead. He elected to accompany Nate and Hannah back to Rymor once the weapon repairs were completed.

The larger items were getting a power source replacement. They had brought a batch of packs with them that could be exchanged with a few clicks. The smaller ones and the PB rifles were being reconfigured at one of the mobile workstations they had on board the shuttle. They had worked through the night and would be leaving soon.

The last thing I wanted was Hannah in the camp with the Jaru mere days away, but I had to admit I had enjoyed watching her handle weapons of various sizes with such confidence.

"Is it just me or does the sight of her tiny hands wrapped around that fat PB rifle diminish the blood flow to your brain," Garren mused beside me.

I punched him on the shoulder.

Agregor snickered.

I glowered at Agregor. "What are you even doing here? Doesn't Tay need some help packing the camp?"

Agregor slunk off.

"Poor kid, he's developed a bit of a crush on Tay, and she's been working him hard day and night." Garren grinned.

I lifted a warning hand. "That's already too much information."

"Well, we've got bigger romantic entanglements to worry about, since Javid is on his way. He found out your mother's new love interest is here and he intends to issue a challenge."

"A challenge!" What the fuck? "We don't have time for a challenge!"

"I was joking," Garren said, laughing. "Javid has begun mobilizing now he has working weapons. You know he wouldn't fool around when there's serious killing to be done."

"Your sense of humor needs some development," I grumbled.

"My sense of humor?" Garren feigned outrage. "I should lock you in a room with Danel and Han for a few days, *then* you would appreciate my humor." He indicated the shuttle. "I heard they were leaving soon and was wondering who was going to kiss her goodbye first, or whether we were just going to squish her between us and go to town."

"How is it that I haven't killed you yet?" I shook my head slowly.

Garren grinned again.

"Don't you have soldiers to organize?" I frowned.

### The Master of the Switch

"No, already done."

"Han and Danel?"

"Already gone. It's just me, three thousand Shadowlanders, four hundred and twenty Rymorian soldiers, and five medics, according to Theo, waiting on your command."

Ahead, Theo jumped down from the shuttle and hurried over. "We've got satellite confirmation on the Jaru. They're closer than we thought."

"How close?" I asked.

"Javid and Arand have moved to block the river crossing. The Jaru will hit them imminently. We've warned them to prepare."

"Distribute whatever is fixed and get everyone mounted. We're moving out," I said to Garren before turning to Theo. "And I need the shuttle out of here."

Garren's shouted orders sent people rushing. The remaining weapons crates were swiftly stowed on board the shuttle.

"Keep in contact," I said to Theo as we walked to the shuttle. "Hopefully, communication—and everything else—keeps working."

"I will," Theo replied. "I'll see you when it's over."

He passed Hannah on the shuttle ramp as she ran down and threw herself at me. I hoisted her up, and she wrapped her arms and legs around me with enough enthusiasm to make Molly proud. "Where's Garren?" she said, peering over her shoulder and reminding me that she was busy thinking about her other mate while in my arms.

It took some getting used to.

Then she spied Garren stalking over and buried her nose against my neck. "Please don't die," she whispered. "I can't lose either of you, okay."

"We won't," I said.

Garren closed in behind her, fisted her hair, and drew her hair back for a hot kiss that had her thighs squeezing around me. Note to self, she really liked being pinned between us. By the time they came up for air, I had to remind myself there was a war.

I kissed her and tried to pour everything I felt into that kiss, until the whirr of the shuttle powering up brought the moment to an end.

"Make sure the base has operational weapons and, if Rymor is as bad as it sounds, make sure you keep yourself safe." I lowered her to her ground, turned her around, and swatted her ass. She ran up the ramp where Red was waiting. He raised his hand in salute.

Fuck, when did life get this complicated?

The ramp lifted, and a blast of air accompanied the shuttle taking off.

Around us lay abandoned tents and supplies that might become a forgotten legacy should we fail to stem the Jaru tide.

*How Gaia would despair.* Was there even a Gaia anymore? It could be years before we had enough technology working to give them concern... on either side of the wall.

"Ready to go?" Garren asked.

I nodded and mounted swiftly. Garren gave the signal, and we rode out of the clearing, followed by the members of the final section.

For some, it would be their first battle.

For some, it would be their last.

∼

An hour from the river, a scout arrived, warning that Jaru had broken through Javid's line.

Soon after, the Jaru swarmed us. The thud of weapon fire reverberated around the forest. The blast decimated both Jaru and trees and sent blood, vegetation, and chips of wood ripping through the air in every direction. As the fighting turned to close quarters, those less familiar with the Rymorian weapons reverted to their swords.

I signaled to Garren, telling him to press forward.

He lifted his hand in acknowledgment and, in slow, painful, hard-won increments, we forced the Jaru from the path. As a gap opened, we surged forward. Garren pulled his horse out of the line

## The Master of the Switch

and shouted orders to his second to continue on. "I'll make sure the rear doesn't get cut off," he called at me.

My horse snorted and danced underneath me before we took off at a gallop for the river. Trees flashed by in a blur, and the hooves created a thunderous drum against the forest path. I tapped my communicator. "Theo, I need an update."

*"Javid has been pushed back from the crossing,"* he replied. *"Some Jaru have broken through."*

"Yes, we've just had to fight our way through. Our plans depend on cutting them off at the river."

*"The Jaru have a Rymorian cannon mounted on a wagon. There are two Rymorian snipers with Javid's group moving into position to try and take the operators out."*

We rode on.

I came upon the combined forces of Javid and Arand. A huge group of some thirty thousand spread to cut the Jaru off. The deep *thud-thud* of the cannon came from somewhere far ahead. It ceased suddenly, and a great cheer went up.

"Theo?"

*"It's down. Han is waiting to talk to you."*

I found Han waiting with his section toward the rear. I dismounted beside him, joined by my ever-present wolf guard and Agregor.

"Danel is to the east." Han gestured over his shoulder where the earlier blasting had come from. "We have contained most of the Jaru who have crossed, but some have got through."

"Yes, we met one or two of them on the way." The Yandue River crossing, while not particularly narrow at half a mile wide, provided some control and forced the Jaru into a bottleneck of sorts. "Can we hold them here and create some breathing space?" It was a month's journey before the river could be crossed again and in a direction that would draw the Jaru further from Rymor. "I need them back on the plains and not wreaking havoc in Shadowland as their consolation prize. If we can break them now, then there is a chance they will flee."

"The gap is too wide to be effective, but better than nothing. They've enough numbers to break through," Han said. "We need to take their leader out. They won't leave while he lives."

So, it had come to this; sooner than I expected. I called my wolf guard, mounted, and headed for the frontline. Here I lost myself in the battle to retake and hold that vital strip of land. We turned the giant Jaru gun around and pointed it back at its former owners. Undeterred, the Jaru kept coming, as Jaru often did, presenting a senseless slaughter as they fell in waves. As Han predicted, it was impossible to hold them all, and the battle continued.

Javid caught up with me as we swapped out the section in the front.

"It makes you sick, does it not?" he said as we watched yet another Jaru tribe try then fail to cross. "They were always foolhardy, but this? I do not wish them to die. Much as it would make our lives easier. What now, eh? What now?"

As night fell, the attacks stopped, and the area turned quiet. The supplies arrived, but I elected to leave them at the back. Without tents and no more than basic rations, we sat in quiet clusters and ate or rested as the medics dealt with injuries.

Dawn brought the first Jaru attack, and in the midst of this, Garren returned with a dozen of his men. I hadn't seen him since we separated yesterday.

"I've got a couple of Rymorians." Garren pointed at two bound men. "They were fighting for the Jaru. They've got implants." He grinned and cracked his knuckles. "It won't take much to make them talk."

He yanked the nearest man down from the horse and directed his men to collect the other. They hit the ground with a thud and grunts before being dragged to their feet. From their wary expressions and disheveled appearance, their capture had not been gentle.

"Do you know who I am?" I asked.

## The Master of the Switch

Neither spoke. Garren punched the man standing nearest to him in the stomach.

"We've seen your picture," the other man said as his companion heaved up air. "You're the terrorist who was exiled."

Garren thumped the nearest prisoner again. I was confident he would have punched him whatever his companion said.

"I received a pardon a month ago." They stared at me blankly. They must have missed that communication... "Who were you working for?"

Neither answered.

"Is this worth dying for?"

Still no answer.

I nodded at the man nearest to Garren. "Kill him slowly."

Garren had landed no more than a couple of blows when both men began babbling about telling us everything.

I put my hand up. Garren paused, fist drawn back, his other hand locked around the man's throat. It was the most farcical interrogation I'd ever experienced.

"If I think the words you speak are a lie, he will die quickly." I pointed at the man Garren was slowly choking.

They nodded swiftly.

"Who were you working for?" I asked again.

Garren tightened his chokehold.

"His name was Ailey." The words tumbled out of the man on the right. "We were part of a reconnaissance team, at least we were to start with." The man on the left turned red and started to thrash. "Shit! Please don't kill him!"

Garren released him, and the man collapsed to his knees, sucking in hoarse breaths. My brother was wearing that overly innocent expression. "I thought it would speed things up."

I turned back to the men. "How many Rymorians are colluding with the Jaru?"

"Colluding?"

Garren didn't like that answer and cuffed him.

"My team was twelve strong. We've been out here for five years, off and on. More arrived this year. I'd say close to a hundred. We were allocated to their warlord, but before that we were working for a Rymorian man called Karry."

I don't remember moving, only that Garren was in my way, gripping my shoulders, shouting in my face.

"Don't fucking kill him!"

The two prisoners had been boxed in by Garren's men, eyes wild with terror. I must have looked pissed. I didn't lose my temper, not with someone I needed answers from. Karry's name was the only one, other than Bremmer himself, who could make me lose control.

"You're the level-headed one." Garren sounded amused. "I'm impressed with myself for thinking to stop you." He leaned in closer and whispered. "We can strangle them both in a bit." He released me and turned his scowl on the two men. "You enjoy torturing women then?"

"What? No!" They both stammered. "We were working for a private agency, but under government direction, or so we were told. It's been weird from the start, but it's gotten crazy over the last year while we've been with Ailey. There's hardly a day goes by that he doesn't kill someone. And K... the *other* person we worked for wasn't much better."

"Where is Ailey now?" I asked, trying to wrap my head around their revelations. If they were working with Karry, they were working for Bill, whether they knew it or not. How the hell did Bill control the Jaru? The last year and all the trouble in Shadowland... might have made sense, but how did this new decision to send them to Rymor fit in?

And why was I even trying to work this out when Bill or someone else had used the Armageddon switch?

"It's not Ailey leading them anymore," the one Garren had choked said. "There's a Jaru religious master from an Outlier tribe. Now they are heading for Shadowland, to destroy—" He stopped, realizing too late that Shadowlanders surrounded him. "But the Jaru master is controlling Ailey using a strange torque he gave to him."

"We think the torque is ancient technology," the other man added. "It has that fine craftsmanship you see on ancient pieces."

"Ancient technology from the Outliers? Even if they found such a thing, they should have no idea how to use it?

"We can only tell you what we saw," the man continued. "We didn't have any choice. We've been trapped out here. You can't just up and leave a Jaru war tribe, and you don't walk away from a man like Ailey. Not easily anyway. Except today we tried."

"It didn't get you very far," Garren said before he turned to me. "They were on their own, and fleeing something, but whether it was Ailey or to save their own skin is hard to tell."

The men fell silent.

"You still haven't told us where Ailey is. And what about this religious master?" I said.

"Ailey was near the river crossing, last we saw. The master stays with the Outlier tribes near the center. Whatever the reason behind this movement, it has the backing of the tribe elders and the tribe elders do the Outlier master's bidding. Until recently, the Outliers have remained uninvolved. But they began arriving a couple of weeks ago. Then, last week, the master arrived."

"How do you know they are Outlier tribes?" I asked.

"Their tents look Rymorian. Their clothes aren't Rymorian, but they dress nothing like ordinary Jaru. And then there are their eyes."

"What about their eyes?"

"They all have gray eyes."

I felt a prickling of unease. "That sounds odd."

"Everything about the Outliers is odd," the man said.

"And how many Rymorian weapons do you have?"

"Not many," he replied. "Only the Rymorians can use them. There's a few hundred of us altogether. Maybe a few less now—everyone wants out."

Yes, I expected they did. "Secure them. I may need to question them again."

Garren nodded to his men, who took the Rymorians away. He thumbed in the direction of the crossing. "We're going over?"

"We are," I said. "Get the leaders together."

It was risky, but so was doing nothing. The Jaru would scatter, whether back to the plains or Shadowland. I might never have another opportunity to take the leader or leaders out.

It seemed unlikely they would go to such an effort simply to retreat.

Time to force them out once and for all.

# Chapter 61

**Ailey**

Yesterday had been a disaster, and today held little promise of being better. It was hot and muggy, with few trees to offer shade on this side of the crossing. After inspecting the crossing site, I returned to the camp and the hide tent where I would find the bastard who had put my head in a golden noose.

I shoved the Jaru man standing outside, sending him reeling, and barged my way inside. Here I found the master sitting cross-legged on a blanket with tiny gold switches, cogs, and parts scattered before him and a pair of magnification glasses on his nose.

"This is pointless now they've taken the big gun." I stared down at the master, fighting to temper my rage. I needed to kill someone. Preferably the master, but since that wasn't an option, someone else would get it. "It's over."

"It's not over," replied the master with that condescending air of his, and taking the magnification glasses from his nose, he placed them beside the golden items on the rug. "Find a way."

"We'll go around," I said decisively. "They've got weapons—we don't. Not enough, anyway."

"We will not go around." The master reached for his glasses again.

"Fuck you!"

The master put the glasses back down.

So far, I'd resisted the urge to try and kill him, but it was riding me hard today. I felt twitchy, like there were ants under my skin. "We're getting nowhere. What do you think I can do?"

"Keep them occupied while I work out how to disable their weapons." He indicated the rug.

"Occupied? This is fucking pointless. All of it. Why the fuck do you want Rymor so much? Why do you care about these Shadowlanders? We could go around. They've too few numbers. They can't stop us all."

"I wasn't expecting them to fix the weapons so soon," the master said patiently, as if explaining to an idiot.

I hated people talking down to me. I killed people who talked down to me.

"An unfortunate development," the master continued. "Since they have, it changes everything. Now they must die. The risk of them regrouping with more weapons is too great and will jeopardize my plans." His eyes narrowed on me in a way that made me sweat worse than I already was from the baking sun. "And I want Rymor, as I mentioned before, because we found it first."

"They have to be destroyed because you found it first? You didn't find it first. You were a bunch of savages. You're still savages. You didn't have enough intelligence to even know what you had or hadn't found."

A tingling in my neck swiftly morphed into a ferocious burn.

I stared back with gritted teeth and ignored the sweat beading on my brow and trickling down my spine. It felt like my skin was peeling off, but it was mild compared to the last demonstration.

"Be careful who you call savage, savage. Your Shadowlander heritage may lift you above the plains-dwelling Jaru, but it does not

## The Master of the Switch

raise you above the Outliers." The pain dissipated. "I want the land inside the wall. That is all you need to know."

"You want us to keep throwing ourselves at their weapons? Until you finish playing with this shit?" I gestured at the rug. "I'm not allowed to kill them, but you're happy to send them to their death?"

"Yes, that is exactly what I want. The moment you cease throwing yourselves at the weapons like the savages you are" He smiled as he spoke, savoring his private joke, "they will become suspicious that we're going around. A reasonable suspicion, since it was your first idea. They will send some of their forces to check. We need to keep them precisely where they are—together—so they are easy for us to kill once I disable the weapons."

"How long is that going to take," I ground out, frustrated with this conversation.

"Soon." This time the master reached decisively for his magnification glasses.

I watched him for a while, the tension rippling through me. I needed an outlet. I needed to kill someone.

I pushed out of the tent and stormed off through the camp. Some of the Rymorian men had deserted. It was time to make an example for the benefit of those who remained.

First, since I couldn't kill the Jaru in person, I would satisfy myself by sending a few thousand of them to their death. I stalked toward the crossing, calling on the leaders of several tribes who happened to be close to the front line. A prestigious location that was about to send many of them to their death. No one balked at my request, eager to show their loyalty and battle prowess to the harbinger. I watched them leave, annoyed that the order wasn't my choice, then mounted and headed past the Outlier tribes to where my tent had been pitched amid the Rymorians.

I grabbed the first Rymorian I saw upon arriving and dragged him to a clear patch of ground.

"What are you doing?" The man stammered.

I pulled a knife from my belt as I shoved the man to the gritty ground, stamped over his wrist, and impaled his hand into the dirt. His yowl hit all the right spots in my violence-hungry soul. I needed this. The other Rymorians scattered back. "Stay!" I growled at them as I took the man's other hand and impaled it to the ground with my second knife.

He screamed. A delightful sound. I pressed my boot against his right leg and drove a decent-sized long blade into his shin. There was a crunch with that one. Yes, I enjoyed the crunch.

"Beg me to end it." I stepped over him, my rifle muzzle poised inches above his chest.

"What have I done?" The man sobbed. A pitiful sight that only increased my loathing.

"Beg!" I holstered the rifle, drew my sword, and hacked the man's right hand off at the wrist.

He screamed and thrashed, blood fountaining from the stump until I stomped my boot over it.

"Beg." I sneered.

"Please!"

I stabbed the blade into his chest, cracking through bone as I drove deep to find the internal organs. When I pulled it out, he was on the way to dead.

I retrieved my knives—I had thrust them good and deep, so it took a fair bit of yanking. When I lifted my head, I found a crowd of frightened faces.

It hit me then that I was a slave, just like them.

I glanced over my shoulder toward the master's tent and realized I didn't have a fucking thing to lose.

I drew the PB rifle strapped to my thigh and studied the setting.

Not a single fucking thing to lose.

Chuckling to myself, I turned it up to the highest setting and hitched the muzzle under the edge of the torque at the side of my neck... And pressed the trigger.

The ringing in my ears was so loud that I thought the master had activated the device again, but it soon faded to a dull roar. I was face

## The Master of the Switch

down on the dirt, a mouth full of slobber and grit. Rising to my hands and knees, I swayed and shook my head. A great glob of blood and a lump landed to the left of my hand.

My ear?

The torque was on the ground hissing, sparking, and blackened on one side from the blast. I started to laugh.

Half my ear, I amended, giving the lump of flesh greater attention. I laughed again and heaved myself to my feet, where I wavered. My sword lay beside my PB rifle. I snatched both up and turned south. The master's tent lay that way. I should go back and kill the bastard. The Jaru wouldn't reach Rymor easily, and not this way. If that hope was over for me, I was going to end the master's plans as well. I stumbled toward my horse and pitched into the saddle, splattering blood everywhere.

"Let your brothers and sisters know it's over," I shouted into the crowd of Rymorians and Jaru. "Go back to your homes, back to the plains, or follow me. The choice is yours."

"Where are you going?" a Rymorian man called.

"To kill the master." My grin held sadistic glee. "Then I'm going to Talin." If I couldn't get to Rymor, then it was time I finished Bill.

I rode back through the heaving, chaotic camp, my rifle in my hand and my mind clear of everything but the need to destroy the bastard who'd dared to put a collar on me.

The master's tent was just visible when a distant roar penetrated the ringing in my ears. I brought my horse to a stop and looked back to find a mob of Jaru heading straight for me. They surged past.

What the fuck was happening at the crossing?

My horse danced beneath me as the mob cut off my access. I still had the PB in my hand. Leveling the sights on the master's tent, I hit the trigger... and was rewarded by a dull click. Nothing. I huffed and grabbed my second smaller PB, only to find it dead.

I tossed them aside. Was it the master's magic trick, or was it something else? It didn't matter anymore. Jaru or Rymorians would finish the master soon enough. Through the approaching tumult, I watched hide tents collapse as the fleeing Jaru whipped the rest of the vast camp into a frenzy.

There was no way against the swarming Jaru tide. It was time to leave and find another fight. I turned my horse and pressed forward to my new destination, Talin.

# Chapter 62

## Tanis

A little distance away, the giant PB cannons started thumping. The Jaru was launching the first attack of the day.

"I'm not sure about this," Danel said.

"Why is my section on point again?" Garren asked.

"We should definitely do this!" Agregor said.

"I've got nothing else on today," Javid said.

"They're Jaru, I say we kill them," Arand said.

"Everyone is ready," Han said.

"Good, we are in agreement, then," I said, aware that I didn't, in fact, have consensus but unwilling to engage in a debate. "If you see this Ailey, and by all accounts he's hard to miss, just shoot the bastard, but I want any Outliers taken prisoner. You know the ways in which they are different. Everyone, get to your positions."

The leaders dispersed, some on horse and some on foot. Javid's section was closest to the crossing and directly in front of mine.

"You know they're stupid enough to keep throwing themselves at the cannons." Garren fell into step beside me. "If we sit tight, they could all be dead in a couple of days."

"That won't give me their leaders," I said.

"Maybe not. But I *am* curious to see how stupid they are."

"Very funny," I said, not about to fall for Garren's mock thoughtful expression.

As we reached their group, Garren began issuing orders to his section, and Agregor went to join the wolf guard. Tay had been tasked with keeping Agregor safe today. Although, I was confident my younger brother wouldn't make any rash moves after his recent near-death encounter.

I checked my weapons while I waited. I hated waiting. Readying my horse, I mounted.

Ahead, the lines of Javid's men began converging on the crossing. The PB cannon sounds muffled and then echoed louder.

"They're moving," Garren said, climbing onto his horse.

With a call to move out, we rode slowly forward.

Then a little quicker.

Then a little quicker, still.

"This is odd." Garren said.

A scout came thundering back toward them. "They are fleeing! All of them are fleeing!"

# Chapter 63

**Talin**

**Ella**

The kitchen was busy when I went to get myself something to eat. I wasn't hungry, but Bill had been arguing with Pope in his office, and it seemed a good idea to be elsewhere.

The one positive aspect of Bill's unwanted attention was my newfound freedom to roam. Not that I could go far since my room was in the segregated section of the fortress. I saw little of what went on outside other than people busy with construction work.

I pretended to get myself food from the fresh produce store. In the end, I picked up an apple. The hairs on the back of my neck tingled and I turned to find a man watching me.

Before he turned away, I saw his look of recognition.

Only I didn't know him, I was sure.

Fearful, I fled the store. Once in the corridor, I leaned against the wall and pressed my hand against my chest, trying to steady my breathing. Why was he watching me? Was he one of my former tormentors?

He couldn't be. He was unusual with that curious mustache. Short, too, not much taller than me, with swirling tattoos poking out the edges of his rough clothes. I would remember someone so unique.

Yet those terrible dark days were a blank, and I'd pressed the memories into a neat little compartment, aware of them as if they had happened to someone else.

"Ella?"

My eyes popped open to find him right beside me.

"What do you want? Who are you?" I edged toward the hall door.

He lifted both hands in a placating gesture that failed to reduce my anxiety.

"Hannah sent me," he said.

"Hannah?" I stared at him blankly. *Hannah?* Not my Hannah?

"I've come to get you out." He quickly glanced up and down the corridor before returning to me. "Please, let me get you out."

"No!" No, this couldn't be happening. It was a trap. It had to be a trap. Not now, when I was so close. It was a test, my final test.

"Please," he coaxed. I could sense his desperation, the way his eyes were never still, alert to danger.

He made a grab for me.

I screamed and fled for the hall. His curses and pounding footsteps chased me. We were almost at the door when his fingers closed around me. I screamed again. His hand clamped over my mouth, but he was too late as the door to the hall flung open, and Pope stood there.

What followed was a blur. The dull thud of fist connecting with flesh before the arm around me disappeared. The stranger on the floor with Pope standing over him.

Men swarmed out of the hall. "Bind him," Pope ordered. The man fought, but they overpowered him and dragged him away.

"What happened?" Pope demanded, drawing me aside.

### The Master of the Switch

"I-I don't know." I was shaking now it was over. Did he really say Hannah had sent him? Had I imagined it? Had I just made a terrible mistake?

I had to finish this now. "Did you leave it there?" I whispered.

His jaw tightened. "It's there. Now tell me what the fuck just happened."

"If Bill stays with me tonight, promise me you'll wedge the door so he can't get out."

"There's shit kicking off inside and outside the fortress, he's not going to stay with you. Now is not a good fucking time, Ella."

The door to the hall burst open again, and Bill strode out. "Ella!" He pulled me against him, his attention shifting from me to Pope. "What's going on?"

I leaned into Bill, but my eyes locked with Pope's, and I mouthed, *promise me!*

A pulse ticked in Pope's jaw. "One of the new men touched her." His eyes cut to Bill. "I'll deal with it. Someone should take her back to her room. I think she's going into shock."

Pivoting, he strode after his men and the prisoner.

"Ella?" Bill asked softly, his fingers gentle as they tipped my chin.

"I'd like to go to my room, please."

He released a heavy breath. "Okay, I'll take you there."

He walked me to my room while my heart pounded, and I tried to work out what had happened and what it meant. Once inside, he turned to leave, but I caught his hand.

"Please stay," I said.

He stopped and turned to face me.

"Please Bill, I want you to stay."

# Chapter 64

## Shadowland

### Tanis

It had been an exhausting day and the turn to evening cast shadows over the former Jaru camp. The trees were sparse due to the rocky nature of the ground, and the lack of cover seemed to emphasize the destruction. Bodies, ruined tents, and discarded possessions littered the ground in a jumble of devastation. The Jaru people were either dead or had fled.

Many had returned the way they had come, snatching up a few possessions and following the line of the Yandue River.

Others had headed toward Talin.

"Any sign of the Outliers?" I asked Garren, as he joined me at the outskirts of the camp. Ahead, Shadowland and Rymorian forces had halted their pursuit of the fleeing Jaru. We had enough rations for a few days, and the ground to make a temporary bed. My wolf guard stood nearby, alert to danger, but unless the Jaru had a sudden and comprehensive change of heart, there was nothing to concern us here.

## The Master of the Switch

"None," Garren confirmed. "Other than their flattened tents. They've fled by the looks of it."

"We need to find them," I said. There had been no sighting of their elusive warlord Ailey, either. Prisoners said he had left earlier in the day and that his destination had been Talin. "Ailey could be returning to Bill. We know he was working for him." The two Rymorians who Garren had captured yesterday had connected themselves to both Karry and Ailey, providing the last missing piece. Somehow, Bill had done the impossible and had infiltrated the Jaru, doubtless in an initial desire to bring about my demise.

Did he turn his attention to Rymor after he was forced to flee?

Did he destroy everything and everyone out of his insane quest for revenge?

"I need to get inside," I said softly.

"Talin?" Garren frowned. "Well, we've the Jaru to contend with first, and fifty thousand Shadowlanders in our way, which won't be easy now the fancy weapons are dead *again*."

"Which is why I'm not going in the front door."

"I didn't realize there was another door." Garren's eyes narrowed as he processed this new information.

"Theo has found me another way."

"We're going to attack him from a different direction, then?" Garren asked.

"No, *I'm* going to attack from a different direction."

"Alone? That's a stupid idea. Your last solo endeavor nearly got you killed," he said heatedly.

"Well, I'm doing it anyway. Nate is on his way via a shuttle, but before I leave there's something I need you to do."

"Me?" Garren raised a brow. "Last time I offered to look after Hannah you threatened to gut me. Wait, how did Nate get a shuttle? I thought everything had been destroyed again?"

"Your communicator is working, isn't it? The technology damage was localized and targeted at weapons this time. Whatever they used wasn't the master switch. And I'm still going to gut you! I just need you to be me."

Garren scowled. "You don't need to be so fucking superior. I didn't think about trying the communication bug in my head... and what do you mean by me being you?"

I smiled. Garren's eyes narrowed.

My smile faded. "Kein has been taken prisoner. He found Hannah's sister, but she called for guards. I can't leave him there." He would've come for me were it the other way around. "I can't leave Hannah's sister there, either. Bill will kill them both if he thinks he's cornered. He's not going to hesitate with Kein either way. There's a tunnel I can use. I need this over, and I need it over now. Even if most of the Jaru flee, we still have the forces from Tain and Techin here. It could take months to overturn Talin. I don't have months. Rymor doesn't have months. I cannot allow myself the luxury of worrying about what is happening there." I drew a deep breath. "I need this over."

A sense of urgency gripped me. For many years, I'd buried my hatred of Bill and let my past go. I couldn't let it go anymore.

It had to be over, and it had to be over now.

"How does me being you help?" Garren's frown said he had doubts.

"It's simple," I said. "I want everyone to think I'm still here. You're going to proceed with the attack on Talin and the Shadowland forces outside to keep them occupied. If Bill is focused on what is happening outside Talin's wall, he won't be expecting me to be inside. Kein is a risk now. He'll talk sooner or later —we all do—and whatever he says will benefit Bill."

"I understand that, sort of," Garren said. "At least it's not as stupid as giving yourself up to the Rymorians. Me pretending to be you, though? That's an even more stupid idea than going to Talin alone. You're the most recognizable man on the planet."

"Not if you are wearing my clothes... and helmet."

### The Master of the Switch

"We don't have your clothes or your helmet," Garren said. "We left everything at the camp, remember."

The sound of a shuttle arriving brought a grin to my face. "Which is why I asked Nate to collect it on his way."

Garren scoffed. "You never manage to keep your helmet on for more than five minutes."

"But you do, and you will, for me," I said as the drone of the landing shuttle increased.

Garren muttered under his breath as the shuttle landed. The engines powered down, the ramp lowered to settle against the dusty ground, and Nate poked his head out.

"Bring your second with you," I said to Garren before hailing two wolf guards. Not Tay and definitely not Agregor. "Get me some basic clothing and armor that will fit me, and another sword, and both you and Alid meet me in the shuttle."

I headed to the shuttle, where I found Nate with my Shadowland armor.

"You've no idea how hard this was to find," Nate complained. "And heavy. I think I pulled a muscle."

I patted Nate's shoulder and nodded my head at Garren.

Garren stripped and dressed in the Shadowlander plate and leather armor that belonged to me.

I, likewise, stripped my Rymorian combats and replaced them with the plain Shadowlander clothes and armor my guards brought.

"Theo has updated Danel and Han, but no one else is to know," I said. "All orders will come through them." I turned to Garren's second, Alid, and the two members of my wolf guard. "My plan depends on everyone thinking Garren is me. Protect him as you would me, and make sure he doesn't take that bloody helmet off by mistake."

"It's a little tight." Garren poked at the armor and flexed his arm as Alid helped him to buckle the main plates into place.

"I know. You're looking a bit fat," I said, face perfectly straight.

"Fat!" His outrage cooled as he noted my smirk. "It's a little tight," he repeated, grinning smugly.

"It's not about the size, Garren. It's how you use it that counts."

"Said no woman ever," Garren quipped.

I barked out a laugh. "Alright, don't let the temporary power go to your head."

"I think you're asking the impossible," Alid said, grinning.

Our goodbyes were swift. I could sense Garren's reservations. "I need this to be over, Garren," I repeated, my hands on his shoulder. My lips tugged up. "Whatever you do, don't tell Javid."

Garren's grunt was noncommittal, but he left, and I knew I could count on him.

The moment had a bittersweet edge. I had found love and friendship with my half-brother. The testing times had cemented my ties to my father, and a relationship that had always been edgy at best had become far deeper and stronger than I could have ever hoped.

I had seen my mother again.

I had let go of how, in the past, I had failed the woman I'd once loved.

And, eclipsing all of that, I had found Hannah. Yeah, the sharing part hadn't been on my list of aspirations but, damn, it was hot, and I'd come around to that too.

I hoped this would work.

*It had to work.*

"Let's go," I said to Nate.

The ramp lifted, and the engines rumbled to life.

*"I've got the labyrinth map ready,"* Theo said through my communicator.

"Good," I replied. I would need Theo's assistance once I arrived, lest I become lost in the maze of underground tunnels.

A sudden thought crossed my mind. "Theo, does Bill still have his communicator?"

*"Yes, I presume so. Although, it might not work. Why?"*

"See if you can reconnect him and put me through," I said.

### The Master of the Switch

"*Is that a good idea?*" Theo asked.

"Probably not, but I'm going to do it anyway."

Theo cursed in a very un-Theo-like way. There was a pause. "*It's done.*"

"*Theo?*" Bill's voice brought a wave of recognition that tightened my gut and set the hairs on the back of my neck rising.

"No," I replied. "It's Tanis, and I'm coming for you, you sick son of a bitch."

# Chapter 65

**Talin**

**Kein**

If I were a thinking man, I would be thinking I needed to find a new profession. This one wasn't going so well for me.

Soon, it would get much worse.

For an abandoned fortress, the tunnels below were in good repair, at least the flash of them I saw as they dragged me into a surprisingly full prison system. There was a battle going on outside. I knew, because Theo had updated me.

Unfortunately, I hadn't been left alone since Ella had raised the alarm, and although I thought the communicator was still on, there was no opportunity to speak.

They threw me into an empty cell at the end of the corridor. It was cold and dark and smelled foul enough for me to feel as if I were already dead and buried. Two soldiers followed me in and took up positions at the door with their swords drawn to watch me. I was

## The Master of the Switch

contemplating how best to kill them when the gray-haired one, called Pope, entered.

The guards stepped outside at his command.

As if sensing my silent consideration, Pope punched me in the face. I dodged, but the blow connected with enough force to make my head ring. Despite my struggles, my manacled wrists were hooked into a chain dangling from the ceiling.

I got a solid kick in, but Pope stepped out of reach, circled, and jabbed me in the kidneys twice. During the blur of pain, he bolted my ankles to the floor.

I was good at finding opportunities to fight back. This moment presented none.

Pope let out a heavy sigh and stalked over to lean back against the door, where he stared at me with a brooding expression that gave nothing away.

"I knew you weren't a farmer," he said. Heaving a sigh, he pushed away from the door. "I'm sorry about this. Real sorry." He retrieved a pair of leather gloves from his pocket and pulled them on. "Someone needs to, though."

He smashed his fist into my stomach, face, and stomach again. I coughed. There was blood pooling in my mouth, and breathing was a challenge. His wiry build was deceptive.

None of this boded well.

There were no questions, just an endless barrage of fists against various parts of my body that found fresh layers of suffering. Pope, unlike the Jaru, knew where to hit without rendering the victim unconscious.

I prayed for the welcoming blackness.

It never came.

Garbled words slipped through the communicator as Theo jabbered away in my head. Or perhaps I imagined it? The strange communication device was unsettling, and such pain overwhelmed my head and body that I didn't know what was real anymore.

Pope stood back and leaned against the cell wall, breathing hard.

He dragged the gloves off and flexed his fingers. His knuckles were red and raw despite the protection.

Little wonder I felt like I'd been beaten apart.

"Want to talk now?" Pope asked.

I struggled to breathe. Speech was beyond me. I spat blood and fought for air.

*"Kein...is...coming."* Theo's words bounced around my head in a scratchy warble. Was the device damaged? I wanted to laugh, because how could it not be?

*"Kein...Tanis...tunnels..."*

I tried to talk, but no words could get through my wheezing fight for breath.

Pope grunted and shoved himself off the wall. He stalked over. "Got something to say now, have you?"

I couldn't see much more than a blur through my right eye. My left was working fine, and I recoiled as the other man approached.

Pope reached up to unhook the cuffs that held my hands, and too weak to brace myself, I hit the floor with a skull-rattling crack.

*"Kein, just...him..."* The voice crackled. It made my head ring.

I groaned and pressed my fingers to the back of my ear.

Pope froze, and I realized my mistake.

He crouched down over me in a flash, fisted a handful of my hair, and dragged my head to the side. "You've got a communicator?" He dropped my limp head. It cracked against the stone floor. He muttered a sharp, vicious curse as he stood.

I began to laugh.

*"Kein, please don't do...stupid."*

I laughed harder. "Too late," I rasped out.

"Who the hell are you?" Pope crouched down over me once more, fisting my hair. "Who—the hell—are you?" He shook me hard, but I laughed harder.

"Tanis told me to tell you he's coming," I croaked. "You're about to—"

Pope hit me, and this time the world turned black.

# Chapter 66

**Ella**

"I can't stay," Bill said softly.

Swallowing, I fought an internal battle for control. "Please." The voice was not mine, and the words less so.

"I need to check what's happening, but I'll be back soon." He turned away, and as the door shut, I heard the familiar clatter of the key in the lock.

This room became my sanctuary after the abuse and torment that followed my arrival in Shadowland. It was a comfortable prison, but it was still a prison; and it wasn't my sanctuary anymore.

I remembered in painful detail the day I was snatched from the street of Azure, cornered by those black-suited men, and thrown into the back of a transport. Little did I know it would be the last time I would see Rymor or my family.

I had been seeking Dan and the answers he might have after my sister disappeared. I still didn't know what had happened to Hannah, but I thought it very likely Bill had something to do with it.

But where *was* Hannah? Not here, and not dead. Not once had I allowed myself to believe her gone, which lead me to consider the possibility that the strange man had been telling me the truth.

My mind lapsed into a reluctant exploration of possibilities and likelihoods as I went over the conversation with him in the corridor. The haunted, desperate look on his face when I didn't comply, followed by the wide-eyed fear when I screamed and ran. Neither was the reaction of a monster. I'd met monsters, and my gut said he wasn't one.

The words *Hannah sent me* and *I've come to get you out* taunted me. The way his eyes shifted, neither hostile nor aggressive but wary of interruption.

It hadn't felt like a trap. Bill had been equally surprised.

I ran my fingers through my hair, gripping handfuls, so mad with myself I wanted to scream. A new threat became apparent, filling me with lethargy, and I slumped to the floor beside the door with my head in my hands.

By exposing the man, had I potentially placed Hannah in danger?

*What have I done?* The wooden floor was rough beneath my knees, but I made no move, lost to a weariness so great I thought I might never be able to rise. Sunlight streamed through the open window and spilled across the bed. It was warm, yet I felt cold inside.

Bill would return, and I must decide what to do. The man Hannah sent and who had been trying to help me would now be questioned. Would he give up Hannah? Would Bill find my sister?

The rattle of a key snapped my head around.

"What are you doing down there?" Bill took my hand and helped me from the floor.

"The man?" My eyes were drawn to the bed. Why hadn't I thought of checking if the knife was there?

"Pope is questioning him." Bill's smile was grim. "Don't worry, Pope will find out all his secrets. He won't trouble you again."

I didn't doubt that Pope would be thorough. My stomach churned. Pope was ruthless. Perhaps he had always been so, or

## The Master of the Switch

perhaps Bill's abuse had hardened him. It didn't matter. The man sent by Hannah would be beaten and tortured until he spoke. Then Pope would have answers; only, not the ones he was expecting. I wished there had been time to speak to Pope before Bill had come upon us. I trusted Pope. He wouldn't consciously reveal something to Bill that would endanger me.

Bill was no longer looking at me but toward the window.

I frowned. "Has something happened?" Belatedly, I recalled the strange urgency in the fortress personnel and in Bill before I was brought to my room.

His blue eyes, clear and vulnerable, met mine. "A ghost from my past—" There was pain behind his careful mask. "We may need to leave."

My heartbeat kicked up.

His face softened. "Don't worry about it. There are troubles outside Talin, but I won't let anyone hurt you."

He cared for me, I realized, in his own warped way. "I know." I pressed my trembling hand to his cheek. "I-I don't want to think about any of that now."

Pulling away, I began to tug my dress fastenings undone.

His unfocused eyes lowered to my busy fingers. Pope's cautionary words flooded my mind. Yet I was resolved to stick to my course of action. Pope wasn't here to dissuade me further, and the echoes of his concerns faded away.

Bill ran his fingers over his face. "Ella, this isn't the best of times."

My dress dropped to the floor.

"The door. Please, lock the door."

He sighed but withdrew the key and locked the door. "This isn't you."

Taking the key from him, I led him toward the bed. His eyes heated as I removed his clothing, placing each item neatly on the rickety wooden chair beside the bed before setting the key on top. When I was done, I pulled the covers back, my fingers skimming over cool cloth before finding warmth where a shaft of light hit the bed.

When he tried to come above me, I pressed my hand against his chest. "No."

He paused, uncertain, until I pressed him back more firmly and climbed over him instead.

"I am so grateful to you," I said, and even now, I still was. My lips trembled as they touched his. My hand slipped under the pillow, halting as my fingertips brushed against the hilt of a knife.

I pulled the blade free as I kissed his cheek. I was blind and lost; the world moving fast yet impossibly slow. I thrust the blade down. Slight resistance, then more, and his breath became a sharp hiss, loud in my ear.

He wasn't dead.

I couldn't look at what I'd done, but he was definitely alive. I gasped as he grasped my wrist, the knife still buried in his chest.

I tried to pull free, but his grip was too tight.

He huffed out a laugh. "I didn't see that coming."

Panic blossomed, and blood pumped so fast through my veins that my temples throbbed with every beat. My fearful eyes cut to the blade gripped within my hand.

His grip tightened. Blood seeped from the puncture, pooling over his skin and trickling to the bed.

God, I'd just stabbed him!

I began to shake. The tremors took over my entire body.

Why did I stab him? I wasn't a killer. Even now, even here, even after everything.

Tears trickled down my cheeks. How the fuck had it come to this?

"I'm sorry." My words were ridiculous. My chest heaved, and my vision tunneled. I couldn't look at Bill or the blood leaking from his shoulder.

*I'm not a killer.* Whatever came next, whatever the consequence, I was glad of that.

"When?" he demanded, gasping my chin and forcing me to face him.

## The Master of the Switch

I knew what he was asking.

My lips quivered. I was naked yet I felt vulnerable because Bill saw me in ways no one else ever had or could. "I don't know exactly. Weeks." I swallowed. "I didn't want to hurt you. I just—" Tears began to pour in earnest. "I just want to go home."

A tic thumped in his jaw. He was still bleeding all over the bed, soaking the mattress beneath him. His fist locked around my wrist.

∽

## Bill

She wanted to go home.

Home? Where the fuck was home? Where had this begun and where would it end?

Fucking home, to her fucking husband and kids. Her betrayal burned, but so did the wound in my shoulder. I'd thought she had been with me. For weeks she had been playing me, stringing me along, waiting for an opportunity to cut me down. Planning to kill me—there was a fucking dagger under the pillow.

I wanted to be angry. *Needed* to be if I was going to survive.

Only I wasn't, and I couldn't find the inner bastard that had colored the greater part of my adult life.

I was just fucking tired.

Exhausted.

*"It's Tanis, and I'm coming for you, you sick son of a bitch."*

I'd imagined Tanis in so many different scenarios: dead, at my mercy, even living his best fucking life in Shadowland, although the latter made me seethe with bitterness. Yet nothing had prepared me for the impact of hearing his voice after so many years. I wanted him to come for me, was ready for it, to pit myself against him, and to win.

Only his voice, that fucking voice, that clear crisp enunciation had brought all the memories back.

. . .

"Do you remember that time he whipped you until you blacked out? What was the count?"

"Twenty-seven," I replied.

"What about that time when he punched you so hard it ruptured your spleen. You had to take a week off school while they grew you a new one in the lab."

"Yes, I remember," I replied.

"And then there was the time he cracked your ribs?"

"It happened more than once," I replied.

"It was actually five separate occasions. I checked my journal—a total of eight ribs."

"How many other broken bones did you suffer altogether?"

"I don't know," I replied, swallowing back the sickness rising in my throat. "Too many to count."

"Yes, that's what I thought. I decided to be generous with my estimate."

How had it all gone wrong? Where?

My blood was saturating the bed beneath me, while the woman above me, around whom I had concocted a fantasy, cried. Was she sad to have hurt me, or that she had missed the mark? I could ask her, but I thought I wouldn't like the answer. When I'd had her captured, I hadn't meant for them to hurt her. I'd just wanted her out of the way. She'd been so full of righteous anger, and I'd wanted to strip her down a peg or two. Then I'd got here, and they had broken her, and everything changed.

∽

## Ella

"You're bleeding," I said unnecessarily.

## The Master of the Switch

"You stabbed me," he pointed out, but he didn't sound mad, only tired. "Get dressed, Ella."

He released me, and I felt so cold and confused as I rose from the bed and fumbled with my dress.

He pulled the knife free with a sharp hiss before sitting and applying pressure to the wound. I claimed no expertise, but I thought the gory rivulets ran too fast. "This isn't the first time I've been stabbed." He gave a disgusted grunt as he studied his chest. "But it appears you found something important."

He eased out of bed, swaying a little as he found his feet. Grabbing his shirt from the chair, he wadded it against the wound before picking up the key.

Beyond the window a rising din penetrated my daze—a battle?

It was only when the key did not yield to his turning that I realized what had been done.

He frowned, tried the key again, then turned to look back at me. "Pope?"

I nodded, fresh tears streaming.

"Pope," he said, his expression smoothing out. "Well, I never saw that coming, either."

He dropped the key to the floor and took a few steps toward the chair before falling to his knees. I stepped forward, then hesitated. Was this him dying anyway? Had I delivered the killing blow? Would Pope come if I called for him? Was he even out there or was he busy with whatever the tumult was beyond the window?

"What was your plan?"

I went to him, fell to my knees, and pressed the cloth to the wound. "I asked Pope to bolt the other side of the door so you couldn't..." I couldn't meet his eyes. "So you couldn't order him to kill me."

He grunted. "You really think I would have him kill you?"

My lips trembled. I didn't know this man before me. He was nothing like the Bill I had met in Hannah's apartment. He was not the same Bill who had ordered Pope to kill Damien. This Bill was tired... this Bill was dying. "You have anyone without an inhibitor killed."

"Better hope I don't die if you care about Pope. Perhaps he was pissed enough not to care about the consequences, or didn't realize how the inhibitor works. If I die, so does Pope. So does every person I've fitted with an inhibitor."

I felt the blood drain from my face.

His smirk shifted to a pained grimace. "I guess you never saw *that* coming."

# Chapter 67

**Tanis**

It took me most of the night to reach Talin's lower tunnels. Once I was close, I found a place to hole up, and snatched a few hours' rest. It wasn't enough, but it was all I could afford before I pressed on.

At first sight of sconces, I discarded my flashlight and headed up into the populated part of the fortress. As expected, there were few people at the lower levels, but it was game on when I reached the prison section.

Stealth had never been my forte, and I was impressed that I had gotten that far. The alert was called, and guards converged on me, forcing me to fight my way through. A thick-necked bear of a man with even thicker arms brought progress to a halt. We clashed swords, and he beat me back with his sheer weight. Snatching up a nearby torch, I smashed him over the head. It was enough to distract him, and my blade found flesh.

The bear grunted in surprise and doggedly tried to fight on.

I shoved him off my sword and into a tangle of guards waiting their turn. The prisoners rattled bars and hooted.

The guards fell one by one until there were none. I was betting someone had gone for reinforcements, but I would make the most of the respite to get some answers.

Breathing heavily, I stalked over to the nearest cell. "Who are you?"

"From Techin," the man responded.

"Deserter scum," another man sneered from the far side of the corridor.

"Piss off," the first shot back.

Shoving my hand through the bar, I caught the man by the neck and yanked his face into the bar. "Did they bring anyone in yesterday? A worker here."

"They took one yesterday. Heard him screaming for hours. At the other end, near the watch."

"He'll be dead by now," another prisoner called.

"Better hope not." I set off at a jog, sickness churning in my gut. Kein couldn't be dead. Not here, not like this.

Three men were waiting for me when I rounded the next corner. One held a shaking crossbow. His two companions flanked him with their swords drawn. I rushed them. He fumbled the crossbow and the panicked shot sent the bolt ricocheting off the nearby wall. I cut down the crossbow holder, then the man to his left. I disarmed the last, dragged up by the collar, and pressed my sword against his throat. "The worker you brought in yesterday?"

The man pointed at the far cell, hand shaking.

"Keys?" I demanded.

He pointed at the fallen man beside him.

"Get them and open the door." I shoved the man to his knees. I kept my sword pointed at him as he fumbled around the bodies.

He sent a nervous glance my way as he found the keys. "Who are you?" The keys jangled. He dropped them twice before he got them into the lock.

I ignored the question and brought the hilt of my sword down on the back of his head.

# The Master of the Switch

The keys swung in the open door as the man slumped to the ground. I grabbed a torch and stepped into the room.

*Don't let him be dead.*

"Kein?"

"Tanis?" Kein's face was swollen and purple with bruises. "What are you doing here?"

"Saving your ass and finishing your job for you."

"I think I'm getting too old for this. I keep getting captured," Kein grumbled as I grabbed his arm and helped him to his feet. "What's happening? Everyone suddenly got called away."

"Bedlam is what is happening. Garren gets the lucky job of being me for the day. I need to get back before the power goes to his head. Is Ella here?"

"She is, or was. I saw her with Bremmer. Looks just like Hannah, a little older maybe."

"What happened?"

"She called the guards on me when I tried to get her out. I should have just gagged her and dragged her aside. Her scream brought fifty men before she drew a second breath."

"Fifty?"

"Well, ten. Your father once advised me that exaggeration is an excellent ploy in these circumstances."

I laughed and decided that Kein wasn't so badly hurt. "Did you tell her Hannah had sent you?"

"Of course, but she didn't believe me. Then she screamed."

"I appreciate the warning." I nodded at Kein. "Are you going to wait here?"

"No, I'm coming with you. I know where she is.

## Chapter 68

**Rymor**

**Hannah**

There was no time for grieving.

There was not even time to breathe.

Deep in Shadowland, a battle was taking place, and two men I loved were fighting to keep us safe. Our dire predicament could get so much worse if the Jaru got through. Only the Jaru wouldn't get through, because Tanis had told me they wouldn't, and I believed him.

Just as I believed Kein would find my sister.

Rymor, as we knew it, was gone. All we could do was drag the pieces together, keep moving forward in any way possible, and keep surviving.

The council members, personnel, and families based at the research facility had been transferred to a secure base beneath the foothills of the northern mountain range. Dan's summer house and

## The Master of the Switch

the picturesque town of Azure were not so far away. I doubted it would be picturesque anymore.

The damage was catastrophic. Everyone and everywhere was impacted, and it was worse in the cities. Had I still been living in Serenity, I would likely be dead.

How could anyone do this?

How could they use the switch?

Why would they?

"How's the droid coming along?" Dan asked, dragging me from my rumination.

We were at a remote droid manufacturing plant—the largest one in Rymor—in the operations room, where we had begun our work by restoring the power.

To my left, an open gangway hung at a drunken angle and overlooked the formerly self-automated vast underground manufacturing plant; it remained eerily quiet.

On the right, windows and a door faced a cavernous loading bay where assembled droids were stored, awaiting transport. During the EMP blast, the droids had exploded, scattering body parts everywhere and, in some places, embedding them in the walls and roof. Only one of the big loading doors was working, but it was enough to get the shuttle inside and out of sight. The security team remained vigilant, watching the outer compound.

"Close," I replied. The viewer in my hand was plugged into the repair droid, and I was trying to restore its power. There was a certain irony to repairing a repair droid, but I would swallow that irony whole for a spark of life from the machine.

"Good. I think the power coupling is fried on this one," Dan replied.

Droid damage manifested in various ways, but most issues were related to the power source. Occasionally, you could find a way to jump-start it, but most often it needed to be replaced.

"Got it," I said as the robot's lights came on and it straightened. I quickly put it through a diagnostic check. Satisfied that it was working, I moved on to another.

We had a chance to restore order for the country at large if we could begin the cycle of self-perpetuating technology. Repair droids would repair other droids, and they would repair the manufacturing plants, producing more droids, which could then be sent out to repair Rymor.

I had done the calculations. It would take months, even years, to reach the most basic level of civilization. People had died, and more would die over the coming weeks and months. People needed medical attention, water, and food. They would get none of those until the repairs were underway. Repairs needed droids.

So here I was, worried and fearful for those I loved, trying to repair a droid in a remote manufacturing plant far from the cities and people, supported by a team that remained alert for any potential threat.

Society had broken down. There was disagreement on how to help it back. The council of twelve was now the council of four, made up to five by the inclusion of Coco. We had a total of three functioning shuttles, three hundred and sixty-one people at the base, and, as of this moment, three repair droids. The dozen security personnel from the research facility, including Red, were with us. Every other person who knew how to use a weapon was out in Shadowland.

Only no one in Shadowland had functioning weapons after the second targeted EMP blast.

I didn't know what was happening in Shadowland, but it kept Nate and Theo busy. Rymor desperately needed help, so I helped in the only way I knew—using my ancient technology skills.

Besides, keeping busy helped to distract me from worrying about what was happening with Tanis and Garren. I'd seen them in action and battle. Neither were the kind to sit on the sidelines. They would be in the thick of it. Too far away to feel anything through the bond other than a determination that they were alive, it was a case of waiting for news like everyone else.

## The Master of the Switch

"Yes, it's running," I added as the system checks reported full operation. I set it to repair the other droids and moved on to the next one.

"This is taking too much time," Joshua complained. "I'm not convinced this is the best course of action. We should have separated."

"We had to start somewhere." Dan leaned back from the droid he had repaired. "Splitting was a risk. The council members are risk averse... Okay, that's five." His viewer bleeped, and he picked it up, frowning. "A couple more should be enough to give the plant a head start. I'll let Scott know we'll be ready to leave soon."

Dan left the operation room to join Scott, who stood just outside the operations room talking to Red. A blast of icy air hit the room as Dan opened and closed the door—it still shocked me when I saw him walking.

"The end of the world worked out well for you, didn't it, Hannah?" Joshua said the moment we were alone. "Still, he can't keep dodging death, not with so much trouble around him. Then where will you be?"

I stared at Joshua, blindsided by the level of vitriol that was extreme, even for him. "Get over it, Joshua! *You* destroyed our wall. Not Tanis. Not me. You. Get over it." My fingers gripped the viewer with such force it was a wonder it didn't crack.

"Get over it?" His face twisted into a sneer. "I didn't have a choice. He was going to kill me! I bet he didn't need to hold a knife to your throat to get you to spread your legs. You saw an opportunity, and you took it. Only you didn't stop at sleeping with him, did you? No, you had to mate him and his brother. I'm surprised you didn't hop into bed with his father to consolidate your plans. Make sure the barbarians keep you safe."

The door opened again to admit Dan.

My fury breathed fire under my skin. "Are you sick in the head?"

"Me? I'm not the one sleeping with our enemy. I know about your parents. Moiety sympathizers. Treachery runs in the family, doesn't it? Guess you can go ahead and breed some little terrorist babies to finish Rymor off!"

"Joshua! That's enough!" Dan said, his young face flushed. "What the hell is wrong with you?"

I wished I'd gone ahead and slapped Joshua. At least one of us would be feeling better. My hand still itched for the feel of it.

"What's wrong is that it's the end of the world and everyone is blaming me, while that monster she's—" he stabbed a finger in my direction, "been sleeping with is the savior of the day. You think I don't know the whispered conversations? Oh yes, I know you've been telling everyone. Spreading the lies."

"You've lost your damn mind." Dan's brow creased into a line. "No one has said a damn thing about you to anyone."

"She did," Joshua spat back, stabbing his finger at me again before barging past Dan and storming out the door.

It rattled in its frame before a gust of wind slammed it shut again.

Red jogged up the ramp and came in. "What the fuck was that about?" My heart was racing a mile a minute, and my tension must have spiked through the bond.

"Just Joshua venting again."

He wrapped his arm around me. "I'm going to fucking punch him. I swear, he's getting worse."

"We've got a problem," Scott said, running up the ramp to join us. "A couple of drones just flew over. The wind is picking up so they didn't hang around for long. They could be friendly and curious, but either way, we need to finish up ASAP and secure the site."

"We'll pack up," Dan said.

Red left with Scott.

Dan's face softened when he turned back to me. "Are you alright?"

"No, not really, but none of us are." It was freezing with the door open, but I thought I was shaking from more than just the cold. "He's been doing this for a while. I'd had enough of it today. I guess arguing brought out his vicious side."

# The Master of the Switch

"I know about your parents," Dan said.

I sucked in a breath.

"Theo told me. He looked into it after. I know they weren't terrorists, Hannah. Any more than John Tanis was."

My chest was heaving. "How does Joshua even know?" I felt trapped, cornered, and very exposed. The world was falling apart, and Joshua wanted to play games. "Who else knows?"

"Theo, me, Grace Claridge... I believe he told Tanis. But, Hannah...no one cares about it. Not everyone in Moiety is a killer, in fact only a very tiny percentage—" Dan's gaze suddenly shifted to something over my shoulder. "What the hell?" He charged out the door at a run. "Stop the shuttle!"

I followed him, confused and reeling from what he'd just said. Everything was coming at me through a tunnel, seeming to move in slow motion. The shuttle ramp was closing. Dan and the nearby security personnel ran over, waving arms and shouting.

Too late. I stared in horror as the shuttle powered up and took to the sky.

Everyone came to a collective stop, staring in stunned disbelief.

"Did Joshua really just take off and leave us here?" someone asked.

*Joshua?*

"God damn it!" Scott pointed at Dan. "Communication?"

"No!" Dan said.

I tried mine—dead.

"We have incoming," Scott called. "Land vehicles moving fast. Everyone inside now!"

We were hustled back inside. Red moved off with Scott to watch whoever was approaching.

It had been a four-hour journey to get here.

Unknown vehicles were incoming.

Joshua had taken the shuttle and left us behind.

# Red

As I watched Joshua take off in the shuttle, I knew we were fucked. I'd had suspicions that something was going on between him and Hannah, but every time I'd asked her, she had denied it. I'd empathized with Joshua at first. He'd been held captive for many weeks, liberated, and then watched a close friend and colleague slaughtered. After, he'd been cast into a world he knew little about, where he had no purpose and very little hope. And in that environment, he'd agreed to help John Tanis to bring Station fifty-four down.

He'd created a bomb and, with that, Station fifty-four was no more.

The guy had some personal baggage but, hey, didn't we all?

I should have pushed Hannah for answers, sat her down, and made her talk to me like Tanis and Garren would have done. Only I hadn't, and now we had potentially hostile forces incoming and no way out.

"They could be curious survivors, but I'm thinking not," Scott said as the team hustled Hannah and Dan deep inside the droid plant. The wind was picking up, so the drones had gone, but they'd gotten close enough to the entrance to see that we had the door open with a shuttle in here. So now we were trapped with no shuttle, no comms. Anything could be happening in Shadowland and Rymor. Who knew how long it might be before someone could come and get us? And it wasn't like we had a heap of functioning shuttles for that to happen. We had precisely three.

Two now.

Where the fuck was Joshua even going?

We stood just inside the doorway watching the dust cloud approach as the loading door slowly lumbered shut. "Has to be twenty or thirty vehicles to kick up that much dust."

"Fuckers are coming in hot," Scott said. "I don't have a good feeling about this."

"Me neither," I agreed. And then, when it was only part-way

## The Master of the Switch

closed, the loading door came to a juddering halt.

"Fucking hell!" Scott roared, running over to the closure mechanism and slamming his hand against the plate several times.

"It's wedged at the top!" someone called.

I stepped forward and looked up, seeing a big crack in the structure where a chunk of fascia had been torn off. That had to be what was stopping the door from closing. We had no fucking time. I tossed my rifle to the nearest team member and ran out to the narrow metal access ladder leading up and onto the roof. "I'm going to see if I can kick it out! Get ready to hit the button."

As I reached the top, my eyes cut to the distance, where the cloud of dust was getting larger and closer.

"We're cutting it fucking fine! If it's not moving, get your ass back down here." Scott called. "Mike, see if there is somewhere we can barricade ourselves inside."

I skittered across the roof, buffeted by the winds, got down and, braced on the edge, kicked at the chunk of fascia board. It creaked and swung about but didn't break off. I kicked harder, putting everything into it. Hannah was inside. I didn't know who the fuck these people were, but they had hacked technology, and I'd sooner have my first conversation with them from behind the vantage of a camera and a reinforced steel door.

"Red! Get down here, now!" Scott called.

"Move, for fuck's sake! Move!" Heel of my boot against it, I kicked again and, finally, it came free and crashed to the ground.

"Red!"

"Coming!"

The great door was lumbering closed again.

The dust cloud was close enough for me to hear the roar of old-fashioned engines.

"Fuck, fuck, fuck!" Only one group of Rymorians used the old motors, and they weren't people I wanted to meet. I half climbed, half slid down the ladder, and hit the dusty ground with a thud, rolling my ankle.

# Chapter 69

**Talin**

**Tanis**

Pandemonium had spread through the fortress. My killing spree on the lower levels and the subsequent release of the prisoners had achieved the desired effect. Most prisoners were deserters from Greve's garrisons who had intended to join me. There were a few hundred men, which wasn't a lot. Bill had been hanging someone every day but what they lacked in numbers, they made up for with enthusiasm.

"This way," Kein said. His breathing was labored, and he needed to rest often. Although I'd suggested he wait in the lower cells, I felt better having him close.

"I need an update on what's happening outside." I communicated to Theo.

*"It's busy!"*

"Busy? What the fuck does that mean?" I gestured at Kein to wait before I turned the corner. "What has Garren done?" It was probably

## The Master of the Switch

unfair of me to assume Garren was up to something, but I had a terrible feeling that the temporary power had gone to his head, and that Theo was being cagey.

*"Just a bit of fighting... Nothing to worry about... I have to go!"*

"Great," I muttered, motioning for Kein to follow me. From the time we'd left the tunnels, where the escaped prisoners were still kicking up a storm, we had met no one. "It's too quiet. Are we in the right place?"

"This part was off limits to the workers. But I agree. It's been abandoned. I hope she's still here."

The doors on either side of the corridor stood open to reveal tumbled chairs, clothing, papers, equipment, and furnishings, both Rymorian and Shadowlander, scattered in a chaotic way that instilled apprehension.

"Why would they leave? Where would they go?" And what the fuck was Garren up to?

"Fled outside perhaps?" Kein paused at a doorway. "Blood." There was another corner ahead, and Kein took off without waiting.

I swore and hurried after him.

He came to a stop. A single door stood at the end of the next turn. Two men lay on the floor before it. One was broken and bloody enough to mark him dead. The other was slumped against the wall, his arm across his belly and enough blood smothering him that dead was also a possibility.

"It's Pope," Kein hissed. "The one who questioned and beat me in the cell."

Pope groaned. I had my sword leveled on him before his eyes fluttered open.

He looked between Kein and me. "Fuck." His rough huff turned to a low moan. "Tanis, I presume?"

"Indeed."

"I'm not your fucking enemy."

"No? Might need you to enlighten me on how that works after you beat the shit out of my friend."

"I didn't know who the fuck he was or what he wanted with Ella. You want Bremmer. Get in the fucking queue."

I raised a brow. "You're not working for him?"

He huffed again. "May as well kill me. Once you open the door, I'm going to be in a world of hurt if I don't obey him. Not sure I have the strength of will to fight it, and I'd rather die than hurt Ella. The best I could do for her was stop anyone else from opening the fucking door."

"You're not making any sense," I said slowly as Kein stalked over to the closed door and pressed his ear against it.

"Don't fucking open it!" Pope's heels skittered against the floor as he tried to gain his feet.

I held up a hand to Kein.

Pope slumped back. "Got me and every other fucker here fitted with a genetic level inhibitor. If you're not familiar, they're a nasty little piece of genetic engineering that makes the recipients compliant. If I try to kill him, I'm dead, slow and painful. You try to kill him, I'm going to die trying to stop you. A few of those he infected left. A few challenged him. Dead by the Jaru or by Bill's human rights violation. Neither option is good." He laughed, low and bitter. "He's got Ella in there with him. She told me to lock them in, and make sure no one else came. I left her a knife. If she's got any sense, she's used it."

My chest compressed, and cold swept the length of my spine.

Bill was within reach, with Ella. They were locked in a fucking room with a knife.

Pope tried to rise again but couldn't get his feet under him—he was no threat to me or anyone.

"It might be a trap," Kein urged.

My fingers shook where they rested against the bolt. "I've not come this far to stop now."

I slipped the bolt open and pushed the door wide.

It was a bedroom.

Bloody smears and dark, sticky puddles covered the floor and bed. A man sat slumped on the floor against the side of a mattress, my

## The Master of the Switch

view of him partially blocked by a woman who knelt before him with her back to me. Both were splattered with a grisly amount of blood, which had dried to a blackened crust.

It was Ella. I knew it instantly, even before she glanced back over her shoulder with tear-stained gray eyes to meet mine.

The man was Bill, and from the looks of it, he was already dead.

Then his head lifted slowly, and his eyes opened.

I sucked in a sharp breath. It trapped in my lungs as a dizzy, heart-pounding sensation hit, and my ears began to ring.

Ten years and a world destroyed, but I would know Bill anywhere.

Hot, potent rage filled me as years of pent-up frustrations spilled over.

"Don't kill him!"

Ella was up and had launched herself at me before I took more than a step. My eyes widened seeing a knife in her hand, which she pointed at me.

"Ella, put the knife down," Bill said.

What the hell?! "Shut the fuck up!"

Kein had moved to stand between Bill and us.

I wasn't blessed with a natural ability to incapacitate without killing. Whenever I tried, I invariably failed. I gave serious consideration to letting her stab me and disarming her after, because Bill was still alive, and I needed to rip him the fuck apart. I shoved my sword at Kein, caught hold of her wrist, and pulled the dagger from her surprisingly fierce grip.

"You can't kill him!" Ella sobbed. "If you do, you'll kill Pope!"

I stilled, chest heaving. "The inhibitor?"

She nodded. Tears streamed down her cheeks. "Please. Not just Pope, but everyone here he fitted with one."

"I won't kill him." *Now, but I make no promises for later.*

"He's already lost a lot of blood."

"Understood."

I set her aside, handed the knife to Kein, and stalked toward Bill.

He was pale, and in a bad way. My former friend and my greatest enemy. "I let you live and you sent people to fucking kill me."

"I know. I'm sorry."

"Sorry? Like sorry is going to cut it? Like sorry comes close?"

"It's all I've got left," he said, his tone bitter. "You've won. You've taken everything."

"Except your life." My hands were on him. I told myself I was rational and understood what Ella was saying, yet as I closed my fingers around his throat, all I wanted to do was squeeze. On the other side of the room, I could hear Ella and Kein arguing, the sound of a scuffle, but I never took my eyes off Bill. "You sent that sick bastard to get Hannah. Do you have any idea what he did to her? Was he following your instructions?"

His eyes widened. "No," he wheezed out.

"Well, I guess that wasn't part of the Bremmer master plan. But you pressed the button, didn't you?"

"Yes."

"Condemned millions to death!"

"Yes."

"I ought to kill you. I want to. The lives of a few thousand people I know nothing about sounds like a small price to free the world from your tyranny." His hoarse choking sounds were music to my ears. I just wanted to fucking squeeze until his eyes rolled back. "But if Ella, the woman who stabbed you and clearly wanted you dead, could stop herself from finishing the job to save them, then I guess I can wait."

I released him, felt my lip curl, and a growl bubble up in my chest as he slumped back.

"Pain is the only thing your sick and twisted mind understands. It will be my greatest pleasure to give you more of that."

I punched him.

Ella screamed, the shrill sound rousing me from the fury-steeped daze into which I had sunk.

Bill was out cold.

"Pope?!" Ella called.

# The Master of the Switch

"Still here."

I guessed I managed to pull the punch enough. Snatching the wadded clothing up, I pressed it against the wound, used my blade to cut another strip from the bedding to tie it off tight. My hands shook. I wanted to strangle the bastard so badly, I could taste it sharp and bitter on my tongue. I tugged the cloth a little tighter, enjoying his unconscious groan.

*Hope you lose your fucking arm. See if they can grow that back in the lab!*

When I turned around, I found Ella holding the knife again... definitely related to Hannah. Kein stood between us with both hands out wide. Pope stood in the doorway using the door frame as a prop.

"Hannah is going to be upset if you stab me," I said, rising slowly. "Not that she hasn't considered it a time or two herself."

"Hannah?" She stilled, and then caught a ragged breath. Her eyes shifted between me and Kein, who watched warily from my side. "She's really alive?"

"Yes, she is."

"My family? What about my family?"

"I don't know. I'm sorry." I closed the distance between us and snatched the knife from her... for the second time.

Pope muttered a curse like he was getting set to interfere. I fixed him with a glare as Ella tried to yank her wrist from my grasp.

"That's not happening until I'm confident you're not about to rush off and find something else to stab me with."

"Is he going to die?" She pointed at Bill.

"Eventually," I replied. "But not today and not from the wound."

She trembled. Likely she was going into shock. "So, you're John Tanis?"

She seemed rational enough and I released her wrist. "I am, and the man you nearly got killed yesterday is called Kein."

"I'm not sorry." She clenched her shaking hands into fists. "He didn't explain himself very well. I thought it was a trick." Her eyes softened as they turned to Pope but hardened when they returned to me. "How does John Tanis, the terrorist who was exiled ten years ago, and who Bill has been planning to kill, know my sister? Are you sleeping with her?"

I raised my brows. "You're amazingly direct."

Pope grunted.

Ella stared back at me boldly, which was impressive given what had gone down in this room...

"I *was* sleeping with your sister," along with two other men, but perhaps now was not the time for that conversation, "but I'm pretty sure I won't be again unless I get you out of here alive."

Her lips twitched like she wanted to smile but had forgotten how. "I hope you're not another psychopath."

A long time ago, as it seemed now, I'd told Hannah that I thought I would like Ella if we ever met. Now, I realized I did. "I'm sure there are a few people who would attest to it, given what I do."

A thud signified Pope nearly pitching over, just catching himself against the door frame in time. Ella rushed to him. Worry lined her face as she checked on his wound. He wrapped his arm around her, and I was struck by the moment. She was married and had children in Rymor. Yet whatever had happened here, she had formed an alliance, perhaps more, with the mercenary working for Bill.

Shadowland. It changed us all, some for the better and some for the worse. Whoever Ella had once been, she was different now.

"I need to get you out of here. There's a battle taking place outside the fortress walls, and within isn't much better since I released the prisoners."

Gray eyes, so much like Hannah's, met mine. "I've waited a long time for someone to say that." Her gaze shifted to Bill, and her lips trembled. "What will happen to him now?"

"Now, we work out how to disable the inhibitor. What happens after remains to be decided." Only as I spoke, something struck me.

I opened my communicator to Theo. "We need picking up from Talin"

# The Master of the Switch

Calling Kein over, I leaned in close. "Get them out. Wait for me. I'll join you soon."

"What are you going to do?" he asked.

"I have a theory. One I need to test."

⁓

As the room cleared, I turned back to the man on the floor.

His eyes were open. He was a tough bastard; I would give him that.

I knelt down before him and removed the hand he was pressing against the wound. I drew my dagger and cut through the binding I'd just put there.

"What the fuck?" Bill coughed out a bitter laugh. "You lied to them? You're just going to kill me? Condemn all the good people to death with me?"

I watched the blood flow faster as I pulled the wad of cloth away. "It was always going to be like this between us," I said, holding Bill's hand away easily as I watched the blood pump out. "Personal. I tried to live my own fucking life to move past it, to fucking forget you, but you couldn't let it go. You couldn't meet me half fucking way."

Bill thrashed, his legs kicking out as he realized my intention, but his struggle was weak.

"There is no genetic level inhibitor, is there? No consequence for Pope or anyone else. My mother is a geneticist. You may have heard of her, she's famous in her field. The inhibitor relied on technology, didn't it? And it died when you pressed the switch. But by them, it had served its purpose and your people were suitably controlled."

I huffed out a breath seeing his mouth work as he tried to form words.

"Someone has to end this. You can't do it. You've tried enough times. I guess this is goodbye, Bill. I hope to god there's no afterlife because I never want to see you, never want to think of you, or hear your fucking name. You found her first, but I will have her last."

I didn't feel even the slightest hesitation as I pressed my blade into his chest. I simply watched his body jerk and held my dagger tight.

"Do you remember that time he whipped you until you blacked out?" I asked. "What was the count?"

"Twenty-seven," Bill replied.

"You know, I was so sure your father was going to manage to do better, but he only made it to nineteen." I gave a humorless grin. "What about that time when he punched you so hard it ruptured your spleen. You had to take a week off school while they grew you a new one in the lab."

"Yes, I remember," Bill replied.

"A surprisingly difficult injury to replicate," I said. "You have to punch someone really hard to make it pop like that. And I mean, really fucking hard. It took me a few attempts... And then there was the time he cracked your ribs."

"It happened more than once," Bill said.

"Five separate occasions—I checked my journal—a total of eight ribs. I rounded it up to an even ten just to be sure... How many other broken bones did you suffer altogether?"

"I don't know," Bill replied. He swallowed. "Too many to count."

"Yes, that's what I thought. I was generous with my estimate."

"Will he live?" Bill asked.

I took hold of Bill's wrist, turned his hand over, and placed a knife into his palm. "That's up to you."

Bill shook his head. "I-I can't-kill him?"

"You can," I replied. "You have to, now. It's him or me."

Bill's face smoothed out. "He'll kill you if I let him live." He stared at the knife in his hand. "I see you've already thought this through."

"I couldn't let him keep hurting you." I placed my hands on Bill's shoulders. "You know I love you, Bill. You've been my friend my whole

## The Master of the Switch

life, and I've watched him destroy you slowly, piece by piece, blow by blow, your whole life. It had to stop."

"It's too much," Bill said. "No one else would help me—not even my mother—no one else ever cared, not like this, not this much."

"It's him or me," I said softly and stepped back. "I'll accept your decision, even if it's not the one I would wish. I'll take the punishment if need be. It'll be worth it, knowing I paid him back."

Bill nodded, his face downcast. He took a deep breath and looked toward his father. Robert Bremmer sat strapped to a chair staring back through his one functioning eye, his breathing no more than a shallow rasp behind the gag, and his body a broken mess.

Bill walked over. He glanced back at me with tears streaming down his face. Then he sank the blade into his father's chest and watched as his tormentor gasped and choked his last breath.

"It's over now," I said.

"Is it?" Bill asked. His eyes searched mine, and then a smile bloomed on his lips. "Yes, it is, isn't it? I feel... free." He studied the dead man slumped in the chair. "I feel odd, empty." A smile ghosted his lips. "Pity I didn't get to watch you do it."

"Well, if you want to watch it, I recorded the whole thing. I didn't want you to be blamed if anything went wrong."

Bill laughed. "I owe you, Tanis. A debt I fear I will never repay. I'll try, whatever you need, I will try to repay you."

Bill had tried to repay me long ago, but it had gained an ever more misguided edge that had eventually led to the cataclysmic point where Ava had nearly died.

I knew my rejection had wounded Bill deeply. In a twisted way, Bill loved me. It was why he'd tried so very hard to kill me.

Had I turned him into a monster? Was it his father's abuse? Or was the monster always there, lying in wait? There was no way to know.

Yet as I stared down at the dying man, my memory stretched back in time to the young boy who had once been my friend and, but for different circumstances, might have remained my friend.

*Consider your debt paid,* I thought. And as the last light left his eyes, the only thing I felt was freedom.

I rose, wiped off my blade, sheathed it.

# Chapter 70

**Garren**

I was enjoying being a temporary leader. People followed my orders a little quicker, were more attentive, and were swifter in their efforts to please me.

Was this good?

No. Now that I thought about it, I hated being the temporary leader.

The battle had progressed into the chaotic stage. Shadowlanders against Shadowlanders was nothing new, but muddled into the mix were Rymorians and the fleeing Jaru, creating a jumble of bodies who all had their own agendas and needs. Our numbers were equal, our weapons were equal, and it was now down to who wanted it more.

I was certain I wanted it more.

The Rymorian weapons had stopped working yesterday just as we had been turning the tide toward victory. My favorite kill toy had been discarded for Tanis's inferior blade.

He was the leader. Could he not find a better weapon than this? Did it hold some sentimental value? Was Tanis sentimental? I grinned down at the Jaru I'd just killed. I would enjoy taunting Tanis about his sentimentality when this was over.

A commotion came from ahead, and a prickle of unease tickled the back of my neck. Soldiers started falling in swathes, and some drew back. Neither reaction was good.

"What now?" I muttered. Was a Rymorian weapon working? My fingers reached down to where the PB rifle should have been, but I'd tossed it aside yesterday, and there was no slot in Tanis' clothes.

Then the scattering crowd parted, and I saw the beast.

"Nice of you to leave this one to me, Tanis." The man had to be taller than Danel, and his chest was half as broad again. The sword he was carrying was almost as long as I was tall. I was going to guess this was Ailey, and Ailey was a beast.

Then the beast's eyes latched onto me.

He charged.

"Fuck me!" There was a great urge to run, but I never ran from a challenge—unless that challenge involved Tanis—but Tanis sure as fuck wouldn't run, and I was playing Tanis today.

I raised my sword and braced as the beast's colossal sword came down. It clanged against mine. I staggered back under the blow, and my arms trembled with the effort of holding him at bay.

The beast pulled his blade back... and slammed it down again.

We danced around, him beating me back with a systematic efficiency that scared the shit out of me. If I was about to die, I wanted to at least die as me.

Only I wouldn't be dying as me, I would be dying as Tanis; and if Tanis died, this whole battle would fall apart.

I could sense the fight still going on around me and the weight of snatched glances. I'd never thought much about the pressures of leadership—didn't spend much time thinking at all. It pissed me off that, while getting pummeled by this lumbering beast, I should be dedicating any of my limited mental resources to thinking about it now.

I couldn't afford to lose this fight because I wasn't only fighting for myself, I was fighting for Shadowland and Rymor.

# The Master of the Switch

The expectation of everyone on the battlefield, and the weight of two different people settled on me. Only it didn't crush me, it lifted me in a way I'd never understood before.

It was a place where all things were possible.

It was a place where I could win this fight.

Han sidled up on the other side of the beast, but I shook my head in a silent *no*. Han wouldn't interfere if this were Tanis. Another vicious blow reverberated the length of his arm as I deflected it. Well, maybe he would; even Tanis had never faced a monster like Ailey.

The beast was surprisingly fast for such a hulking man, but his technique was poor. His attack relied on brute force to crush whoever was in his way, which *was* working for him. It was time to change the pace.

I'd been sparring with Danel and Han for the last five years, and knew how to fight men bigger than me. The two brothers had ten times the skill of this beast.

I shifted back, giving myself a little space. Alid was behind me, covering my back, allowing me to keep all my focus ahead. Adjusting my grip on the hilt of my sword, I launched a counterattack.

There it was, that awakening when the enemy knew you had their measure and as a result they became no longer sure of themselves. Sometimes it happened after the first blow, and sometimes, you had to work for it. Today I was working for it.

The blows kept coming, thick and fast, in both directions, but the beast was no longer pushing me back. I grinned. "You're screwed now, beast-man."

Tanis often complained that I talked too much and that my constant jabbering during a battle would one day get me killed. Still, Tanis failed to understand the power of a well-timed insult or curse.

The beast didn't either until my—Tanis'—sword slipped through a gap and stabbed into the base of his throat. I yanked it out and jumped back, ready to counter another blow. Blood gushed—the blade had caught the jugular. He reached to try and stem the flow, but the wound was deep, and the giant slumped to his knees with a thud I felt through the soles of my feet.

A thunderous cheer rose.

The nearby Jaru began to flee.

I wavered a little. "That was harder than I thought, and I thought it was fucking hard."

Alid clamped me on the shoulder. "Impressive. Tanis' reputation has not been damaged during your watch."

"Fuck it," I muttered, straightening my weary stance. "No one will believe it was me."

# Chapter 71

**Tanis**

Talin was mine. I promised pardons to the former prisoners who'd helped me. To a man, they had been caught deserting Greve or Falton, and their loyalty had already been mine. They would keep the fortress secure while I dealt with their former lords.

Nate collected us, dropping Kein and me at where my forces had camped overnight before leaving with Ella and Pope for the Rymorian base.

It had been my second night without sleep.

Rubbing gritty eyes, I ignored the pull of exhaustion. It was time for me to finish this and regain control of Shadowland.

The great portcullis at Talin remained closed, and the forces of Techin and Tain were in my sights. It was early morning, and the fighting had yet to begin. The opposing sides sat in their respective camps, licking yesterday's wounds and preparing for another day.

The members of my wolf guard did a double take as I neared. Garren was to one side talking to his second, still dressed as me, complete with helmet.

I grinned and ignored the hostile glares from my guards, who realized they'd been duped. Agregor directed a confused look between Garren and me.

Seeing the ruse was over, Garren snatched the helmet off. "About time." His worried eyes searched mine. "You got them out okay?"

"Yeah. Kein was in a bad way. Hannah's sister... That's going to take some time, but she was okay." I grimaced, remembering the conversation. "Tenacious and a survivor—I can see where Hannah gets it from. Nate took them back to the Rymorian base." I nodded my head at Garren. "I hear you've been busy."

"No shit! Nice of you to leave that big bastard to me." He rolled his eyes before grinning and flexing his arm. "And this is still too tight... By the way, you look like shit."

"Thanks, I feel like it." It felt good to be back, listening to Garren being Garren. "Right. I want Greve and Falton's heads."

"Javid is on his way," Han said as he joined us. "I believe he will kill you this time."

"Who told him?" I pinned Garren with a look.

Garren raised both hands. "It was Danel. You know how pessimistically dramatic he can be. He was convinced you were dead. Thankfully, we got the message you were on the way back before Javid could get himself properly riled up."

"Wonderful!" I said sarcastically. "Where is Danel so I can beat him within an inch of his life."

"You're wasting your time," Garren said. "You'll wear yourself out before he notices something is amiss."

"Why is everyone standing about gossiping when we have traitors to kill!" Javid chose that moment to arrive.

I eyed my father warily. "No greeting punch?"

"You've already lost your edge," he said amiably. "Wouldn't want to knock the rest out of you." He indicated Garren. "Your brother has done an impressive job while you've been gone." Garren puffed up a little under the praise. "A few more blows to the head and that's all you'll be good for, too." Javid continued,

## The Master of the Switch

oblivious to Garren's glare. One day, Garren would stop rising to the bait.

One day, we both would.

I hoped that day never came, that I would suffer through a long lifetime of Javid's questionable fathering techniques and Garren's antics. I wanted time to claim my mate, to learn about her, to get to know Red, the beta who had claimed a place in Hannah's heart. I wanted it all, but I had business to finish here first. "What about the Jaru and the Outlier tribes? Losing Ailey must have been a blow, but what about the rest?"

"Most of the Jaru fled before we took Ailey out," Han said. "The rest scattered after his death. We captured several who we believe to be Outliers. We had scouts following and it was easy enough to pick them off. The rest were too intent on flight to care about their supposed masters. The Outliers were unarmed and offered no resistance."

"Let's hope we've got the one who the Rymorian deserters referred to as the master. If he's not among them, then I think it's time we venture into the Jaru lands once this is over," I said. "We can't let them band together again."

"Got any working weapons?" Garren sounded hopeful.

"None. Rymor is in a state of disarray still. They've transferred critical personnel to a secure underground base, but that's as much as I know."

A scout came thundering up. "Techin are calling for a meeting!"

Javid let out a guffaw.

"What sort of meeting?" I asked.

"Lord Falton wishes to speak to you! There is a messenger waiting at the front."

"Either he's drunk, foolhardy, or has a trick up his sleeve," Javid muttered.

"All right, I'll speak to him." I glanced around. "Where are the field scientists? I need whoever has Theo's disabler, just in case they have a functioning weapon." Tay nodded, heading off to find them.

I motioned to Agregor to fetch my horse.

"You can't be serious about talking to them?" Garren said. "It has to be a trap."

"Probably," I said. "Garren and my wolf guard, you're with me. Let's go and see what he's up to. I don't believe Falton has enough cunning for subterfuge, but either way, I'm not about to accept his surrender, even if I actually believed he was offering it."

Tay returned, accompanied by a Rymorian man.

"Any signs of active weapons?" I asked.

"Nothing in a five mile radius. After the last EMP, they don't even show up here as muted. Theo said the possibility of someone circumventing it was statistically impossible. It's not going to happen."

That was all I needed to know.

Together with my party, I rode out to the front line—a stretch of corpse-riddled ground. Beyond stood the ruinous Talin and, to the forefront, the armies of Techin and Tain.

A cluster of men and horses waited in the center of the dead zone, Tain's standard flapping in the light breeze.

A twitchy messenger stood beside a horse at the edge of my forces. He took a few unsteady steps back as we drew close.

"No harm will come to you," I said. "Speak plainly. What does he want?"

"He wishes to issue a challenge!"

"A challenge?" I failed to keep a note of incredulity from my voice.

Garren snorted a laugh, which drew the messenger's nervous attention.

"To what end does the traitor challenge me?"

"He seeks to avoid further bloodshed!"

"So, when I kill him, will his forces surrender to me?"

"I believe my lord is confident of his ability to win."

I raised an eyebrow. "Are you confident?"

"Me?" The messenger squeaked.

# The Master of the Switch

"Yes, you. Do you believe Falton will win?"

"I-I believe Lord Greve was concerned."

Garren chuckled again. "I think you should call it. It'll be entertaining if nothing else."

I gave Garren a *shut-up* look before returning my attention to the messenger. "Tell him I accept, but I want Greve there with fifty of his men. I'll be bringing my guards. Return to me once everyone is assembled."

The messenger nodded, turned, and launched himself into his saddle before tearing back across the dead zone.

"It's not a trick. That idiot thinks he can win," Garren said when we were alone. "Or maybe he has a spy in the camp who has seen what you look like?" He raised a questioning eyebrow. "Sounds like Falton and Greve have not been seeing eye-to-eye. Greve always thought Falton was an idiot. Fuck knows why they aligned."

In the distance, a group peeled away from the right of the opposing army. Amid them was the Techin standard. "Everyone thinks Falton is an idiot." I pointed at my helmet in Garren's hand. "Want to take this one for me again?" I asked casually.

"Fuck no!" Garren unbuckled my sword and passed it over. "This one is all yours. Need your armor?"

"What I've got is fine." Nudging my horse close to his, I took my sword from Garren.

"You think Greve is going to fold?" Garren asked.

I buckled the sword on. "Yes."

"Yeah, I think he will too," Garren agreed.

The thud of approaching hooves heralded the return of Falton's representative. "They have assembled, Lord Tanis."

"Right, let's get this done." We rode to meet with the cluster of representatives.

Falton's face lit with an arrogant smirk and unconcealed glee as he took in my disheveled appearance. Greve's, by contrast, was expressionless other than for a faint tightening around his eyes.

I handed my horse to where Agregor stood waiting. My younger brother's face was solemn, but he was handling the situation well.

I inclined my head to Greve before offering Falton a flat stare. "Falton, a pleasure to see you in such high spirits."

"You look tired, Tanis," Falton said, grinning.

"I've been busy. Your new associate is dead." I gestured toward Talin. "Talin is under my control, and the Jaru have fled. I'm prepared to accept your death as due payment for failing in your allegiance. Garren said it would look poorly on me if I killed all your living relatives."

Falton's face turned a deep shade of red. It was clear he had no idea which points to address first.

"I make no such concession to your family." Falton sneered in Garren's direction.

Garren's grin was all teeth. "Try it."

"Let's finish this farce," Falton growled. He stepped back, ushering his men away with an impatient shooing motion.

Garren touched my shoulder once before walking away with everyone else.

We drew our swords and approached with measured steps. Around us, the select crowd fell silent. Falton attacked first, an aggressive strike filled with overconfidence and years of latent hatred. Our blades rang as they met. I followed up with a swift counterstrike. We danced around, trading hits, giving me a chance to get a feel for his skill. I'd seen him fight but had never sparred with him. He was clumsy, and I could smell alcohol on his breath. I was also a little awkward, but that was down to tiredness. A gentleman might have told him to sober up. I wasn't a gentleman. I was an alpha with much to live for, and he needed to die.

I jabbed my sword up to strike Falton under the ribs... and cleaved up into his chest cavity.

Falton stared down, eyes wide and incredulous. His fingers lost their grip, and his sword clattered to the ground.

I yanked my blade out, and Falton sank to his knees. His mouth

## The Master of the Switch

worked in silence as he collapsed to the ground, twitching through his death throes.

"Stay!" I leveled my blade on Falton's second-in-command. The remainder of his men had backed up and looked set to flee. Greve's men made a subtle move to block their escape. "Take another step, and you will die."

They halted, their eyes turning wild as they realized they were trapped.

I pointed at the ground with the tip of my sword, my steady gaze on Falton's second. "You can kneel or die. The choice is yours."

His face twisted up, and his lips trembled. It would make life easier for me if he knelt, but I wouldn't back down from either choice. He was no blood relative of Falton, but he'd been with Falton's father, and the loyalty to the family would run deep.

He knelt. A moment later, so did the rest of Falton's men.

"Get up," I said, furious now that it was over but more furious about what must happen with Greve.

"Tay, please fetch Javid to supervise Tain's surrender."

Greve met my eyes, nodding once. He knew what was coming. At his side was his daughter Edile, a striking alpha woman on par with her father and, by all accounts, a lethal sword master. She was Greve's only child and would be sure to make a difficult situation hell.

"Is it true about Talin?" Greve asked.

"Under the temporary control of your deserters," I said.

Edile's fingers were white around the hilt of her sword, but Greve reached to place his hand over hers. He leaned in to talk to her, and she slowly released her grip.

"There is no way back from this," he said, I suspected for the benefit of his daughter as much as anyone else.

"None."

"Sometimes there's no easy choice." Greve's smile was tired. "Bremmer was an arrogant bastard. I can see why you wanted him dead."

Behind me came the clank and clatter of soldiers as Javid brought his men up from the south.

"Javid, I will need you to handle Tain's surrender. Kill anyone who hesitates to cooperate." My gaze settled on Falton's second, who stood beside his leader's lifeless body. "Falton knew the consequence of his actions in going against me. I will leave Javid to decide your fate."

"My pleasure." Javid growled, his lip curled. I thought Falton's second would likely be dead before day's end.

"We will return to your camp," I said to Greve, "where you will make the announcement. Tomorrow you die. It is your choice how."

Greve offered his acceptance.

Falton's death meant nothing to me, but Greve was a necessary act I would regret.

# Chapter 72

Rymor

Tanis

With the Jaru gone, Shadowland could begin the healing process. The elusive Outlier master had been captured, as confirmed by Ailey's Rymorian deserters.

Danel and Han were charged with managing Greve's former home, which would be a challenge in more ways than one since they had been mooning over Greve's indomitable daughter for years. That I'd removed the fortress leader's head would surely sully the situation.

Javid had sent half his forces back to Luka. The rest would be heading to Tain to oversee Falton's former home until I could decide on his replacement.

As for Talin, it felt like the right time to reinstate the fortress to its former glory. As the nearest fortress to the wall, it would make a valuable stepping-stone for supplies to Rymor. Likely we would soon be using Talin and the additional capacity of all the Shadowland fortresses for refugees. That Bill had started the work would soon be forgotten, along with the man.

The lines had gotten blurred between the two parts of our world. If I had my way, a line would never exist between us again. Once upon a time, I had wanted change. Now there was change. I wondered, had I wanted it too much?

I witnessed the impact of the tragic fall of a great civilization through the shuttle's window as we traveled. Long lines of people fleeing the destruction. Their destination, Shadowland.

Yet these were problems for another day. Today, and right now, I had something far more important to do.

Nate had collected us from the field where Falton's reign had come to an end. Hannah, Red, and a team were at a remote droid-processing plant. Communications had gone down between them and the main base.

Then, a short time ago, Joshua had arrived at the Rymorian base on the shuttle—alone—taken his family, and fled. With no soldiers there, no one had stopped him.

I'd been aware that something had been playing out between Joshua and Hannah. Red had mentioned it when I visited the research center, and so had Theo. To say I was tense as we took the long flight to the droid plant where they were last seen was an understatement. I didn't think Joshua had it in him to kill—he wasn't a Marcus, AKA David Renner. That didn't leave me feeling any better about whatever the fuck had happened for him to abandon his team.

Assuming the team was even at the base.

I spent the entire flight pacing the shuttle, which wasn't easy when it was packed full of my best Shadowland forces. We weren't close enough yet, and so the bond revealed nothing save an echo that told me Hannah and Red were alive.

"Red will keep her safe," Garren said.

Unlike me, he wasn't pacing, just sitting beside Nate at the front with his jaw locked tight and his tension pummeling the bond. Nate

## The Master of the Switch

was busy controlling the manual flight—we were beginning our descent, and he was focused on the task.

As we dropped below the cloud line, pain assaulted me through the bond. Sweat popped out across the surface of my skin, and I had to swallow down bile lest I be sick. Was it Hannah or Red?

"It's Red." Garren surged up from his seat. "He's hurt."

I didn't question his determination. We were descending fast. Beyond the shuttle window, a mass, I estimated close to a hundred, gathered around the loading doors of the facility.

"We've got comms!" Nate said. "Scott! It's Nate. I've got Tanis with me. We're landing."

"*About fucking time,*" Scott replied. "*Joshua left, taking the shuttle. A mob turned up. The fucking door wouldn't shut and Red went to kick the blockage out. The bastards closed in and cut him off. I don't know what they're doing to him, but Hannah is going nuts. She says he's alive but hurting. Be careful. We don't want to chase them off with him, nor do we want them to kill him.*"

"Hold tight," I said. "We'll get this done."

How, I didn't fucking know. No way was Red about to die. Not after all we'd been through, and sure as fuck not like this. Garren was growling and pummeling tension into the bond. If we could feel Hannah and Red, then they could feel us.

I took hold of Garren's shoulders and got in his face. "Control! Find some fucking control or you're going to fuck this up before we have a chance. He's hurting. So is Hannah, for him. Lock down what you're feeling. Find the calm you need before battle, find the place you were when you took the Jaru leader down, and project the shit out of that. We can do this, Garren. We can do anything we need to, and we will."

∽

# Red

I was going to die... in horrible pain.

I was already in terrible pain. Death would be a relief. My right eye was gone. I couldn't open it to try and see, but I knew in my gut whatever they'd done to it was terminal. My ribs were busted, every finger on my right hand was broken... They were pissed they couldn't get in and were making me pay.

Well, fuck them. I would do it all again in a heartbeat. Hannah was in there. Her mates would come for her and fuck these assholes up. Throwback preppers. End-of-the-world junkies—they were the only people thriving in this worst of times.

"Tell them to open the door. We're not interested in you or your friends. We just want the base." When I didn't answer, the leader, a toothless maniac with bad breath and a big fist, punched me in the gut.

I doubled over and heaved up bile, which only delivered agony all over again.

Like I would fall for his bullshit.

Like I would tell them to open the door.

Like Scott would open the door even if I did.

I was on the road to death. Nothing short of a miracle would bring me back, and the only thing that kept me hanging on was knowing the pain it would cause Hannah when I died. As for Joshua: if I ever met that spineless bastard, I'd... I didn't know what the fuck I would do, but it would involve a lot of pain.

She was hurting for me, and that was destroying me worse than any prepper blow.

They started arguing. Someone shot at the door.

I was slipping, sinking into the dark place, going under, thoughts scattering. Out of the darkness came a feral kind of rage, a storm lashing me, rousing me from the brink of nothingness.

*Garren.* I didn't know how I knew it was him, but I felt him like he was under my skin, like his consciousness was melding with mine.

### The Master of the Switch

Then calm. A deadly kind of calm, only it wasn't directed at me.
I started laughing.
The crazy bastards all went quiet.
My ears were ringing from the blows so it took me a while.
The whirr of a shuttle coming into land.

An explosion rocked the ground. The manufacturing plant doors opened... and chaos erupted, screams and shouts drowned out by the roar of weapon fire.

I tried to move, to stand, to find my fucking feet, but nothing was working. I lumbered up, then pitched straight over into the dirt.

Cold and pain faded. The only thing I could feel was the bond... and then not even that.

∼

## Hannah

It had been many hours since Joshua had abandoned us in the repair droid manufacturing plant. I had counted every second in misery.

There were criminals outside.
They wanted in.
They couldn't get in. Frustrated, they were hurting Red.

I'd begged Scott to open the door. Screamed at him and told him I would shoot him if he didn't get out of my way.

"I don't have close to enough numbers," Scott said, face drawn. "There is nowhere for you and Dan to be secured." A tic thumped in his jaw. "Red will die for nothing if I let the bastards in."

I hated him, hated how his words had the ring of truth.

Hated that he spoke like Red was already dead, when he wasn't, when I could still feel him with me, deep inside. Despite his many years as a field scientist, he was a gentle man—everyone liked Red.

And I loved him.
I was broken down.
I didn't think life could break me anymore, but as the minutes

blurred and Red's suffering turned my heart to dust, I realized I didn't understand broken and that there was always more.

Dan worked close by, trying to create a transmitter out of the parts he'd found. I should have been helping him, but my fractured mind wouldn't stretch that far.

I retreated inside myself, found a corner of the operation room, and curled up on the floor, holding onto the connection to Red, pouring all my love into it, begging him to hold on, to not leave me, because I needed him.

I existed only in that single golden thread of pure light shrouded in darkness.

Pure, potent rage ripped me from the inky prison.

*Garren.* I felt him inside, pounding into me, and I jerked to alert.

I blinked. Dan's head swung my way. All around him, plasma plates and switches, his hair wild and his face drawn. "Hannah?"

Calm. I flinched as it hit me, sucking the fear from my gasp. My chest vibrated with a purr, my broken sorrow snatched from my grasp and held firmly out of reach.

"Hannah, what is it?" Dan was kneeling beside me, holding my hand.

"They're here," I whispered, my eyes searching his.

Dan's cobbled-together communicator suddenly crackled.

Scott surged into the room, beating Dan to the response plate. "Scott here!"

"*Scott!*" Nate communicated. "It's Nate. I've got Tanis with me. We're landing."

"About fucking time," Scott replied.

I didn't hear the rest. I cried because beneath the forced calm, I could feel Red slipping away.

∼

# The Master of the Switch

## Garren

"Do they have tower-dweller weapons?" I asked Nate.

"Yes, and they're unregulated," Nate said. "We outnumber them. I'll get you close."

Great. They had the fancy shit, and we had... swords.

"Helmets on, and make sure your suits are sealed," Tanis said into the communicator. "They've got unregulated weapons so brace yourself and move fast."

To me, he said, "We're up. Keep focused."

He flipped his helmet visor down, and I did the same. On the screen was a small white dot—Red. Thank fuck each field scientist was fitted with a tracker.

The shuttle touched down, and the lowering ramp sent a draft of frigid air over us. A cluster of road vehicles and the bastards who'd ridden them here waited outside the base doors. The shuttle ramp had yet to touch down when we charged.

I took a hit to the right shoulder. Waves of pain radiated outward, and I tightened my grip on my sword as our two sides met in a clash of blades and PB fire. I took two men down in swift succession before another PB blast hit my right shoulder again. This time I dropped my sword. I punched the PB owner in the face with my numb fist. The crunch was satisfying, and Tanis cut him down from the other side.

I didn't care who the fuck was in my way or what they hit me with. I could feel Red's pain and the sense of him fading, even as Tanis flooded the bond with icy calm.

Then I saw him swaying on his hands and knees, blood dripping from his mouth, and some bastard leveling a weapon on his unprotected head.

I roared and charged.

~

## Tanis

There had been many times in my life when I had seen life and death hang in the balance. Those fleeting moments between one state and the next, where fate can fall in any direction, and time seems to stop. As I watched Garren charge toward Red, I knew this was one such time. I raced after him. The thugs, already sensing the tide of the clash was not going their way, were scattering back to their vehicles.

The weapon pointing at Red fired, but Garren was already barreling into the thug, and the man missed Red and shot one of his own. Garren and the thug went down, and I snatched Red out of the way.

He didn't make a sound, and I swear the weight of his unconscious body and the waning light on his side of the bond brought a mindless sense of panic. Garren staggered up and stamped his boot down over the thug's skull with a satisfying crunch.

Only none of that mattered.

Garren's head snapped around as I staggered up, hoisting Red's lifeless body in my arms.

"Nate, we need the scanner!" Garren roared into the communicator.

We met Nate halfway to the shuttle. He had a medic with a scanner, and they got to work immediately.

I felt Hannah before I heard the patter of feet and turned to snag her around the waist before she could launch herself at Red. "Steady, Hannah. Let the medic treat him."

"Red!"

I held her tight, purring, trying to calm her, though knowing it wouldn't work.

She sobbed as Nate and the medic worked. It had only been a few days since I'd last seen her, but it felt more like a lifetime.

The world had fallen apart in between.

As Red gained consciousness, I carefully released Hannah—so she could go to his side, where she clung to his unbroken hand and

### The Master of the Switch

told him how much she loved him, how he must never leave her like that again.

Any bitterness I might have felt in sharing her was long gone. Instead, I felt only fierce respect and pride in Hannah's chosen men. One of us would always be there for her.

"He's stable, we can move him aboard the shuttle," the medic said.

Red tried to stand—Garren waded in and picked him up.

"For fuck's sake! I'm not dead!" Red grouched.

Hannah clamped her hand over her lips and emitted a sound between a sob and a laugh.

"He's going to be fine," I said. "Let's get him back to the base."

Her hand felt small and precious in mine, and she looked up at me and smiled; I knew everything would be fine.

# Chapter 73

**Hannah**

Tanis brushed the tears from my cheeks and leaned in to press his lips to mine. "Now the emergency is out the way, there's something I need to tell you."

"What?" I demanded, not sure I was ready for any more shocks.

"The war is over. The Jaru have fled, and the fortresses who opposed me have been crushed." His eyes searched mine as I gulped and tried to take all that in. "We have your sister, Ella. We got her. She's okay."

I burst out crying.

She had been gone so long and had been with Bill for much of that time.

Tanis sat me down and explained what had happened to Ella in plain, uncensored language, telling me the worst kind of things, which broke my heart. She had always been the strong one who cared for me when no one else could.

As for Bill. He was gone. Dead. Something in me died along with this knowledge. He was the first man who didn't make me feel ashamed. The one who showed me the beauty of being an omega. I

## The Master of the Switch

would be forever grateful to him for that. What came after would haunt me.

Yet the scars his actions had left upon me were nothing compared to Ella.

"She is doing okay, Hannah," Tanis said. "She's tough, like you, but you also need to understand it will have changed her, and she will need time to talk to you about it when she is ready."

I remembered nothing more of the shuttle ride back to the Rymorian base. I held Red's hand the whole time and tried not to think, which was harder said than done when Red lay with a bandage over his missing eye. My pain for what he had endured was all muddled up with thoughts of my sister.

"It looks worse than it is," Tanis said.

"He'll be able to see again?"

His lips tugged up. "Eventually. It's amazing what they can grow in a lab."

∽

My world turned into an emotional pinball machine as I was taken through the sprawling underground bunker, mostly unused. Refugees would begin arriving, or so I'd been told before we left for the droid manufacturing plant. The great tunnels were bare and joyless, and it was devastating that anyone should have to call them home.

Garren went with Red to the medical bay, and Tanis took my hand and led me in the opposite direction.

I knew he was taking me to see Ella and I was braced for it. Yet when he stopped in front of a door, it suddenly hit me that she was really here. My heart rate rocketed, and I was terrified that I would find her changed. I wanted *my* Ella, the brave sister who'd always protected me, who had told me Bill was a bad idea in both words and attitude.

"Hey?" Tanis placed a finger under my chin, waiting until I lifted my eyes to meet his. "Let everything go for now, Hannah. Just hug her, tell her you love her. She will be going through a lot of adjustments. Slow and steady."

Tears pooled in my eyes. "Does she even want to see me?"

He pressed a kiss to my forehead. "According to Nate, she has been demanding to know where you are," he said dryly.

I snorted an inelegant laugh. Yeah, that was my Ella.

He knocked. The door opened, and I sobbed from the very first look. I didn't remember moving, but we were together. We clung to one another, crying, trying to choke out coherent words, and failing.

We held each other and wept.

We pressed our heads together and finally found the words, but nowhere near enough.

"I'm here. I'm home," she said. "With my husband and my beautiful boys. It changed me being out there. I met someone, a man who risked his life to save me. He gave me unexpected hope, and I learned to trust again, even in that desolate place. And now I've seen you safe and well, that's everything I need. It's going to take time, Hannah, time to accept what happened and to heal."

Quiet settled around us. I became aware of Tanis on my periphery and looked up.

"Come on," he said. "Ella needs some time with her family."

Of course, she did. Nicholas had remained with us, but my nephews were with his mother. They needed time as a family.

We shared one more hug, secure in the knowledge it wouldn't be the last.

Taking my hand in his, Tanis took me from the room, back along the corridors as uniform and as confusing as Thale, until we arrived at the medical bay.

Red was sleeping when we entered, a bandage covering his right eye and his chest rising and falling in an easy rhythm. Garren sat beside the bed, and I climbed onto his lap and shared a hug.

"Is he okay?" I asked softly.

"Yes," Garren said. "Going to take a week for his eye to grow." He

## The Master of the Switch

shuddered. "Tower-dweller technology still freaks me out. He's out of it. You should go and get some rest with Tanis. I'll stay with Red."

"I want to stay, too."

"Not a fucking chance," Tanis said, plucking me from Garren's lap. "You can see him in the morning. Don't think I can't feel your exhaustion, because the bond is screaming with it."

"You know what Red's like," Garren added. "He gets all feisty if he thinks you're in discomfort."

I smiled at a memory of Red insisting Garren put a blanket under me before he rutted me on the floor, despite the fact that Garren had been in full growly alpha mode after discovering me in bed with Red.

"Fine," I relented. "So long as you message me the moment he wakes up."

Tanis led me to a functional room not far away. He stripped me down, put me to bed, and presented me with a T-shirt. It was Red's and covered in his scent.

I curled around the t-shirt.

Tanis curled around me and purred.

I woke rested, the comfort of Tanis's scent all over me, Red's under my nose... and Tanis's head between my legs. I groaned loud and long, a sudden climax side-swiping me out of nowhere. He crawled up the bed, wiping his mouth with the back of his hand, lined up, and filled me in a single thrust.

I arched up at the delicious stretch, feeling alive, feeling whole.

"I've been thinking about this all fucking night," he said, voice low and growly beside my ear. He began to pound into me, a fast, hot rhythm that had me climbing fast, the thick bulge of his growing knot making nerves spark and flutter as he slammed in and out. "I've been so close to losing everything over the last few days, yet all I could think about was you. I've had the operation reversed. Couldn't stand that Garren might breed you when I could not. Don't think you're getting through another heat without getting bred."

I should have been appalled by his words, his actions, yet my body launched me into a shuddering, breath-stealing climax that made a mockery of any indignation. I bit him hard enough to draw blood and ground my teeth to make sure.

He hissed. His knot bloomed, locking us together, and a hot flood bathed the entrance to my womb.

"I think someone likes the thought of being bred," he said on a gusty breath. "Maybe we should get Red to have the procedure done while he's in medical."

My pussy spasmed around his cock and knot.

He chuckled.

My teeth released their lock on his throat, and I glared up at him.

He smirked. "He's awake, by the way."

"Red?" I slapped my hands against his chest. "Get off! I need to see him."

He didn't budge—he was a heavy mass of muscle pinning me to the bed... and then there was the matter of his knot.

His deep chuckle shifted toward a purr. "We might need to give it a moment. The way your cunt keeps clamping down on my knot is making me hard all over again."

~

I got cleaned up in record time, throwing on yesterday's clothes and not even caring, I was so impatient to see Red.

He was dressed in loose sweatpants and sitting up when I entered. Tanis made some excuse about leaving and ordered Garren out with him. I didn't spare them a glance.

Faint bruises covered Red's chest. His hair was a little damp, and he smelled clean like he'd just gotten out of the shower... there was a patch over his right eye.

I burst out crying.

"Shit!" He grunted as I threw myself into his arms, purring manically. "Please stop or they'll come back in and accuse me of upsetting you!"

### The Master of the Switch

He pulled me onto his lap, and there we stayed, holding one another as I came to terms with all that I might have lost.

"Promise you won't do that again."

"Hannah." His voice held a soft warning.

"That's not a promise, Red."

"Baby, you know I can't."

He wasn't anything like Tanis or Garren, though he was as determined to protect me. Red was gentle, caring, and everything I needed in my third mate.

"You look like a pirate," I blurted out as I traced a fading bruise on his cheek.

"Yeah? A hot kind of pirate?"

I nodded.

He smirked. "Pity they are growing me a new eye, then."

"Can they do that? I thought Tanis was lying to make me feel better."

"Apparently so."

His one good eye lowered to my lips. He was hard against my hip. I was feeling needy. "I love you, Red." My hand skittered between us to settle over the bulge. "I want to show you how much."

"I'm, ah, not supposed to engage in physical activities for a few days."

"Really? That's a shame." I nipped at his throat. He groaned, and his dick kicked against my hand. "I had better do all the work, then."

I slipped from his lap to my knees and pulled his sweatpants down to liberate his beautiful cock.

"Fuck! This is not a good idea. Garren is going to kick my—fuck!"

I hummed as I sucked him into my mouth, amused by how swiftly that argument was won.

∼

# Red

I was getting the best head of my life when the door burst open, and Garren and Tanis stormed in. Better them than the medic.... My emotions were going haywire so I shouldn't have been surprised.

Garren chuckled.

Tanis growled.

I went off down Hannah's throat.

She sucked it down like the greedy little omega she was. I swear I'd found heaven on earth and didn't even care about the two alphas watching me embarrass myself in such a short time.

They'd seen me do worse.

"The fuck! We left you alone for five minutes," Tanis growled. Even his scowl didn't bother me. I was high on Hannah... along with whatever drugs the doctor had pumped into me.

Her lips popped off. "I was showing Red how much I love him.

"How can you be so sweet and so filthy at the same time?" I cupped her cheek, then pulled her up toward me and kissed the hell out of her.

She gave my cock an experimental jack. I shuddered. I was hard. "Why am I still hard?" I muttered, frowning.

Ah, fuck!

Hannah decided now was a good time to drop down and suck my cock into her hot, wet mouth again. My face flushed. Garren and Tanis were still fucking standing there watching. Usually, everyone was involved. Usually, I wasn't the front and center of the show.

"Hannah, Red's blood pressure is through the roof," Tanis said dryly. "Maybe give the man a break before the medic charges in here."

Her growl was adorable, but she stopped, much to my disappointment... and even tucked me away.

"Damn, I think you broke my cock. I'm still fucking hard."

"Get used to it," Tanis said. "Being with an omega changes betas. More so over time."

### The Master of the Switch

"I'm not going to grow a knot, am I?" My voice came out a little high toward the end.

Garren emitted a deep guffaw. "Not a chance."

"Good, because I like how it fits easily everywhere."

"Red!"

Garren chuckled. "Don't mind Hannah's blush or fake outrage, we all know it for a lie."

∼

## Hannah

A knock sounded on the door, and the medic stepped inside to check on Red. We waited. I snuggled against Garren, who purred for me as I wrung my hands. Finally, the tests were completed, and Red was announced well and free to leave.

"Good," Tanis said. "It's about time we went home."

"Home? I don't know where home is anymore." My thoughts returned to Ella.

"Today, your home is Thale. Tomorrow, we can figure out what happens next for Rymor and Shadowland, but for now we're going home. All of us. The people of Thale need to see me. I've been absent too long, and after so much conflict they need to know how important they still are to me."

I was alive, Tanis, Garren, and Red were all here, and I had seen Ella. All my needs had been met.

I remembered promising myself months ago that one day I would go home. At the time, I had thought my home was within Rymor, but so much had changed since then.

Today, I was going home to a new home and a wildly different life.

Today I was going home to Thale.

# Chapter 74

**Shadowland**

**Tanis**

Talin's hall had been turned into a temporary base for operations between Shadowland and Rymor. With more functioning shuttles coming on board, I could now fly between Thale, Talin, and the Rymorian base with speed.

"What are you going to do with him?" Jon asked. He had remained at Talin after the armies dispersed back to the various regions of Shadowland. Refugees were pouring over the Rymorian border, fleeing in the wake of the great civilization's collapse.

For some, Talin would be a stepping stone to other Shadowland locations and, for some, it would be their permanent home.

"Talk to him," I replied. The Outliers were unlike any Jaru I knew, leaving me curious about who they were. I'd always assumed they were simply a remote-living version of the Jaru, but everything I'd learned told me those assumptions had been wrong.

"Well, he's an odd son-of-a-bitch, that's for sure," Jon said. "Sit-

## The Master of the Switch

ting there in his pristine clothes wearing a benign smile. You'd think he was on holiday instead of locked in a cell."

I smiled at Jon's candid description as I left him overseeing the next batch of arrivals and made my way down through the warren of tunnels to the prison section of Talin. Here I found the elusive master, sitting as Jon had described, neatly and in immaculate clothing, on his cell bed.

He stood as I entered, and I asked the guard outside to lock us in.

"You are not Jaru." I got straight to the point. The unusual tents, the ancient technology, and the other artifacts we found in the Outlier part of the camp—none of it made any sense. Neither Moiety nor Rymorian terrorists felt more likely. So how did he come to live among the Jaru, and why?

His laughter was strangely melodious. "I am, assuredly, the closest thing to a true Jaru you have ever met."

I studied him, noting the cognizance behind his intelligent eyes. There was no feral anger present—some masked uncertainty, despair too, but not the flat dead anger the Jaru typically gave off.

"You're a member of Moiety?" I said.

He shrugged. "I sympathize with the Jaru displacement, but I am no more a terrorist than you are."

His answer had the ring of truth, yet it opened more questions. "You want Rymor?" He nodded. "Why?" I asked. It was the one question I still couldn't answer. Rymorians had lived on the land far too long for a residual sense of displacement to linger in any Jaru—Outlier or not. "Do you really feel wronged still, after so many lifetimes? Rymor doesn't have records stretching that far back. How can you trust in events so long ago?"

The man bobbed his head. "I'm inclined to answer you for selfish reasons, since I'm certain I'm about to die. It's my greatest wish for at least one worthless Rymorian, even one from the lowly warrior caste, to know what your masters did. Although you were called Aterra back then."

A deep unease prickled the hairs on the back of my neck. "I think you have me confused. My father may be a Shadowlander, but my mother is Rymorian."

"A half-breed? How the Aterran genetic elitists of old must be turning in their graves." I smiled. "The Rymorian masters abandoned their warrior caste long ago. Still, you served your purpose, and continued to serve the same stupid purpose after they cut you from their warm embrace."

"You're not telling me anything new. But how does a lowly Jaru come to know so much about Rymor?" There was a strange sickness roiling in my stomach. The same sensations had assailed me when I'd learned of ancient technology in Outlier hands.

"I will tell you first what I told the savage you knew as Ailey. We want Rymor because we found it first. The Jaru are not indigenous to this planet. This was a dead hunk of rock when our interplanetary probes discovered it. We brought plants, animals, and technology. We built this world, as we built many worlds, incubating it over many millennia, allowing the world to flourish before coming to claim our prize. We took too long to return, many years passed, and when we arrived the Aterra had claimed it as their own."

"The ship you searched so hard for wasn't yours, it was ours. The switch you fear so much was ours. We are the ancients whose technology you rely on. Everything that lives here, does so by our design. Everything that exists here, and you call your own, the city and the power to support it, does so by our design."

"A fanciful story," I said, but the sickness made my stomach clench, and I began to sweat. "The Jaru I know are not the creators of worlds."

"No, they are not." The man smiled a sad smile. "You see, while our people were technologists, the Aterrans were the masters of genetic manipulation—genetic warfare. They didn't want to relinquish the prize they had stumbled upon, and they didn't want to share it, either. They didn't even want us to live in peace on the land you now call the Jaru Plains. We arrived expecting a world ready to accept our people. Never suspected we might have to start anew or

## The Master of the Switch

fight for what was ours. We were world builders, and we knew little of war.

"Aterra knew a lot about how to fight, and they knew the threat we posed as the creators of your technology. We were too great a threat. They created an airborne virus. A few captives of our race were all they needed. They sent it out to our defenseless colony, and it worked. It worked well. It regressed us and turned us into the mindless savages you see today. Only there was a problem. Some among us had a genetic defect that prevented the virus working on a small subset of the population. The same genetic defect that gives us gray eyes."

I felt the urge to empty my stomach. I swallowed. A dull thud had begun pounding at the base of my skull.

"What is worse, I often wonder? To be mindless, or to be mindful of what we once were? Most with the genetic defect were killed in the aftermath, turned upon by our own."

Outwardly, I remained impassive, but my ears started ringing, and the roiling angst in my gut said this wasn't such a fanciful tale.

"They thought we would kill ourselves, turn on each other like rabid beasts, and we did: many of us died by our own hands. But as time passed, and we formed basic society, we began to pose a threat again, there being so many of us, and so very savage. It was then that they created the alpha caste, built a wall to keep us out, and put the warriors between them and us. So here we are, the last of a people, the last few true Jaru, the last of the ancients."

I swallowed again, but the sickly sensation remained, and the thud of my blood had risen to a roar in my ears.

"We destroyed your station when we saw that, for the first time, a half-breed had united the savage ones, and this gave us hope. We had two plans. One to find the records of what was done to us so that we might reverse it. Another to destroy the city and the Rymorians there so we could rebuild it for ourselves and uncover the records that way. It was a hope, a distant hope, it now seems."

"Why didn't you use the master switch before?"

The man smiled sadly and shrugged. "It is hard to destroy such beauty. Destruction is your forte, and I'm glad it was your hands that took it away."

The sickness had settled to a hard lump.

"You will kill us now because we still offer a threat," the man said, his tone regretful.

"Are you telling me that you don't?"

"It matters no more. You are genetically designed to protect the Aterrans, the people you now know as Rymorians. Your biology compels you to eliminate the threat."

He was right.

I wished he wasn't, wished my hands weren't shaking and that my blood wasn't thundering through my veins.

I walked over, took out my knife, and slit his throat.

The master's eyes slipped closed as his blood poured, and he slumped to the floor.

In an instant, the sickness abated, the thud tormenting my skull eased, and my pounding blood returned to a steady pace.

"The thirty-second rule of Rymorian warfare," I said. "Is one of my favorite rules. If you cannot implicitly trust, then you must distrust. If you distrust, then the subject is a threat. You always eliminate the threat."

# Epilogue

**Tanis**

We found Joshua thirty days after he fled.
The shuttle had crashed.
His wife and son were dead.
He was walking in circles around the crash site.

We patched him up and then dropped his ass outside the biggest, nastiest prepper community we could find.

"Why are you doing this to me?" he demanded. He might have been broken but he still had a fucking mouth. "I destroyed the wall for you. I have skills. I can be useful. More kills than the omega slut you're so enamored with."

He still didn't get it.

I punched him. Not hard. I didn't want to kill him. I wanted him to live long and to suffer for all of it, to question his life choices and personal failings that had resulted in the death of his wife and son.

"Hannah is my mate. You fucking abandoned her and your team to a bunch of preppers then fled on the shuttle. You're not fit to breathe the same air."

The big metal gates of the prepper compound had slowly swung open. Ground transports swarmed out, tearing through the dust toward us.

"I help those who help me. I have no fucking time for those who don't. You betrayed *me* when you betrayed Hannah, when you betrayed Red. I want to end you, but I want you to suffer more. Welcome to the end of days, Joshua. You made your choices; time to live with them."

He begged, screamed at me, and threw himself at my feet.

I kicked him away, turned and boarded the transport. As it took to the sky I watched the prepper mob swallow him up.

# About the Author

Thanks for reading *The Master of the Switch*. Want to read more? You can read the prequel duet, Predictive and Variant on Amazon! Amazon: https://www.amazon.com/author/lvlane

Where to find me...
Website: https://authorlvlane.com
Blog: https://authorlvlane.wixsite.com/controllers/blog
Facebook: https://www.facebook.com/LVLaneAuthor/
Facebook Page: https://www.facebook.com/LVLaneAuthor/
Facebook reader group: https://www.facebook.com/groups/LVLane/
Twitter: https://twitter.com/AuthorLVLane
Goodreads: https://www.goodreads.com/LVLane

# Also by L.V. Lane

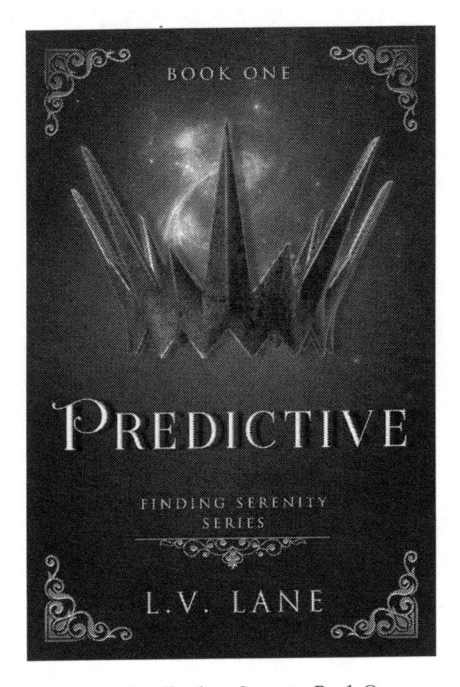

*Predictive, Finding Serenity Book One*

**Serenity, where it all began...**

*International Bestseller in Military Sci-fi, Colonization, Space Marine, Space Fleet and Metaphysical Sci-fi on US, CA, and AU!*

**I can tell when someone is lying.**

And I know when they speak the truth.

I predict about the future, about our civilization,

And I've predicted that we are going to lose the war.

I'm not afraid to use predictive skills to break the rules, to break people, if it's necessary for the greater good.

My relationship with my brother may be strained, but he's in trouble, And I'm going to get him out...whatever it takes.

Predictive and Variant are the prequel to *The Girl with the Gray Eyes*, and tell the story leading to the founding of Serenity.

Made in the USA
Monee, IL
21 March 2024